...e you read them all:

One Perfect Christmas and Other Stories

'Paige introduced us to characters old and new in this witty, heartfelt and romantic collection of short stories' *My Weekly*

'Like a delectable Boxing Day buffet, this tasty collection reunites some much-loved characters from Toon's fifteen novels in nine never-before-printed short stories' *Heat*

Five Years From Now

'Filled with warmth and poignancy, *Five Years From Now* is a page turner and a delight' **Catherine Isaac**

'Full of living-in-the-moment and what-might-have-been contrasts, this tender read pulls at the heartstrings' ***Fabulous***

The Last Piece of My Heart

'Wonderfully heartfelt... her best book yet!' ***Heat***

'A gorgeous, warm novel' **Adele Parks**

The One We Fell in Love With

'You'll love it, cry buckets and be uplifted' **Marian Keyes**

'I blubbed, I laughed and I fell in love… utterly heart-wrenching' **Giovanna Fletcher**

The Sun in Her Eyes

'Paige really ratchets up the tension. You'll be in a reading frenzy by the end' **Lisa Jewell**

'Paige Toon's epic bestseller shows how life can change in a heartbeat' ***Glamour***

Thirteen Weddings

'Witty, fun and impossible to put down!' ***Closer***

'A brilliant piece of chick-lit' ***Fabulous Magazine***

The Longest Holiday

'Will bring a smile to the face of anyone who has been unlucky in love' ***Daily Express***

'Pure, sun-drenched escapism… the perfect summer holiday read' ***Heat***

One Perfect Summer

'Drama, heartache and tears aplenty – a refreshing take on the happy-ever-after tale' ***Marie Claire***

'Sweet, charming and true to life… had us reminiscing about summer loves… amazing' ***Cosmopolitan***

Baby Be Mine

'If you want escapism, this is perfect' ***Cosmopolitan***

'Heart-warming and gut-wrenching (yet funny and addictive), will warm the cockles of your heart' **Giovanna Fletcher**

Pictures of Lily

'An absorbing and emotional narrative – brilliant!' ***Heat***

'Another perfect summer page-turner from Paige Toon' ***Mirror***

Chasing Daisy

'A fast-paced and funny read… with great jokes
and a thoughtful heart' ***Daily Express***

'Laugh-out-loud funny and touchingly honest' ***Company***

Johnny Be Good

'Pacy, highly enjoyable insight into life in La-La Land!' ***Closer***

'All the warmth and fun that I've grown to expect
from the talented Ms Toon' **Freya North**

Lucy in the Sky

'I loved it – I couldn't put it down!' **Marian Keyes**

'A fab debut and a great summer read' ***Elle***

Also by Paige Toon

Lucy in the Sky
Johnny Be Good
Chasing Daisy
Pictures of Lily
Baby Be Mine
One Perfect Summer
One Perfect Christmas (eBook short story)
The Longest Holiday
Johnny's Girl (eBook short story)
Thirteen Weddings
The Sun in Her Eyes
The One We Fell in Love With
The Last Piece of My Heart
A Christmas Wedding (eBook short story)
Five Years From Now
One Perfect Christmas and Other Stories

Young Adult

The Accidental Life of Jessie Jefferson
I Knew You Were Trouble
All About the Hype

paige toon

if you could go anywhere

SIMON & SCHUSTER

London · New York · Sydney · Toronto · New Delhi

A CBS COMPANY

First published in Great Britain by Simon & Schuster UK Ltd, 2019
A CBS COMPANY

1 3 5 7 9 10 8 6 4 2

Simon & Schuster UK Ltd
1st Floor
222 Gray's Inn Road
London WC1X 8HB

Simon & Schuster Australia, Sydney
Simon & Schuster India, New Delhi

www.simonandschuster.co.uk
www.simonandschuster.com.au
www.simonandschuster.co.in

A CIP catalogue record for this book
is available from the British Library

Paperback ISBN: 978-1-4711-7946-4
eBook ISBN: 978-1-4711-7947-1
Audio ISBN: 978-1-4711-8495-6

Typeset in the UK by M Rules
Printed and bound by CPI Group (UK) Ltd, Croydon, CR0 4YY

For my oldest friend, Jane Hampton
This one's for you, Janiekins!
Love Paigiepoo xxx

Prologue

And then I see him, a black shape against the stormy sky.

Hope blasts away the cold grip of fear, but the feeling is fleeting: he's standing near the edge and I know he's committed to jumping.

'Wait!' I scream, but the sound is snatched away by the wind. I lose my footing and stumble to my knees. Gripping hold of the slippery rock with ice-cold fingers, I push myself back up.

I've come so far: from the driest, flattest of lands to the soaring peaks of windswept mountains. I'd go to the ends of the earth for him – and beyond.

I still don't know if I stand a hope in hell of changing this tortured man's mind, but I had to try, whatever the cost, whatever the consequences.

God knows how I'll make it down from here alone.

Drawing as much air into my lungs as I can, I open my mouth and give it everything I've got…

Chapter 1

If you could go anywhere, where would you go?

I was thirteen years old, the first time I asked that question. School had just broken up for the summer and my best friend Louise and I were lying in the cargo tray of her dad's ute, staring up at an ink-black sky glittering with stars.

'I dunno,' Louise replied with a shrug. 'Adelaide?'

'You're always going there!' I exclaimed. 'And it's not even out of the state.'

'I like it,' she grumbled. 'It's "green".'

When you lived in a part of the country that resembled Mars and the moon, colour was everything.

'Come on,' I urged. 'If you could go anywhere? Anywhere at all? Use your imagination.'

'I told you, I *don't know.* Where would *you* go?'

Now that she'd asked... 'France, Holland, Germany, the Czech Republic, Austria, Italy and Spain.' I reeled off the list I'd memorised, glad I hadn't stumbled.

It was only later that I learned I'd been mispronouncing 'Czech'. *Kerzetch.*

'You're just repeating the countries stamped on your mum's passport,' Louise sniped. 'How is that "using your imagination"?'

'I'd go *anywhere*,' I stated, piqued that she'd caught me out. 'Anywhere but here.'

'Why would you want to leave Coober Pedy? It's the opal mining capital of the world,' she parroted.

This much was true. It was also in the middle of nowhere.

If you type Coober Pedy into Google Maps, all you will see is a vast mass of orangey-beige land in the middle of South Australia, riddled with the cream-coloured wiggly lines of empty creeks, gullies and ridges. It looks like a slab of marble or a medical diagram of blood vessels in the human body.

Click to zoom out once and you'll see more of the same. It's only when you zoom out twice that the names of other towns begin to appear.

There's Oodnadatta to the north, William Creek to the east and Tarcoola to the south. Tallaringa Conservation Park is to the west and that's it. Of the towns, William Creek *looks* the closest, but it's actually a six-and-a-half-hour drive away. It had a population of ten the last time I checked.

All these years later, Coober Pedy is still the opal capital of the world. According to the 2016 census, almost 1,800 people live here, but Louise isn't one of them. She and her family moved to Adelaide when she was seventeen, but she's long since given up asking me to visit.

And I've long since given up asking the question:

If you could go anywhere, where would you go?

It repeats now on a loop inside my head. I must've asked it a hundred times as a teenager and been given a hundred different responses in return.

I had planned to see the world, travel the same tracks as my mother and make new tracks of my own. But I'm twenty-seven and I've never been anywhere; never so much as stepped out of the state in which I was born.

All that is about to change and I'm not quite sure how I feel about it.

Nan's hand is cold in mine. I used to be able to transfer my warmth to her, but nothing helps now. Her skin is unbearably fragile, paper-thin and peppered with liver spots, and her white hair has thinned to such an extent that each and every follicle stands alone. She has shrunken away into a different person altogether, a pale imitation of the mighty woman who raised me.

If you could go anywhere...

Stop thinking about it! I don't know where I'd go! I don't know anything anymore! I've been anchored to this place since the day I was born and soon I'll be cut loose, but all I feel is numb.

A hand covers my shoulder. 'She's gone, Angie,' Cathy, Nan's nurse and now my friend, says gently. 'I'm sorry.'

I lean forward and rest my forehead against my grandmother's brittle hand. Relief swells inside my chest, squashing the grief I know I'm supposed to feel. It's like a bubble, expanding and expanding, until, *POP*! A needle of guilt stabs me through the heart, exploding my relief and filling me with shame.

I can go anywhere now. I've never felt more lost.

Chapter 2

Heat engulfs me as I step outside, like a gust of hot air from an oven turned up full blast. We're supposed to be coming into winter, but the desert is defiant.

I can't imagine a world in which people go to saunas, but it happens: people actually sit inside small wooden cabins and ladle water onto searing rocks to create clouds of hot steam. Then they take off their clothes and sweat. On purpose. For pleasure.

Aada told me about it, and Laszlo too. Aada is Finnish and Laszlo is Hungarian, just two of over forty-five different nationalities that live in this multicultural town of ours.

I used to find the knowledge of the people who had travelled here fascinating. I would hang on their every word, soaking up the tales of the places they'd come from and the things they'd seen. I used to think, *One day I'll see these things for myself.* That was when dreaming didn't hurt me, when it didn't make me ache from the inside out.

A cabin made out of wood! Even the thought of a wooden building is alien; trees are so few and far between here. The first tree in Coober Pedy was fashioned out of scrap iron and planted up near the lookout so the local kids would have something to climb. I burnt my hands once, trying to climb it in the summer.

Why am I thinking about metal trees and saunas? Am I in shock? It's not like I haven't had time to get used to the idea of losing Nan. Alzheimer's stole her from me years ago, after a mining accident robbed us of my grandfather.

They were the only parents I'd ever known – the only family I had – and now they're both gone.

A screen door squeaks on its hinges and my neighbour, Bonnie, comes out from the shelter of the veranda. As soon as she sees me, she knows.

'Oh, Angie,' she murmurs. She enters my front yard via the gate that no longer needs to be locked and gathers me into her arms. 'I'm so sorry. Come over to mine? I'll make you a cuppa.'

I shake my head, the weight of responsibility still pressing heavily on my shoulders. 'I can't. Cathy—'

'Go,' Cathy interrupts.

I don't know what I would have done without her these last few days. She understands death in a way I don't think I ever could.

'I'll wait for Bob and see him inside,' she adds.

The funeral director.

He's coming to take Nan away.

A sudden, desperate urge to flee overpowers everything else. I can't imagine how I'll bring myself to step inside my home ever again. I know I'll have to, but right now I want to run. Mumbling a thank you, I dazedly follow Bonnie next door.

My neighbour fills up the kettle. The clock on the wall says it's half past eleven. Mick, her husband, will be home soon for lunch.

I've known Bonnie and Mick my entire life – they were good friends of my grandparents and are now good friends of mine. In their early sixties, Mick is as tall and as thin as a post with a shiny bald head and a bushy handlebar moustache. Bonnie is shorter, and a darn sight cuddlier, with rosy pink cheeks that flame red when she's had a few drinks. She used to work at one of the pubs in town but leads a quieter life these days, while Mick shows no sign of retiring. He still seeks the addictive rush that comes from mining and not without reason: he's done well out of prospecting over the years – well enough to buy his own home and help his two grown-up children buy theirs.

Less than half of the population in Coober Pedy live in ordinary above-ground houses, while everyone else – Bonnie and Mick and myself included – live in 'dugouts', which are caves carved out of the rock.

The outback temperatures are severe – bitterly cold in the winter and often soaring well past forty degrees and even into the fifties in the summer – but below the earth it's consistently cool. Coming home after a day in the hot sun is like stepping into an air-conditioned room.

Our dugouts are carved out of a hill so entry is on flat, level ground with the kitchen on the left and the bathroom on the right, set back under a veranda that keeps the rainwater out.

Deeper into the hill is a warren of rooms – a dining room and a living room, off which three bedrooms lead.

It's been over thirty-five years since Bonnie and Mick emigrated from South Africa, but their interior still pays homage to their homeland. African masks and woven baskets hang from burnt orange and ochre-painted walls, and colourful throws, cushions and rugs adorn the sofas and floor. Bonnie's collection of miniature elephants sits in pride of place in the various nooks and crannies carved out by Mick with a jackhammer.

Mick also put in the electricity, stringing wires directly over the rock, and a warm glow emits from backlit shelves and up-lit walls. All the rooms are arched and roughly sculptured spaces, and as there are no windows, they're also completely dark and soundproof. Many of the hotels and motels are underground too: the tourists who come here to see if we really are modern-day versions of the Flintstones often say they've never had a better night's sleep.

Although the layout of our two dugouts is similar, Nan's home is far less exciting with its white walls, antique furniture and kitchen décor that is firmly stuck in the 1950s. I've always liked it at Bonnie's – it's the one place I dared to escape to on a whim when Nan was napping, although I never stayed long in case she woke up and I wasn't there.

She'll never wake up again.

A memory of my grandparents hits me: Grandad's blue-brown eyes twinkling with merriment and his smile half hidden by his crazy, out-of-control beard, and Nan, on her hands and knees, pulling brightly wrapped Christmas presents out from under our silver tinsel tree. Her hair was short and white, the way she always wore it, and when she glanced over her shoulder at me, her bright pink lipstick was still firmly in place.

It's the way that I try to remember her, the way that I *want* to remember her and, at that moment, it consumes me – grief – bubbling and boiling out of me like black ants pouring from the anthills in the desert.

'Oh, darling,' Bonnie says, putting down the mugs so she can comfort me. 'You were the best granddaughter she could have wished for. The best *daughter*,' she adds fervently, hugging me hard as I shake with silent sobs. 'We're all so proud of you, love. You know that, don't you? You couldn't have done more for your nan.'

Bonnie was one of many who used to urge me to put my grandmother into a home.

'We hate to see you wasting your life away!' I remember her saying once.

But I couldn't abandon Nan. Nor could I take her with me if I'd wanted to move to another part of the country. The first would have been a betrayal of the worst possible kind, something I never would have forgiven myself for, and the second was, quite simply, impossible. Nan had spent most of her life in the outback and she hated change. She refused to consider leaving the desert after Grandad died and her anxiety only worsened as her dementia took hold.

Bonnie and other friends tried to ease my burden, encouraging me to take holidays or even day trips. But Nan panicked when I wasn't there and I couldn't bear to put her through hell for the sake of a few hours of respite for myself. I only dared to leave the house for short periods when she was asleep and someone was available to sit with her. I even work from home, doing the laundry for one of the motels.

Before my ex-boyfriend lost his sense of humour about my circumstances, he told me that I reminded him of 'a fairy tale princess, locked up in a castle'.

'Don't you mean dungeon?' I replied, casting my eyes around the windowless room.

I was in the laundry room at the time, pressing pillowcases, and he was leaning up against the doorway arch, watching me.

'Soon you'll be free,' he said with a smile.

I didn't like his comment, or his tone of voice – it felt disrespectful – but I let it slide because I didn't want another argument.

He was right, though. It might have taken another three years, but now I *am* free.

I barely remember what my life was like before this. I'd been hurtling towards my eighteenth birthday, desperate to stretch my wings and fly like my mother had at my age. I'd unearthed Mum's passport years earlier and seeing those stamps from around the world had stirred something in me.

Nan had taken my travel bug personally, as though my longing to see the world had been a personal slight against her and my grandfather. She had been like that with my mother too. Bonnie told me about it once, about the arguments Mum and Nan had had in the lead-up to Mum leaving. Nan hadn't wanted Mum to flee the nest either, but Mum's wings couldn't be clipped.

Unlike mine.

Grandad's sudden death forced me to put everything on hold.

Losing him devastated me, but it destroyed Nan. I couldn't desert her until she was back on her feet, but as the months stretched into years, her general forgetfulness developed into something altogether more sinister. At first, unable to fathom why she couldn't set a table correctly or put an electrical plug into a socket the right way up, she thought she had a brain tumour. She'd forget things that had happened earlier that same day and struggled to grasp words she was looking for in conversations. She was constantly misplacing her car keys and even walked out of the supermarket a couple of times without paying. It was confusing, worrying and frustrating for her, and upsetting for others when she'd make hurtful or inappropriate comments or forget birthdays and important anniversaries. But it was all manageable, much easier to deal with than what came later.

She forgot how to wash…

She forgot how to dress…

She forgot how to cook…

She forgot how to eat and drink and go to the toilet…

She forgot how to talk…

She forgot me.

'Don't *you* ever put me into a home,' she used to say darkly, even as we were leaving the care home in Adelaide where her own father had resided until his death at eighty-nine.

The irony, it seemed, was lost on her.

When she was diagnosed with Alzheimer's, she begged me to stay in Coober Pedy. And I promised her again and again that I would.

Some said she never should have asked such a thing of me,

but I understood. I was all she had left. She had raised me like a daughter, hoping to fill the gap left by the one she'd lost.

Three days after giving birth to me, my mother had developed an infection that led to septic shock and multiple organ failure. She'd been only a few weeks pregnant when she'd returned to Coober Pedy after being away for almost two years, travelling first around Australia before heading overseas. According to Bonnie, she'd rarely called home in all that time, preferring to send letters and postcards rather than endure her mother's wrath over the telephone.

Nan couldn't bear the thought of me taking after my mother.

But it hadn't always been that way. When I was a child, she and Grandad used to find the similarities between us heart-warming. I remember countless times, growing up, when they'd glanced at each other with delight and exclaimed that I looked 'just like Angie', or sounded 'just like Angie', or done something that Angie would have done. We even have the same name, Mum and me: Angela Samuels.

Personally, I couldn't see any comparison – from the pictures I'd studied, I didn't think I resembled my mother at all. Where her hair had been long, glossy-straight and dark, mine was a mass of frizzy blond curls. Where her eyes were the colour of a sunny daytime sky, mine were more of a milk chocolate. Her complexion was fair and freckly while mine was honey-hued in colour. She was taller than me by three inches: five foot seven compared to my five foot four, measured against the markings on the kitchen wall on our respective seventeenth birthdays.

Our likenesses, my grandparents had insisted, were in our

smiles and in our actions, in the way that we spoke, danced and played. None of these comparisons were tangible to me, but I welcomed every one. I was glad my grandparents could see my mother in me; they said they knew nothing of my father.

There had been one night, though, when I'd questioned the truth of that claim. It was New Year's Eve and I was ten or eleven. I'd been speculating out loud about whether my father might be out there somewhere, waiting for me to come and find him. Nan had had a few drinks and she'd muttered – I'd heard it as clear as day – that he was a 'bad man'. I'd jumped to my feet in shock, demanding to know what she'd meant, but she'd immediately denied saying anything at all.

But I couldn't forget those two words. They chilled me to the bone. And although I'm still curious about my biological father, part of me wonders if I'm better off remaining ignorant about who he is and where I came from.

Chapter 3

Five days later, I find myself back at home. After the funeral director came, I kind of crashed out.

'You've been holding up your nan for so long, it's no surprise your walls have crumbled,' Bonnie said as she made up her daughter Helen's bed for me that first night.

I suspect I'm now four parts blood and bone and one part chicken noodle soup, but it was nice to be mothered for a change.

Nan's funeral is this afternoon and I'm trying to rustle up the energy to get dressed. I've been lying on my bed for the last forty-five minutes, staring up at the world around me.

I used to ask everyone I met to send me postcards when they went on holiday, moved away or returned to wherever it was that they'd come from, and I still have them stuck to the rough, domed ceiling and walls of my bedroom, a mosaic of colours and countries from all over the globe.

The awe-inspiring pyramids of Egypt and the crumbling

ruins of Rome. The Northern Lights of Scandinavia and the crystal-clear waters of Greece. Thailand's white-sand beaches and Switzerland's snow-capped mountains. The purple heather of England's moors and the green hills of Ireland's Emerald Isle. Oceans and savannahs, sunrises and sunsets, skyscrapers and shepherd's huts. Paris's Eiffel Tower and China's Great Wall and many, many more.

The sharp trill of the doorbell pierces the air. Friends have been coming by Bonnie and Mick's to offer condolences, but word must've got around that I'm back in my own home. I wearily swing my legs off the bed and drag myself to the front door, opening it to find a glamorous blonde bombshell before me.

'Louise!'

My oldest friend steps forward to hug me hard.

'I'm so sorry about your nan, Angie,' she mumbles into my hair.

'What are you doing here?' I withdraw to stare at her, unable to believe it. It's been over five years since I last saw her.

'I've come for the funeral! As if I wouldn't!' she chastises. 'Let me in, it's like a furnace out here. My face is melting.' She bustles me into the hall.

Growing up, Louise used to hate her curves, but when she moved to Adelaide and got a job at a beauty salon, she embraced them. Gone are the drab, baggy T-shirts of her teenage years, replaced with a wardrobe of brilliantly coloured, figure-hugging outfits. She's wearing an uncharacteristically demure navy dress today, presumably for the funeral, but is still rocking the red lipstick and false eyelash look that I'm familiar with from her Instagram posts.

'Why didn't you tell me you were coming?'

'Thought I'd surprise you. I was shocked when Bonnie called. Well, not shocked. I mean, we knew it was coming, but still. I can't imagine how you feel.'

Bonnie offered to call everyone who had known Nan to tell them of her passing. I was too shattered to do anything besides acquiesce.

'Are you wearing that?' Louise asks, belatedly noticing my faded blue T-shirt dress.

'No, I haven't changed yet.'

'Oh. Phew,' she says.

I think she's done with the sympathy. It was never her strong point.

'What about your hair and make-up?'

My hair is… I don't know how to describe it, much less know what to do with it, so I choose to ignore the question. 'I haven't worn make-up in years,' I say instead.

I stopped wearing it at around the same time Nan stopped wearing her trademark pink lipstick.

'Well, thankfully, I have my kit with me – including waterproof mascara,' Louise adds meaningfully, 'so there's no need to panic.'

I wasn't panicking. She could dress me up as a Tellytubby and I'd probably go along with it.

'Come on,' she urges. 'Let's see what's in your wardrobe.'

In my bedroom, she pushes a red curtain aside, revealing a rectangular space filled with clothes. Grandad cut the wardrobes out of the rock for my mother – this was once her bedroom – but he never got around to hanging proper doors.

'I remember this from when you were sixteen!' Louise

exclaims, pulling out a yellow dress on a hanger. 'And this!' She yanks out a navy and white striped skirt, although the navy has faded to a washed-out purple now. 'You need a serious wardrobe overhaul, girl.'

'Don't get a whole lot of chances to go shopping.'

Her expression morphs into pity. 'When are you going to come and see us in Adelaide?'

I perch on the end of my bed and fight the urge to climb under the covers. 'Soon,' I promise. 'I'm desperate to meet the girls.'

Louise hasn't wanted to drag her children the nine or so hours it takes to drive here. They're only two and four years old.

'I suppose you'll be wanting to follow in your mum's footsteps and go to Europe before you do anything else.'

'I'm not sure what I'm going to do.'

'You've had enough time to think about it.' She casts a significant look around my room.

'I can't afford to go travelling.'

'But you will once you sell up, right?'

Her casual question causes my insides to convulse. This dugout might've been my prison, but it holds a myriad of happy memories. The thought of packing up Nan's things and saying goodbye forever…

'I'm sorry!' Louise gasps, seeing my face. 'There's no rush for you to do anything, of course there's not. Adelaide – and we – will be waiting for you whenever you're ready.'

I nod and she squeezes my shoulder before returning to my wardrobe to rifle through the rest of my clothes. 'How about this?' she asks of a black knee-length cotton dress.

'I wore that to my grandad's funeral,' I mumble as she dusts it off.

'Does it still fit?' She holds it up and gives me the once-over.

I might be softer around the edges than I used to be, but I haven't put on that much weight in the last ten years, mostly thanks to exercise DVDs.

'I reckon it does,' she answers her own question. 'Lucky cow. Come on, chuck it on and let's get started on your hair and make-up.'

Like I said, sympathy is not her strong point. I don't think I mind.

Houses aren't the only things that are underground in Coober Pedy: some hotels, motels, restaurants, bars, shops, galleries and even churches are.

It is in the front row of one of these churches that I find myself sitting that afternoon, with Louise to my left, Bonnie and Mick to my right and Nan's small, frail body resting in the casket in front of us. Behind us, the seats are full and many are standing. Nan had lived in this town for over fifty years and she meant a lot to the people here, just as these people now mean a lot to me.

Each and every person I'd call a friend, but I'm unused to being around all of them, all at once. The reverend is the first to repeat what Bonnie told me – that I couldn't have done more for Nan and that I was the best granddaughter she could have wished for – but he's not the last. Although I know the words come with the best of intentions, I'm uncomfortable hearing them, and by the time we reach the pub for the wake, I'm feeling overwhelmed. All I want to do is return to the solace of my quiet, secluded dugout, but I feel an obligation to stay.

Towards the end of the evening, I go to the bathroom and sit on the toilet with my eyes closed and my head in my hands. It's only a momentary respite.

'You okay in there, hon?' Louise asks with a rap on the cubicle door.

'Yes, fine.'

'Bonnie and Mick want to make a speech before people start to drift off.'

'Really?' Bonnie spoke at the funeral – what else could she have to say?

I flush the loo and come out to see Louise waiting. She smiles at me. 'Despite everything, you look lovely.'

I pull a face, unused to compliments, but as I wash my hands, I am slightly taken aback at the sight of my own reflection in the mirror over the basin.

Earlier, Louise styled my frizzy mass of honey-blond curls into a tight, high bun. She accentuated my cheekbones with peachy blusher and made my light-brown eyes look wider and more almond-shaped with a sweep of jet-black eyeliner and mascara. The make-up, remarkably, is still intact.

'Can I?' she asks me now, holding up a compact of pressed powder.

I stand self-consciously, allowing her to remove the shine from my nose, but I turn down her offer to apply colour to my bee-stung lips.

'Lip-gloss, then?' she asks hopefully, brandishing a rose-pink wand.

'Vaseline,' I barter, spying some in her handbag.

We head back to the bar area. The room is quieter than it was when I left it, but now it falls completely silent.

My eyes graze over my friends in the crowd to seek out Mick, one of the tallest men in the room. Beside him, I find his rosy-cheeked wife, who smiles warmly and beckons me over.

'We all know that Ginny, Angie's nan, thought of Angie as more of a daughter than a granddaughter,' Bonnie begins when I'm at her side. 'But she had a bit of competition in later years because Mick and I think of Angie as a daughter too.' There are a few chuckles. 'And we're not alone,' she continues, addressing the room. 'All of us have spent time in this young lady's company and I've heard some of you say that she feels as much like family to you as your own flesh and blood. We want you to know, Angie,' she says, turning to look at me directly, 'that you're not alone, love. You'll always have family and friends here in Coober Pedy, and even when you're off traipsing around the world, we want you to remember that. This will always be home.'

A stinging starts up behind my eyes and Bonnie takes me in her arms, squeezing me tight to the sound of sympathetic murmuring from all around. After a moment, I pull away and try to compose myself.

'Thank you,' I say, turning to look at the sea of smiling faces before settling on Grandad's old mining partner, Jimmy, at the front. He's leaning on his walking stick, his left eye twinkling – his right is hidden behind an eye patch. I feel a rush of affection for him as I add, 'Thank you all for coming.'

'We're not finished, Angie,' Mick interrupts, prompting a few laughs from the crowd. 'How many of you,' he addresses everyone, 'have had young Angie ask you where you'd go if you could go anywhere?'

Over half of the people in the room raise their hands, including Jimmy. I think he was the only person aside from my grandmother who'd replied that he was happy right where he was, thank you very much.

Mick turns back to me and grins. 'We know you might not be ready to think about this yet, Angie, but we hope you don't leave it too long before getting out there and seeing the world like you've always dreamed. Bonnie and I, and everyone here, want to give you a hand in making that possible.'

'Wherever you want to go,' Bonnie adds, 'whatever you want to do, we hope this will help.'

Mick steps forward and places a grey leather pouch into my hand. It's about the same size and weight as a bag of sugar, and beneath my fingers, I can feel the objects within clinking and rubbing against each other. I stare at Mick and Bonnie with wide-open eyes and carefully prise open the drawstring at the top of the pouch to peer inside.

It's full of opals.

Chapter 4

There are two broad classes of opal: precious and common. The internal structure of precious opal causes it to diffract light, resulting in what is referred to as play of colour as it's tilted or rotated. Common opal is more of a milky colour, often blue or green.

The opal I'm holding between my forefinger and thumb is most certainly precious. It flashes with layers of brilliance as I turn it this way and that, displaying every colour on the visible spectrum, from luminescent orange, fiery red, pink and violet, to bright blue, yellow and green.

As a child, it used to surprise me that the opals my grandfather brought home didn't glow in the dark – they looked like they should. But later I learned that all they needed was a little help from a special black-light torch.

Grandad used to take me noodling – sifting through the rock ejected from the mineshafts in search of opal inadvertently discarded by miners. Sometimes, at night, he'd drive me out to the opal fields, carefully steering me around gaping mineshaft holes with thirty-metre drops. When he turned on his UV torch, the colour that would jump from the rock heaps would make me gasp with wonder. It wasn't just the opal that would light up – agate and fossilised wood would, too, and scorpions: Grandad always warned me to look twice before scooping anything up.

Over the years, I collected enough small pieces of opal to enable my grandparents to have them made into jewellery for me for birthday and Christmas presents. I'll always treasure those pieces: bracelets, rings and necklaces, held together with sterling silver.

But the piece of opal I'm holding now is something else. I can't take my eyes off it. It's about two inches in diameter and could well be a hundred carat. Colour sparks and flashes under my reading light as I tilt it backwards and forwards. Only about three quarters of it has been polished and I like that traces of the creamy rock from which it was hewn continue to cling to it in parts. It reminds me of my childhood when I'd watch my grandfather preparing his own finds. Seeing him grind, cut and polish to uncover the jewel from beneath the rough, dull sandstone was nothing short of magical.

This opal reminds me of him for some reason, more than any of the others, but it can't have been his because all of his precious opal was sold after his death to keep us afloat. Bonnie and Mick don't know where it came from – about two dozen opals were donated anonymously at the wake after Mick raised the idea with some of his mining buddies.

I'm still reeling.

'You mean a lot to the people around here, Angie,' Bonnie

said to me last night when we said goodbye outside our respective homes. 'Your kindness and generosity, and the love and devotion you've shown your nan, have really warmed the hearts of the people in this community. They wanted to give you something in return. Now all you have to do to make them truly happy is stretch your wings and fly. But come back – even if it's only to pack up your nan's dugout. Come back when you've decided what it is you want to do for the rest of your life. We can't wait to hear all about what you get up to so make sure you send plenty of postcards!'

Her words brought me to tears – again.

At the sound of the doorbell, I slip the opal into its pouch.

It's Louise.

'Good morning,' I say with a smile, opening the front door wide.

'How are you feeling?' she asks, stepping into the hall.

'Okay, I think.'

'Not too tired? Bonnie told me you've been wiped out. I hadn't realised. Do you think you might've had the flu or something?'

'Maybe. I think it just hit me – all of it, all at once. I feel better today.'

'Good, because I thought we'd spend it out and about – you've been stuck inside for too long.'

'What did you have in mind?'

Her face breaks into a megawatt grin as she realises I'm going to go along with her plan. 'I thought we'd take a tour of our past, starting with breakfast in town.'

'Okay.'

'Great! I'll make us a cuppa while you go and get ready!'

The wind is ferocious today, but despite the dust that collects up our noses and cakes our skin and hair, I feel the stirrings of lightness in my chest.

After breakfast, Louise and I meander around the grounds of our old high school and pass by her former dugout. We drop in on the Umoona Opal Mine and Museum where we both did stints as tour guides one summer holiday when we were sixteen, and we even revisit the location of my first kiss which happened, randomly, inside the shell of an old spaceship that was left over from a movie they filmed here.

Eventually, we end up at the pub. We used to come here as teenagers when we weren't quite legal, and if Beryl, the owner, was in a good mood, she'd turn a blind eye. Put a foot wrong and we'd be dragged out by our ears.

Beryl is serving behind the bar tonight.

'It's good to see you out and about,' she says when I go up to order a second round.

I know she means well, but her comment needles my conscience. Louise and I have been laughing about a failed double date we went on as teenagers when her parents had parked right next to us at the drive-in. Now I'm wondering how I can find anything funny when we buried my grandmother only yesterday. It feels wrong.

'You've been through so much, Angie,' Louise says when I return to the table in a sombre mood. 'You've got to embrace life now. No one is going to hold it against you.'

'I'm sorry, but I no longer feel comfortable being here.'

'How about we take a bottle back to yours?' she suggests.

I'm not ready to call it a night yet, so this seems like a good move. Then I remember that we don't need to buy a bottle.

'Let's crack open one of Grandad's fancy reds instead.'

Louise's eyes light up. '*Loving* this plan.'

The thing about living in a cave is, if you need a shelf or another bedroom, you can carve one out of the rock. If you're lucky, you might even unearth treasure while you're renovating: one of the local motels uncovered so much opal that it paid for the extra rooms they were excavating.

In Grandad's case, he wanted a wine rack, so he bored half a dozen bottle-sized holes directly into the living room wall and happened to find enough colour to pay for a no-expense-spared trip to Adelaide to visit the wineries with Mum and Nan.

It was the first of many such trips that they took and, in later years, I went instead of my mother.

I still remember those endless green hills and the rows of grapevines that seemed to go on forever.

The wine-tastings bored me half to death, but the swims in the cool, clean ocean that inevitably came towards the end of our holidays easily made up for it – they're some of my best memories.

Grandad added to his wine rack over the years, drilling out new holes and filling them with bottles, but he never again found opal. And Nan and I never drank any of his wine. Nan was more of a sherry drinker and the thought of tucking into her husband's cherished collection made her feel too sad, so it stayed there while her health dwindled.

I certainly didn't feel right drinking it myself. I've barely drunk a drop of alcohol in years. I was worried I might sleep too heavily and miss something I shouldn't, like Nan switching off the fridge-freezer at the socket. She did this on my birthday a few years ago and I woke up the next morning to face, not only a pounding headache from the wine I'd drunk the night before, but a freezer full of defrosted meat. I had a lock installed on the kitchen door after that.

'I know nothing about wine,' I tell Louise as I pull a random bottle from its dusty hole and brush my hand over the label. 'Lockwood House Creek Shiraz.'

'I know that winery!' Louise exclaims. 'It's up in the hills. The guy who runs the cellar door is hot.'

'Made with grapes from sixty-five-year-old vines planted down by the creek at Lockwood House,' I recite from the label.

'Give me that,' she gasps, swiping the bottle. 'This is their really good one. Probably worth a few hundred bucks,' she says. 'Don't waste it on us.'

I laugh and make a mental note to give this one to Jimmy before sliding it back into its hole. It hits the rocky wall at the end with a clunk.

A few bottles later, I'm wondering how on earth Louise knows so much about wine. She's recognised every winery so far and even knows which years to look out for.

'Mark and I often tour the wineries. It's our thing,' she tells me. 'You should sell these, they'd be worth a packet.'

'I thought I'd give them away as leaving presents.'

She looks delighted. 'So you're leaving? Definitely?'

I give her a smile and nod. 'I don't know when, but soon. After the dust has settled.'

Not that the dust ever settles around here.

'Have you still got a passport?' Louise asks.

I nod. I applied for it when I was nineteen, before Nan was diagnosed. She made me feel horrible when I asked her to dig out my birth certificate, and I still remember the additional sting of: *father unknown*.

'Where will you go?'

'I haven't decided.'

'Come to Adelaide and we'll check out some travel agents!' she urges. 'We can go shopping and *update your wardrobe*.' She pulls a face as she says this. 'Then I can take you to the airport and see you off!'

Louise's words bring about a warm glow inside me. Is this what proper excitement feels like? It's been so long, I hardly recognise it.

'Come on, let's toast the adventures you're going to have.'

Three bottles later and I'm out of patience.

'They're all good!' I cry. 'Pick one. Any one you want!'

'Are you sure?'

'Absolutely.'

'In that case, let's go for the Cab Sauv.'

'Which one was that again?' I stare at the wall.

She points. 'There, I think.'

I pull out a bottle, but it's dusty, not one of the ones we've already looked at. I slide it in the hole with a clunk and pull out another. 'Oh, for goodness' sake,' I snap when I see that it's another dusty bottle. 'We're drinking the next one, no matter what it is.'

'Deal,' she says with a clap. 'Lucky dip for grown-ups.'

I slide it back in, but this time, there's no *clunk*. I pull the bottle out a little and slide it in again. The surface at the end gives, as though it's made out of something soft. It's certainly not rock.

'What's wrong?' Louise asks as I pull the bottle out fully and peer into the hole.

'Can you pass me the torch from the shelf?' I ask. There's some sort of rough material at the end. I pinch it between my fingers and it comes loose, bringing with it a small dust cloud.

'What are you doing?' Louise asks as I turn over the crumpled piece of canvas. 'Wait,' she says before I can put my arm into the hole again. 'There could be a snake nest down there for all you know.' She hands me the torch and I direct the light inside.

An envelope, folded in half, is wedged in at the end. I frown and pull it out. It's addressed in neat, rounded handwriting to someone called Giulio Marchesi in Rome. My heart skips a beat at the sight of my own name and address on the back.

No, not my name: it must be my mother's.

'What is it?' Louise asks as I hastily open the envelope and scan the words written on the two pages of white paper inside.

I glance up at her.

'It's a letter from my mother to my father.'

Chapter 5

Earlier, my heart was pounding in my ears, but at the sight of Bonnie's face, it plummets to the depths of my stomach.

'You *knew* about this?'

'I wasn't aware that she'd kept the letter,' she replies in a shaky voice.

'Who? Who kept it? Mum or Nan?'

'I think it must've been Ginny,' she replies miserably.

It's after ten at night and I felt bad when Bonnie answered the door in her nightgown, but I couldn't bring myself to wait until morning to run this by her. Louise is back at my dugout, checking behind the other bottles to see if there's anything else we missed.

'You'd better come in and sit down,' Bonnie says, indicating the kitchen table.

As soon as we're seated, she begins to talk.

Bonnie's daughter, Helen, who lives in Port Lincoln with a family of her own, was the person who told Bonnie that my mother had wanted to contact my father. Helen was eighteen when Mum returned from overseas, aged twenty, and although they hadn't been close, they had, on occasion, hung out together.

Shortly before I was born, Helen popped next door and found my mother in tears.

'Up until that point, your nan had been telling everyone that Angie planned to raise the baby on her own, that the father wasn't on the scene and never would be. She made it very clear to us all that we should butt out and mind our own business.'

But Helen must have happened across my mother in a moment of weakness because Mum told her everything. She said that she met my father whilst working as a waitress at an Italian restaurant in Rome.

I look now at the word under Giulio Marchesi on the front of the envelope: *Serafina's*. Could that be the restaurant's name?

'She'd written to your father a couple of months earlier, but he didn't reply,' Bonnie continues. 'Your nan kept saying that he obviously wanted nothing to do with her. She urged Angie to forget all about him, but Angie told Helen in confidence that she planned to write again or try to phone him after you were born. She still held out hope that her first letter had simply been lost in the post.'

'But Nan never sent it,' I murmur.

When my grandmother told me that my father was a 'bad man', I'd thought those two little words meant something truly terrible, but there's nothing in this letter that implies violence. Quite the opposite…

Caro Giulio,

Firstly, I'm sorry for leaving without saying goodbye. It was the last thing I wanted to do, but I had thought a clean break would be better for everyone. Things were so intense there at the end – not only between us, but also between you and Marta, although I know that was a different kind of intensity. I hope she's feeling better now? She's been preying on my mind a lot.

You probably didn't think you'd ever hear from me again and, in truth, you weren't supposed to. I had planned to complete my travels, return home and try to forget all about what happened between us in beautiful Roma, but fate, it seems, had other plans.

I've wanted to write to you countless times in the last few months, but I haven't known where to start. There is no easy way to say it so here goes: I'm pregnant. Seven months, to be exact – that night at Serafina's, right before I left.

I know this will come as a terrible shock, and please believe me when I tell you that I don't expect you to be involved, but I thought you had a right to know. And if you would like to have a relationship with your son or daughter, then I promise that I will do everything possible to make that happen.

Do you think you could give me a call one night when you finish work? Ideally between midnight and 1 a.m. your time, Sunday through Thursday? Sorry to be so exact, but South Australia is eleven and a half hours ahead of Italy which means it'll be lunchtime on the following day here and my mum should be out, taking lunch to my dad at work. I'd rather talk without them eavesdropping!

Frankly, though, you can call me any time – I'd really like to hear your voice. It's been a frightening few months, to be honest, and I'm desperate to talk all of this through. My number is below.

Ciao,

Angie x

Mum wrote her telephone number below her name – it's the same one that I have now.

'Who's Marta?' I wonder out loud.

Bonnie clears her throat. 'She was your father's wife.'

I feel as though I've been winded. 'My mum had an affair with a married man?'

Bonnie nods reluctantly.

I'm already experiencing a whirlwind of emotions, but now I can add disappointment to the mix.

I'm also oddly relieved. I had always feared that my biological father had physically hurt my mother, but is the fact that he was married what Nan meant by him being a bad man? I don't like that he cheated, but I'm glad he wasn't violent.

'Did Helen tell you?'

Bonnie nods. 'On the day of your mum's funeral. She'd kept Angie's confidence until then, but broke down and blurted it all out. Later, your grandmother confirmed it.'

Oh, this is too much…

'You *spoke* to Nan?' My voice cracks on the question.

And neither of them ever told me?

'I brought it up with her a couple of times,' Bonnie replies with mounting distress. 'It always resulted in her getting very upset and angry. She said that your father had had his chance to come out of the woodwork, that Angie had written to him and he hadn't even had the decency to reply. She claimed she had no way of contacting him herself – she said she couldn't even remember his name, let alone which restaurant he worked at – and she seemed convinced that he wanted nothing to do with you because he was married. She believed that telling you all of this would only cause you pain and...' Bonnie hesitates. 'And I thought she might be right.'

I have such a lump in my throat, it's hard to talk around it. 'But it was all a lie!' I slap my hand down on the envelope. 'My grandparents had a name and address for my father all along!'

'I knew nothing about that,' Bonnie states firmly, her eyes shining.

I can't believe I'm twenty-seven and I've gone all these years thinking that, once my grandparents passed away, I'd be alone in the world. But now it seems that I might have a father out there who doesn't even know I exist!

Bonnie reaches over and takes my hand as tears spill down my cheeks. 'Your grandparents were crushed after Angie's death. With their daughter gone, you were the only thing that made them smile. They would have been terrified of losing you, darling,' she says, her own tears breaking free. 'They'd lost your mother once when she'd disappeared on her travels for two years – that was hard enough on your nan. Your grandad missed her too, of course, but he had his work to distract him whereas your nan was like a little lost sheep when Angie went away. When your mother returned, your nan would have done everything she could to convince her to stay and raise you here. Maybe she planned to tell you about your father one day,' she says. 'Maybe she kept the letter for that very reason. She might've even forgotten she had it!'

I stare at her desolately, my tears continuing to fall. 'I'll never know now, will I?'

Chapter 6

When I return to my dugout, Louise is putting the last of the bottles back into the wine rack.

'The rest were all solid rock,' she replies in response to my silent query.

I slump down on the sofa.

'What did Bonnie say?' she asks.

'I'm going to need a drink before I tell you.'

We're half a glass down by the time I've finished filling her in. I've barely even registered what the wine tastes like, but Louise manages to get in that it's a 'very good drop'.

'Where's your laptop?' she asks at last.

I fetch it from my bedroom, then settle down next to her on the sofa as she copies the address from the envelope into the browser and hits return.

We might live in caves, but thankfully we have access to the internet. It's kept me blissfully connected to the outside world while I've been stuck inside.

I'm not really expecting Louise to find anything, so I almost spit out my mouthful when she cries, '*Serafina's*! It's a pizza restaurant!'

'It still exists?'

Sure enough, it's right there on Google Maps with a 4.7 star rating. My eyes drift down to the telephone number under the listing and then to the line beneath.

Open now.

My pulse speeds up. I have no doubt that the wine is giving me Dutch courage, but something else makes me act on impulse – the part of me that doesn't want to waste another minute of my life.

'Are you calling him now?' Louise asks with astonishment as I reach for the telephone and dial the number with a shaking hand.

'There's no way he'll still work there,' I reply bravely, pressing the phone to my ear. 'But someone might know what's happened to him.'

There's a long, unfamiliar-sounding ringtone. Does it mean the line is engaged? I'm a little relieved, but then the phone clicks and a woman answers.

'*Ciao, Serafina's*.'

'Er, hello,' I reply, jolting to attention. 'Do you speak English?'

'You want to make a reservation?'

'Um, no, I'm trying to track down a man called Giulio Marchesi. I think he used to work there.'

There's a rustling sound and I hear the woman bark a name: Alessandro.

A moment later, a man comes on the line. 'How can I help

you?' he asks smoothly. As with the woman who answered the phone, he has an Italian accent, but his is not as strong.

I fight the urge to hang up, suddenly having second thoughts about rushing into this.

'Um, I'm wondering if anyone there might know someone called Giulio Marchesi?' I ask hesitantly.

'Giulio Marchesi?' he repeats, and it sounds different to the way I said it. Better. With proper pronunciation.

Joo-Lee-oh Mar-*chay*-see.

'Yes!' I exclaim, nerves engulfing me.

'He's not here right now.'

The blood drains from my face. 'You mean, he still works there?'

Louise's eyes are out on stalks – I'm pretty sure mine are too.

The man at the other end of the line lets out a short laugh. 'Where else would he be?'

There's a pause and I can hear the bustle of restaurant noise in the background. It must be lunchtime there.

When the man next speaks, he sounds wary. 'Who are you?'

What do I say? I hadn't thought about this, hadn't planned it, hadn't even imagined for one second that my father would be so easy to track down. Am I about to blow his whole life apart?

'Is he still with Marta?' The question bursts from my mouth before I can think about it, and a second later, blood flows back up to my face and burns me from the inside out.

Louise sits forward and stares at me with horror. It's clear to both of us that I don't have the faintest idea what I'm doing.

'Marta passed away many years ago,' the man replies after a long pause. 'Who is this?' he asks again, and this time his tone is more demanding.

'My name is Angela Samuels,' I reply, blundering forth like a bull in a china shop. 'I believe Giulio is my father.'

Chapter 7

Nerves dance around my stomach, pulling my insides into knots. I check my seat belt again to make sure it's tight enough and look out of the window at the airport staff loading the last of the bags onto the plane. How can something so big take off from the ground and fly through the air to the other side of the world? It defies belief. I glance around at the dozens of people in the cabin, but nobody seems worried. The teenage boy beside me is engrossed in his game on his iPad while his dad, to his right, casually flicks through a magazine. The small children in the row directly in front of us are chattering away to their mother, practically bouncing on their seats with excitement. They're all taking it in their stride, completely unfazed by the journey ahead.

Did my mum take it all in her stride too? Or was she terrified like I am? I'm not sure how much of my anxiety can be apportioned to a fear of flying and how much is because I'm on my way to meet my father for the first time.

*

The last few weeks have been surreal. Alessandro from *Serafina's* called me back the morning after we spoke and introduced me to my father by speakerphone.

'Angela?' Alessandro asked when I answered.

'Please, call me Angie,' I replied.

And then another deeper voice came on the line. 'You sound just like your mother.' His accent was thicker than Alessandro's, but his shock was clearly detectable.

'Angie, this is Giulio,' Alessandro interjected, and for a moment, we were all speechless.

Giulio broke the silence. 'My Angie... She never tell me. How could this happen? I cannot believe I have a daughter!' he exclaimed. 'Why she never write or call?'

'She tried,' I told him. 'She wrote to you before I was born, but I don't think my grandparents ever sent the letter. I've just uncovered it.'

'But where is Angie now?' Giulio asked.

I paused. 'She... She died three days after I was born. She developed an infection. There was nothing anyone could do.'

The silence that followed was deafening. It was Alessandro who next spoke and his tone was gentle. 'What did your mother's letter say? Perhaps you could read it aloud?'

I did, and afterwards, Giulio exhaled heavily. I had a feeling he was trying to take it all in.

'Will you come to Italy?' Alessandro asked.

'*Si!* You must!' Giulio interrupted before I could contemplate the question. 'I send money for your ticket! How soon you come?'

'It's okay, I have money,' I replied, dazed by the strangeness of it all.

'Then when can you come?' Giulio asked again.

I felt slightly railroaded into promising, 'Soon.'

I think Bonnie would have had me take a while to come to terms with Nan's death before jetting off, alone, to the other side of the world, but Jimmy encouraged me to 'just get on with it'.

I've known Jimmy all my life, but we've become close in recent years. He damaged his leg and an eye in the same accident that killed Grandad and I became quite protective of him after that. Only a year earlier he'd lost his wife Vicky to cancer.

'The longer you spend thinking about it, the scarier it'll become,' he said in his usual no-nonsense manner. 'Go ahead and book your ticket and the rest will fall into place.'

I did book my ticket, but much of what else has fallen into place has come down to Alessandro, who seems to have taken the reins in getting everything ready for my arrival. He's arranged for me to stay with one of *Serafina's*' long-term waitresses – a girl called Cristina, who has a spare room. Giulio has only a one-bedroom apartment above the restaurant, and living with him would certainly have felt like too much too soon.

I've spoken to Giulio three times since our initial conversation, once only briefly because Alessandro was not around. I find speaking to my father quite daunting, not least because his accent is strong and he can be overly exuberant, but I'm hoping it'll be easier face-to-face. Giulio and Alessandro have told me a little about the rest of my family. I have two aunts, Eliana and Loreta, who are married to Enzo and Boris respectively. Between them, they have four children aged between seventeen and thirty-five. My cousins' names, and it has taken me a while to memorise them after asking Alessandro to write them down in an email, are Valentina, Jacopo, Melissa and Francesca.

Loreta runs a hotel with her husband in Venice, and Eliana lives in Tivoli, a town outside Rome.

I also have another grandmother who is alive and well and living in Tivoli with Eliana. *Serafina's* was actually named after her by my grandfather, Andrea, and inherited by Giulio when Andrea passed away. I can't wait to meet her.

I'm still not entirely sure where Alessandro fits in. His email address revealed that his full name is Alessandro Mancini, but I have a feeling he's more than a simple employee. When I thanked him for his part in getting everything organised, he replied that he was happy to help, adding that he owed Giulio a great deal. He didn't elaborate further than that.

The plane is moving now. *The engines are so loud.* They make my whole body vibrate. Needing a distraction, I hook my foot beneath the handle of my bag and drag it towards me. Soon I have it in my hand: my opal.

The teenage boy beside me is too distracted with his game to pay me any attention, but I turn towards the window anyway and rotate the opal under the sunlight.

Mick's friend Trev, a licensed opal valuer, valued this opal alone at nine thousand dollars – worth more than any others in the pouch by a mile. But when it came to handing it over for sale along with the rest, I couldn't let it go.

'Can I keep this one?' I blurted.

'You can do anything you like, dear, it's yours,' came Trev's wily reply.

I stare down at it now, mesmerised by the colours that flash from brilliant red and orange to gold, green and blue. If I needed to, I could sell it at any time, but until then, it will remind me of home wherever in the world I am.

I can't believe I'm going to Rome for the summer.

Ever since seeing the stamp in my mother's passport, Italy has been one of the places I've dreamed about visiting. She spent four months there – longer than in any other country, according to her immigration stamps – and left only to go to Spain for a few weeks before heading home.

Giulio says that my mother can't have known she was pregnant when she fled Italy because they were 'together only once', right before she left. It's likely she found out after she'd returned to Coober Pedy and we know from her letter that it took her several months to pluck up the courage to write to my father. I can't imagine how alone she must have felt during that time.

I feel closer to her right now than I ever have, going on this journey to the country where I was conceived. Mum claimed in her letter that she would do everything she could to help Giulio have a relationship with me if that was what he wanted. The fact that I'm seeing her wishes through makes my heart ache in an unfamiliar way.

It was hard saying goodbye to everyone in Coober Pedy, but especially Bonnie, Mick and Jimmy, who all came to wave me off.

Bonnie was emotional. 'I'm sorry, darling,' she said for the umpteenth time as she squeezed me hard. 'I'm sorry I didn't tell you sooner.'

'Please, Bonnie. You really have no need to apologise,' I tried to reassure her. 'I understand.'

But I sense she'll give herself grief for a good while to come.

As for Jimmy...

'Go on, off you pop,' he urged, shoving me towards the bus.

'You're acting like you're glad to see the back of me!' I cried indignantly.

'I am!' he shouted, hooting with laughter and stamping his walking stick on the dusty ground.

I know he loves me really, the old codger.

I've spent the last few days in Adelaide with Louise and her lovely family. We never did make it to any travel agents – there wasn't any point because I'm destined to go to Italy – but we did hit the shops and I have several new outfits in my suitcase as well as the skinny jeans and blue and white striped jumper that I'm wearing.

My friend also sorted me out for make-up and frizz-controlling hair products, but after approximately twenty-four hours of intensive air travel, I pop to the loo for a final freshen up and am mortified to come face to face with a wild-haired cave woman. Singapore's tropical flora and fauna was amazing, but the humidity has done my hair no favours. My head has been crackling and fizzing with static electricity against the plane seat over the course of this horribly long flight and now I realise I don't even have a hair tie with me.

I'm bouncing between exhaustion, an irrational urge to cry, relief that the flight is finally over and debilitating nervousness at the thought that my father is picking me up from the airport.

When the plane touches down on Roman soil, the long wait to get off the aircraft is followed by an even longer delay at passport control and yet more time spent waiting for my suitcase. The airport is crammed with people – it's even busier than Adelaide and Singapore – and when I finally trek out through customs, I'm feeling a bit beside myself.

I've only seen one picture of Giulio, which he emailed at my request. Bonnie thinks we have the same milk-chocolate eyes and eyebrow shape, but to me, he looks like a dark-haired, mahogany-skinned, fifty-something stranger.

I scan the crowd for this stranger.

But my attention is captured by a younger man, holding a white sign that reads *Angie*.

Could it be Alessandro?

One of his hands is raised as he shields his eyes from the bright morning sunlight streaming into the airport terminal behind me. When our gazes collide, he smiles and lets his hand drop, coming out from behind the barrier.

I'm a little taken aback. Alessandro sounded nice on the phone, but I didn't think too much about what he might look like. He's lean and attractive with green eyes and chestnut-brown hair that has been tied back into a small knot, the rest of it falling free at the nape of his neck. He has dark stubble that is not quite a beard, and although he's not *very* tall, he's still taller than me by almost half a foot.

I smooth down my bird's nest with my free hand and hold out my palm. His grin widens at the sight of my attempted handshake, but he obliges, and our skin connects with an almighty shock.

'I'm so sorry!' I cry, pain zipping up my arm and, no doubt, his too from the look on his face. 'My hair is full of static electricity!'

He throws his head back and laughs while I stand there, wondering how on earth those words found their way out of my mouth.

'In Italy, we greet each other with kisses, but I'm not sure I dare touch you again,' he teases, before bending down to kiss my flaming cheeks, one after the other. 'I'm Alessandro,' he adds, extracting my suitcase from my hand.

'Angie.'

'I gathered.'

'Where's Giulio?'

His amusement vanishes, and when he speaks, it's with regret. 'I'm afraid he couldn't come. He had to go to hospital last night.'

My stomach drops.

'But he'll be out later today,' he quickly assures me.

'Is he okay? What's wrong with him?'

'High blood pressure. He works too hard,' he mutters. 'He wasn't feeling well last night so I insisted he get checked out and they kept him in for observation. He was very angry. Angry with *me*,' he clarifies, flashing me a meaningful look. 'He really wanted to be here. That man is as stubborn as an ox,' he adds darkly, but I detect an undercurrent of affection. 'You'll see for yourself. Come. My van is this way.'

I assumed he meant a worker's van of some sort, but when we reach the car park, he leads me to a high-top VW campervan.

It's olive green in colour and utilitarian in appearance, sort of chunky with a big, black grille. It's not one of the 1960s vintage ones – this is more 80s in style.

'This is cool,' I comment.

'My humble abode,' Alessandro replies casually, opening the front passenger door for me and sliding open the side door to put down my suitcase.

Over his shoulder, I notice a bench seat with a quilted orange throw and built-in cupboards facing the door. Clothes spill out of a cubbyhole at the back.

'You actually live in this?' I ask, spying a crumpled sleeping bag lying flat out in the roof space.

He nods proudly. '1985 VW T3 Westfalia Synchro.'

'I have no idea what you just said.'

He smiles and shrugs. 'She's my baby.' He pats the van fondly and goes to slide the door shut so I step out of his way.

'But how do you manage in such a confined space?'

'I don't need much room,' he replies, walking around to the driver's door. 'I have the essentials: a cooker, fridge, solar power.' He climbs into the van and I do the same, buckling up while he turns on the ignition and raises his voice over the loud rumble of the diesel engine. 'When in Roma, I usually eat at *Serafina's* and if I want a hot shower or need to do my washing, Giulio lets me use his facilities.'

'And when you're not in Rome?' I ask. Where else does he spend his time?

'I make do.'

He looks over his shoulder as he reverses out of the parking space. He's wearing faded black jeans, partly worn through at the knees, and a black shirt with white buttons, rolled up at the sleeves and layered over a black T-shirt underneath. I catch a glimpse of a thin gold chain around his neck as he turns to face forward again.

'I will take you straight to Cristina's so you can get some rest,' he says as he sets off in search of the exit.

'Thank you. Do you know her well?'

'Too well,' he replies wryly, leaning across me to open the glove box. I move my knees to the side. 'She likes to boss me around like a big sister, even though she's five years younger than me.' He finds the sunglasses he's after and slots them onto his nose.

'How old are you?' I ask with interest.

'Thirty-five,' he replies. 'Cristina's a good person. I think you'll like her.'

'We haven't actually talked about the rent, yet.' *I hope it's not too expensive.* 'Do you know how much she's charging?'

He waves me away dismissively. 'Giulio is covering it. You don't need to worry.'

'No, no, no, *I'll* pay!'

'He won't hear of it. He feels it's the very least he can do,' Alessandro continues over the sound of my protestations. 'You will insult him if you do not allow him to do this one thing,' he says firmly.

I'm distracted by the fact that we're driving on the wrong side of the road – or should that be the *right* side? We drive on the left in Australia.

'I will bring Giulio over this evening and we will take you out for dinner,' Alessandro says as he joins a busy motorway.

'Will he be well enough?' Concern overrides my surprise that Alessandro will be joining us.

'I think so. He wanted you to come to *Serafina's*, but I thought you might prefer somewhere quieter.'

'Thank you.' He's right. I can't imagine meeting my father for the first time in front of a bunch of strangers: customers *or* employees.

Speaking of employees… I need to get to the bottom of who Alessandro is and what he means to my father.

'How long have you known Giulio?' I ask.

His eyebrows jump up. 'All my life. Giulio didn't explain on the phone?'

'No.'

I presume he means during the last conversation that Giulio and I had when Alessandro wasn't around. We didn't speak long because, frankly, it was awkward.

'Ah.' He sighs. 'He was supposed to.' He pauses before continuing. 'Marta was my mother.'

My mouth drops open. *Alessandro is my half-brother?*

'Giulio is my stepfather,' he clarifies, letting me know that we're *not* related. 'He married my mother when I was young.'

'I see!' Now it all makes sense: Alessandro is a part of the family, not an employee.

But hang on a second… Giulio cheated on *his* mother with *my* mum. Isn't he bitter? He's been nothing but nice to me since he found out I exist.

Perhaps he can sense my confusion.

'It was complicated between Giulio and my mother.' He sounds jaded. 'My mother wasn't well. I'm sure Giulio will tell you all about it sometime.'

I think that's my cue to leave it there for now.

Respecting his wishes, I change the subject. 'Do you work at *Serafina's* too?'

'Yes, but only for part of the year.'

'What do you do the rest of the time?'

'I roam,' he replies.

'Roam?'

'Roam,' he repeats.

'In this?'

'Yes.'

'Wow. Where have you been?'

He laughs wryly. 'It would probably be easier to tell you where we *haven't* been.'

'We?'

'Frida and me,' he replies, tapping the steering wheel.

Oh. Is that his girlfriend? Or his wife? He's not wearing a wedding ring, but that doesn't mean he's not married.

'Is Frida your...?'

'My baby,' he replies, tapping the steering wheel again and waving his hand around the interior of the van.

'Wait. *This* is Frida?'

He nods.

I laugh. 'I thought she was your wife or something.'

'No!' He looks horrified at the thought. 'No, no, no. It's just me.'

A blue car comes out of nowhere and slots into the already too-small space between the van and an enormous lorry. I gasp and hang on to my armrest for dear life. A red sports car roars past us in the fast lane and, a second later, the blue car darts out and almost crashes into a white Mercedes following the sports car.

'The drivers in Roma are all crazy,' Alessandro comments flippantly as my heart hammers against my ribcage. 'You'll get used to it.'

I'm not sure that I will.

The rest of the journey to Cristina's is so nerve-racking that I don't attempt to strike up another conversation. Instead, I focus my attention away from the action on the road to the countless high-rise apartments flying past. When will I get a chance to see the sights that Rome is so famous for?

My spine straightens when we come to a river, crossing over it on a wide bridge lined with magnificent white-stone pillars and giant eagles sitting atop plinths. The sparkling surface below glints in the early morning sunshine.

Rivers, oceans and lakes are such novelties to me. I don't think I'll ever tire of seeing copious amounts of water, not even when I'm old and grey.

The trees on the other side of the bridge are like the ones I've seen in television shows about Italy: umbrella-shaped pines.

'Stone pine,' Alessandro tells me when I ask for the name.

'They're beautiful. What about that?' I point at a tall, skinny conifer. I've seen a few of these on the journey from the airport.

'Cypress.'

'There aren't many trees where I come from,' I reveal.

'No?'

'No. I live in the desert.'

'Aah.'

As we make our way through the suburbs of Rome at a more leisurely pace, the tension in my body begins to dissolve. I'm transfixed by the view outside my window. One minute we're driving along a quiet, leafy residential street with ornate houses behind tall iron gates, the next the streets are wide and busy, packed with traffic lights and pedestrian crossings. Some districts are awash with shops and restaurants, others seem to have only one or two tiny establishments. It's all so different to the flat, barren landscape of the desert.

'*Serafina's* is along there,' Alessandro says after a while, pointing. 'The one-way system around here is a pain, so I won't take you there now, but it's easy to get to if you're on foot.'

'How long does the walk take?'

'Ten to fifteen minutes, but Cristina rides a scooter so you could always hitch a lift with her.'

I don't think so, not with the drivers I've seen.

Soon we're turning into a curving street flanked with apartment blocks. There are cars parked on both sides of the road, facing towards us and away, and it's so narrow I can't believe it's not one way. Alessandro winds uphill and comes to a stop, manoeuvring his van into an impossibly titchy space. He switches off the engine and nods further up the hill.

'Your new home,' he says, opening his door and climbing out of the van. I follow his lead, hesitantly hooking my carry-on bag over my shoulder. While he retrieves my suitcase, I take in my surroundings. There are apartment blocks all around, each six or seven storeys high. They're cube-like in shape, the floors stacked one above the other with balconies bursting with greenery and laundry hanging out on lines. I can hear a couple of dogs barking and look up to see a little brown pooch on one of the balconies nearby, woofing down at us with great gusto. My gaze takes me higher to the rooftops, which are adorned with orangey-red tiles, gleaming against the blue-sky backdrop.

I can't believe there's so much life packed into such a small area. There are probably more people living in these surrounding apartment blocks than in the whole of Coober Pedy.

The sound of Alessandro shaking his keys draws my attention back to him. 'Watch your step,' he cautions as he sets off uphill, pulling my suitcase along behind him. He's carrying a bulging shopping bag in his other hand.

The footpath is not wide enough to walk side by side so I follow, carefully stepping over the uneven paving stones until we come to a stop outside a gated courtyard. Alessandro presses a button on the buzzer and nods slightly left at a crooked wall, alive with creeping ivy. 'Cristina's terrace is behind there.'

'She's on the ground floor?'

'Yes.'

The gate latch makes a clicking noise and Alessandro pushes it open, leading me across the courtyard and in through a glass door that has been propped open with a terracotta plant pot.

Inside is a reception area, within which a middle-aged man sits off to the left behind a desk. Alessandro greets him in Italian and gestures towards me. 'This is Salvatore, the doorman,' he tells me. 'He's here between nine in the morning and eight at night. Outside those times, you will need to use the key Cristina will give you.'

It's nine thirty now.

'*Buongiorno*,' Salvatore says.

I've tried to memorise a few phrases and I know that this means good morning. I repeat the greeting to him with the best accent I can muster. He looks pleased and rattles off a few words and I nod and smile, pretending to understand, while Alessandro goes up to the first door on the left and raps sharply.

The front door opens, revealing a beautiful, barely dressed girl with long, tangled, dark-brown locks and stunning cat-like green eyes.

Alessandro recoils. He starts to speak rapidly in Italian, sounding far from happy, while I stand there, wondering why he's not introducing us. The girl responds equally irately and turns away to storm through a door off the hall, shouting something over her shoulder at him as she goes.

Alessandro sighs and ushers me in, but doesn't offer a word of explanation as the girl continues to rant out of sight. A moment later, she reappears, wearing a thigh-length plaid skirt and a white T-shirt. She pulls on her shoes and coat and then goes out the front door, slamming it shut behind her.

Alessandro's jaw twitches with annoyance.

'Was that Cristina?' I ask.

'Cristina?' He looks momentarily entertained at the thought before shaking his head firmly. 'No. That was Rebecca, her ex-girlfriend. Well, she's *supposed* to be her ex-girlfriend,' he says drily as he goes to stand in the doorway of the room that Rebecca just exited.

'Cristina,' Alessandro says loudly while I stand there digesting this information. 'TINA!'

Groggy mumbling comes from within.

I wait in the hall, awkwardly, while Alessandro says something in Italian. I hear the name Rebecca, to which Cristina mumbles a sleepy response. Alessandro raises his voice, as does

Cristina, and then he turns on his heel and stalks out, pulling the bedroom door shut firmly behind him. He mutters what I'm almost certain is a string of swear words before turning to stare at me with resigned eyes.

'Sorry about that,' he says in perfect English. 'Coffee?'

I have a feeling that life here is going to be interesting.

Chapter 8

While Alessandro gets on with making our drinks, I give myself a tour of the apartment. It doesn't take long. There are two bedrooms off the hall, one of which is to be mine. Placing my bags inside, I note a double bed made up with a pale-green bedspread and two windows hung with long white net curtains with a view over a large central courtyard. A wardrobe with curved edges sits against the wall to my right, alongside a low-slung chair, and to my left is another door leading to an en suite bathroom. A couple of empty shelves are fixed to the wall.

The shared spaces are open-plan. Six vibrantly coloured chairs sit around an oval-shaped dining table to the left, and to the right is the living room and kitchen, separated from each other by a bar top, under which two metal stools are tucked. The living room has a large grey sofa with loudly patterned cushions and a leather armchair facing a flat-screen TV. There are vintage ski posters hanging on the walls, and shelves filled with books and knick-knacks. I spy an old Chupa Chups tin, but have a feeling the lollipops are long gone.

The apartment is light, bright and airy, as far from my dark, dated dugout as you could get. This has a cool vintage vibe about it, in line with some of the home make-over shows I've seen on TV.

Beyond the dining area are double doors opening up onto a terrace. Peering through the glass, my eyes widen at the sight of all the succulents and leafy green plants lining the walls. There's even a palm tree.

The space is divided into two by a low wall covered with bright blue tiles reminiscent of the swimming pool in Louise's back yard. Behind it, to the far right, is a wooden table shaded by a faded orange sun umbrella. Directly in front of me is a bench seat, two orange wire chairs and a coffee table, upon which sits a couple of empty wine glasses, two empty wine bottles, and an ashtray, half full.

I didn't think to ask if Cristina is a smoker.

Alessandro appears to be making himself at home in the kitchen. He catches my eye as he places two tiny white cups on the bar top. I walk over and pull out a stool, facing him. On the hob, a gas flame glows beneath a metallic-silver contraption. It's almost kettle-like, with a spout and a black plastic handle, but its insides are pinched in towards the middle in an hourglass shape.

'Moka pot,' Alessandro tells me, noticing my perplexed expression. 'Italian coffee maker. You haven't seen one of these before?'

I shake my head.

He picks up the pot by its handle and pours thick black liquid into the cups.

'Is Cristina okay?' I ask as he pushes one of the cups towards me.

'Sugar?'

'No, thank you.' I wouldn't mind some milk, but it's not offered, so… *When in Rome…*

I take a sip. *Jeez, that's strong!*

'She's very hungover,' Alessandro answers my question, propping his elbows on the bar top. 'We won't be seeing her for a while.'

'Says who?' a voice calls from the hallway.

Alessandro raises his eyebrows at me expressively. 'I spoke too soon.'

And then Cristina – for I'm assuming there are no other random women in this small apartment – appears in the kitchen.

'Hi!' I exclaim, hopping down from my stool. 'I'm Angie.'

'Cristina.' Her look is surly and I tense up as she comes around the bar top to greet me.

She's around my height but stockier – straight-up-and-down as opposed to curvy like me. Her hair is short and dark and her ears are pierced several times all over with gold hoops. She looks a bit worse for wear.

Alessandro says something to her in Italian.

'English, *please*, Alessandro, where are your manners? And where's *my* coffee?' she demands to know.

He tuts, but turns back to the hob, and when Cristina returns her attention to me, there's a wicked glint in her eye.

'I'm sorry about Alessandro,' she drawls and, when he tuts again, she smirks. 'And he thinks Rebecca is rude.'

'You won't be defending her when she cheats on you again,' Alessandro interjects ominously as Cristina collapses on the sofa, her boobs bouncing freely beneath her light-blue tank top.

She rolls her eyes. 'It'll be different this time.'

'Sure it will.' Alessandro walks over and hands her a cup of coffee before settling in the armchair and stretching his legs out in front of him.

'Giulio is in hospital,' he says as I return to my stool.

As he fills Cristina in, a heavy fatigue settles over me, not unlike the weariness I felt after Nan passed away.

I've been sitting here listening, and they've spoken in English so as not to exclude me, but I've still felt separate from their conversation. It's not something anyone can help, but it is a reminder that I'm going to feel like an outsider here for a while, at least.

'I might have to lie down for a bit,' I say when their conversation comes to a natural conclusion.

'Of course.' Alessandro jumps to his feet. 'But try not to sleep for more than three hours or your jet lag will be insufferable.'

I'll take his word for it.

I head into the kitchen and surreptitiously pour the rest of my coffee down the sink. The shopping bag that Alessandro brought in earlier is on the countertop and I peek in to see that it's full of supplies, including a few bottles of beer and other booze. How thoughtful.

'Leave your cup, I'll put it in the dishwasher,' Cristina calls out to me as I look around for a washing-up brush.

'Oh, okay, thank you.'

Alessandro walks me into the hall.

'Thank you for picking me up,' I say.

'It was my pleasure. Sleep well, but not too well.' He places his hands on my arms and bends down to kiss my cheeks. 'I'll be back at seven o'clock with Giulio,' he adds, staring into my eyes.

There might not have been an electric shock when we touched this time, but I can feel energy radiating from the place where his hands held my arms, even as I head into my bedroom.

Is this another thing I'm going to have to get used to?

Chapter 9

I climb straight into bed, not bothering with a shower, but I do remember to set my watch alarm to wake me after three hours. When it goes off, however, I feel so disorientated and exhausted that I cancel it and promptly fall into a deep sleep.

Knocking on my door rouses me.

'Angie!' Cristina calls from the hallway. 'Are you still sleeping? It's half past six!'

I sit bolt upright. 'I'm awake!'

My father will be here in half an hour!

'I've got to go out, but I've left something for you on the terrace,' she says as I struggle against the heaviness that wants to pull me back down again.

'Okay! Thank you!'

I can barely think straight as I hunt out my toiletries from my suitcase, but I feel better after washing my hair and brushing my teeth. A glance out the window tells me it's still a sunny day, but I have no idea if it's cool or warm so I play it safe with layers, pulling on a pair of black jeans with a mint-green top, light-grey cardigan and ankle boots. Tying my damp hair into a bun rather than attempting to dry and style the frizz, I try to disguise the dark circles under my eyes with the make-up Louise mercifully insisted I buy.

At seven o'clock exactly, I walk out onto the terrace to find the table laden with bowls and plates of food. Olives, slices of cured meats, cubes of cheese, pretzels, savoury crackers... My stomach rumbles at the sight of it all and I realise that I haven't eaten since they served breakfast on the plane. I mentally thank Cristina as I throw a pretzel into my mouth and eye a tall wine glass filled with what looks a bit like Fanta on ice. Sitting down on one of the wire chairs, I take a sip.

Ooh, that is *not* Fanta. This has a bitter orange aftertaste and is almost certainly alcoholic.

The air is cool, but the sun is warm, a blissful combination if only I were at ease enough to enjoy it. The dog from the first-floor balcony begins to bark at me, so I turn to look at it until it grows bored and jogs into its house, its tail wagging perkily.

I still haven't got used to having no responsibilities. In the few weeks since Nan died, I've been jolting with dread at this feeling that I've forgotten something. I had to do so much for her, whether it was helping her to get dressed or go to the toilet or eat her dinner, but now the only person I need to worry about is myself.

She would have loved this garden, I think with a pang.

I'm still finding it hard to reconcile the woman who raised me with the woman who withheld the truth from me for all those years. I'd give anything to be able to have one last lucid conversation with her. It isn't easy to forgive someone who can't give you an explanation – or an apology.

Voices coming from the roadside wall drag me out of the rabbit hole I'm going down and simultaneously prompt the dog to come rushing outside and go absolutely mental.

The gate latch buzzes and, a few seconds later, I almost jump out of my skin at the sight of Alessandro's top half appearing over the courtyard wall. He's propping himself up on his arms.

'You started without us!'

He's wearing a black T-shirt and the sight of tanned arms and lean muscles is distracting.

'Are you ready?' he asks.

I nod and swallow, and then an older man's raised, animated voice starts up. He's speaking in Italian and Alessandro looks over his shoulder at him and replies with a few words as he drops to the ground. They disappear into the reception area where Salvatore's voice joins the mix.

I'm a bag of nerves as I hurry inside. I try to take a deep breath to steady myself, but I'm barely able to expand my lungs at all because I'm so on edge.

I open the door and there, in front of me, is my father.

Chapter 10

Giulio is not much taller than me, but is substantially broader, with deeply tanned skin and thick black hair speckled with grey. He's wearing blue denim jeans and a cream-coloured shirt, and his brown eyes are crinkled at the corners as he drinks me in.

Do we have the same eyes? I think so.

'Angie!'

My feet seem to have glued themselves to the spot, but *my father* steps forward and embraces me, squeezing me tightly.

I could not feel more bizarre as I squeeze him back. He smells of cologne and wood smoke – sort of homely and welcoming – and for a split second, my senses are flooded with the memory of what my grandfather used to smell like. But before I can capture the memory and make it stick, it drifts away again.

'I cannot believe it,' Giulio says, withdrawing. 'You are here. My *daughter*.' His eyes roam around my face, from the top of my forehead to the tip of my chin. 'You don't look like your mother,' he muses, cocking his head to one side.

'No,' I reply, vaguely aware of Alessandro watching our exchange.

'Have you a photo of her?' Giulio asks.

'Yes. Would you like to see?'

'Later, later,' he replies, releasing me and clapping his hand on my back with a laugh. 'First we have a *birra*.'

'Let me,' Alessandro says. 'You go out to the terrace.'

My father takes the bench seat and delves straight into the cured meats, deftly folding two slices of salami in half before popping the whole parcel into his mouth.

'Are you feeling better?' I ask awkwardly as he chews and swallows.

'Fine, fine. Big fuss over nothing.' He throws a dirty look at the inside door before patting his jeans pocket. 'I have pills to take. No worries. That's what you Australians say, right? No worries?'

'Yeah.' I laugh nervously as he pops an olive into his mouth.

This is so weird.

'When you gonna come see me at *Serafina's*?' he asks. 'Tomorrow?'

'You should be resting,' Alessandro interrupts, appearing at the terrace doors with a glass of beer for Giulio and a can of lemonade for himself.

Giulio makes a noise of disgust.

Alessandro sighs and sits down, picking up the glass of *NotFanta* and passing it to me. '*Salute*,' he says.

'*Salute*!' Giulio responds enthusiastically. 'Welcome to Roma!'

'Thank you,' I reply.

'*Grazie*,' Giulio corrects me.

'*Grazie*,' I obligingly reply.

He beams at me.

I feel oddly disconnected as I take a sip of my drink. 'Cristina made this for me,' I tell them, trying to rustle up my small-talk skills. 'I don't know what it is.'

'Aperol Spritz,' Giulio replies. 'Prosecco with Aperol Bitters and soda water. Very popular drink, here in Italy. Where is Cristina?' he asks, eagerly looking around as though she might be hiding somewhere.

'She's out this evening,' I tell him.

'How did you sleep?' Alessandro asks me.

'Well. Too well,' I add with a wry smile. 'Cristina woke me about half an hour ago.'

'But that's a disaster – you won't sleep tonight.'

'He knows all about the jet lag,' Giulio chips in. 'He's always travelling around.'

'In his campervan?'

'*Si*, *si*, but before that he flew.' Giulio moves his hand through the air to denote an aeroplane. 'All around the world.' Now he waves his hand above his head in a circle like a helicopter. 'He's seen more than anyone I know.'

And I have seen nothing. Could we be less alike?

It's not long before we set off for dinner at an Italian bistro a few minutes' drive away. It's situated on a street corner and is triangular in shape with big windows and about a dozen wooden tables lit by candlelight.

Giulio orders for us, which surprises me, but as Alessandro doesn't bat an eyelid, I'm guessing this behaviour is typical.

He must know what he's doing if he's worked in the restaurant trade for years.

When a golden platter of deep-fried deliciousness arrives at our table, I breathe a sigh of relief.

'*Frittura alla Romana*,' Giulio declares, pushing the plate towards me. 'Fried vegetables, veal brains and lamb sweetbreads.'

My hand freezes mid-air. I used to think I'd be adventurous when I went travelling, but the last few years have taken their toll. My gut churns as I search wildly for what might be a nice green vegetable, but I can tell by the expression on Giulio's face that I won't get away without trying a little of everything. Bravely choosing something brown in colour, I attempt to remain poised under his scrutiny.

And scrutiny is the right word for it. Giulio watches me like a cat staring at a hole in the wall, waiting for a mouse to appear. Thankfully, the sweetbread or whatever it is tastes quite nice and his face lights up like a lantern when I tell him so.

This experience is repeated continuously over the course of the evening and I'm giddy with delight at the sight of a simple *spaghetti alla carbonara* appearing before me. It's the original Roman recipe made with no cream or mushrooms, just egg, grated parmesan and diced pancetta, but it's gorgeous. We also have grilled, juicy, marinated lamb cutlets and fava bean *scafata* made with cherry tomatoes and pancetta.

As the night wears on, it becomes clear that food is the one subject that is guaranteed to capture my father's attention.

He doesn't ask me much about myself, but he's happy to talk and I do my best to listen. I hear about the time the mayor came into his restaurant, and another occasion when he met the Pope, along with countless other anecdotes. It's hard to keep up with what he's saying, not least because he occasionally switches from English to Italian halfway through a story, but when the conversation drifts to his family, I concentrate because they're my family too.

What I really want to know is what he's not telling me: what happened during Mum's stay in Italy? What was his relationship with her like? How did he come to fall in love with her? And why did she leave so suddenly? I hope one day I'll feel comfortable enough to broach all of this, maybe when Alessandro is not around. I still can't believe that he's being so welcoming to the offspring of his stepfather's mistress, but I'm grateful for his presence and the way he's acting as a buffer between Giulio and me, translating when necessary and filling the gaps when I'm lost for words.

I find watching my father fascinating. He gesticulates wildly and becomes very animated when he's talking about something he cares about, which seems to be most things, but particularly the food that arrives at our table.

What was he like twenty-eight years ago when my mother met him? What attracted her to him?

'Do you have any photos from when you were younger?' I ask Giulio as we walk back to Alessandro's van at the end of the evening.

'*Si*, *si*, when you come to *Serafina's*, I show you. I also teach you how to make pizza, how to make pasta,' he adds nonchalantly.

'Give Angie a chance to settle in, Giulio, she's here for the whole summer,' Alessandro points out.

It's early June, now.

'Why you say only the summer?' Giulio demands to know. 'She might decide she like Italy enough to stay. We find her a nice Italian boy. She get married and never leave.'

Now I laugh out loud. *He's had too much to drink.*

'Is possible,' he adds with a shrug.

Finding a man and settling down is the last thing I plan on doing. I've waited my whole life to see the world – there's no way I'm getting tied down again so soon.

'One step at a time,' Alessandro replies mildly, giving me an apologetic look as he opens up the side door.

I climb in and buckle up. I'm not tired in the slightest so I'm glad when Alessandro says he'll take a yawning Giulio home first. I could do with drawing out the evening as long as possible.

We pull up in the car park behind *Serafina's*.

'Tomorrow I show you inside,' Giulio tells me abruptly, getting out of the van.

Alessandro says something to him in Italian and Giulio responds boisterously before opening up my side door and beckoning for me to get out. He kisses both of my cheeks, making a loud, wet suction noise, which is not nearly as unpleasant as it sounds.

'It is good to meet you,' he says, switching to English. 'You more like your mother than you think. You have her smile!'

His comment has a radiator effect on my stomach, which may or may not be linked to the wine I've consumed. He stumbles ever so slightly as he turns away, then laughs and waves dismissively at the van before making his way heavily up an external staircase that leads to his apartment on the first floor.

'Is he going to be okay?' I ask Alessandro through the still-open passenger door. He's frowning at Giulio through the front window, but he turns and gives me a weary smile. 'He'll be fine. Hop in,' he adds, patting the seat next to him.

I climb in, looking up through the window in time to see Giulio closing his apartment door behind him.

That was undoubtedly one of the strangest nights of my life. I have a father and his name is Giulio and he's fifty-five and he likes to talk and I *think* he likes me and I *think* I like him, but it's all a bit crazy, and I can't get my head around any of it. I'm not sure what I feel.

'Right,' Alessandro says, checking his watch.

Disappointment makes my insides wilt. He's going to take me home now and I'm going to be stuck there for hours, on my own, mulling over everything while sleep evades me.

'How about a tour of Roma?'

I stare at him. 'Are you serious?'

He shrugs and puts the van into drive. 'Sure. Why not?'

I clap and bounce on my seat like a child and he pulls, smiling, out of the car park.

Chapter 11

We drive at a comfortable speed along the wide streets of what Alessandro tells me is the Parioli district, or the second quartiere of Rome, identified by the initials Q.II. There are a few other cars on the road, but it's not busy. From the number of outdoor tables under canopies, I gather the restaurants normally spill out onto the pavements, but right now the staff are shutting up shop for the night, and when we stop at a set of traffic lights, I watch as they stack chairs and close shutters.

'What's it like, where you come from?' Alessandro asks out of the blue.

I turn to look at him. His face is half cast in shadow and half lit by the glow of an electric billboard outside his window.

'Tatooine,' I reply with a smile. Will he get the reference?

'Luke Skywalker's home planet in *Star Wars*?'

'Exactly!' The light turns green and he sets off again, the diesel engine threatening to drown out our conversation.

'So you live in a desert.' He raises his voice, unperturbed.

'Yes.' I twist towards him in my seat, tucking my left foot under my opposite knee to get comfortable. 'People who fly in say it's like looking down on the surface of Mars. That's how they imagine it, anyway, with the red sand. But the town and the surrounding area look more like the moon. We have over seventy opal fields with about two hundred and fifty thousand mineshaft entrances – they look like craters from above, with cream-coloured rock piles beside them.'

Opal was initially discovered in Coober Pedy in 1915 by a fifteen-year-old boy called William Hutchison. He was part of a syndicate prospecting for gold, along with his father. He wandered into the bush in search of water, but returned with opal – masses of it. A mad mining rush followed.

'It must get very hot out in the desert?'

'Yes! And windy and dusty. It gets really cold in winter, too, but I live in a dugout – that's a cave underground – so the temperature is pretty stable: between twenty-one and twenty-four degrees.'

Alessandro throws me a look of confusion. 'Did you just say you live in a cave?'

I nod. He listens intently as I tell him about my dugout, asking the occasional question. It's unusual for me to be doing so much of the talking. I haven't had a lot to say in the last few years, preferring to hear about what Nan's and my visitors have been up to.

I'm in the middle of telling Alessandro about Louise's old bedroom, which was decorated like an underwater mermaid's cave, complete with silver fish hanging from the ceiling and shells carved straight out of the sandstone walls, when he reaches across and places his hand on my knee, silencing me instantly.

I stare down at his hand and it squeezes.

'Angie,' he says.

My eyes dart up to look at his face, but he nods straight ahead, letting me go as I turn to see what has got his attention.

I literally gasp out loud.

The Colosseum is right there at the end of the street.

I sit forward in my seat so I can get a better view as it looms closer and closer. Each of its arches is lit up and it's glowing like a beacon in the night sky.

We drive right up to it and almost the whole way around, while I stare out of my window in astonishment. I've seen dozens of pictures, but nothing compares to the sight of this enormous structure in real life. Evidence of its age is clear in the pockmarked stone. It's mind-boggling to think that it was built almost two thousand years ago, especially considering the oldest surviving public building in Australia – Old Government House in Parramatta – is only around two hundred years old.

As we come almost full circle, Alessandro points out Palatine Hill and the Forum. The unlit buildings look brooding and ancient in the darkness, making me long to return in the daytime so I can explore properly.

'Make sure your bag is secure,' he advises when I say this out loud. 'Unfortunately, we have a lot of pickpockets in this city.'

We pass what he says is the Monument of Vittorio Emanuele II, or Altare della Patria. It's a huge, white monument situated high at the top of some steps with statues and fountains and curved rows of backlit columns. Alessandro tells me that, in daylight, it reminds him of a wedding cake, but we fly by too quickly for me to pay it as much attention as I'd like, the van leaning heavily as we take the corner at speed. It's a relief when we begin slowly zigzagging through narrower roads.

Alessandro points out a building that looks like a giant, brown-brick drum. 'That's the back of the Pantheon.'

Surely he's not being serious. Is he really able to get us this close?

He pulls onto the kerb and cuts the engine.

'Come,' he urges.

I climb out of the van and follow him into a nearby square.

We're right in front of the Pantheon's main elevation.

The portico looms over us, completely obstructing our view of the domed roof. It's lit up, but it looks dark and shadowy behind its eight giant columns.

'It's incredible inside,' Alessandro says. 'It's one of my favourite buildings. Almost two thousand years after it was built, it's still the world's largest unreinforced concrete dome. You know about the oculus? The big, round hole in the middle of the roof?'

I shake my head.

'It's open to the elements. When it rains, you get wet.'

'Doesn't it smell of damp?' I ask. 'If water gets into one of our dugouts, it reeks for about two years.'

'Is that right? Well, no, because the floor inside is slightly convex. The rain runs into still-functioning Roman drainpipes underneath.'

Refuse collectors are at work nearby, carrying rubbish bags

from outside cafés and dumping them into an awaiting truck, so we move on before we get caught behind it.

As we drive, I stare out of the window at the chunky rough stonework on the buildings lining the narrow streets. Everything seems so old, so full of history.

Alessandro pulls over again and we cross the road and head down a short passageway, coming out in a long piazza. Three marble fountains, with jade-coloured water lit from within, are spaced equally along its length.

'Piazza Navona,' he tells me as I do a slow about-turn, staring up at the yellow-painted buildings lining one side.

I've seen this place in films. I shake my head, stunned. I feel as though I'm in a wonderful, bewildering dream. I've wanted this for so long.

'There's a good gelato place nearby,' he says. 'I'll take you sometime.'

'This is incredible,' I murmur as we return to his van. 'I can't believe we're driving around the centre of Rome. You seem to know it like the back of your hand.'

'I've lived here for a long time,' he replies.

'How long?'

'On and off, all my life. But tell me more about Coober Pedy. I've never heard of anywhere like it.'

It doesn't take an idiot to work out that he's trying to deflect attention away from himself.

But I'm not sure why.

Chapter 12

'Your football team had to drive a nine-hundred-kilometre round trip to play matches?' Alessandro asks with a laugh. 'But that's insane!'

'At least we *had* a football team,' I point out good-naturedly. 'Even if it was "just" Aussie rules.'

He pointed this out earlier, the nitpicker.

I used to go to some of the Saints' matches myself when I was growing up, and I didn't mind the long journey. It was nice to visit somewhere different. Roxby Downs, where the rest of the league's teams are located, is bigger than Coober Pedy and more modern, but ultimately, it's another outback mining town.

'Okay,' Alessandro says, reverting to the business of being my tour guide. 'This is Ponte Vittorio Emanuele II.'

Ahead is a stone bridge flanked with statues. On our left, the surrounding up-lit buildings reflect prettily in the dark water, but it's the view to our right that takes my breath away.

'Castel Sant'Angelo,' Alessandro says of the towering cylindrical building on the other side of the river.

A pedestrian bridge, also lined with statues, runs right up to it. The rampart defences are lit with an orange glow against the navy blue sky, and a single statue at the very top shines with bright white light.

'Once the tallest building in Rome,' Alessandro tells me. 'Commissioned by Emperor Hadrian as a mausoleum for himself and his family, but later used by the popes as a fortress and a castle. Now, it's a museum.'

There are so many places I want to visit. I experience a thrill of excitement at the thought that I'll have plenty of time to explore in the coming weeks.

Once over the bridge, Alessandro turns left and at the end of the street is a very familiar, very famous sight: the dome of St Peter's Basilica. I've seen it on the news countless times and in movies. They even screened the film adaptation of a Dan Brown novel, in which it appears, on the flight over.

Alessandro finds somewhere to pull up, mounting a steep kerb that would stonewall a normal car.

As we walk across St Peter's Square – or Piazza San Pietro – he tells me that we are no longer in Italy but in the Vatican City, the world's smallest country.

The colonnade, with its forest of columns, curves symmetrically on either side of the plaza, and the cobbles beneath our feet are shiny and smooth from foot traffic over the years, so shiny that the lights from all around are reflected in them.

'You'll have to go up to the rooftop one day,' Alessandro says, nodding ahead at the dome. 'You stand right amongst the statues. The view is very special.'

He points out the entrance to the museums and the Sistine Chapel on our right.

'How many times have you been?' I ask.

'Once. That was enough.' He shudders. 'I don't like queues. Or people.'

I laugh, assuming he's joking, because he seems like a pretty sociable guy, but maybe he prefers his own company if he travels alone in Frida.

'Why did you name your van "Frida"?' I ask. 'Are you a Frida Kahlo fan?'

He doesn't seem fazed by my abrupt change of subject.

'Her paintings intrigue me, but I'm not particularly drawn to her work. I like the name, that's all.'

'Where did you and Frida go most recently?' I'm curious.

'Most recently? We spent a bit of time in the "Stans".' Alessandro catches my confused look. 'You know, Kazakhstan, Uzbekistan, Turkmenistan… Came home via Russia, Georgia, Turkey, Greece and ferry from Albania.'

'Have you ever been to Australia?'

'That's one place I haven't been. What about you?'

'Me?'

'What were the last countries you visited?' he asks.

'I've never been anywhere.'

He thinks I'm pulling his leg.

'I'm serious. Until yesterday, I'd never stepped out of South Australia.'

He comes to a stop and stares at me. 'You haven't travelled anywhere?' Now he's not only disbelieving, he's disappointed. *Disapproving*, almost.

'Not out of choice,' I feel compelled to explain. 'I'd

planned to go travelling when I turned eighteen. But then my grandfather died and my grandmother was diagnosed with Alzheimer's. I couldn't leave her.'

I explained some of this in one of our first phone conversations, but I didn't go into detail. I wouldn't expect Alessandro or Giulio to know what it was like to be a full-time carer. Few people understand.

His eyebrows pull together. 'Your grandfather was an opal miner?'

I wasn't seeking his sympathy; I just couldn't bear the look on his face.

I nod.

'How did he die?' he asks tentatively.

'A section of his mine caved in.' I still find it difficult to say the words out loud, even after ten years.

Nan and I were there when he was brought out from under the ground. He hadn't a hope of surviving, but we had hoped anyway. That hope had been crushed with the weight of a couple of tonnes of rock.

My grandfather had seemed so small in death but, in life, he'd been the heart and soul of our world. He was always up for a laugh, and when he found opal, his energy would soar to stratospheric levels. Those were the best days, the days when he'd whack on his music and dance around the living room, twirling me in circles to the likes of Johnny Cash and Roy Orbison.

We stopped playing his records after he died. I've always felt as though a part of us died with him.

'He was like a father to you?' Alessandro asks quietly, and I nod.

'And your grandmother… She was your mother.' He says it as a statement, not a question. 'You must have been heartbroken to lose her.'

A darker emotion twists and coils around my grief.

'I lost her a long time ago.' I swallow down the lump in my throat and begin to slowly walk forward.

I *was* heartbroken, but more so years ago. I think they call it anticipatory grief. Those moments when I realised she was slipping away from me, the first time she forgot my name and the second and the third… The days I found her out in the yard, rattling at the gates and trying to get out because she wanted to take lunch to my grandfather, even though he'd long since passed away… The blank look on her face when she couldn't recall the recipe for the Anzac biscuits she often used to make…

I try to explain what it was like as we head in the direction of Alessandro's van. 'But right now…' I hesitate, but can't stop the words from spilling out. 'Right now I'm too upset with her to feel sad that she's gone. I'm sure she had her reasons, but it hurts that she lied. She lied to me *and* to my mother. I'm pretty sure both of my grandparents did.' I imagine the letter, squirrelled away in my grandad's wine rack, and I feel so racked with frustration, resentment and hurt that everything else – sorrow, relief, guilt at feeling that relief – is momentarily blasted away. 'They kept my father from me, all of these years. How can I ever forgive them for that?'

My eyes fill at such a speed that I drag my sleeves hurriedly across them. I mutter an embarrassed apology and pick up my pace.

We reach the van in silence and I know I'm going to be kicking myself about this later. *Talk about too much, too soon.*

But when we're buckled up and Alessandro's hand is hovering over the key in the ignition, he says to me in a low voice: 'You will forgive them. One day, you will forgive them. You must.'

A glint of gold catches my eye when I turn to look at him. I notice that the chain hanging around his neck has broken free from beneath his black T-shirt, revealing a small gold cross pendant.

'Are you religious?' I ask, distracted.

I don't know why I'm surprised – this is a devoutly Catholic country, after all – but I didn't get a sense of reverence coming from him in the piazza just now.

He reaches up and tucks his pendant back beneath his T-shirt. 'I have a tumultuous relationship with God,' he mutters, bringing Frida noisily to life. 'Right! I think it's time to bring a smile to your face!' he shouts over the engine.

I'm glad we're leaving the darkness behind.

At least for a little while.

Chapter 13

The next morning, Cristina wakes me up soon after nine. She literally bounces on my bed until I roll out of it and somehow manage to land on my feet.

'Sorry!' she says, not sounding the least bit apologetic as she backs out of the room. 'I'm under strict instructions from Alessandro. He's been texting me. Jump in the shower and I'll make you a coffee!' she shouts over her shoulder as she heads in the direction of the kitchen.

Because I tied my hair up while it was still wet yesterday, it's in an interesting place this morning. And by interesting, I don't mean good. I don't bother to wash it again, but I do dampen it down and secure it into a bun.

I rarely bothered with my appearance in Coober Pedy – there seemed little point as no one cared what I looked like, or at least I didn't mind what anyone thought. For some reason I don't feel nearly so nonchalant now.

*

Last night, after we left Piazza San Pietro, Alessandro and I skirted along the banks of the river for a while before returning to the centre. He pulled up on a corner – I didn't know what we were doing or where he'd brought me. Then, outside my window, the Trevi Fountain burst into life.

It was so big and bright and beautiful – the largest Baroque fountain in Rome, Alessandro said. It definitely brought a smile to my face.

The view fell dark again and we realised that the fountain lights were being tested. It was after two in the morning, but there were still a dozen or so people about when we climbed out to take a closer look.

Alessandro stayed in his van for the next stop, shouting, 'Spanish Steps!' out of his window at me as I peered over some railings at a set of wide stone steps leading to a fountain at the end. He'd said that would be our last stop, but he must've had a change of heart because he parked up not far from Villa Medici and took me to a viewpoint.

'At sunrise, it is even more beautiful,' he said as I gazed at the rooftops stretched out before us. 'The sun rises behind, backlighting the trees in the park and casting morning light on the church domes all across the skyline. But I am too tired to wait until sunrise, I'm sorry,' he said with a small smile.

I shook my head with wonder. 'This has already been one of the best nights of my life. Thank you.'

He didn't say a lot after that. I hope it wasn't another case of too much, too soon, but I've always worn my heart on my sleeve and I find it hard to shut up when gratitude is due.

*

Cristina is in the kitchen when I emerge and she's dressed and ready for the day in smart black capri pants and a white shirt. Her hair is fashioned into a spiky style that sits high on her head. She's not wearing make-up, as far as I can tell.

'Hey,' I say, my eyes widening at the sight of what looks like a latte on the countertop. She pushes it towards me. 'Thank you!' I exclaim, relieved that it's not a strong espresso.

'Lots of milk,' she replies knowingly.

Did she catch me grimacing yesterday?

'How was last night?' she asks.

'Oh, it was amazing.' I shake my head with awe. 'We went to the Colosseum, the Pantheon, St Peter's Square, the Spanish Steps, the Trevi Fountain… Where else? All over the place. I can't believe I've seen so much of Rome already.'

She seems perplexed. 'With Giulio?'

'No, with Alessandro,' I reply.

And then it dawns on me that she had been asking what it was like to meet *my father* for the first time.

I realise I've barely thought about our encounter since I woke up.

'Alessandro took you on a tour of the city?' Cristina asks with even more surprise than the thought of Giulio accompanying me.

'Yes. But, oh, meeting Giulio was great!' I tell her hastily. 'We went for dinner at a bistro and had a good chat. It was great,' I repeat lamely, failing to find a sufficiently eloquent description on the four hours of sleep I've had. 'Thank you for the drink and snacks, by the way.'

'Aperitivo,' she replies. 'Italian word for pre-dinner drinks and snacks,' she explains.

'I see! I liked the Aperol—'

'Spritz.'

I wasn't speaking particularly slowly, but I suspect she's naturally a faster-paced person than I am. I think it's that, rather than impatience, that has her completing my sentence for me.

'Are you going into work today?' I take a sip of my latte and hope I'll soon come to feel less daunted by her.

'Yes, later.'

'Is black and white the uniform?'

She lets out a wry laugh and glances down at her outfit. 'No, we don't wear a uniform. Giulio tried to introduce one once, but Alessandro wouldn't be seen dead in red. He's picking you up at ten o'clock.' She snatches a set of keys from the benchtop. 'These are for you. Let me show you how the door works; it's a bit tricky.'

She leaves shortly afterwards – off to meet a friend for brunch. I didn't dare ask if that friend is Rebecca, the vixen from yesterday morning.

Alessandro arrives ten minutes later, wearing a faded black T-shirt and the well-worn jeans from yesterday.

'How did you sleep?' he asks after we've exchanged kisses.

'Not as well as I would have had Cristina not woken me up by jumping on my bed like a nutcase.'

His lips lift at the corners. 'Good. We'll have your jet lag sorted in no time. Shall we go? Giulio is keen to see you.'

'How is he this morning?' I ask as I grab my keys.

'Fine. Chirpy.' He opens the door, touching his hand to my lower back as he ushers me through.

On the way to the restaurant, Alessandro talks me through the journey, pointing out the short cuts I would take if I were walking. I'm not sure I'll remember – in fact, I'm almost certain I won't – but I do my best to keep up with his directions.

He parks behind the restaurant, then leads me around the outside of the building to the front door rather than taking me in through the rear entrance.

'Giulio will want you to see it in its best light,' he explains.

Windows line the front of the building as we pass, and a glance in reveals bench seats with black padded backs fixed to the walls. The space between them is filled with wooden tables and chairs, and the walls are whitewashed with minimal decoration. The eating area appears to be on a lower level to that on which we're walking, and when we enter through a glass door, I notice a few steps leading down to it.

On the left is a bar area with bottles lined up against the wall and straight ahead is a tall, slender desk, on top of which sits a telephone and a reservations book.

At the back is a large serving hatch, and beyond is a big orange dome and a couple of people at work. Giulio bursts out through the kitchen door and spies us, opening his arms wide.

'My daughter!' he cries, beaming from ear to ear. 'You are here in the Marchesi restaurant!'

Grasping my upper arms firmly, he kisses each of my cheeks. His kisses are different to Alessandro's – they land with intent, whereas Alessandro's are not much more than cheek brushes.

'This is great,' I say, looking around. 'Has it changed much since my mother worked here?'

'*Sì*, it used to be full of, how you say? Knick-knacks.' Giulio points to the walls. 'Shelves. Ornaments. Red walls. Strings of chilli, garlic. I thought it was a little too…' He clicks his fingers as he thinks of the right word. '*Cluttered.*' He points at the ceiling. 'My father, I don't think he like this. He call it boring.'

I assume he means his father wouldn't approve from the afterlife. He passed away a few years ago.

'I like it,' I say with a smile. 'It's fresh and clean.'

'I think so too,' he agrees with a decisive nod. 'I introduce you to Maria and Antonio.' He beckons me towards the kitchen while Alessandro heads behind the bar.

The two people in the kitchen could be brother and sister, they look so alike. They're both about my height, but a good few stone heavier, and they have short dark curly hair with shocks of white at the temples. Their round faces grow even wider with smiles at the sight of me.

Giulio introduces us and they simultaneously burst into excited Italian, wiping their hands clean on their aprons so that they can greet me like an old friend.

They don't speak English, so I ask Giulio if they're related.

'Married forty years,' he replies. 'They worked with my mother and father and now they are here with me,' he says fondly, squeezing Antonio's shoulder.

I glance past them to the counter. 'What are you making?'

'They make dough for pizza,' Giulio replies. 'They are the best.'

What I didn't realise about *Serafina's* is that it is *still* a family-run restaurant. I'd assumed that Giulio had taken over completely from his parents, but he spends part of the morning explaining that much of the produce that is used in the kitchen is grown on the family's land in Tivoli.

Giulio's sister Eliana, her husband, Enzo, and two of their three children who are still living at home, Jacopo and Valentina, prepare much of the produce, such as the pork and fennel sausages, ricotta and antipasti pickles. Many of the vegetables, herbs and salad come from the two families' gardens, and the wild mushrooms used in some of the dishes are foraged from the surrounding land. A few gelato flavours are made at home by Eliana with fruit from the orchard, goats produce the milk that makes some of the cheeses and free-range hens provide the eggs used to make the pasta. Serafina is still in charge of the ravioli, but the rest of the pasta and sauces are prepared by Giulio and his team at *Serafina's*, as is the pizza dough. Maria and Antonio make it fresh every morning. That giant dome that I saw when I arrived is a wood-burning clay pizza oven which gives the pizzas a distinctive taste.

Giulio put his fingertips to his lips and blew a kiss while making a brilliantly clichéd 'Mwah' sound when he told me this.

I still can't get my head around the fact that this exuberant Italian man is my father.

By the time Cristina appears for lunch service, I feel as though I've been at *Serafina's* for several hours, but in fact it's been less than two. My body is weary with exhaustion and I feel hungry, but I know I'm not, from the way Giulio has been making me try various morsels in the kitchen. It seems jet lag has well and truly kicked in. It's so strange to be finally experiencing it.

'I'll make you a coffee,' Alessandro says when I prop myself up at the bar next to Cristina.

Giulio has ushered me out of the kitchen now that it's about to get busy.

'Maybe you should go for a walk, get some fresh air?' Alessandro suggests.

'I think I'm too tired. Is your van outside? Can I go for a lie down instead?'

He claps me over the top of my head and makes a tsk sound. I laugh and bat him away. At that moment, a petite brunette walks through the door and stops short, her face like thunder.

Alessandro says something to her in Italian. She glares at him as he checks his watch, then tosses back her long hair and struts over to the cash register, ignoring him. She barks something at Cristina and flicks her gaze in my direction. Cristina answers in English.

'This is Angie, Giulio's daughter,' she explains, gesturing to me and then the girl in turn. 'And this is Teresa.'

She's about my age, tiny but well-proportioned, with an oval face and a small, upturned nose.

'*Ciao*,' she says, without cracking a smile. I'm glad of Maria in the kitchen, because the Italian women I've met so far haven't exactly exuded warmth.

Teresa picks up a pencil from behind the cash register and twirls her dark locks up into a bun, slotting the pencil into her hair to secure it.

Show-off.

I turn at the sound of Alessandro placing an espresso in front of me. His eyes are still on Teresa as he absentmindedly passes me a sachet of sugar. I think of milk, longingly.

The next thing I know, Cristina is behind the bar, upending the contents of my tiny espresso cup into a larger cup and adding hot milk from the coffee machine.

Alessandro splutters something at her in Italian.

'Pay attention!' she berates him in English, passing me a frothy cappuccino.

He stares at her, then he stares at the cappuccino cup, and finally, at me. I must look like all of my Christmases have come at once. *Milk – yay!*

The door whooshes open and a guy saunters in. He's tall and broad with short dark hair, high sculptured cheekbones and a strong chiselled jaw.

Cristina beams – *beams*! – and I watch with amazement as she comes out from behind the bar to clasp his face in her hands.

I've barely seen her cracking a smile – not even when she was bouncing on my bed like a two-year-old.

The guy exchanges a couple of curt words with Teresa, but he greets Alessandro with a handclasp before turning his attention to me.

Wow. Check out the length of those eyelashes.

'Stefano, this is Angie. Angie, Stefano,' Alessandro introduces us as Cristina disappears through the door at the rear of the restaurant.

'Aah! Giulio's daughter!' he exclaims with a smile that is so bright and sparkling that it makes me want to hunt out my sunglasses. He bends to kiss me, taking his time about it, and my cheeks feel well and truly warm when he's done.

'How are you finding Roma so far?' he asks.

'I'm loving it.' And, I have to say, it's improving by the minute.

Cristina returns with a stack of folded cream-coloured fabric, chucking one piece to Teresa, another to Stefano, and keeping one for herself. I watch as all three of them put them on: aprons!

Stefano works here? He looks like a model, not a waiter!

Giulio bursts out of the kitchen, shouting in Italian and gesticulating wildly. Stefano, Cristina and Teresa scatter while Alessandro speaks to Giulio in a calm, collected manner. Giulio returns to the kitchen and Alessandro comes out from behind the bar.

'What was that about?' I ask as he picks up the telephone.

'The seafood supplier didn't turn up today,' he replies, dialling a number. 'We need prawns, *pronto*.'

I sip my coffee as he makes a call.

'Good,' he says when he's hung up. 'Our friends at another restaurant will help us. You want to come with me for the walk?'

'Sure!' I finish off the last of my coffee and hop down from the stool.

He calls out to the others to let them know what we're up to. Teresa gives us a filthy look. What's her deal?

'How long have Teresa and Stefano worked with you?' I ask, trying to make sense of Teresa's mood as we walk out of the door and take a right along the wide, well-kept pavement.

'Stefano, about four years. Teresa, one.'

'Cristina and Stefano seem to get on,' I comment casually.

'Yes, they are very good friends. Stefano has been on holiday. Cristina has missed him, I think.'

'And Teresa? What's her story?'

'I'm not sure what you mean,' he replies.

Is it my imagination or does he seem uncomfortable?

'She doesn't appear to fit in as well as the other two.'

He shrugs. 'She's not really part of their gang. It was Stefano who introduced Cristina to Rebecca. They go out together a lot.'

Interesting. 'How did Stefano and Rebecca meet?'

'They were in the same class at university, studying law.'

I glance at him. 'But Stefano didn't go into law?'

'No, he hated it. He quit university in his second year. He wants to be an actor, but his parents do not approve.'

It's cooler than yesterday, and I didn't bring my jacket, but Alessandro keeps a brisk pace so I'm feeling warmer as we walk. Tall trees line the road and sunshine streams through the leaves overhead, dappling the pavement with light. We pass a lively café, a couple of boutique clothes shops and a greengrocer with a jewel-like array of fruit and vegetables out on display. A stout man in a black apron calls out a buoyant greeting to Alessandro and he replies with a cheerful one of his own.

I'm glad of the chance to see more of the Parioli district – it seems like a nice place to live and work.

'That's *Bruno's* over there.' Alessandro points across the road at a restaurant with an ivy-covered trellis out the front, dripping with fairy lights.

I bet it's pretty at night.

As soon as Alessandro steps off the pavement, I dart past him at a run.

'I'm not used to this many cars,' I tell him as he walks towards me, a look of bemusement on his face at my apparent eagerness to reach the other side.

Everything is new and exciting to me right now, even traffic.

The restaurant owner, a man in his fifties, greets us when

we enter the restaurant, and he's even more effervescent when Alessandro introduces me.

'Giulio is very happy to have you here,' Bruno tells me with a wide smile.

His friendly son, Carlo, also comes out of the kitchen to be introduced, bringing with him a polystyrene container for us.

'That was nice of them,' I say when we're on our way again.

I try not to run across the road this time, but I do walk fast. Very fast.

'The restaurant trade is like one big family,' Alessandro replies. 'We help each other out.'

'How many people work at *Serafina's*?'

'Apart from Stefano, Cristina and Teresa, there is Dario, Edgardo, Marcella and Susanna. Dario and Marcella help out in the kitchen, but the others are part-time. You'll meet them on Friday night and at the weekend.'

It's Wednesday now.

It's only when we arrive back at *Serafina's* to a cold look from Teresa that I realise I retrieved no information about her at all.

Chapter 14

On Friday morning, I decide to walk to *Serafina's*, reasonably confident that I'll be able to find my way after Alessandro's repeated directions. The sky is blue, but I take my raincoat anyway, not trusting that the weather won't turn as it did yesterday. Alessandro has given me a lift home the last couple of evenings, but I imagine it'll be busier tonight and he might not be able to get away.

Listening out for traffic and looking left and right several times before daring to cross the road, I bound up a few steps and enter a small triangle of parkland. It's so dense with trees that the sky overhead is mostly obscured. I'd probably feel vulnerable taking this short cut if it weren't for a teenage girl walking her dog nearby.

I wish her a good morning in Italian and she repeats '*Buongiorno*' back to me.

Coming out onto the road, I head uphill past several identical apartment blocks, enjoying the sensation of my thighs burning. After Nan passed away, I went all over Coober Pedy on foot, making the most of being able to visit the homes of friends who had previously had no choice but to come to me. But all I've done here in the last couple of days is sit around. Alessandro has let me take up residence at a table in the corner of the restaurant and I've been on my laptop, replying to messages on Facebook and determinedly trying to learn Italian via an online course. More than anything else, though, I've been watching what's going on around me.

I think I've got a pretty good grasp now of how it all works. Giulio seems to be, on the whole, a well-liked boss, full of smiles for staff and customers and only throwing the occasional tantrum when something goes wrong with kitchen supplies. On Wednesday it was the prawns, and yesterday Enzo was late with the ravioli delivery. Giulio berated him fiercely, but the two men quickly resolved their differences and it was delightful to meet the husband of the aunt I never knew I had.

Antonio and Maria, I adore, even though they barely speak a word of English. Dario and Marcella don't either – the former is in his late teens and does the washing up, and Marcella is a few years older and helps mainly with food preparation.

I like Stefano a lot – he's friendly and funny – and Cristina has also grown on me in a big way. She notices everything and has a brilliantly dry sense of humour, but with Stefano, she really lets her guard down and it's been a joy to watch the two friends banter with each other, something they often do in English so I feel included.

Teresa, however, is hard to warm to. She's often sour and

moody, but when she's serving, she dials up her charm to full power and her smiles make her impossibly beautiful. The customers clearly can't tell that they're false, because her tips are better than everyone else's – I know this because she makes a point of counting them out at the end of each service.

Stefano also seems to fare well on the tip front, but Cristina's surly demeanour does not reap rewards. I like her all the more for being genuine.

As for Alessandro, he mans the bar and manages the restaurant as Giulio spends most of his time in the kitchen, only coming out to occasionally converse with his regulars. Alessandro is professional with customers, but somewhat aloof with staff, which came as a bit of a surprise to me after our night drive around Rome. His personality seemed warmer then, but at work, he's remote.

At the end of the road is a small café and the sound of coffee beans being ground reminds me of the noise that Grandad's opal-polishing machine used to make.

Under other circumstances, the memory might make me feel sad or nostalgic, but instead, I'm filled with elation. It has just hit me: I've done it. I've left Coober Pedy and I'm in Italy on the other side of the world. I'm *free*.

On impulse, I head into the café and buy myself a warm, flaky pastry to eat on the rest of the journey to *Serafina's*.

I'm still smiling when I arrive at the restaurant.

Yesterday, Giulio promised with his hand on his heart that he would dig out some photos for me and I'm pleased to find he has them ready and waiting. We sit at the table in the corner, side by side on the bench seat.

'This is when I was seventeen years old,' he says, passing me a photo of a tanned teenager in light-blue shorts and a yellow T-shirt. I bring the photo closer to my face and study it. His hair is longer – a very dark shade of brown – and there isn't an ounce of fat on him.

We flick through a few more photos, and as he ages, his shoulders broaden out and his hair lengthens until it comes to shoulder level. He almost always has his same friendly smile, and everything about him glows with youth and vitality. I can see what my mother saw in him: he was a very good-looking guy.

'Is this *Serafina's*?' I ask, studying a photo of him standing with his father. They're both wearing white T-shirts and jeans.

I knew straight away that it was my late grandfather, Andrea, because he looks so much like Giulio. Andrea must've been about the same age that Giulio is now – mid fifties – and Giulio is about twenty-five. He met my mother when he was twenty-seven.

The walls behind them are painted red and covered with knick-knacks: shelves full of copper pots and pans, decorative plates and figurines, and long strings of garlic, chilli and bunches of dried herbs hanging from the ceiling.

'*Si*, yes, *Serafina's*. See what I mean? Cluttered.'

'Yes,' I reply with a smile, and despite what I said about liking the fresh, clean style of today, I can totally see the appeal of the old look. It reminds me a bit of Jimmy's home. His wife, Vicky, used to collect figurines and painted plates and she'd hang up dried herbs in the kitchen too – Jimmy never took them down after she passed away and they were coated in dust when I went to his dugout a few weeks ago, having not been there in years.

'Leave it,' he growled when I reached for a sponge, wanting to wipe down a surface or ten. 'If I'd known you were going to fuss about, I would have come over to yours. I've lived with the dust all my life, girlie. It's a war I've never tried to win. Now, what's this you've got to tell me?'

I rang him earlier that morning to ask if he was in, having just spoken to my father for the first time. I wanted to bring Jimmy up to date and it was a relief to see his stunned expression at the news. The world wouldn't have spun quite so perfectly on its axis if I'd discovered that Jimmy had lied to me as well.

The thought of my old friend at home alone in Coober Pedy makes my heart squeeze. I hope he's okay.

'How old are you here?' I ask Giulio, returning my attention to the photos.

'Twenty-four.'

He's sitting on a deckchair in the sunshine and beside him is another dark-haired, attractive man of around the same age.

'Who's this?'

'That is Giorgio,' he replies, and something about his tone makes me glance at him.

'He was my best friend,' he tells me. 'He died a couple of years after this photo was taken. A rare brain tumour.'

'I'm so sorry,' I say softly, glancing at my father. Sadness has pulled his features down, making his shoulders droop. I've never seen him like this and my insides swell with sympathy. But his sombre mood lasts only a moment.

'Giulio and Giorgio!' he exclaims perkily, making me jolt. 'We were like brothers. We grew up together in Tivoli.'

Out of the corner of my eye, I see Alessandro approaching with a couple of coffees.

'Thank you,' I say as he places them down on the table: an espresso for Giulio and a latte for me.

His corresponding smile warms my insides. I think he likes seeing Giulio and me together.

'Aah, Giorgio,' he murmurs, peering over my shoulder at the photo. This is followed by a few words in Italian, clearly meant only for his stepfather's ears.

My curiosity is piqued. It's rare for him to exclude me.

Giulio replies in Italian and I sense unwillingness, but when Alessandro persists my father seems to concede to whatever it is he is suggesting.

'Giorgio was my wife's brother,' Giulio explains. 'Alessandro's uncle.' He says something else to Alessandro in Italian, then reaches over and pulls out the chair opposite, indicating that he should sit down. I don't think Alessandro was expecting the tables to be turned, but he obliges.

'Marta, my mother, was Giorgio's younger sister,' Alessandro says as Giulio falls quiet.

I remember that Alessandro had wanted Giulio to tell me about Marta – and him, her son – over the telephone, but my father had swerved that conversation.

'My mother had depression,' Alessandro says. 'I didn't know that's what it was back then – I'm not sure any of us did. She had been like this for years…' He moves his hand up and down, up and down. The next time his hand goes high, he keeps it up there. 'She fell pregnant with me when she was up here.' He returns his hand to the table. 'When I was older, she told me that she had been careless many times. She did not know who my father was.'

My eyes widen. He's also gone through life knowing nothing about his father? We have more in common than I thought.

Alessandro looks at Giulio as he continues. 'When Giorgio fell ill, he asked Giulio to take care of his younger sister. Giulio married Marta and took us in. I was seven years old.'

Following Alessandro's gaze, I turn to look at Giulio myself. He's motionless, staring down at his folded hands resting in front of him on the table.

'So it was almost like an arranged marriage?' I ask.

Giulio erupts into life. 'I had known Marta her whole life,' he says. 'I loved her, *si*, like a sister, but I *cared* for her. When I met your mother, Marta was…' He stops speaking abruptly.

Alessandro helps him out with the right words. 'She was at a low point.'

'*Si*,' Giulio agrees solemnly.

'Giulio and my mother had only recently got married. Giulio tried to help, but it was very difficult,' Alessandro explains.

'Very difficult,' Giulio repeats and even after all these years, he sounds incredibly weary at the memory.

Alessandro returns his attention to me. 'Your mother could not have been more different from my mother.'

'Did you know her?' I ask with surprise.

He nods. 'She was like a breath of fresh air.'

'I need to go and check on the *abbacchio alla cacciatora*,' Giulio says abruptly, heaving himself to a standing position.

I immediately get to my feet too.

I have always given hugs easily – compassion is something that comes naturally to me – but Giulio hugs me hard in return, and when he pulls away, his eyes are damp.

'I will tell you more about your mother. I promise,' he assures me.

'I would like that,' I reply, my eyes tracking his journey to the kitchen as I sit down again.

That was intense.

'He loved her,' Alessandro says quietly, reflectively.

I look at him.

'Giulio loved your mother,' he repeats. 'The news of her death, even after all these years, has hit him quite hard, I think.'

The restaurant door whooshes open and Teresa appears. She glares over at us, and I give her a nod that she chooses to ignore.

Alessandro stands and collects our coffee mugs, but before he can turn away, I press his hand.

'Thank you for explaining.'

His eyes rest on mine for a moment and then he nods curtly and turns away, barking something at Teresa. She raises her voice stroppily in return and I hide my smile.

I'm glad that I've seen again the softer side Alessandro displayed during my tour of Rome. I have a feeling that he doesn't show it often.

Chapter 15

There's another waitress on tonight, one of the part-time staff. Her name is Susanna and she's tall and curvy with bright red lipstick and a blinding smile. She's friendly and chatty and I like her the moment we're introduced.

Alessandro has mentioned that it's going to be busy tonight, but he says I can hang out with him at the bar. Of course, what he really means is that I'll have to give up my favourite table.

I'll probably head back to Cristina's early. I've been leaving the restaurant at around eight o'clock the last few nights, reading in bed until I can't keep my eyes open any longer. I may be over the worst of my jet lag, but I'm still waking up on and off throughout the night and it can take me a while to fall asleep again.

It doesn't help that it's so noisy here – cars going up and down the street, dogs barking, people arguing, sometimes in the reception area right outside the apartment.

Actually, Cristina said this morning's argument wasn't really an argument: the two men were discussing football. Italians often sound like they're angry when they're simply having an animated conversation, I've discovered.

It's all very different to the life I had at home where my room was so quiet and dark that I could've heard a pin drop.

Not that I slept well there. The slightest noise had me bounding from bed with worry about what trouble Nan might be getting herself into.

As I'm packing up my laptop, I spy Stefano sniggering to Cristina nearby.

'What are you two whispering about?' I ask.

'We're waiting for the fireworks to start,' Stefano replies, casting a look over his shoulder at Susanna.

She's behind the bar with Alessandro and although she has her back to us, there's something coquettish about her body language. Alessandro is cleaning out the coffee machine while she watches. I think he's listening to something she's saying because he nods occasionally, although he doesn't look at her.

'What fireworks?' I ask with confusion.

Teresa flies through the door in her usual hurricane-like manner and Stefano looks like he's about to spontaneously combust.

Teresa's eyes make a sweep of the room, coming to a stop at the sight of Susanna and Alessandro behind the bar. Susanna stiffens and her smile freezes in place. Teresa looks away again and begins her usual arriving-to-work routine, checking the reservations book and twisting her hair up into a bun and securing it with a pencil. She doesn't acknowledge any of us, but her eyes are flashing with even more annoyance than usual.

It's like watching a soap opera. If only there were subtitles.

'I can't believe I was on holiday when it happened!' Stefano mourns loudly when I follow him and Cristina into the stockroom-cum-office-cum-cluttered-little-cupboard-space at the rear of the restaurant.

'When what happened?' I ask, barely managing to squeeze into the tiny room.

'When Alessandro and Susanna got it on,' he replies, making rude gestures with his hands.

Cristina makes a noise of disapproval. 'You don't know for sure that they did it,' she brushes him off, before saying to me, 'Susanna has been all over Alessandro since the day he arrived.'

'Since the day *Alessandro* arrived? From where?'

'From his latest travels.'

'But what's the deal with Teresa?'

'Teresa is so last summer,' Stefano replies gleefully, waving at me in a mock dismissive, highly camp manner.

'Alessandro slept with Teresa last year?' I ask with surprise.

'And the rest,' Stefano replies slyly.

What? This is an unexpected revelation.

Cristina makes that same noise of disapproval again. 'Too much gossip is bad for you, Stefano. Your cheeks have gone pink. What shall we listen to tonight?'

As they argue over which music to play on the sound system, my gut twists unpleasantly.

And there was me thinking I was getting to know Alessandro.

I come out of the stockroom and look over at him. He's polishing glasses behind the bar. Susanna is in the kitchen – I can hear her chatting away merrily to Maria and Antonio – and Teresa is setting tables, putting down knives and forks with such intent that each piece of cutlery hits the wooden table with a clunk.

Loud – and I mean *loud* – rave music fills the room and Stefano bursts into the restaurant area, fist pumping the air and enthusiastically marching across the floor beside the bar. Cristina follows him, laughing, and the two of us stand side by side in hysterics as Alessandro throws his hands up in outrage and shouts something that none of us can hear.

Giulio went out a while ago – I don't think anyone would attempt to get away with this sort of behaviour if he were around, but then again, I'm surprised Stefano is being this ballsy with Alessandro.

I glance at Alessandro to see that he's stopped shouting and is now staring resignedly at Stefano. His lips twitch at the sight of him trying to get Teresa to dance.

Blimey, he's managed to get her to crack a smile.

Susanna comes out of the kitchen and erupts into peals of laughter. Stefano, spying a potential new dancing partner, bounds up the stairs from the lower level to the top and gyrates past the bar in the direction of Susanna.

Alessandro flicks his ear with the cloth he was using to polish glasses.

'Ow!' Stefano exclaims, clutching his head.

I can't hear him, but I can read his lips.

The music abruptly cuts off and I look to my left to see that Cristina is no longer beside me.

As Stefano protests loudly, the music changes to 'A Little Respect' by Erasure, the volume reduced considerably.

Stefano's irritation endures only a couple of seconds before he shrugs and begins to nod his head along to the music. The first customers walk through the door as Cristina reappears beside me.

'That broke the tension,' she mutters, watching Teresa greet the customers with her brightest smile. 'For now.'

As the restaurant fills up and the orders pile in, I sit at the bar, feeling like a spare part.

Alessandro is preoccupied dealing with multiple drinks orders, so I pick up the cloth he was using and continue to polish the glasses he was doing earlier. When he turns around and sees me doing this, he looks surprised.

'I'm happy to help, you know,' I tell him.

Everyone else is flat out and I've been sitting here, sipping the red wine that Giulio poured for me earlier. I could go back to the apartment, but the thought of being alone tonight makes me feel, well, lonely.

I'd offer to help out in the kitchen, but I'd only get in the way. Too many cooks and definitely not enough room. And I can't serve tables as I don't speak Italian. Not yet, anyway.

'Maybe I can help you with the coffees later?' I ask Alessandro as I polish. He taught me how to work the machine earlier.

He eyes me thoughtfully as he makes a couple of Aperol Spritzes.

I reckon he could probably prepare most drinks blindfolded.

'You're bored?' he asks.

'A bit.'

'I'm sorry.'

'Why are you apologising?' I've appreciated him taking me under his wing since I arrived in Rome, but I do want to learn to fly soon.

Next week, I plan to venture into the city centre to check out the sights in daylight. I'm petrified at the thought of trying to work out the public transport system, but it's all part of the adventure, I keep telling myself.

'Perhaps on Monday you could go to Tivoli to meet some of Giulio's family?' Alessandro suggests.

'Aren't they your family too?'

He shrugs and returns his attention to the drinks, but his nostrils flare.

Have I upset him?

Susanna comes over to collect her drinks order, saying something coy to Alessandro. I think she's asking him to get a move on and she's doing it rather flirtatiously, but his expression remains impassive.

Susanna smiles at me and winks as he pours a glass of beer from the tap. He doesn't look at her as he places it on the tray. She picks up the tray and, in what seems like slow motion, turns and crashes straight into Teresa.

Glasses go flying, smashing into smithereens on the floor. Both Teresa and Susanna get soaked, and the whole restaurant falls silent at the commotion.

Along with every other pair of eyes in the room, I watch the two women stare at each other in shock.

And then Teresa lets rip.

She begins *screaming* a tirade of abuse at Susanna and, a moment later, Susanna starts to give as good as she gets.

I'm aghast, seeing this go down in front of the customers, so I can't imagine how Alessandro feels. He's frozen, regarding them both with horror.

Giulio comes out of the kitchen with a similar expression on his face, but to my surprise it's Stefano who jumps to the rescue, ushering both Susanna and Teresa out the back.

Cristina appears with a mop and a broom and I slip off my stool immediately to help her clear up the mess. I hear Giulio mutter a few angry words to Alessandro and glance up to see him striding in the direction of the kitchen, shoving the door open with menace. Cristina breathes in sharply and, after some awkward tittering from the tables, people return to the business of eating and drinking.

When I straighten up, Alessandro is still standing behind the bar, looking shell-shocked.

'Are you okay?' I ask him tentatively.

He comes to his senses, nodding tersely and getting on with redoing the drinks order.

'Which table is it for?' I ask when I've returned to the bar after discarding the broken glass and putting away the cleaning supplies.

'Table 4.' He nods at a table by the window.

I pick up the completed order and deliver it to the table.

The people sitting there are two middle-aged couples, and I'm glad to discover that they're American.

'What were the waitresses arguing about?' they ask me conspiratorially when they realise I speak English.

'I wish I knew,' I reply with a smile.

Stefano is at the bar when I return, saying something about Susanna to Alessandro.

'Teresa?' Alessandro asks him.

Teresa reappears, shooting daggers at Alessandro as she returns to work.

Stefano follows her lead.

Alessandro seems defeated. It's obvious that he doesn't want to talk about it, so I get on with polishing glasses, but when Susanna doesn't return and a harassed-looking Cristina is flagged down by yet another of Susanna's customers, I can't stay quiet.

'Has Susanna left?' I ask Alessandro.

'Yes,' he replies wearily, and then a family of five walk through the door: two adults and three young children.

I can hear the mother speaking English and an idea comes to me.

'I could serve the English-speaking tables if you like?'

Alessandro looks hopeful. 'You could?'

'Of course.'

'Thank you!' He breathes a sigh of relief. 'Put them on Table 1 at the bottom of the stairs. If you could also take over Tables 4 and 6, which is the one in the middle,' he says, pointing it out, 'I'll let Teresa know.'

Without delay, I hurry over to the door to welcome the family, grabbing a pen, notepad and menus from the stash beside the till.

'Are you Australian?' the mother asks me as I settle them and mention the fixed-price deal for the children. I've overheard the drill.

'I am,' I reply with a smile. 'Where are you guys from?'

'Britain,' she replies.

'Awesome. When did you arrive?'

As we chat, I notice Teresa returning from the Americans at Table 4. She halts in her steps and stares at me.

'Can I get you a drink right away or should I give you a few minutes?' I ask, feeling Teresa's eyes boring into the side of my face.

'Ooh, I'd love an Aperol Spritz,' the mum says.

'Great choice,' I reply, turning to smile at the dad and trying not to be put off by Teresa's death stare.

'I'll have a beer, please. Which Italian ones do you have?'

I reel off the ones I've noticed in the fridge and on tap, hoping something will appeal.

He chooses a Peroni Gran Riserva, plus peach juice for the kids.

Teresa is at the bar having a full-on hissy fit. It doesn't take a genius to know what she and Alessandro are arguing about, albeit in low tones so the customers can't hear. I place my drinks order at the bottom of Alessandro's pile and hurry past them to the stockroom to grab myself an apron. When I come back, Teresa has returned to work.

'That didn't go down too well?' I ask Alessandro, who sighs and shakes his head.

He's having a bad night.

'Americans give the best tips,' Cristina explains, materialising at my side. 'And Brits tip better than Italians,' she adds.

'She can have the tips, I don't care,' I reply with a shrug.

'No, she will *not*,' Alessandro interjects sharply.

'That American table at least,' I reply, trying to reason with him. 'And surely Table 6,' I add, even though they're still studying their menus, so all she's done is take them to their table.

'They're your tables. End of discussion.'

I don't have time to argue with him, we'll sort it out later.

Antonio calls from the serving hatch and Alessandro jerks his head in his direction. 'Table 4.'

I hurry over, take the garlic bread and calamari to the Americans and then return to the kitchen for the rest of their starters. There's no way I'm going to attempt to carry more than two plates at a time without practice.

Afterwards, I pay Table 6 a visit and take their order.

Chapter 16

The next couple of hours fly by. There's so much to remember. I've never waitressed before, but I end up doing six tables that are dotted around the room, including serving two additional British families and an American couple who come in.

My head is full to bursting. Every time I walk through the restaurant area, someone calls out for something: glasses of water, fresh cutlery, drinks. Sometimes I understand the Italian and am happy to help out with small requests like refilling water carafes, but often I have to apologise and seek out their server – I do this cringingly if that server happens to be Teresa.

We're supposed to open bottles of wine at the table using a one-handed corkscrew, but I've found this contraption impossible to master. When Teresa saw me struggling on my first attempt, she actually laughed, enjoying my mortification. Luckily, Stefano stepped in and opened the bottle for me, doing it with a smile and flourish. He's done the rest of my bottles since in the same amiable manner. I'll have to practise at home in case I need to help out again.

The Americans are the first to finish up. They pay in cash and leave an enormous tip. I don't know what to do with it.

'Please put at least some of that in Teresa's tin,' I implore Alessandro, placing the plate with the money in front of him.

The servers all have tip tins with names on them, under the bar.

He shakes his head at me and tsks. I give him a beseeching look over my shoulder as I hurry back to my tables and, from his expression, he seems to be coming around.

I might not love the girl, but I don't want to make an enemy of her.

Unfortunately, I think I'm too late for that. Teresa's smile that she reserves for customers drops off her face as she passes me on the stairs. I hear her whisper something under her breath and I know that it's hateful.

My heart sinks. I'm not used to animosity.

Soon I'm down to one table. The others in the restaurant are finishing up as well. When my last customers settle their bill, I take my tip to Alessandro and place it on the bar.

He nods at the stool opposite. 'Sit down, I'll get you a drink.'

I do as he says, the soles of my feet stinging as I revel in the feeling of finally being able to take a breather. I check my watch and see that it's almost midnight. Oddly, I don't feel tired. I seem to have got my second wind.

'I'll take you home soon,' Alessandro promises as Cristina appears with her tip plate.

'Can we tempt you to come out with us instead?' she asks

me hopefully as Alessandro calls out '*Grazie, arrivederci*' to the last of the customers.

'Yes! Come!' Stefano cries, joining us. 'Give her a shot or something,' he urges Alessandro.

Alessandro looks at him and then at me. I don't know why I'm not putting this idea to bed – bed is certainly where I thought I was headed – but I'm strangely flattered to be asked to join them.

Alessandro, noticing me hesitating, lines up some shot glasses. Stefano claps with glee as Alessandro reaches for a bottle of something yellow in frosted glass.

'Teresa!' he calls, pouring alcohol into the line of glasses.

She looks over, but turns up her nose.

Alessandro mutters something under his breath and picks up his glass. We all follow suit, chinking them together before knocking them back.

Eesh! That was strong.

Alessandro smiles at the look on my face. 'Another?' he asks.

'Yes!' Stefano cries on my behalf.

I shrug and nod, so he pours a second round.

After that, we set about cleaning the restaurant. Stefano whacks on some loud music and tries to get me to dance with him.

I didn't have many friends my own age in Coober Pedy – it had been that way my whole life. A combination of being a shy child and some of the other girls coming across as overly dominant made me withdraw into my shell.

Louise was my only friend at school, but she lacked confidence too. In time, we each grew into our own skin, but when she moved away, I was left out on a limb.

Cristina and Stefano are a dominant pairing, but I'm no longer daunted by strong personalities. Even Teresa I can handle, although I might not enjoy being the unfair recipient of her hostility.

The idea of becoming part of Stefano and Cristina's gang is appealing. It's probably about time I had some friends my own age. I feel a prickle of guilt as I think this, though I know the crowd back home wouldn't hold it against me.

I wasn't aware of this until about five minutes ago, but every service ends with pizza for the staff. Alessandro pours glasses of red wine, while Stefano and I wait by the serving hatch.

'So, are you coming?' Stefano asks me.

'Yes, I think I will.'

'Excellent!'

My feet are still stinging, but the couple of shots I've had have helped. I reckon I could manage some dancing.

We carry the pizzas to the bar top as Teresa marches out of the stockroom with her bag slung over her shoulder. She goes straight to Alessandro, demanding something or other of him. He opens the cash register to pay her, I suppose, and gets her tip tin out from beneath the bar.

Meanwhile, Cristina hands out glasses of wine and Stefano gingerly begins to separate the piping hot pizza slices to cool them down and make them easier to eat.

Teresa counts out her money and mutters under her breath. Did Alessandro share some of my tips with her? I hope so.

He speaks sharply and pointedly glances at me before returning his attention to her.

I think that's a yes.

She glances at me with annoyance then raises her voice at him. Stefano sucks air in through his teeth and Cristina averts her gaze. I'm glad Giulio and the others are still in the kitchen, but I wish I knew what was being said.

Or maybe it's better that I don't.

Alessandro throws his polishing cloth down and leans over the counter, staring Teresa directly in the eye. I can feel the tension radiating from him as he says something low and furious to her. Her mouth promptly snaps shut. And then she reaches for one of the pizzas on the bar top – one that hasn't yet been divided into slices by Stefano – and slams the entire thing against Alessandro's chest.

We all cry out as boiling hot tomato sauce and strings of molten mozzarella fly everywhere, some landing on the bottles behind the bar. But most of it lands on Alessandro himself and he gasps with pain as he hastily pulls his T-shirt fabric away from his chest. I stare with alarm at the sight of a slab of cheese on his hand. He seems to notice it at the same moment and his eyes are wide with pain as he peels it off, a huge blister bubbling up before our eyes.

Giulio bursts from the kitchen, demanding to know what's going on as Teresa shoves open the front door and leaves. Alessandro begins to explain and Cristina rushes behind the bar to grab an ice bucket, filling it with ice.

'No, no,' I say at once, manoeuvring her out of the way and turning on the cold water tap. I take Alessandro's hand and hold it under the stream. Surprise makes his explanation to Giulio falter as he turns to stare at me.

Then Giulio kicks off. I don't know what he's saying, but he's raging. He shouts and gesticulates madly and

Alessandro's eyes are downcast as he gently removes my hand from his.

'It needs to stay under for twenty minutes,' I tell him quietly as Giulio turns on his heel and storms out the back door.

The music is still playing at top volume, although no one is in a party mood now.

At least, I'm not.

As Cristina goes to turn off the music, Stefano retreats behind the bar to help clean up the mess. Alessandro wearily tells us to leave it.

'I'll do it later. Go to your club. Please,' he adds, reaching for what I now know is Limoncello. 'Take Angie if she still wants to go.'

One-handed, he lines up a few shot glasses, pulling the cork out of the bottle with his teeth. He fills them and passes them out.

'Ding-dong, da-da, da da,' Stefano says, humming the tune to 'The Witch is Dead' from *The Wizard of Oz*. He chinks Alessandro's glass.

Alessandro is tight-lipped, but he knocks his shot back regardless.

'Was that Teresa quitting, then?' I ask uncertainly.

Stefano looks at me and bursts out laughing.

'What?' I ask.

'Yes,' he replies, giving me a look that implies I'm a bit dim. 'That was Teresa quitting.'

Chapter 17

The first time Nan burned herself, I panicked. She was baking cookies and she forgot to put gloves on when she retrieved the tray from the oven. Her fingers blistered instantly and her yelps of pain felt like a blow to my solar plexus.

I didn't think twice about putting ice on the injury, but later I learned that it was the wrong thing to do. You should never use ice or iced water, nor should you use creams or greasy substances like butter when treating burns. My research came in useful again, I'm sad to say.

Alessandro and I are the only people remaining at *Serafina's*. I sent Cristina and Stefano on their way, promising that I'd join them when they next asked me on a night out.

I'm still cleaning up despite Alessandro's protests that he'll do it.

'Twenty minutes,' I repeat firmly and he reluctantly obeys, because whenever he takes his hand out from under the stream of water to help, his features pinch with agony.

The Ibuprofen will kick in soon.

I go to hunt out clingfilm from the kitchen and when I return, he's knocking back another shot.

'This will help too,' he says drily as I pull up a stool opposite him. With his non-injured right hand, he grabs the open bottle of red wine from earlier and pours a couple of glasses.

'I'm sorry to have spoiled your night.' His voice already sounds thicker with alcohol.

The shots have also gone to my head and he's had even more of them than I have.

'It's all right. I'm sure I can go some other night. Will Susanna come back?'

He stares into his glass, swirling the russet liquid around as he replies. 'I don't think so.'

'What will you do?'

'Edgardo comes in tomorrow, but he's only part-time. Jacopo or Valentina might also be available to help. Saturdays are busy.'

Jacopo and Valentina are my cousins who still live with my aunt Eliana in Tivoli.

'Do you have many English-speaking customers?' I ask, pulling out a length of plastic.

'Almost always. Why?'

'I'd be happy to help out again.'

'You would?'

'Yes, I enjoyed it.'

He opens the cash register. 'I forgot to pay you.'

Pulling out a few notes, he also retrieves my tips from under the bar top. I wasn't sure I'd get paid – I was happy to do it as a favour – but I know it would insult him if I turned down the money and, anyway, it wouldn't hurt to have a few extra euros to play with.

'Time's up. Give me your hand,' I prompt.

He shuts off the tap and brings out his injured hand from under the benchtop, wincing as the pain kicks in.

'Have you thought about having a joint tip tin to share out between everyone at the end of the night?' I ask as I carefully lay the plastic over his injury. 'I know tips are an incentive, but no amount of money is going to encourage Cristina to smile at the customers. I'm sure you wouldn't want her to be false, in any case, but she and Stefano work as hard as each other.'

He nods as I fold the ends of the plastic under his hand so they stick together. 'This is true.'

'And I noticed the kitchen staff don't get tips. Shouldn't they be rewarded for the food they prepare? People don't only tip for good service – if the food is awful, they tip less, if at all.'

'This is also true. I will speak to Giulio. He will like that you have made a suggestion.'

He looks down at his hand and then up at me with surprise. 'It hardly hurts at all.'

'It will if you take the plastic off – I think the air makes it more painful – so leave it on as long as possible. Have you never had a burn?'

'Of course, but I just deal with it. How did you learn how to treat them?'

'My nan had a couple of accidents.'

'Ah.' His gaze drops. He needs no further explanation, but that doesn't stop me from feeling a terrible pang of guilt for the part I played in one of her mishaps. I left the kitchen door unlocked and she went upstairs to make herself a cup of tea, as she had every day for most of her life. But on this occasion she poured boiling water straight into the teabag tin, and when she realised her mistake, she panicked and knocked it over. The boiling water scalded her arms and hands.

But it could have been worse. Much worse. Forgetting to light the hob once the gas has been turned on is a fairly common occurrence for people with dementia – and the consequences can be catastrophic.

I had a gas sensor installed after that. We all make mistakes and it wasn't worth the risk.

'Right,' I say with a sigh. 'I guess I'd better go home.'

His jaw drops. 'I've had too much to drink!'

'I know,' I reply with a laugh.

'I can't drive you!'

'I'm happy to walk.'

'I'll walk with you.'

'You don't need to.'

He tsks at me in a manner that I'm becoming accustomed to and comes out from behind the bar, stumbling slightly as he bumps into it with his hip. I think he might be drunk.

I'm pretty tipsy too, I realise as I wait outside in the fresh air. Alessandro has locked up the restaurant and is getting a clean T-shirt from his van. When he reappears, he's wearing a black leather jacket. With his hair tied back, he has a bit of a rock star thing going on. Susanna and Teresa clearly thought as much too.

We come to a big intersection with a series of pedestrian crossings. Alessandro leans against the traffic light to steady himself and puts his hand out to make sure I wait until the pedestrian signal turns green. He's definitely not thinking clearly – there's no way I'd walk out into traffic.

Eventually, we find ourselves on a long, straight stretch of road, although you wouldn't know it's straight from the way we keep gently colliding. I'm feeling very light-headed.

'Tell me about Susanna and Teresa,' I say. 'How did you get yourself into that mess?'

He shoots me a look of alarm. A moment later, his features blacken and he rolls his eyes. 'Stefano has been gossiping in the stockroom again.'

'I might not be able to understand Italian, but I know a scorned woman when I see one. Don't you know it's a terrible idea to mix business with pleasure?'

Alcohol is definitely at play. I wouldn't normally be this direct.

He sighs dejectedly. 'Yes, I know. Sometimes I do too much of this and not enough of this.' He mimics drinking a bottle of alcohol and then taps his temple with his index finger.

'It happens,' I say.

'Do you have a boyfriend at home?' he asks.

'No.'

'Maybe we will find a nice Italian man for you to marry after all. Such as Stefano,' he adds with a cheeky grin.

This makes me laugh slightly hysterically. 'He *is* very good looking, but I question his sexual orientation.'

Alessandro chuckles. 'I do too, sometimes, but I assure you, he likes women. You might be too young for him, though, with his penchant for older ladies.'

'Seriously?'

'You didn't see him flirting with Table 15 earlier?'

I shake my head. I was too run off my feet to pay attention to anything other than the customers I was serving.

'How did you learn to speak English so well?' I'm thinking of his use of words like *penchant* and *tumultuous* and *insufferable.*

'I've spent a lot of time in English-speaking countries.'

'Which ones?'

'America and Canada, mostly.'

'What were you doing there?'

'Travelling around.'

'I'm envious,' I say wistfully.

What a life.

I glance at him and catch an oddly melancholic expression on his face, but then he smiles and lifts one shoulder.

'I'm lucky,' he says.

After a while, we pass the bistro that we went to on my first night in Rome. I go to cross the road, but Alessandro grabs my arm, stopping me.

'No. This way.' He nods ahead to a dark residential street.

I look right, down the other street. I'm sure that was the route I took on my way to work this morning. He pointed it out as one of the short cuts I could take on foot.

'Isn't it down there?' I'm convinced he's making us go the long way round.

'It's this way,' he replies sharply, adding in a gentler tone: 'I prefer the view from up here.'

We walk in silence for a few minutes and then, out of the blue, he says, 'Does it bother you that you have the same name as your mother?'

'Er... No... Not really,' I stutter. 'Maybe it used to, on and off, over the years.' I glance at him. 'You said earlier that you remember her?'

He nods. 'She started work at *Serafina's* a few weeks before my eighth birthday. We had a party at the restaurant and she gave me a pack of cards as a present. *Uno*. We would often play during down times at the restaurant. I liked her a lot.'

This blows me away. It's been hard to comprehend, but at that moment it hits me: he really did know my mother. He was here, in Rome, on the other side of the world to where I've spent my whole life, and *he knew her*. He knew her well enough for her to buy him a birthday present.

'What else do you remember about her?'

'She had long dark hair that she usually wore in a braid, and bright blue eyes. She was pretty, especially when she laughed, which she did a lot. She made Giulio laugh too. I remember her teasing him. At first I didn't think he liked it – he would cast his eyes heavenwards and tut – but I was only a boy, I didn't understand flirting,' he says with a small smile. 'When she left, there was no more laughter, not for a long time. Back then, I felt as though I was as miserable as Giulio, but now, of course, I realise that his sorrow was greater.'

I still can't believe how understanding he seems of my parents' affair.

He comes to a stop outside Cristina's apartment. We could have been walking around the streets of Pompeii and I wouldn't have noticed.

'Do you want to come in?' I ask hopefully, not ready for him to stop talking yet.

'I need to use the bathroom,' he replies apologetically.

It takes me ages to find my keys, but finally I pull them out of my bag and unlock the courtyard gate. The inner door to the apartment has a tricky double bolt system so that takes me even longer.

'Sorry,' I mutter, managing it at last. 'You can use the toilet through there.' I nod at my bedroom door. 'Do you want a drink?' I call.

'Um... Maybe a beer,' Alessandro replies over his shoulder.

The toilet flushes and I hear the bathroom door open, but he doesn't reappear immediately. I wander down the hall to my doorway. He's staring at the stacks of postcards piled up on the shelves.

'Here you go,' I say.

'What are these?' he replies curiously, taking the bottle.

'Postcards,' I reply.

'I can see that. There are hundreds. Do you collect them?'

'They were sent to me.'

'Can I take a look?'

'Sure.'

He puts down his beer and rifles through the pictures, turning one over to study the name at the bottom. He turns over another, and another. 'Who are all these people?'

'Friends... People I used to know... People come to Coober Pedy from all over the world. Some stay, others leave – whenever anyone used to return home or go on holiday, they'd send me a postcard. Everyone knew that I wanted to travel.'

He lifts his head and stares at me for a long moment. The light from the bathroom is behind him so I can't see his expression very well, but I'm guessing it's pity.

I step forward to collect the postcards and, as his hands brush against mine, I register the alien presence of plastic.

'How's your hand feeling?' I ask.

'Fine,' he replies. 'I think I could take this off now.'

'Let me check.' I carefully peel away the clingfilm. 'Does it hurt?' It's so quiet that I find myself speaking in a whisper.

'No,' he replies, matching my low tone.

I glance up to find his green eyes glittering back at me. We're so close that I can make out freckles on his nose.

Our stance feels overbearingly intimate, but I fight the urge to step away because I'm not done checking his injury.

I'm grateful that now it's *my* face that is cast in shadow.

'Angel,' he whispers, prompting me to glance up at him again. He's wearing an odd expression. 'Angel,' he says again.

'What are you talking about?' I ask uneasily.

'You look like an angel again. The light is behind you, but you've lost your halo.'

How drunk is he?

'Your hair,' he explains, his face breaking into a sweet smile. 'When you came out of the airport doors, the sunlight was streaming in from the window behind you and your curly hair was all lit up. It looked like a halo.'

'How drunk are you?' I ask the question out loud and I can't help but sound amused.

'Not very,' he replies, then waggles his head from side to side. 'Maybe a little. Okay, maybe a lot, but it's true what I'm saying. I'm going to call you Angel from now on.'

I start laughing and pat his stomach, about to say that he'd better stop drinking, but his face contorts with pain.

'What's wrong?' I ask.

He shakes his head, but I reach down, concern making

me unthinkingly push aside his leather jacket and lift up his black T-shirt.

'Alessandro!' I'm dismayed at the sight of an angry red mark defacing his skin, another burn from where the pizza first landed. 'Why didn't you say anything?'

His stomach is toned, flat and tanned, a trail of dark hair leading from his navel downwards. Before he can pull his T-shirt down, I glimpse a long, jagged scar stretching from his waist down to his hip-bone.

'How did you do that?' I ask with horror.

'Accident.' He steps away.

'Wait! What about your burn?'

'You can't wrap me all up. I'll be fine.'

'At least take some Paracetamol,' I insist, disappearing into the bathroom.

When I come out, he's in the hallway.

'I should go.' He accepts the painkillers and knocks them back with a few glugs of beer.

I wish he'd stay and tell me more about my mum, but it's late.

'Thanks for walking me home,' I say.

'Shall I come and get you tomorrow?'

'No, I'll walk. What time do you need me?'

'You really want to work at *Serafina's*?'

'Absolutely,' I reply.

'I'll see you at eleven thirty then.'

He gives me one last smile and opens the door, heading off into the night.

Chapter 18

Giulio is still in a foul mood the next day. He arrives shortly after Stefano and me, but I don't think he notices us in the stockroom.

'What's he saying?' I hiss at Stefano.

I'm not sure what it is about him, but I feel as though I've known Stefano for years, rather than days.

'He's making Alessandro promise not to sleep with any more waitresses.'

I listen intently and realise that Alessandro is not taking it lying down as he did last night.

'What's Alessandro replying?' I ask urgently.

'He's threatening to leave!'

'What?' I screech-whisper. 'He'd rather quit than stop shagging around?'

Stefano snorts. 'It's not about that; he says he'll go anyway if Giulio no longer wants him here.'

'What—'

'Shh,' he snaps, trying to listen as the two men rant at each other.

'What—'

'Shh!' He whacks me on my arm and then the shouting abruptly stops.

'What did they say?'

'Nothing, they're still angry at each other,' he replies.

'Is Alessandro going to quit?'

The thought of this makes me feel quite ill. What would I do without him?

'Of course he won't quit,' Stefano brushes me off. 'He needs this job too much.'

'He could get another one.'

I really would appreciate some reassurance here.

'Another job that lets him disappear out of the door for six months of the year and return whenever he likes? I don't think so.'

'Is that how long he goes away for?'

'If you have questions for me, you can ask them directly,' Alessandro says from the doorway.

Stefano pulls a face and awkwardly ducks out of the stockroom.

'Sorry, I didn't mean to pry,' I mutter as he ambles over to the stereo and unplugs Stefano's phone, replacing it with his own.

'*Are* you leaving?' I blurt.

He tuts under his breath and shakes his head, but it's a gesture of mock disgust, not the denial I'm seeking.

'If I could understand what you were saying to each other—'

Alessandro turns to face me and places his hands on my arms, cutting my sentence short.

'I'm not leaving. Not anytime soon.'

My heart skitters as I stare into his emerald-green eyes. He abruptly lets me go and walks out of the stockroom, but I'm startled at my body's reaction to his touch.

Uh-oh.

Oh no.

No, no, no, no, no.

I do not want to have a crush on Alessandro.

I dreamt about kissing him last night, and he was my waking thought as a result. Obviously I dismissed the dream as nonsense, but he hasn't been far from my mind this morning. The idea of seeing him today has been making me feel edgy, but I've dismissed those feelings too.

It's hard to ignore these ones. It's been years, but I haven't forgotten what desire feels like.

I hastily tie my apron around my waist and walk out into the room. It's only then that I register his song choice: 'There Must Be an Angel (Playing with My Heart)' by Eurythmics.

'Did you put this on?' Stefano asks me with delight.

I shake my head, but he's already too busy strutting around the room to care who's responsible.

Alessandro is cleaning out the coffee machine with his back to me, but he glances over his shoulder and our eyes lock.

'You thought I was joking?' he asks with a raised eyebrow.

Alessandro calls me Angel for the rest of the day. At first it makes me blush, then I'm too run off my feet to care and, by the end of the night, I'm answering to it.

'Angie belonged to her mother,' Alessandro told Stefano

and Cristina, the first people who noticed. 'She should have her own name.'

He said this in such a calm, reasonable manner that, to my surprise, they merely shrugged and returned to work.

Giulio reappeared at lunchtime, his earlier argument with Alessandro seemingly forgotten. He seemed a little surprised when he overheard the nickname, but then he good-naturedly agreed that I *was* an angel and left it at that.

Now it's close to midnight and we're about to tuck in to pizza.

Stefano and Cristina carry the plates over to a table instead of the bar, but before I can sit down, Alessandro passes me an unopened bottle of red wine and the bottle opener.

He promised to teach me after I admitted I was struggling.

While the others sit and chat, we stand off to the side, and I'm hyper aware of his close proximity as he watches my technique.

I have no problem getting the screw into the cork, but I can't for the life of me lever the cork out with only one hand. I'm used to a corkscrew with two arms.

'Like this.' Alessandro's hands cover mine.

I've been trying to reassure myself that crushes are fleeting, but my butterflies have not yet got that memo.

'Thanks,' I mutter, breaking away from him to pour the wine.

Cristina covers her glass. 'Not for me.'

She was hungover today, and when Stefano suggested going for a few drinks, she told him that she wanted an early night. Alessandro has offered to drive us back to her apartment.

We take the same route home that we took last night, and as Alessandro and Cristina chat in the front, I puzzle over his claim that he preferred the view from this higher road. I took the short cut on my way to work and now I'm staring out of the window, wondering how they differ.

This road *is* prettier, I concede, with houses rather than apartment blocks.

'Do you want to come in for a drink?' I offer hopefully when we arrive.

There are no parking spaces next to our block, so Alessandro has stopped in the middle of the road.

'Another time,' he promises.

'Okay.' I try not to feel deflated as I follow Cristina to the courtyard gate. I hear the van pulling away when we're safely inside.

'I'll have a drink with you,' Cristina offers as she unlocks the front door.

'I thought you were hungover?'

'Herbal tea. Want one?'

Our paths at home haven't crossed much with her late nights and my jet lag, so I say yes, not wanting to turn down the chance to bond. We could do with having a chat, just the two of us.

'How long have you worked at *Serafina's*?' I ask as Cristina brings the tea over to the sofa area. It's too cool to sit out on the terrace.

'Almost twelve years,' she replies, handing me a mug.

'Did you know Alessandro and Giulio before you started working there?'

She shakes her head and sits down at the other end of

the sofa. 'Only since I joined. Giulio, at least. I've known Alessandro for about nine years.'

I'm confused. 'How come only nine years? Where was he before that?'

She shrugs and pulls a face. 'Who knows?'

'He was away for three years straight? He never came home?'

'He was away for a lot longer than three years,' she replies. 'I didn't even know he existed until he turned up one day. Giulio almost had a heart attack.'

'I don't understand.'

'None of us do. Alessandro is an enigma, Angie. Be warned.'

I stare at her. Has she already managed to work out that I'm attracted to him?

'There's no need to warn me.' I inwardly curse her all-seeing eye.

'No, I know,' she replies flippantly. 'He'll never lay a hand on you. And not only because Giulio has vowed that he'll be out on his ear if another waitress quits because of him.' She sighs and stares at me in a resigned manner that makes me feel deeply uncomfortable.

'Alessandro loves Giulio,' she tells me. 'He'd never disrespect him by sleeping with his daughter.'

'I would never have slept with him in any case,' I reply indignantly. 'I'm no Teresa.'

'I'm glad to hear it.'

Chapter 19

The next morning, I feel awkward at the thought of seeing Cristina. My conversation with her has done the trick of dampening my crush, at least.

It's not like I thought it would ever go anywhere, even if Alessandro *had* been attracted to me in return. I'm here to forge a relationship with my father, not complicate matters wildly by falling for a family member, especially one who recklessly sleeps around.

I'm at the dining room table, making my way through a bowl of granola, when Cristina comes out of her bedroom. She's up earlier than usual.

'I hope I didn't annoy you last night,' she says as soon as we've exchanged good mornings. 'I have a habit of saying what's on my mind to people.'

'Not at all,' I reply, suppressing a smirk. *Talk about getting straight to the point!* 'At least I know where I stand with you.'

This comment seems to please her and it's the truth. I

value honesty in people. It feels surprisingly natural to level with her now.

'It was only a fleeting reaction to being around a hot-blooded male. It's been a while since I've had a guy in my life.'

'Alessandro has just called me,' she says.

I nod, trying to seem unfazed but, goddammit, I blush. I press my hands to my cheeks. 'I'm going to feel self-conscious every time you say his name,' I notify her. 'But I'll get over it.'

She grins – properly, now, which makes me laugh.

'What did he say?' I ask, lowering my hands.

'Valentina and Jacopo are coming to help out at *Serafina's* today, so you're not needed unless you want to go in to say hello, but he also pointed out that you'll meet them in Tivoli tomorrow, so you shouldn't feel pressured. You told him you wanted to buy a mobile phone?'

'Yes.' I mentioned it last night. I had no need of one at home because I never left the house, but I think I should have one here. I'll feel safer if I'm out on my own.

'I'm going into the centre for lunch, so you can come with me if you like? Alessandro was worried about you getting there on your own.'

'That sounds perfect.'

I could do with a break from *Serafina's* and probably also a break from Alessandro, but I'm glad I'll meet my cousins tomorrow. The restaurant is closed on Mondays.

Cristina tells me that the easiest way to get into town is on her scooter, but the thought of this terrifies me and I tell her so.

'Fine, we'll go by metro,' she says a little grumpily.

On the walk to the station, I ask her who she's having lunch with.

'Rebecca,' she replies shortly.

'Aah, Rebecca.' I flash her a significant look. 'What's the story with you two, then?'

'Are you getting back at me for last night?'

'Can you take it?'

She laughs under her breath and shakes her head. 'Probably not, but I will try.'

'How long have you been seeing her?' I ask.

'On and off for about two years, though I've known her for four. She's a friend of Stefano's, but she had a boyfriend when we met.'

'I see.'

'Yes. This is the problem,' she adds resignedly. 'She doesn't know what she wants. Or at least, she knows what she wants and then changes her mind. Again. And again. And again.'

We've been making our way through a maze of apartment blocks, down steps and across roads riddled with grass breaking through cracks in the asphalt. Cars are squeezed into small spaces, and there are some teeny tiny ones parked perpendicular to the other vehicles, front-facing into the kerb. Cristina tells me they're called Smart Cars.

I should be memorising the route, but I'm distracted, my mind on our conversation.

'Why do you put up with it?' I ask.

'I love her,' she replies simply.

'Does she love you?'

She shrugs. 'I don't know. At the moment, she says she just

wants to be friends. She says that last week was a mistake. I think she's seeing someone.'

'A boy or a girl?'

'A boy, of course.' She sounds bitter. 'She only dabbles with me. At least, that's what she tells me.'

'And you believe her?'

She nods. 'I think so.'

We buy our tickets from a kiosk on the way so we're able to head straight to the station platform. When the train pulls in, I stand and stare with amazement and apprehension as it glides to a stop.

'You okay?' Cristina asks as the doors whoosh open.

'I've never seen a train in real life,' I admit, hesitantly stepping on and looking around. I jolt as the doors slide shut.

'Okay, how did that happen?' Cristina demands to know as she manoeuvres me towards a couple of vacant seats.

She spends the rest of the journey badgering me about my upbringing.

We get out at Flaminio rather than take the one stop on the metro to Spagna, which is where many of the shops are situated.

'Spagna brings you out near the Spanish Steps,' Cristina tells me as we walk through a huge, arched entryway into Piazza del Popolo.

I look all around at the vast, oval-shaped space surrounding us. There are fountains at each end and a tall obelisk in the middle. Something about it feels oddly familiar and, when I peer up at a nearby hill, I notice several people gathered on a terrace, staring at the view.

'What's that place called?' I ask Cristina.

'Terrazza del Pincio,' she replies.

'I think Alessandro took me there the other night.'

'Huh,' she says and, once again, I sense that she's surprised about our night drive. I ask her why.

'I like Alessandro – I get along well with him – but he can be very selfish.'

I'm perplexed.

'He's been better since you arrived,' she adds with a shrug, noticing my expression. She points out three big roads leading away from the piazza. 'If you take that one,' she says of the road heading diagonally off to our left, 'you'll come to the Spanish Steps.' She points at the centre road. 'At the end of this one is the Monument of Vittorio Emanuele II.'

'I remember it.' Alessandro said that it reminds him of a wedding cake. 'And beyond it is the Colosseum, right?'

'More or less. The Trevi Fountain is in that direction and the Pantheon is over there,' she adds, pointing roughly to our left and then our right. 'You'll see signs for them.'

'Okay, thank you. In what way is Alessandro selfish?'

'He does what suits him,' Cristina replies as we walk down the central road. 'He works when it suits him and he disappears when it suits him. Giulio will go for months without hearing a word and I know this upsets him. Then, *poof*! Alessandro reappears, ready to work to earn enough money to fund his travels and whatever else he gets up to.'

'What do you think he gets up to?' I ask with a frown.

She shrugs. 'Who knows? He's vague. Like I said, he's an enigma. I think there is darkness in him, but he hides it well.'

Cristina stays with me while I buy a phone, a relief because the various plans involved are complicated and the shop assistant doesn't speak much English. I only want a cheap, super-basic model for making phone calls – nothing fancy: I have my laptop if I need to use the internet.

My new flatmate stores a few numbers for me and then we part ways so she can go and meet up with Rebecca.

Her words about Alessandro linger.

I ponder our conversation as I wander the streets, partly attempting to follow directions on my city map, but mostly looking out for signs. I go to the Trevi Fountain first and barely recognise it. I've never seen so many people crowded into such a tight space. *And I thought it was busy at two o'clock in the morning!* In the daylight the stone statue is the colour of pearl and the water is pale blue and crystal clear, but to begin with I can only see it from a distance. As the crowd in front begins to disperse, I manage to move forward, and then I'm able to stand and behold one of the most famous fountains in the world. In the centre is a statue of the Greek God Oceanus standing under a triumphal arch. His shell chariot is being pulled by two seahorses, one wild and one docile.

There's a tightness in my chest as I think of my mother. Did she stand in this exact same place? How did she feel? Was she overawed or underwhelmed? It's hard to contemplate that thought, with so many people chattering loudly and jostling into me.

I'm not sure I could ever live in a city, I think to myself as I push through the throng with some difficulty. *The crowds would get to me.* This thought leads me back to Alessandro and what he said to me in Vatican City about not being able to stand queues or too many people.

Somehow I end up on a busy street lined with pavement

cafés and restaurants. It's lunchtime and people are crowded around tables outside in the sunshine. I hear the chink of spoons against coffee cups and inhale the scrumptious smells coming from plates piled high with pasta, fresh from the kitchen and wafting with steam. My stomach rumbles and for a moment I imagine myself sitting at a table on my own and ordering lunch, but instead of feeling a thrill, I experience a pang of loneliness.

Glancing through the window of a nearby café, I spy stacks of paninis, spilling over with ingredients, lined up behind the glass counter. I make a snap decision to join the queue and, when it's my turn to order, I point at a panini and breathe a sigh of relief when it's placed, freshly toasted, in my hands. Grabbing something to drink, I pay up and head out onto the street, almost immediately spying a sign for the Pantheon.

A couple of minutes later, I'm standing in front of the famous structure with its majestic triangular-shaped portico and grand Corinthian columns.

The square around me is lined with buildings painted every shade of orange, from the palest peach to the colour of the red desert sands of Australia. One alone is as blue as the sky above.

There are quite a few people hanging out on the white marble steps surrounding the square's central fountain and I take a seat amongst them, unwrapping my lunch from its wax paper and cracking open a can of lemonade. I've gone for a combination of oozing mozzarella and tangy sun-dried tomatoes and as I eat, I soak up the ambience. The fountain is playing a soundtrack of cool clean trickling water and all around I can hear conversations being spoken in different languages. There are so many nationalities in Coober Pedy that I've picked up a few words here and there. I can tell that the nearby students with their brightly coloured T-shirts are German, the gaggles of girls taking non-stop selfies are almost certainly Chinese and I *think* that the blond-haired couple beside me are Norwegian.

I sigh happily and lick my fingers. I've had toasted paninis back home, but *that* was something else.

The queue to get into the Pantheon is long, but it moves quickly, and soon after I've eaten I find myself standing inside the enormous domed space. The air is blissfully cool against my sun-kissed skin and I'm reminded of walking into my dugout and escaping the hot desert air.

But that is the only way in which the Pantheon makes me think of home.

I am in *awe*.

I crane my neck, staring with wonder at the unsupported roof with its big round hole in the centre. There are lots of people here, but everyone is speaking in hushed, reverent whispers and there's no jostling for position as there was outside the Trevi Fountain.

I can see why Alessandro calls this his favourite building – it's *stunning*.

Yet again, my thoughts have led me to him.

I realise that I've barely thought of Giulio today at all. He was the person I came to Italy to meet, but we haven't spent much time with each other. Our closest bonding moment was when we looked at his family photos together and he and Alessandro told me about Marta. He still hasn't asked to see my photos of Mum.

But I know he's happy I'm here – yesterday at *Serafina's* he was introducing me to some of his regular customers as his long-lost daughter. He seemed proud of me, standing there with his arm around my shoulders. It was nice. But it still feels surreal and I'm struggling to get used to the fact that he's my dad.

Maybe, I reason with myself now, I don't need to get used to it. It's not like he's ever going to *be* a dad to me. My grandfather was the one who made up bedtime stories to tell me and taught me how to ride a bike and play the piano. Maybe the best that I can hope for Giulio and me is to be friends.

A shrill ringtone pierces the hushed silence and I look around, feeling embarrassed on behalf of the culprit. To my alarm, people nearby turn to look at *me*. Aghast, I realise the sound is coming from my new phone, so I quickly answer it, speaking in a hushed voice into the receiver as I hurry away from those I've offended.

'Hello?'

'Angel.'

'Alessandro!' I feel slightly breathless. 'How did you get my number?' I whisper.

'Cristina. Where are you?'

'I'm in the Pantheon. It's amazing.'

'Want to call me back?'

'Sure. What's your number?'

'It's in your phone, Angel,' he says with amusement, ending the call.

Yes, all right, I haven't had one of these things before.

I leave the Pantheon before I'm quite ready in order to call him.

'It's slow here this afternoon,' he tells me when he answers. 'I'm not needed. Would you like to meet for gelato? I can give you a ride home.'

'I'd love that. The place near Piazza Navona?'

'You remembered.'

We arrange to meet in half an hour and I set off, wondering how Cristina could ever have called him selfish.

Chapter 20

I see a figure, dressed in black, standing by the middle fountain in Piazza Navona, and know immediately that it's Alessandro.

He smiles when I reach him, bending down to give me two quick kisses.

A few wings flutter – there's no denying that he looks gorgeous today in his faded T-shirt and ripped jeans – but I sternly remind my butterflies of Cristina's warning and that helps to bring them under control.

'Do you only ever wear black?' I ask as we walk.

'Pretty much,' he replies.

'Why?'

He shrugs. 'It's easy.'

'Cristina said Giulio once tried to get everyone to wear red T-shirts at *Serafina's*.'

He snorts. 'No one wanted that.'

'She blamed it on you,' I tell him teasingly.

'Stefano didn't want to wear them, either,' he responds haughtily. 'Cristina's the only one who doesn't care what she looks like.'

I didn't think he came across as caring much about that sort of thing himself, but I remember his sexy leather jacket and wonder if his level of vanity is another thing I know nothing about.

At the gelateria, I'm mesmerised by the incredible display. Every colour of the rainbow is laid out before me – I count at least six different shades of green, from pale pistachio, lime and melon to vibrant apple, kiwi and mint. Even the traditional flavours seem superior to anything I might have had in the past: lemon looks as light and airy as the clouds, wild strawberry is as pink and vivid as my nan's favourite lipstick and chocolate is so rich and dark that it looks almost black. I have no idea how I'm supposed to choose, but somehow I manage it.

'How's Giulio today?' I ask on our way out, cones in hand.

'Good. Try this.'

'Wow. That's amazing. What is it?'

'*Bacio.* Chocolate hazelnut cream.'

I'll be having that next time. 'You want some of mine?'

'No, it's okay. *Pesca* is one of the flavours Eliana makes.'

Pesca means peach. I know because I ordered it, not because I'm making a whole lot of headway with my Italian.

'Giulio is looking forward to taking you to Tivoli tomorrow,' he says.

I glance at him. 'Giulio is taking me?'

'Yes.'

'What about you?'

'I thought it would be a nice thing for you to do together.'

'Won't you join us?'

His brows pull together as he glances at me. 'You want me to come?'

'Yes, I do,' I admit.

'Why?'

'I don't know Giulio like I'm getting to know you. I'm not as comfortable with him,' I find myself confessing. 'I'm nervous about meeting the rest of my family. I know you'll help me get through the day without too much stress.'

He doesn't say anything for a little while, but he's not eating his gelato either.

'If you really want me to come, I'll come,' he says mildly.

Relief chases away my worries, but it's followed by a stab of uncertainty.

'Are you sure you don't have plans to do anything else?' It's his day off, after all. What if he's seeing Susanna? *Or someone else.*

'No plans,' he assures me, catching a gelato drip with his tongue.

I tear my gaze away and simultaneously remember, *Aren't they your family too?*

It was a question I asked him a couple of days ago when he referred to Giulio's family as exactly that: 'Giulio's family'. Does he not feel welcome around them? He's not a blood relative so do they make him feel like an outsider? Is that why he doesn't want to go?

Maybe I should give him an out...

But before I can say anything else, my attention is caught by a young Hungarian couple on the street. They're studying their map with confusion and I can hear that they're trying to work out how to get to Piazza Navona. I pause to tell them that it's in the direction we've just come from.

Alessandro splutters with astonishment as soon as we walk away. 'You speak Hungarian?'

'Only a little,' I reply. 'I recognised a few of the words they were saying and I know how to say, "It's over there."'

'Why Hungarian? How did you learn?'

'An online language course.' It's very similar to the Italian one I'm taking at the moment. 'I only speak a little,' I repeat. 'I learned as a favour to a friend.'

'Which friend?'

'Two, actually,' I correct myself. 'Vera and Laszlo. Vera was my nan's friend, but she and I became close.'

'And Laszlo?'

'Laszlo is a widower who came to Coober Pedy on a whim from Hungary a couple of years ago with dreams of finding opal. He barely spoke any English, but I sensed that Vera liked him – her husband had passed away the year before and Laszlo had lost his wife – so she and I did a language course together so they could get to know each other. She would have found it too daunting to attempt something like that on her own.'

Alessandro shakes his head. 'You're full of surprises, Angel.'

'It was no big deal.' And honestly, it wasn't. It's the sort of thing anyone would do to help a friend. 'Anyway, how do *you* know how to speak Hungarian? You understood what I said.'

He shrugs and walks on. 'I can get by in most European languages.'

'That's *awesome*.'

'Languages are the one thing I seem to be okay at,' he

mutters, polishing off the last of his cone and checking his watch. 'I wonder if Cristina is finished with Rebecca.'

'You know that's where she is today?'

'She told me earlier. Maybe you can help pick up the pieces,' he says darkly, getting his phone out of his pocket and dialling a number. He speaks in Italian and ends the call, shaking his head. 'She doesn't want a lift home. They're already out at some bar, drinking. I doubt you'll see her tonight.'

'Oh. Okay.' I was planning on cooking steaks for dinner – I picked them up yesterday during a break from *Serafina's*. Before I can think better of it, I turn to him: 'Have you got dinner plans?'

Chapter 21

'Can I ask you something?'

Alessandro and I are sitting on the sofa, side by side, facing each other. An empty bottle of red is on the coffee table, but there's still some left in our glasses.

'Fire away,' Alessandro replies.

'When did you find out about my parents' affair? Was it when I first spoke to you at *Serafina's* or did you already know?'

He stares at me. Then he looks down. 'I already knew.'

'How?' I ask with surprise.

He swallows. 'I saw them together one night. At *Serafina's*. It may have been the night your mother refers to in her letter.'

I'm shocked. *He saw them having sex?*

'I was too young to understand what I was seeing, but I understood that what they were doing should be kept a secret.'

My heart goes out to him. 'You must've wanted, so badly, to talk to your mother.'

'No.' His response is sharp. 'That was the *last* thing I wanted to do.'

'Because of her depression? You were worried about her?'

He nods deliberately.

'Did you live upstairs, above the restaurant?'

'No.' He shakes his head once. 'We lived in an apartment not far away. Andrea and Serafina lived upstairs.'

'And you were staying with them that night?'

I'm trying to put two and two together, but once again he shakes his head.

'I had walked to the restaurant alone. My mother had taken sleeping pills. I couldn't wake her and was worried.'

I'm appalled. 'But you were only a child!'

'Yes.' He nods gravely.

'Was your mother okay?'

'Yes,' he replies. 'That time, she was okay.'

From the way he said *that time*, I have a horrible feeling that there was *another* time when his mother *wasn't* okay. I know Marta passed away years ago, but I haven't heard how she died.

'Do you mind if we talk about something else now?' he asks with a small smile.

'Yes, of course. I'm sorry, Alessandro. I didn't mean to be nosy.'

He nods at me. 'You've got your halo on today.'

'What? Oh, my hair.' I smile ruefully and tug at my frizzy curls.

'Wear it like that tomorrow,' he says.

'Why?'

'You'll see.'

I'm intrigued, but his smile is secretive and I doubt I'll get it out of him.

He edges himself down so his head is resting on the back of the sofa and his legs are stretched out before him.

'You look tired,' I comment.

'I am. Can I sleep here tonight?'

'On the sofa or in your van on the street? You can't drive.' That's for sure. He's had a couple of beers as well as the wine.

'I like this sofa. Sleeping on a hill is no fun.'

I smile. 'I don't know what Cristina will say, but I don't have a problem with it.'

'She won't care. I've slept here before.'

'It's settled then.'

'Good. I'll wash my hair and shave here in the morning before I see Nonna.'

'Is that what you call Serafina?' I ask with glee, loving that he's being more open in this sleepy, drunken state.

He nods.

'So she *is* like a grandmother to you?'

'She tried to be.' Or was that, 'She *tries* to be?' It sounded like the former, but I probably misheard.

His sleepy smile has faded a little so I don't ask. His eyes fall closed.

I stand up and gather the empty glasses and bottles together and take them to the kitchen. When I look over at him, he's shuffled down to lie on his side, taking up the whole sofa. I attempt to hunt out a spare duvet with no luck. I can't even find a blanket.

Remembering his sleeping bag in his van, I don't think twice about snatching up his keys from the coffee table. Luckily I do manage to think twice about closing the front door before I go, realising at the last second that I'll need my own keys to get back inside. I don't imagine the other residents would have appreciated me banging my door down, trying to rouse Alessandro.

Out on the pavement, I look left and right for Frida.

That's right, we walked uphill. I find the van just around the corner. I unlock it and slide the side door open, climbing in and reaching up to grab the end of Alessandro's sleeping bag from the roof space. It falls on top of me as I pull it down. I'm about to bundle it together and get out of the van when I recall his comment about needing a shave. He can get his razor himself in the morning, but what about a toothbrush? Surely he'll want to brush his teeth tonight.

I decide to open a couple of cupboards to see if his toothbrush is easy to spot. The first I try is full of black clothes and smells of his deodorant. I smile to myself and go to close it, but a flash of pink catches my eye. Thinking it might be a washbag, I reach into the cupboard and pull out a stuffed toy. It's a rabbit, a pink one.

Did an old girlfriend give him this? She must have meant a lot to him if he still has it. I feel an unwelcome prickle of jealousy and stuff it back in the cupboard. I can't even ask because he'll think I was snooping.

On that note, I decide to give up on the toothbrush idea, but as I'm about to slide the door shut, I spy a dark-grey washbag on a shelf on one of the open cupboards.

Bullseye.

I grab it and return to the house.

Alessandro is snoring lightly and it's clear he was never going to be brushing his teeth tonight in any case. Unzipping the sleeping bag and laying it flat over him, I turn out the lights and go to bed.

Chapter 22

The next morning, as we're preparing to leave the apartment, a postcard slides under the door. I swoop down and pick it up.

'You have your mail hand delivered?' Alessandro asks as I turn it over. 'Why doesn't Salvatore put it in the mailbox along with everybody's else's?'

'Dunno.' I shrug. 'Maybe because I make him coffee.'

'When?'

'The last couple of mornings. There's enough for two in that Moka thingie, and Cristina has been sleeping in.'

I read the postcard with a smile.

Dear Angie, am I the first? I reckon I had this in the mail before your bus dust had settled. I listened to the audiobook last night. You do Scarpetta better than Patricia Cornwell. I miss you, but I'm glad you're gone. Love Jimmy

'Who's it from?' Alessandro asks.

'Jimmy, my grandad's old mining partner.'

'What does he mean, *Scarpetta*?'

'You've never heard of Patricia Cornwell?'

'Yes, but...' He shakes his head, confused.

'She writes crime books about a medical examiner called Kay Scarpetta,' I explain. 'Jimmy loves them, but he finds reading difficult as he only has one eye. He was in the same mining accident as my grandfather.'

'Ah,' he says, but once more he frowns. 'Sorry, I still don't understand. What does he mean, "you do Scarpetta better"?'

I laugh. 'I'm sure he's joking, but I read to him. We were only part way through the Scarpetta series when I left, so I sorted him out for audiobooks. Patricia Cornwell herself must've read the last one he listened to.'

Jimmy and I would sit outside under the palm trees in our front yard – we didn't have a back one because the dugout was built into a hill, although we did have a bench seat up top where Nan and I used to watch the sunset.

When I first started reading aloud to Nan, that's where we'd go, but Jimmy came over one day as we were about to get started and asked if he could listen in as well. He couldn't manage the hill with his bad leg so we moved to the front yard. We sat there every evening for years.

Alessandro is quiet as I lock up. I think he's feeling as rough as I am.

When we arrive at *Serafina's*, he sends me upstairs to retrieve Giulio from his apartment.

'*Buongiorno*!' my father exclaims, giving me a hug. 'You ready to meet everyone?'

'Yep!' I reply brightly.

'Ah, Alessandro is here,' he says, spotting Frida. 'Good. I thought he change his mind about coming to Tivoli. After he call me last night, I didn't see his van in the car park.' He sounds ominous.

'He stayed at Cristina's,' I explain.

The look on his face... '*With you?*'

'Not like *that*!' I reply, laughing and blushing simultaneously. 'He slept on the sofa. Cristina was out so he kept me company.'

'I see. Okay.' He seems to decide that this is acceptable, but when we get in the van, I'm sure he questions Alessandro about it.

Alessandro brushes him off, waving his hand dismissively and tutting at whatever it is he's saying as he drives, shaking his head, out of the car park. After that, they switch to English.

The journey to Tivoli takes less than forty minutes, beginning on the motorway but changing to country roads as we near our destination. Out of my window, fields and farmyards zip past. Everything is so green. I've never seen so many trees in my life.

Alessandro tells me that we might get a chance to visit the hilltop town of Tivoli later, but the family's land is on the outskirts, situated to the north-west of the medieval centre. A bumpy dirt track leads us up to it.

They must've heard us coming – it would be hard not to, with that diesel engine – because when we arrive, we have a welcome party. Serafina, Eliana, Enzo, who I've already met, and my cousins, Valentina and Jacopo, are all here.

I have a strange knot in my stomach as Serafina walks

towards the van with her arms open. It's not anxiety; it's something else.

She can't see me behind the darkened windows, but when Giulio climbs out to greet her, her smiling attention remains focused on the side door.

Alessandro is on his way around the back of the van, but I don't wait for him to open my door for me. I feel a bit odd about being presented.

Serafina's face lights up as I tentatively slide my own door open, and even though the rest of the family is behind her, at first, she's the only one I see.

Her eyes are narrow and her nose quite big, but her whole face is smiling, her cheeks bulging like a chipmunk with a mouth full of nuts. Her shortish hair is grey and thick with tightly packed curls and she's wearing a blue and white checked apron. When I step out of the van, she embraces me. I'm taller than her by several inches, but I can feel the strength of her embrace. The knot tightens and my nose prickles with emotion.

Oh, Nan… I'm overwhelmed with grief at the thought of her and desperately, *desperately* sad that she kept this part of my family from me.

Serafina pulls away from me and clasps my face with her hands, looking intently at my features. She exclaims something and touches her hand to my hair, turning around to beckon excitedly to Valentina.

My seventeen-year-old cousin steps forward. She's beautiful, with high cheekbones and almond-shaped eyes, and she's wearing a pretty fifties-style red and white polka dot headscarf that's tied into a knot on the top of her head.

At Serafina's insistence, Valentina removes the scarf, and I gasp. We have the same thick, frizzy curls!

I have always wondered where my hair came from and now I know: my father's side of the family.

My hair is medium-blond, whereas Valentina's is dark, but it's the same texture and length, although she wears it much better than I do.

Valentina and my grandmother chat away animatedly to each other as Eliana steps forward.

'My mother had hair like this too,' she says, translating what Serafina is saying as my grandmother touches my hair with amazement. She seems absolutely delighted. I think she might now be saying that I have Giulio's eyes, from the way she's gesticulating and looking between her beaming son and me.

Alessandro has told me that the whole family speaks English, although not necessarily fluently. In the heat of the moment, I don't think it's occurring to my grandmother that I can't understand a word of what she's saying.

Eliana is stockier than her mother, but with the same bulging cheeks. Her hair is black, threaded through with grey, and tied up in a bun, and she's wearing thick black horn-rimmed glasses.

Enzo, Eliana's husband, and I met at the restaurant the other day. His white T-shirt is splattered with cooking sauce and he smells of tomatoes when we hug. It reminds me of Giulio's promise of a feast on our arrival.

Last but not least, I meet Jacopo, Valentina's twin brother. He's been hanging back, talking to Alessandro, and he seems a little awkward and gangly as he steps forward to greet me.

His features are still a bit too large for his face, but I suspect he will grow into them.

I look over at Alessandro. Serafina has his face in her hands and is chattering away to him as he smiles down at her.

She breaks away from him and guides me towards the house, a warm, soft arm around my waist. I feel oddly at ease with her. Maybe it's because I'm comfortable around people of my nan's generation. I know enough of them at home.

The house is nestled amongst tall skinny cypress trees, but it's a bit of a shambles, with old brickwork peeking out beneath patches of broken plaster. What remains of the plastered walls is painted salmon, but it's obvious the colour has faded dramatically over the years and is washed-out in places. The many small windows are each fitted with wooden shutters, some open, some closed. The building looks a bit as if it's on its last legs, but, inside, it's a different story. The walls are whitewashed and clean with terracotta floor tiles and the cosy rooms are crammed with rugs and wooden antique furniture. The kitchen, by contrast, is as modern as they come: shiny stainless steel, the kind of thing a Michelin-starred chef would be proud of.

I don't stay inside long before venturing out into the warm sunshine with Alessandro, Eliana and my cousins on a tour of the grounds.

The Marchesis own about four acres of land on a steep hillside peppered with fruit trees, stone pines and sprawling, ramshackle outbuildings.

The higher land behind the house contains pens for the pigs, two goats and chickens. Valentina tells me that the goats are called Fiocco and Nocciolina – 'Bow' and 'Little Nut'. It's her responsibility to milk them every morning. She and her brother are generally responsible for the welfare of the animals.

'Can I feed them too?' I ask Valentina when she swoops down and pulls up a handful of grass, tempting Fiocco and Nocciolina over.

'Of course!'

I laugh as their teeth tickle the palm of my hand. I've never seen a goat in real life before.

Nor pigs! I feel a bit sorry for them, knowing what I know about pork and fennel sausages, but they seem happy, especially when Jacopo and Alessandro scratch them between the ears. I copy them, giggling when the pigs snort loudly at me and try to nibble the sleeve of my shirt. I thought goats were supposed to be the ones that ate your clothes.

Part of the land is terraced – flattened-out expanses with retaining walls made of stone. The herb and vegetable garden sits on one of these terraces and it's *huge*. Eliana makes me promise to visit later in the summer when it's in its prime.

There's also an orchard with lemon, fig and peach trees growing in abundance, and a vineyard that Eliana tells me was planted by her husband ten years ago. He and Jacopo have been making wine, but only enough for the family. They'd like to plant vines up on the higher slopes one day and maybe even buy some extra land.

At the bottom of the property is a river rushing noisily downhill. The flora and fauna here have been left to their own devices and everything is so green and lush. It honestly feels like heaven on earth. I can just imagine myself sitting amongst the swaying grasses, relaxing in the sunshine.

High up on the other side of the river is the town of Tivoli, a mass of medieval buildings of various sandy shades, from cream to pale orange. I stare up at a bell tower topped with a pyramid-shaped roof and sigh with contentment.

Eliana tells me that Serafina used to walk to town at least three times a week when she was younger. Sometimes she, Giulio and Loreta, their little sister, would be dragged along as well. It would take them at least an hour to get there – longer if Loreta was dawdling – but the 500-metre climb was much easier in reverse, and of this they were thankful because they were always laden down with shopping bags from the market.

The land closer to the house is also terraced with neatly mown grass edged with vibrant flowerbeds. Remnants of a happy childhood are visible in the rope swing hanging from a nearby tree and an old wooden playhouse.

What a lovely place this must've been for Valentina and Jacopo to grow up, not to mention Giulio, Loreta and Eliana. The home has been in the Marchesi family for decades.

We eat outside on a long trestle table and every one of the dishes is delectable. Along with the usual vast array of antipasti, there are fried artichokes that are shatteringly crisp on the outside and tender within; *cacio e pepe*, literally translated as cheese and pepper, a rich but simple Roman pasta dish that packs loads of flavour, made with Pecorino Romano cheese and freshly ground pepper; rich savoury and sweet Roman oxtail stew with slow-cooked, fall-off-the-bone meat, plus vegetable dishes such as cauliflower parmesan, and chicory, sautéed Roman style, with garlic and chilli pepper.

'This really *is* a feast,' I marvel. 'It's incredible.' I'm full but reluctant to stop eating.

'Come to Tivoli for Christmas!' Eliana exclaims. 'So much food! Loreta, Boris, Francesca and Francesca's husband Pepe – they all join us, and Melissa, too, will return from Venice, maybe with Otello this year.' Melissa is Eliana and Enzo's eldest daughter – she's twenty-one and, along with her boyfriend, Otello, is studying environmental sciences.

'*Sì, sì*, you must!' Serafina exclaims, and the table is full of loud, vocal agreements, a cacophony of sound.

The thought of it... The thought of being surrounded by this vibrant, welcoming family... I have a return ticket to Australia booked for early September, but I can't imagine Christmas in Coober Pedy without Nan. Who would I celebrate with? Jimmy, Vera and Laszlo, like last year? They came to my dugout for a very simple meal – I did a roast chicken with roast potatoes and a few veggies, but didn't feel up to making all of the extra trimmings. Nan was very frail and barely touched her food.

'Maybe you can get Alessandro to join us,' Jacopo chips in.

A hush falls over the table.

'Francesca is pregnant!' Serafina tells Giulio. 'She called me this morning.'

Everyone begins to talk about my eldest cousin, wondering if the baby will arrive by Christmas.

I glance at Alessandro to see that he's smiling, but then I realise: that's not a smile. Not a real one.

Why wouldn't he come home for Christmas?

*

I try to help clear up after lunch, but I'm shooed away. 'Take Angie into Tivoli,' Giulio suggests to Alessandro. 'Valentina and Jacopo might also like to go.'

Valentina eagerly makes a suggestion in Italian and everyone else appears to agree.

'They want you to see Villa D'Este,' Alessandro explains.

'Very beautiful gardens,' Valentina says in English. 'Lots of fountains – it is magical.'

'Spectacular,' Giulio agrees.

Serafina grabs her son's arm on their way inside, but he shakes his head at her and waves his hands at the table and in the direction of the kitchen. I think he's saying that he's too busy to join us. Serafina tries to persuade him, but he rebuffs her and as she follows him inside, she seems disappointed.

Alessandro has vanished so I ask Valentina if she can show me where the bathroom is.

On my way back into the hall via the living room, I pause to take a closer look at the photo frames crammed onto a side table.

There are so many pictures, old and new. I bend down and peer closely at a black-and-white one of an elderly couple with a man, woman, boy and girl. There's something about the little girl's chubby-cheeked smile that makes me think she's Serafina.

I need someone to point out who's who. I'm sure my second aunt, Loreta, will be here somewhere, and my other two cousins. I can guess who they might be, but I'd like to know if I'm right.

Another photograph catches my eye and I gasp when I

realise it's Giulio on his wedding day. He's wearing a sky-blue suit with yellow flowers in the buttonhole and, next to him, Marta – for that's who I'm assuming it is – wears a dress of very light blue with ruffles around the collar, cuffs and hemline. Her face is gaunt and she appears startled, as though the photographer caught her unawares, and Giulio's smile seems fixed, not the face-splitting beam I've become familiar with.

But I'm most interested in the small boy peeking out from behind a fold in his mother's dress. Alessandro eyes the camera cheekily, his eyes dancing. He, at least, looks happy.

Outside, I hear Frida roaring into life. A moment later, Valentina appears.

'Ready?' she asks.

'Please tell me who some of these people are.'

She's fast about it, pointing from one photo to the next. I'm not sure I'd be able to recite it parrot-fashion, but the whole family seems to be here, going back generations.

'And who's that?' I ask, pointing at a little girl sitting on the grass in front of a flowerbed full of bright pink flowers. Valentina had skipped past her.

'That's Carlotta,' she replies.

The child is just a toddler, with bobbed brown hair and big brown eyes and she's laughing at whoever is behind the lens. It's hard to place when the picture might've been taken – she's wearing a red pinafore dress over a navy blue and white striped long-sleeve T-shirt, and the colours are bright and vibrant. It could have been snapped in the last ten to thirty years, for all I know.

'Come, we must go,' Valentina says. She's her perky self

again as she ushers me out the door, but I'm left wondering why she sounded so melancholic when she said Carlotta's name. It's the first time I've heard her mentioned.

I have a bad feeling in the pit of my stomach as Valentina pulls the heavy wooden door shut behind us.

Chapter 23

Alessandro, my cousins and I meander along narrow, cobbled streets in the hilltop town of Tivoli. Some properties are daubed with graffiti, others have grilles on their windows. Most houses have wooden shutters and crumbly walls with faded paintwork and sections of broken plaster and exposed brick. The beauty of the buildings still shines through and, anyway, after seeing inside the Marchesi residence, I'm not judging anything by its outward appearance. Who knows what lies behind these walls?

Villa D'Este is entered from a doorway on Piazza Trento, next to the entrance of the church of Santa Maria Maggiore.

The sixteenth-century villa once belonged to Cardinal Ippolito D'Este, who had ambitions to be Pope. Inside, the rooms are large and extravagant, with colourful frescoes adorning walls and ceilings, and intricate mosaics on some of the floors.

The view from the sun-drenched rear terrace stretches for

miles – Jacopo points out the direction of the family home, behind the medieval centre. I spy the bell tower that I saw from the house, with its pyramid-shaped roof and arched windows, and can roughly see how far we've come.

But if I thought the Marchesi land was heaven on earth, nothing prepares me for the terraced hillside Italian Renaissance gardens of Villa D'Este.

Famous for its profusion of fountains, I've never been in a more enchanting, fantastical place.

The Aniene, the river that runs along the bottom of the Marchesi property, was diverted to furnish water for the complex system of pools, water jets, channels, fountains, cascades and water games. Sunshine streams through trees, sparkling on water and bouncing off spray from fountains.

There are grottos and follies, niches and nymphaeums, crumbling walls thick with soft fluffy moss, tall sculpted pines and flowerbeds bursting with colour.

My thighs are burning as we climb the stairs, forty-five metres from top to bottom. The air is pure and clean and everywhere we go we can hear the sound of running water, whether it's trickling or cascading.

Right now, we're walking beside a long straight channel where a series of goggly-eyed creatures are spurting water from their mouths in our direction.

Jacopo and Valentina become distracted by a fountain on the other side of the pathway, laughing themselves silly at the sight of water squirting from a statue's breasts. I do a double take and realise that the statue is half woman, half horse, or maybe those are angel wings... Whoever created it had a vivid imagination.

Alessandro and I walk on. I point at one of the people on the wall on our left.

'Is that a person or a monkey? Check out the ears on that one!' I'm as immature as my cousins.

He smiles but doesn't laugh.

'You're very quiet,' I muse. 'Are you hungover?'

He frowns and shakes his head. 'No. Sorry, I was lost in my thoughts. How did you enjoy lunch?'

'Oh, it was amazing. I wish I could cook like that.'

'You will find plenty of teachers if you want to learn.'

'I'd love to spend more time out this way. They're such a lovely bunch of people.'

'They are. The best.'

'How often do you come here?'

He shrugs. 'Not much. I'm usually busy working.'

Valentina and Jacopo haven't caught us up yet, so I give in to my curiosity.

'I saw a picture of a child at the house. Valentina said she was called Carlotta.'

He looks as though I've sucker-punched him. He turns away, but not before I've seen his stricken expression.

'She told you what happened to her?' he asks in a strange, strained voice.

'No.'

I feel awful – he's clearly distressed. Seconds tick by without him elaborating and I'm certainly not about to press him for information.

Valentina and Jacopo appear, laughing. 'Come and see this,' Valentina urges, taking my hand.

I cast a look over my shoulder at Alessandro as I allow her

to drag me away. He's nodding along to something Jacopo is saying, but he looks pale.

If he wanted to talk about it, he would have.

Who was Carlotta? What did she mean to him? And what happened to her?

I sense I'd better tread carefully if I'm going to find out.

Chapter 24

Giulio is sitting out on the patio with Enzo and Eliana when we return, a glass of red wine in his hand. From the enthusiastic way he greets Valentina and me, I think he's on the Tipsy Train, destination: Drunk.

I smile and sit down on the chair he's pulled out for me.

'Giulio was telling us that your grandfather was an opal miner,' Eliana says.

'Yes.'

Valentina wants to know what an opal is, so I pull up the sleeve of my top to show her my bracelet. She gasps, leaning in closer to study it.

'My grandfather used to polish and prepare the opals himself,' I tell her. 'These are ones I found myself in the rock piles.' They're mostly blue and green. 'But the colours on some opals are unbelievably vibrant – red, pink, orange… I have one back at Cristina's apartment. I'll show you sometime.'

Enzo asks about my hometown so I tell everyone about life

in the desert, and after a while I realise that Giulio is listening intently. It's the first time I've dominated a conversation that he's been a part of. I don't think he knew much at all about where I've come from.

No one can believe it when I say that I live in a cave 'like the Flintstones'. Eliana and Serafina clap and look at each other with delight, and they're even more animated when I admit to not knowing what a lawnmower was until I was twelve. Giulio wants to know where Coober Pedy is on a map, so I make the shape of Australia with my hands. 'You know Uluru, or Ayers Rock, the big, red rock in the centre?'

They nod.

'Adelaide, the capital of South Australia, is here.' I point near the bottom. 'And Coober Pedy is here, roughly halfway between the two. It takes about nine hours to drive from Adelaide.'

Jacopo comes out of the kitchen with a glass of what looks like lemonade in his hand. He sits down and his mother quickly brings him up to date on what we've been saying.

I wonder where Alessandro is.

'Have you seen *Mad Max 3*?' I ask Jacopo. '*Beyond Thunderdome* – you know, with Tina Turner?'

'*Si, si*,' Enzo chips in eagerly. Jacopo nods hesitantly. I guess it's a bit before his time.

'Part of it was filmed in the area around Coober Pedy.' I think most of it was shot out on the Breakaways, which is the end of a mountain chain about twenty miles north of the town. 'What about *Pitch Black*?' I ask Jacopo. 'The space movie with—'

'Vin Diesel!' he interrupts. 'Yes?'

'Also filmed in Coober Pedy. One of the old spaceships that they used on the set is still sitting in the town centre.'

The Adventures of Priscilla, Queen of the Desert was also partly filmed in Coober Pedy, but my favourite is an indie film called *Opal Dream*, which was based on a book I love by Ben Rice: *Pobby and Dingan*. It's about a mining family and a little girl who has these imaginary friends called Pobby and Dingan. When they get 'lost' down a mine-shaft, their 'disappearance' has a knock-on effect for the whole family. It reminds me of the stories my grandfather used to tell me, except his stories were about the garden gnomes that Jimmy gave Nan for Christmas. Henry and Henrietta lived in our front yard and Grandad claimed that they came alive at night to throw parties down the mineshafts. I used to look for them when Grandad took me to the opal fields.

It's late afternoon now and the sun is on a downward trajectory. We decide to move indoors, but first I do a sweep of the landscape. Alessandro still hasn't returned.

I catch sight of him, down by the river. He cuts a lonely figure: dark and solitary against the green landscape.

'Is Alessandro all right?' I ask Giulio, tugging on his arm before he steps over the threshold.

He follows the line of my sight. 'He is okay. Being here hard for him sometimes, remind him too much of his mother.' He points down the hill to a cream-stone house with orange terracotta roof tiles. 'That is where Giorgio and Marta grew up. Alessandro spent much time there as a boy.'

'That house was his family home?'

'*Si*, yes. Come, is cold. We go inside.'

There's a piano in the living room with a music book open to Claude Debussy's 'Clair de Lune'.

'Do you play?' Eliana asks when she spies me looking.

I nod. 'This was one of my nan's favourites.'

Serafina overhears. 'Play it for us!' she exclaims.

'No, no, no.' I shake my head, embarrassed.

'*Dai ti prego*,' she implores. 'Andrea, my husband, played to me. Valentina, she is learning, but...'

'I am terrible,' Valentina chips in and everyone laughs.

'Please,' Eliana says with a smile, switching on the nearby lamp in preparation. 'It would mean a lot to my mother.'

I take a seat at the piano. I don't really need the music book, this one is so familiar to me.

The room breaks out into applause when I've finished, no one clapping louder or more enthusiastically than Giulio.

'Will you teach me how to play it?' Valentina asks.

'Only if you teach me how to use one of those.' I nod at her vintage headscarf.

Her eyes light up and as she dashes out of the room, I notice Alessandro standing in the doorway. His expression is warm and open, his eyes glinting as they meet mine. He turns to address Giulio. 'We should go. We need to get back for the wine delivery.'

Everyone else protests, but Giulio agrees, wobbling slightly as he stands.

Valentina reappears with a light-blue headscarf in her hands. I wait as she slips it underneath my hair and fashions it into a knot on top, prompting Giulio and Serafina to cry, '*Bella!*' simultaneously.

As I settle myself on the back seat of the van, repeatedly

promising to return soon, I can't help but wonder why Alessandro doesn't feel more at ease here. I don't believe this lovely family could make him feel anything less than utterly welcome.

Before I slide the door shut, I notice Serafina giving Giulio a bunch of bright pink flowers. He climbs into the front seat and closes his door, winding down the window to call out his final goodbyes.

Alessandro gets behind the wheel and glances across at Giulio's lap, his brow furrowing. He says something and Giulio shrugs, still waving enthusiastically.

But when we're out of sight of the house and the window has been wound up again, Alessandro again speaks in Italian. His voice is low and deep and it carries a warning.

Giulio responds irately and Alessandro does in turn. I watch with a sinking feeling as the mood in the van deteriorates and then Giulio raises his voice and Alessandro abruptly falls silent.

What was that about?

'We need to make a detour,' Alessandro tells me after a minute or so.

'Okay,' I reply.

Soon afterwards we pull into a car park. A *cemetery* car park.

So that's what the flowers are for. But whose grave are we visiting? Marta's? Or someone else's?

'He'll only be five minutes,' Alessandro tells me as Giulio gets out of the van and shuts the door, still looking slightly unsteady on his feet as he walks away.

'Don't you want to go with him?' I ask gently.

He exhales heavily and after a long moment, nods. He doesn't say another word as he gets out of the car.

I watch as he walks away, and then something inside me snaps. Maybe it's because of Nan and Grandad and the secrets that they kept, but I find myself doing something very uncharacteristic. Leaning forward, I pluck the keys from the ignition and climb out of the van, locking it behind me.

I walk amongst tombs and crypts, beneath tall cypress trees and past marble headstones and stone statues of urns, angels and crosses. My feet crunch on the gravel, my footsteps occasionally softened as they land on grass growing through. The longer and further I walk, the more I begin to doubt myself.

I'm about to give up when I see them, Giulio and Alessandro. They're standing before a white stone statue of an angel, their heads bowed.

They begin to turn around so I duck behind a tree, almost high-tailing it out of there in an attempt to make it to the van first.

But I can't do it, not when the truth could be here for the taking.

They slowly walk away in the opposite direction and I realise I might still have a chance of getting to the van before them if I hurry.

Coming to a stop in front of the stone angel, my head begins to spin as I try to make sense of what I'm seeing. It's a family tomb with more than one person buried inside. Names jump out at me: Andrea, Marta, Carlotta... There's also the same photograph of Carlotta that was sitting on the table – the pink flowers have been put into the vase beside it.

Mindful that I don't have long, I study the dates beside Marta and Carlotta's names. Only the years of birth and death are inscribed, but they died the same year.

Carlotta was only two.

For some reason I think of the small pink bunny in Alessandro's van and the vice around my heart tightens.

Was Carlotta Alessandro's sister?

I tear myself away, my walk transforming into a jog as I hurry along a dark, shady path beneath the trees.

I'm still trying to compute the information. How long ago did they die? I manage to do the maths as I run: twenty-one years ago.

Wait. I'm twenty-seven. My brain races as I work out that Carlotta was born four years *after* me. Were Marta and Giulio still married?

My heart crushes to a pulp.

Did I *have a little sister?*

Chapter 25

I approach the van, no longer running. Alessandro and Giulio are waiting, their expressions wary.

'Was Carlotta your daughter?' I ask Giulio.

He nods dejectedly.

I turn to Alessandro. 'I had a half-sister?'

He's looking wretched, but now he's also confused. 'I thought Valentina told you earlier?'

'That Carlotta was my sister? No! All she told me was her name!'

'We were going to explain,' he says in a low voice, glancing at Giulio. 'It was hard to find the right time.'

They're obviously both still deeply affected by these deaths. I'm hurting knowing that I had a small half-sister who was lost, but they *lived through* losing her. They knew her. They loved her. I'm only mourning the *idea* of her.

'What happened to them?' I ask in a choked voice.

'It was an accident,' Giulio replies.

Alessandro glances at him and then looks away. When his eyes find mine, they're full of suffering. 'Carlotta—'

'It was an accident!' Giulio cuts him off, raising his voice in anger and distress.

Alessandro's shoulders slump. '*Si*, it was an accident,' he tells me resignedly. 'She fell from the balcony of our apartment.'

I gasp.

But he's not finished. 'And two days later, my mother followed her down.'

I stare at him in shock and horror.

'It was an accident,' Giulio repeats, but he's broken.

'It was not an accident,' Alessandro tells me, enunciating every word quietly but firmly. His eyes well up with tears. 'Keys, please,' he commands, holding out his palm.

I mutely hand them over and he unlocks the van.

Never has a silence been heavier than on that journey home.

I sit in the back, brushing away tears as I try to comprehend what this family went through. Giulio lost his daughter and then his wife. Alessandro lost his sister and then his mother. Two days apart.

How can anyone ever get over that? Alessandro was just fourteen years old when his mother committed suicide. I understand why Giulio wanted to call both deaths an accident – if Marta was mentally ill, as they knew she was, then she was unlikely to have been in control of her actions.

I can't imagine the grief she must have felt, losing her little girl. It must have been overwhelming. Who wouldn't have considered doing what they could to escape the pain, even without depression blackening their lives? How could *anyone* come through that?

And yet Giulio did come through it. He's here, surviving. And clearly still suffering.

My poor father.

And oh… Alessandro. I think of the pink bunny again and have an overwhelming urge to unclick my seat belt and climb between them to tell them I'm sorry.

I act on my impulse.

Alessandro jolts when I appear at his side, but he keeps his eyes on the road as I place one hand on Giulio's knee and the other on his.

'I'm sorry,' I whisper.

Giulio covers my hand with his and squeezes it hard, and then Alessandro takes my other hand and brings it to his lips, giving my fingers a brief kiss.

'Put your seat belt back on, Angel,' he says in a husky voice. 'We don't want to lose you too.'

Chapter 26

I stand and stare at the apartment blocks lining this stretch of road. I'm walking to work, taking the short cut.

Did Alessandro and Giulio live with Marta and Carlotta in one of these apartments? Did Carlotta fall and Marta jump from one of these very balconies? Alessandro told me that they lived nearby. Is that why he wanted to avoid coming this way when he walked me home on Friday?

Last night, I found it difficult to sleep. In the end I gave up, retrieved my new phone from its charger on the windowsill and called Bonnie, bringing her up to date on the past week. I needed someone sensible to talk it all through with.

'So you and Alessandro share a sister,' she mused. 'But you're not related.'

'No.'

'And he still seems happy that you're there?' she asked.

'Yes. At least, he was until yesterday when I found out about Carlotta.'

I had my opal in my hands and was rotating it absent-mindedly, watching the colours flash under my bedside table lamp.

'If Giulio lost a daughter all those years ago, maybe Alessandro is pleased that he has a second chance to be a father.'

This made me freeze. 'You think he sees me as some sort of replacement for her?'

'I didn't mean that. But you don't know what Giulio was like before you got in touch with him. Maybe Alessandro knew that he was missing something from his life. Maybe that's why he's pleased you're there.'

'Maybe.' I rubbed my thumb over the rough sandstone still clinging to part of the opal's surface. 'Anyway, how are you? What have you guys been up to?'

'Oh, same as always, darling. Not much changes here.'

'Mick still showing no signs of retirement?'

She laughed wryly. 'What do you think?'

I took that as a no.

'Jimmy seems to be slowing down a little,' she divulged.

'Is he okay?' I asked worriedly.

'Just getting old. He and I have been listening to those audio CDs you left for him.'

I was surprised. Bonnie always had her nose in a book – I didn't think she'd be interested in… Ah. Reading between the lines, I gathered she'd been doing it to keep Jimmy company.

'Has Jimmy been lonely?'

'He's absolutely fine, my love, don't you worry about a thing.'

'I'll call him in a bit,' I told her. 'But can you give him a hug from me when you next see him?'

'Of course I will. He'll probably hit me with his walking stick, but anything for you.'

This made me laugh, but how I missed Jimmy. I missed all of my friends and the familiarity that came with them. I was with my family, but they didn't feel familiar to me. Not yet.

'What is it, darling?' Bonnie asked gently when I sighed.

'I'm still not entirely comfortable around Giulio,' I admitted. 'I don't know how to *be* around him. He's a nice man, everyone likes him, even the people who run the restaurant down the road, and you'd think they'd be in competition with each other. He has people working for him who've been there since his parents ran the place and they're still there now. It's like they're one big family, but *I'm* his blood and I don't feel like family.'

'It's early days, love,' Bonnie replied. 'Give it a while. It must be very strange to suddenly find you've got an adult daughter. He may well feel quite intimidated by you.'

I remembered Serafina trying to persuade him to come to Villa D'Este with us and wondered if that could be true.

'Do you have anything in common? What are his interests?' she asked.

'Food, food and food.'

'That's a good start. Why don't you bake something for him? Or perhaps you could ask him to teach *you* something?'

'Mm, that's a good idea.'

One thing was certain. It was going to take a lot more than a hug and a hand squeeze before we'd feel at ease in each other's company.

When I arrive at *Serafina's*, Alessandro is behind the bar. I spy Giulio in the kitchen, but he has his back to the serving hatch.

'Hey,' I say to Alessandro.

I came in early so that we could clear the air.

'*Ciao*,' he replies curtly.

I place Cristina's Chupa Chups tin on the bar top.

'Lollipops?' He's mystified.

'Cristina let me borrow her tin.' I open the lid to show him what's inside. 'Kolaczki cookies. I baked them this morning.' They're made from circular-shaped dough, folded in at two opposing edges with jam in the middle. 'They're Polish. Would you like one?' I offer nervously.

'Er, sure.' He reaches into the tin and takes one out.

'What do you think?' I ask.

'Yum,' he murmurs, shaking his head in bewilderment before meeting my eyes. 'Speaking Hungarian, playing the piano, and now baking. How *did* you learn how to play like that?'

'My grandfather taught me. Actually, he only taught me the basics. I wasn't very interested when I was younger, but Nan loved hearing him play, just as Serafina did Andrea.'

He eyes me thoughtfully. 'So, after your grandfather died, you learned for your grandmother?'

I shrug. 'It was the one thing that calmed her down when she was feeling anxious.'

It was also a way to break the silence.

It was strange: she couldn't bear to listen to Grandad's old rock records, but she liked hearing the piano.

My mother used to tinkle the ivories as well. I was never sure if Nan was referring to Mum or me when she'd tell visitors, 'Angie will play for us!'

Nan often spoke about Grandad and Mum as if they were still alive. It was not only confusing but devastating for her to be reminded that they were gone, so I learned to let her mistakes slide. It seemed kinder to both of us.

Giulio exits the kitchen.

'Giulio, try one of these.' Alessandro beckons him over.

'What is *these*?' Giulio asks.

'Kolaczki cookies,' Alessandro replies with perfect pronunciation. *Kolach-ki*. 'Angel made them.'

Giulio glances at me and peers into the tin. He pulls out a cookie and takes a bite, his eyes widening. 'Who made you these?' he asks me.

I'm not sure if he means who taught me or is wanting to know how they're made, so I give him both answers. 'They're made with lots of butter, cream cheese and flour. My friends, Jakub and Jan, two brothers from Poland, gave me the recipe.'

'Come!' he exclaims. 'I teach you how to toss pizza!'

I shoot Alessandro a look and he laughs under his breath as I follow Giulio into the kitchen.

Antonio and Maria have already made the dough and are currently shaping it into balls.

'*Perfetto*!' Giulio declares at their timing. He takes one of the dough balls and presses it flat against a floury surface. Maria and Antonio beam and chatter away when they realise a lesson is taking place.

Giulio places the flattened dough on his knuckles and starts to spin it around in a circle. The dough stretches and stretches and then he tosses it in the air and it turns as it comes down again. I watch, hypnotised, as the small disc grows bigger and bigger. Out of the corner of my eye, I see Alessandro leaning against the doorframe with his arms crossed over his chest.

'We toss the dough for three reasons,' Giulio tells me. 'First, to get the right size. Second, to build a crust – as you're throwing the dough in the air, you're making it thicker at the ends and thinner in the middle. And, most importantly, we need to dry out the crust so it's crunchy on the outside and light and airy in the middle.'

He places the flattened pizza dough on the countertop. 'Now, you try.'

After washing my hands at the sink, I press one of the balls into a disc shape on the counter. I'm nervous as I lift up the dough and balance it on my knuckles.

'No jewellery!' Giulio cries, realising I'm wearing a ring. It's an opal and sterling silver one that my grandparents gave to my mother on her sixteenth birthday, and later to me on mine. 'Wait,' he says, stepping closer as I take it off. 'This was Angie's ring.'

I glance at him with surprise. 'You remember it?'

'I do.'

I hand it to him and, when it becomes clear he's not going to say any more about it, I begin to spin the dough on my knuckles. It flies straight off and hits Maria on her ample bosom, making her eyebrows jump up with surprise. They hit her hairline when her husband makes a grab for the dough and manages to get himself a handful of breast while he's at it. We all fall about laughing, including Alessandro.

'I show you again!' Giulio cries, and then he pats Alessandro on the back and points at the sink. 'We all do this.'

I don't think I've ever laughed so much in such a short space of time, and it's uplifting to see Alessandro and Giulio working together after the drama of yesterday.

I'm grateful to Bonnie for making the suggestion.

Chapter 27

On Friday, the temperature soars. I've been helping out in the kitchen on and off throughout the week, but it's too hot for me now. It's still mild when we finish work close to midnight.

Stefano is trying to persuade Cristina to go clubbing, but she's not in the mood for dancing. I think she had an argument with Rebecca yesterday.

He turns to Alessandro and me, but Alessandro puts his palms up to ward him off. 'I don't do clubs, as you well know.'

'Angie?' Stefano turns to me beseechingly. 'Angel?'

I laugh. I would have gone if Cristina was up for it, but I'm not sure about Stefano and me going out on our own.

He makes a noise of disgust and takes his phone out of his pocket, presumably to line up someone else.

'Unless we all go to Cristina's instead?' I suggest, glancing at my flatmate.

She nods. 'It's warm enough to sit outside.'

Stefano claps, satisfied with the back-up plan.

'Will you come?' I ask Alessandro hopefully.

He hesitates, then shrugs. 'Sure, why not?'

We don't have much booze in so Alessandro pilfers some alcohol from behind the bar before we head outside to his van. Stefano persuaded Alessandro to drive so we wouldn't have to walk. Honestly, that guy has more energy for dancing than anyone I know, but walking? No.

It's been an up and down week – emotionally draining, but also rewarding. I've helped out in the kitchen when the restaurant hasn't been busy, and Giulio has been teaching me how to cook some of the basic dishes. In turn, I've been bringing in baked goods.

Today it was Oskar's Estonian Suussulavad Kaerakupsised oat cookies, yesterday it was Pasha's Russian Pryaniki spiced biscuits, and the day before it was Magnus and Astrid's Norwegian cardamom-flavoured Krumkake.

I've found all the ingredients I need in the supermarket down the road from *Serafina's* and luckily Cristina has a well-stocked kitchen, including an electric whisk and baking trays, so I haven't had to buy anything new.

I had to improvise a little with the Krumkake, having found an Italian *pizzelle* buried in a kitchen cupboard. The decorative two-sided iron griddle is not dissimilar to the waffle irons they use in Norway – Cristina said that her grandmother gave it to her a few years ago for Christmas, but she'd never used it.

She seemed riveted watching me wrap the thin, flat still-hot cookies around a piece of plastic I'd formed into a cone shape. I had to work quickly or I would have risked burning my fingers.

Every day, Giulio has erupted with excitement and demanded to know the recipes.

Bonnie was right: we seem to be bonding over something we're both passionate about.

'Two more postcards!' Alessandro notes with surprise when we open the front door to find them on the floor.

'She also had one yesterday,' Cristina points out as I swoop down to pick them up. 'Popular girl.'

I laugh when I see that they're both from Trudy. She can talk the hind legs off a donkey. I read them while the others sort out drinks.

Darling Angie, Bake Club celebrated its 7-year anniversary yesterday – you were missed! We've got two new members: Mustafa and Oya from Turkey! They're gonna show us how to make Stained Glass Coconut Cookies – how cool do they sound? I'll share the recipe with you on Facebook! Running out of room, so starting another postcard…

Angie! I've sent you another postcard too – hope they arrive together! Wanted to add that I hope you know how much we all miss you. Saying that, none of us want you to come home anytime soon. But when you do, bring some recipes! Love ya! Trudes xxx

And then in tiny writing at the bottom:

Whose stupid idea was it to write you postcards? There's never enough room!

'What's Bake Club?' Stefano asks, picking up the first postcard from the counter where I've put it down.

I don't mind him being nosy. That's the thing about postcards: the news is out there for anyone to see.

'It sort of began as an attempt to matchmake,' I tell him with a smile.

Alessandro passes me a glass of prosecco. 'That sounds intriguing.'

He presses me to explain as we settle ourselves outside.

'My single friends, Trudy and Rita, were at my place a few years ago when these two brothers, who had not long arrived from Poland, brought over some Kolaczki cookies.'

Jakub and Jan, both in their thirties, had moved into the dugout next to Bonnie and Mick, who'd told them that Nan had once loved to bake.

Trudy and Rita had recently come through terrible divorces, one of which involved domestic violence and the other adultery.

Sensing chemistry between the two couples, I asked if the men would teach us how to make the cookies sometime. They agreed. Not wanting to be a spare part, I invited a couple of other friends. Even Nan joined in, although we had to be very careful with her and the oven at that point.

It was so much fun that we decided to do it again and Bake Club was formed. We held it at mine because it was hard for Nan and me to leave the house, but somehow we always managed to fit into the space, even as our membership grew.

There were times, of course, when I couldn't host or participate. If Nan was having a bad day, someone else would host at theirs. Everyone understood if I had to cancel at the last minute – they'd wait on standby until I could give the go-ahead.

'It's like "Fight Club"!' Stefano exclaims.

This makes me laugh. 'About the complete opposite,' I say, thinking with fondness of some of the old-age pensioners in the group.

A couple of years ago, I decided to collate all of the recipes and get them printed as books to give to Jakub, Trudy, Rita and Jan as wedding presents. They got married in a joint ceremony the Christmas before last and everyone from Bake Club provided pastries and cookies for dessert.

I couldn't go – Nan wasn't up for leaving the house at all by that point – but everyone told me about it and I saw the photos.

The cookbooks were so popular that the local bookshop asked to stock them. We put the proceeds towards a hip replacement operation for one of our members, Astrid. She and her miner husband Magnus moved to Australia from Norway twenty-five years ago and were two of my grandparents' closest friends. They were some of the first people I asked, *If you could go anywhere, where would you go?*

I still remember their answer. It was Preikestolen – also known as Pulpit Rock – back home in Norway. They sent me a postcard of it while visiting their son, Erik, in nearby Stavanger: a steep cliff soaring over six hundred metres above the Lysefjord. At the top is a square plateau of about twenty-five by twenty-five metres. The postcard showed a girl standing on the edge of a large flat rock platform with a sheer drop beside her.

I felt dizzy even looking at it, but Astrid told me that tens of thousands of people take similar photos every year. It's one of the many places I'd love to see for myself one day.

Someone shouts over the wall. Cristina and Stefano's faces light up, the latter leaping excitedly to his feet and shouting back. Cristina hurries inside and Alessandro groans and covers his face with one hand.

'Rebecca is here,' he tells me when I ask what's going on.

I sit up straighter. *About time I met her properly!*

'This could be my cue to leave,' he mutters.

'No, don't! Please stay,' I implore him.

He sighs as Rebecca's voice carries through from the hallway.

'Why do you dislike her?' I whisper.

'It's the way she treats Cristina.'

He cares about her more than she realises.

Rebecca is in a much merrier mood than the one she was in when I first encountered her. She's seemingly pleased to meet me, and even though the greeting she and Alessandro exchange is cool, it's not laden with animosity.

Stefano pours his friend a prosecco and we raise our glasses.

'*Salute*!'

Rebecca launches into a string of Italian and Cristina puts her hand on her knee to stop her.

'English,' she says, nodding at me.

'Sorry!' Rebecca exclaims, taking a moment to light herself a cigarette.

I remember the ashtray on the terrace when I first arrived. To my knowledge – and relief – Cristina doesn't smoke.

'I've come from the bar,' she adds.

'Bar drinking or bar in a lawyer sense?' I ask, remembering that she and Stefano studied law together.

'Drinking!' She laughs. She really is a stunner, with those feline green eyes and tumbling dark locks.

The sound of the buzzer reverberating around the apartment makes Stefano leap to his feet once more. 'The cavalry has arrived!' he declares.

I glance at Cristina.

'Stefano brings the party with him wherever he goes,' she tells me with a wry smile. 'He was texting people on the way here.'

A stream of people steps out onto the terrace, including Cristina's former flatmate and her boyfriend. There are seven in total, four girls and three boys in their late twenties, early thirties.

'Can I use your bathroom?' Alessandro asks me after everyone has been introduced. I've gone inside to help Cristina carry glasses – her friends came armed with booze.

'Of course, as long as you promise to return.'

He wavers.

'*Alessandro*!' I berate him. 'Live a little! I've been stuck in a cave for twenty-seven years, the least you can do is hang out with me while I make some new friends.'

'Emotional blackmail!'

'Is it working?'

He rolls his eyes, but nods. 'I'll be back in a bit.'

When I go outside, all the seats crammed around the coffee table are taken, but Stefano pats his knee. 'Come here, Angie.'

I eye the girl sitting in Alessandro's vacated chair and imagine *her* sitting on *his* knee. It's not a welcome thought. But I go ahead and perch on Stefano's knee anyway.

When Alessandro reappears, the girl in his seat apologetically hops up and squeezes onto the chair next to him with her friend – they're both so tiny, they fit side by side.

'You okay there?' Alessandro asks me.

'She's fine!' Stefano cries on my behalf, hooking his arm around my waist.

Alessandro takes a swig of his beer, exposing the back of his hand. His burn looks a lot better, but he still has patches of dry skin. At least the injury is no longer red-raw.

'Have you taken a look at the accommodation I sent you?' one of the girls, Lindsey, asks Cristina. She's Canadian, but has been living in Italy for three years. I'm glad I'm not the only one who speaks English as their first language.

'Yeah, but I think it's still going to be out of my budget,' Cristina replies. 'Might have to be hostels again.'

'What's this?' I ask.

'Snowboarding. We go every year,' Lindsey replies. 'It's where half of us met,' she adds, indicating the others.

I look over my shoulder at Stefano. 'Do you go too?'

He shakes his head and shudders. 'No, I'd break my neck. You snowboard, though, don't you?' he asks Alessandro.

'Sometimes.'

'Not that anyone has ever seen him,' Cristina chips in. 'He never wants to come with us.'

'I've seen him,' one of the guys, I think his name is Fabio, interjects.

'Where?' Cristina demands to know.

'Chamonix,' Alessandro enlightens her.

'You went to Chamonix and never told me?' she asks him,

and I remember that she has vintage ski posters of the town hanging on the walls in the living room.

'Where are you going?' I ask Cristina to deflect the attention away from Alessandro, who's looking a bit uncomfortable.

'The plan is St Anton am Arlberg in Austria in February,' Cristina replies. 'But I'm still trying to save enough money. You should come!'

'I'll be in Australia by then,' I tell her regretfully. 'I'd love to see the snow one day.'

'Angie has never been out of Australia before now,' Stefano tells his friends.

They want to know what I've done since I arrived in Italy. 'I've only been here about ten days, but I've checked out the city, obviously. And I went to Tivoli.' I smile at Alessandro. 'I'm hoping to do a few trips over the next couple of months. I really want to see Venice. And Florence. And I'm desperate to go to Pompeii!'

'You could do Pompeii on a day trip,' Lindsey says. 'There are bus tours.'

'That's a great idea!'

The night wears on. A couple of people leave, but Stefano, Rebecca and Cristina are still going strong.

Whenever I try to slip off Stefano's knee onto a free chair, he grabs me and pulls me back. He's being increasingly flirtatious, but I can't say I mind. He's so ridiculously attractive and it's been years since anyone my own age has paid me attention.

Anyway, I'm drunk again and don't mind admitting it. '*About time you let your hair down!*' my inner Louise keeps shouting at me. I haven't yet got over the rush at realising that I'm now allowed to have nights like this.

'How did your audition go?' I think to ask Stefano. It was so busy tonight at *Serafina's* that I completely forgot earlier.

He went for a small part on an Italian soap opera.

'It was so-so. It's hard to tell with these things. Have you ever thought about acting?'

'Me?' I scoff.

'Or modelling?'

I bend over and howl with laughter.

'Why not?' he demands to know, hitting me on my back and pulling me into an upright position, his arms still looped around my waist. 'You're beautiful.'

I look over my shoulder at him. 'You're drunk.'

Yeah, I know, I can talk.

'Yes, I am very drunk, but I'm not lying. She's beautiful, isn't she, Sandro?'

Sandro?

Alessandro meets my eyes momentarily. 'Yes, she's beautiful, inside and out,' he replies as my cheeks flame.

Stefano guffaws. 'Such a Romeo!' he cries. 'This is how he woos the ladies.'

Alessandro reaches for his beer, a smile playing about his lips.

'You *are* beautiful, with your big hair and golden eyes,' Stefano insists. 'You remind me of a lion!'

'Big hair, maybe, but golden eyes? You're hilarious.'

'They have a bit of gold in them,' he maintains, turning my face towards him. We're about four inches away from each other, staring into each other's eyes. Oddly, I don't feel uncomfortable.

It's about then that I decide I could never fancy Stefano.

Alessandro gets up and collects a few empties from the table before disappearing inside.

'Let me go, I need the loo,' I tell Stefano.

I'm a little unsteady on my feet as I stand and gather some empty bottles. I take them to the kitchen where Alessandro is sorting out the recycling.

'I'm going to call it a night,' he tells me.

'Don't leave me with him!' I protest, jokily.

'You're not interested?'

I shake my head and pull a face. 'No! I'm still convinced he's gay.'

'I think you'll discover tonight that he's not.'

'What?' I wave my hand dismissively. 'I need the loo,' I mutter, zigzagging into my bedroom.

When I come out again, Alessandro is reading the postcard I received yesterday – I left it out on the dresser in the hall.

'Do you mind?' he asks, glancing up at me.

'Not at all. I doubt it'll be very interesting if you don't know him, though.'

'You say that, but what on earth is your "old spaceship"?'

I laugh and tipsily lean against the wall. 'If you hadn't disappeared when we were with your family in Tivoli, then you'd know that they filmed a movie in Coober Pedy called *Pitch Black*. Have you heard of it?'

'It rings a bell.'

'It's a space movie. The film crew left behind a spaceship in the town centre. I had my first kiss inside it,' I tell him with a cheeky grin.

'With...' he studies the name on the postcard. 'Pieter?'

'Exactly.' Aussie-born son of German immigrants. 'He was my first love.'

'And he's a photographer now?'

Pieter says in his card that he's recently done a fashion shoot in Coober Pedy, using 'our' old spaceship as a backdrop for a couple of shots.

'Yes, quite a good one,' I reply to Alessandro. 'It's what he always wanted to do.'

What are you good at? What are you passionate about?

Those were the questions I'd ask friends who were struggling to decide what they wanted to do with their lives – that's if I didn't already know the answers, which more often than not, I did.

'Why does he say, "*And all because of you*"?' Alessandro asks.

I shrug. 'I encouraged him to do it, helped him to line up work experience with some photographers. Wrote a few letters and urged him to chase his dream.'

English was never Pieter's best subject, whereas I was quite good at it – and school generally.

'You mean so much to the people you've left behind,' he muses thoughtfully, turning the postcard over and placing it on the dresser.

'I didn't leave Pieter,' I correct him. 'He left when he was eighteen. He lives in Sydney and is a fashion photographer now. His pictures are often featured in magazines.'

'So you encouraged your first love to leave you behind to follow his dreams. Who encouraged *you* to leave and follow *your* dreams?'

'Everyone did,' I reply, sobering.

He cocks his head to one side, his brows pulling together quizzically.

'They all knew I wouldn't abandon Nan, but when she passed away, everyone gave me opals to fund my trip. I sold all but one of them. It was so special, I couldn't part with it.'

He looks taken aback. 'Can I see it?'

'Sure. It's in my bedroom.'

I flick on the overhead light and get the opal out of the bedside table.

'Who gave this to you?' he asks with wonder, tilting it one way and then the other.

'I don't know. It's a mystery. They were all donated anonymously.'

'Amazing,' he murmurs.

'Some people think opal is gaudy, but I think it's beautiful.'

'It reminds me of the Northern Lights,' he says. 'The greens and blues, at least.'

'I would love to see them. Have you?' I ask.

He nods. 'A few years ago.'

'Wait. Check this out.' Hunting out my special UV torch, I turn it on and switch off the main bedroom light. The opal glows like something out of a science fiction film. 'People use these when they go noodling.'

'Noodling?'

'Fossicking, but specific to opal.' I explain how people sift through the rock piles, searching for opal the miners have missed. 'Other things also glow in the dark. You have to be really careful after it's been raining as all of the scorpions come out.'

'The scorpions light up?'

'Yes,' I reply as his arm brushes against mine, the warm heat of him colliding with my skin. I didn't realise how close we were standing in the darkness.

Stefano bursts into the room and stumbles towards the en suite, slamming the door shut behind him.

We both laugh and I walk across the room to turn on the bedside lamp.

'I think Cristina has been without a flatmate for too long,' I say drily. 'I don't mind *you* using my bathroom,' I add hastily as he hands me the opal.

'I was about to take the hint,' Alessandro replies.

Stefano opens the bathroom door and looks at us both. His face breaks into a wide drunken smile and then he cries, 'Amigos!' and rushes us.

It happens so quickly that neither of us is capable of reacting. Stefano bundles us both onto my bed, an arm hooked around each of our waists. We're flat out on our backs, our feet still on the floor, and Stefano is sprawled out on his front, two thirds of him on the bed, his bottom third off.

Alessandro and I look at each other and laugh. I give Stefano a shove, but he's motionless.

'Is he okay?' I ask, struggling to remove his heavy arm from my waist.

'He's passed out,' Alessandro replies drily. Stefano's face is turned towards him.

He rolls out from under him and I do the same, then we stand at the foot of the bed and survey the situation. Alessandro grabs Stefano's arm and prepares to heave him from the bed.

'Can you give me a hand?'

'Wait!' I say.

'What?'

'He'll end up on the floor.'

'Yes, and then we can drag him out of your room.'

'But then he'll be passed out in the living room while there's a party going on.'

'So?'

'Don't be mean,' I chide. 'Leave him there. The bed's big enough.'

Alessandro looks puzzled. 'But where will you go?'

'I'll stay here,' I reply with a shrug. 'He's out cold. Anyway, if I'm under the covers, his hands won't be able to get to me.'

He hesitates.

'Are you concerned for my virtue?'

'I am a bit. You're a little naïve, Angel. I'm not sure you know what you're doing.'

My mouth falls open with indignation, but then I shrug. 'Yeah, you're right. It's been a while since I had a boyfriend. I'm a bit out of practice. You can crash there if you want to protect me.' I point at the space to the left of Stefano. 'It's that or sleeping on the hill,' I remind him, sensing his reluctance. 'You can move to the sofa when the party's over, if you want.'

I've done enough drinking for one night so I brush my teeth and change into my PJs in the bathroom. When I come out, Alessandro is sitting on the bed, leaning against the wall, still seemingly unconvinced about this plan. I climb under the covers and edge down until my head is on the pillow. Once I'm settled, he gets into a sleeping position as well, but he stays on top of the bedcovers. It's still warm and he's fully dressed in black jeans and a black T-shirt.

I turn on my side to face him. Stefano is a bit further down the bed so his head is not blocking our view of each other.

'Do you mind if I leave the light on for a while? The room is spinning.'

'Sure.' He seems concerned. 'Too much to drink?'

'Way too much. Again. You?'

'I'm okay. I stuck to beer.'

'Giulio seems to drink quite a lot,' I muse.

Alessandro nods. 'He always has. Not always,' he corrects himself. 'But he has done for years.'

'Why did you come back nine years ago?'

His eyes widen at my direct question – alcohol has well and truly loosened my tongue.

'Please tell me. We shared a sister! That means we're family.'

He breathes in deeply and heavily exhales.

'Talk to me,' I implore.

Seconds tick by, but he *does* answer. 'I bumped into an old school friend in America who told me that my grandparents were ill. I wanted to see them before they died.'

My heart clenches. 'What was wrong with them?'

'Cancer.'

'Both of them?'

'Yes. They passed away within three weeks of each other.'

'Did you make it home in time?'

He nods. 'I had four weeks with my grandmother and seven with my grandfather. I think we made peace.'

'Why weren't you at peace with each other before that?' I ask with confusion.

He sighs again. 'I had been away a long, long time. An unforgivable absence.'

I'm amazed he's answering my questions, considering how reticent he normally is.

'How long were you away?'

'I left the year after my mother committed suicide.'

I'm stunned. 'You left when you were fifteen?'

He nods.

'Where did you go?'

'I slept rough for a bit, hooked up with a bad crowd.' He swallows. 'And then I got lost.'

'Metaphorically or literally?'

'Both.'

'Do you still get lost?' I whisper.

For a while we just look at each other, and then he replies, 'Sometimes.'

The expression on his face makes me feel so sick and sad.

'Is that what happens when you leave? Every six months, you go off and get "lost"?'

'Not in the same way as I used to,' he explains. 'I no longer poison myself with drugs, but I drink and sometimes too much. Mostly I roam, hoping to see as few people as possible.'

There are voices out in the hall. We wait and listen as Cristina and Rebecca say goodbye to the last of their friends and then head into Cristina's bedroom.

Stefano lets out a noise that sounds like a pig snorting and we both start with surprise.

'I forgot he was there.'

'I didn't,' Alessandro replies drily, propping himself up on one arm and regarding the wayward waiter.

I sit up and lean over to peer at Stefano's face. 'He is *so* good looking, but I just don't fancy him one bit.'

Alessandro's eyes cut to mine, his lips curving into an amused smile. He's taken his hair tie out and his hair is falling down around his face, brushing against his stubble.

I pull my gaze away from him and notice that his T-shirt has ridden up, his scar shimmering under the lamplight. He follows the line of my sight and tugs his T-shirt down, returning his head to the pillow.

'*Was* it an accident?' I ask seriously. Did he hurt himself on purpose while he was abusing his body in other ways?

He looks disappointed at the question. 'Yes, it was an accident,' he replies firmly.

'Then what happened?'

He sighs and stares at me for a long moment, his pupils dilated in the low light so his eyes are more black than green. 'Don't tell Giulio,' he warns at last. 'Or, God forbid, Serafina. I'd never hear the end of it. They thought I did it mountain biking.'

I'm alarmed. What on earth is he going to say?

'How *did* you do it?'

'Wingsuit proximity flying.'

Eh?

'It's when you jump off a mountain, wearing a special wingsuit, and glide down.'

My eyes widen. 'That sounds dangerous.'

'It is a bit.' He lifts up his shirt and studies his scar. 'This one almost took me out.'

I'm too distracted by what he's saying to even appreciate his six-pack. 'Why do you do it?'

'Because it's fun.' He gives me a slightly sheepish, wholly adorable smile. 'You get to *fly*, Angel.'

'But you could die,' I point out.

'At least I'd die doing something I love.'

Jesus! 'How often do you do it?'

'Don't make me regret telling you,' he cautions. 'Not often. A few times a year.'

'What are you doing the rest of the time, just driving around, or are there other ways you try to—'

I manage to stop myself, but he finishes my sentence for me.

'Other ways I try to kill myself?' His expression grows dark.

I said it flippantly, but there is nothing flippant about suicide, and after what happened to his mother... My face burns.

'I don't do it to die,' he tells me seriously. 'I do it to survive.'

That makes no sense to me at all, but I decide to let it go.

His expression softens. 'How are you feeling now?'

'Okay, I think. You want me to turn off the lamp?'

He yawns. 'Give it a try.'

I reach behind me and glance across at him for a second. He looks so gorgeous, his face lit by the warm light.

My eyes dart to Stefano's lumbering, snoozing body between us and I have to shake my head. What a completely bizarre sight.

Click. The room falls dark and the air is filled with the sound of Stefano's gentle snoring.

'I'll take you to Pompeii on Monday if you want to go,' Alessandro whispers.

'Will you?' I almost sit up again in my excitement.

'I haven't been since I was a boy. I'd like to see it again.'

'I'd love that.'

'It's settled then. Night, night, Angel.'

'Goodnight, Alessandro.'

Chapter 28

'You've got very varied music tastes,' I decide, picking up Alessandro's phone once again to check what's blaring through his van's speakers. We're on our way to Pompeii and he has his substantial music collection on shuffle. So far we've had 'Vienna' by Ultravox, 'Suntoucher' by Groove Armada, 'Run' by Yonaka, 'Just Dropped In (To See What Condition My Condition Was In)' by Kenny Rogers & The First Edition, and now the shouty, sweary rock of 'Killing in the Name' by Rage Against the Machine has morphed into Frente's slow, sweet 'Bizarre Love Triangle'.

'Not that I know,' I add. 'I haven't listened to music properly in years. The piano was the only thing Nan could bear.'

'And that's why you learned to play so well.'

'I've promised Valentina I'll go to Tivoli next week to teach her,' I tell him casually, fighting the urge to ask if he'll also come.

Giulio has said he'll take me when the restaurant is closed on Monday and I know it'll do us good to spend some time alone together, even if it is only for the journey there and back.

'She'll love that,' he replies.

Valentina came to help out at *Serafina's* again yesterday, although apparently Alessandro has recruited two more servers, one of whom starts tomorrow.

My cousin was disappointed to see that I wasn't wearing my headscarf – she had brought me an emerald-green one. I haven't had the confidence to run with the look since I left Tivoli, but I'm wearing the new one today.

'Toy Soldiers' by Martika starts up.

I glance at Alessandro and laugh.

'I'd get bored if all my music sounded the same,' he says with a smile. 'My songs are the only thing that keep me company when I'm roaming.'

'Where else do you go when you *roam*?' I ask.

'No one place,' he says. 'That's the point of roaming.'

I look over my shoulder. 'Does the bench seat fold down into a bed as well?'

'Yes. I sometimes use it if I want to store stuff up above.'

'I'm not sure I could live in such a small space for months on end.'

'You don't *live* in the van. You *live* out there.' He looks across the fields, drenched in sunshine. 'You only sleep in the van.'

I smile at him, but his eyes are on the road. It's just as well, with all the crazy drivers. Luckily I'm too consumed with what he's saying to pay them much notice.

*

Cristina gave me grief when she realised Alessandro had slept in my bed on Friday night. It was ridiculous, considering we had a great, big, drunken lump sprawled out between us the whole time.

Stefano woke us in the early hours of the morning when he heaved up his guts in my bathroom. Afterwards, he stumbled out of the front door and we haven't seen him since.

Alessandro, bless him, took it upon himself to clean up the mess. Then he showered and emerged wearing only his black jeans.

With his damp hair and bare chest… Honestly, it was like somebody had fed my butterflies speed.

'And that was a good idea, how?' Cristina asked when Alessandro had left.

'Hey, my night was innocent. How was yours?'

Rebecca was still in her bed. Cristina had only come out to the kitchen to get her a coffee.

'She's seeing someone, Cristina,' I pointed out, as the tips of her ears turned pink.

I'd heard Rebecca talking about her boyfriend the night before.

'They're going to break up,' she snapped.

'Sure they are.'

I like that we're able to be upfront with each other, but I also kind of wish she'd butt out where Alessandro is concerned.

She no doubt wishes I'd do the same with Rebecca.

Pompeii is located near Naples and the modern suburban town of Pompei, nowadays written with one 'i'. It was buried under a layer of ash and pumice in the eruption of Mount Vesuvius in AD 79 and because of the lack of air and moisture, the objects that lay beneath the city were well-preserved for centuries. There are mosaics on floors, fountains and statues, paintings on walls, and even clay pots lining the walls of taverns.

It is absolutely mind-blowing to see so much raw history in every direction. I could not feel more removed from the town where I grew up. I want to pinch myself.

In the Forum, a giant square that was once the centre of Pompeii, I stare up at a large bronze statue of a centaur. His human arms have broken off, but his horse hoof is raised in frozen motion. I get out my camera.

'You know you're taking a photo of one of the only new things in Pompeii,' Alessandro says with a smile. 'This statue isn't old. It was crafted by a Polish artist called Igor Mitoraj in the eighties.'

'Oh.' I laugh and take a photo of it anyway. I still like it.

The skies are streaked with cloud and the air is clear and cool. I'm glad it's not too hot. There isn't much shade, so walking around in the direct sunlight could have been taxing.

'I'd love to see the Garden of the Fugitives,' I tell Alessandro.

A friend in Coober Pedy told me about it after coming here on holiday a few years ago. Cathy, actually: Nan's retired nurse friend.

Alessandro consults his map. 'We need to take a right.'

The properties are open to the elements in this part of the city and grass grows between crumbling walls that no longer hold up roofs.

Alessandro comes to a stop.

'I think I remember this place,' he says quietly, stepping over a low wall into what was once a house.

'You came here when you were a boy?'

'Yes.' He peers through an arched doorway into a small room where weeds grow in abundance.

It's so peaceful down this way. Most of the visitors are up in the main part of the city. We've wandered off the beaten track.

He points at a low crumbling wall. 'Carlotta wanted to climb that wall, I think, but fell off onto the grass.'

My heart contracts at the mention of our sister's name. 'Was she hurt?' I'm surprised – and touched – that he's talking about her.

He shakes his head, a sad smile gracing his lips. 'No, she laughed her little head off. Villa D'Este also reminded me of her,' he admits, glancing at me. 'That was the first time I had gone to the gardens since she died. I kept picturing her wobbling about, trying to put her hand in the water.'

So that's why he was quiet that day.

'What was she like?' I ask.

'Very funny,' he replies with that same sad smile. 'You saw the picture of her.'

'Yes.'

'That was her, through and through. She was always laughing, always giving everyone that same cute, cheeky grin. I barely remember her crying at all, but I'm sure she must have. She would chatter. Gobbledegook mostly, but she'd look at me and I'd have these completely nonsensical conversations with her. "Is that right, Carlotta? And what did you do before that?"' He mimics a baby babbling and then his features contort with grief.

'Alessandro,' I murmur, feeling a rush of tenderness as I step forward to give him a hug. The muscles in his back ripple as he lifts his arms to return the gesture and we stand like that as the seconds tick by, my face buried in the crook of his neck and his head resting against mine. He's so warm and solid beneath my palms. Then, all of a sudden, I feel wildly jittery. We break apart at the same time, looking anywhere but at each other, but our eyes find their way back and lock fleetingly before we both glance away again.

We walk in contemplative silence along a grassy path until we arrive at the Garden of the Fugitives. Here, thirteen hollow spaces were found in the hardened layers of ash. The spaces were filled with plaster and became the statues of thirteen people – the largest number of victims found on one site.

Archaeologists believe that they died attempting to flee the city on the second day of the eruption, when hot toxic clouds of gas and debris blasted down from Vesuvius and killed everyone who had not yet left.

As we stand and stare through the glass window of the building that was erected here to host the statues, I feel chilled to my bones. There are adults and children, probably members of one family. The sight of a child lying face down on the ground, his or her arms raised around his or her head, prompts me to look at Alessandro.

His traumatised expression makes me wonder if he saw Carlotta's body after she fell. If so, he'll never be able to rid himself of the image of her, just as I'll never be able to rid myself of the image of Grandad being brought out from the mine. Sometimes it's the only picture of him that I'm capable of seeing.

I place my hand on Alessandro's taut back and he jolts. 'Let's go,' I suggest.

He nods quickly and follows me out onto the track. In the distance up ahead, Mount Vesuvius looms.

He consults his map again and points to our right. 'The amphitheatre is this way.'

'The thought of gladiators slaughtering lions will cheer you up?'

'Rather the other way around,' he replies with an evil grin.

When we're standing inside the large oval-shaped space, I hear a man nearby call what sounds a bit like 'Alley' as in alleyway.

Alessandro looks sharply in his direction and then his face explodes into the biggest, widest grin.

'Logan!' he cries.

The man comes running towards him with his arms open wide, shouting 'ALLEZ-ALLEZ-ALLEZ!' They slam into each other, embracing in a full-on man hug, slapping each other's backs so enthusiastically that the man's baseball cap falls off, revealing a head of shaggy, dark-blond hair. They break apart and grin at each other.

Alessandro beckons me over as the man swoops down to pick up his cap. At the same time, a striking woman in maybe her late thirties, with bright pink hair pulled up into a high bun, joins us with a smile.

'Angel, this is Logan,' Alessandro says. 'An old friend of mine.'

'Angie,' I say with a smile, shaking his hand.

Logan is a little taller and broader than Alessandro with a short blond beard, and he looks a bit more weathered – I'd place him in his early forties.

'This is Lea,' Logan introduces his partner as she pops her sunglasses up on her head, revealing a pair of bright blue eyes. 'This is Allez,' he says to her. *Alessandro for short*, I realise. 'Remember me telling you about him?'

Lea's face breaks into a proper smile of recognition and she steps forward to give Alessandro a hug. 'It's so great to meet you!'

'Where have you *been*?' Logan demands to know, slapping Alessandro's back again as Lea and I exchange warm hellos. 'I haven't seen you in years!'

Logan is British with a regional accent, but I'm not sure where he's from exactly, and Lea is either American or Canadian – again, I can't tell.

'I lost your number,' Alessandro replies. 'Kept thinking we'd cross paths one day and we never did. Until we did.'

Logan grins at him and holds his arm out for Lea to step into. 'Lea and I have just tied the knot. We're here on honeymoon.'

'Congratulations!' Alessandro exclaims.

'Where are you from?' I ask with a smile.

'Liverpool originally,' Logan says, 'but now we live in California near Lea's family.'

'What about you?' Lea asks me.

'I'm here from Australia.'

'Cool! Which part?'

'South Australia, the middle of it: right in the desert.'

'We scuba-dived the Great Barrier Reef a couple of

years ago. It was one of the most incredible things I'd ever done.'

'Wow, how cool.' Another thing I'm desperate to do.

One day…

Lea pops her glasses back on and looks around the amphitheatre. 'Isn't this place amazing?'

'Out of this world.'

Alessandro and Logan start up a conversation between themselves, but Lea stays with me as we gradually make our way towards the exit.

'Have you been to Italy before?' she asks.

'This is my first time. You?'

'First visit for me too. Logan's been before. It's somewhere I've always wanted to visit. We're doing a big tour, flying out of Rome the week after next.'

'Maybe we could meet up when you're there?' Alessandro interjects, overhearing.

'That would be great,' Logan replies, turning around and walking backwards for a few paces. 'Are you guys staying nearby tonight? Want to get a bite to eat?'

'We're driving back to Rome,' Alessandro replies. 'But we could still have dinner?' He casts me a questioning look as he says this.

'Absolutely,' I reply, nodding. 'How long have you guys known each other?'

'Jeez.' Logan scratches his beard and eyes Alessandro. 'Must've been about fifteen years?'

Logan is a friend from the lost years?

'When did you last catch up?' Lea asks.

'Six or seven years ago,' Alessandro estimates.

'Zakynthos Island, Navagio Beach!' Logan recalls. 'That was fun.'

'Are you doing the Dolomites while you're here?' Alessandro asks.

'Nah.' Logan pulls a face at his wife. 'Lea's banned me from jumping.'

'Damn right I have,' Lea replies firmly. 'Do you still let him?' she asks me.

'This conversation is going right over my head,' I admit self-consciously.

Logan gives Alessandro a look of surprise. 'You quit base jumping?'

Base jumping?

Alessandro shakes his head dismissively before jerking his chin in my direction. 'No, I haven't quit. Angel doesn't know... We're just friends. We're not together.'

Lea and Logan look at us again and recalibrate their assumptions.

'How long have you two known each other, then?' Lea changes the subject before I can get to the bottom of what base jumping is. I'll ask Alessandro later.

'Not long at all,' Alessandro replies, smiling at me. 'It's a bit of a story. Might be one for dinner.'

'Deal,' Lea says.

Logan and Lea were on their way to the Garden of Fugitives, taking the route we've been on in reverse, so we part ways, exchanging phone numbers and the address for their hotel.

Alessandro and I walk on together.

'They seem nice.'

'Logan's the best,' he replies, still smiling.

'What's base jumping?'

He walks a few paces before answering, perhaps considering how much to tell me. 'Skydiving,' he replies at last. 'Off fixed structures.'

'Not like skydiving out of aeroplanes?'

'Very different to skydiving out of aeroplanes. You jump off bridges, cliffs and buildings, so you're much closer to the ground. BASE is an acronym for Building, Antenna, Span and Earth.'

'And you do it?'

He hesitates. 'Between us?'

I nod. He can trust me not to tell Giulio.

'Yes. I do.'

'Is it the same thing as wingsuit... What did you call it?'

'Wingsuit proximity flying. The gear you wear is different, but you still jump off fixed structures, although I also know guys who leap from planes and helicopters. Wingsuiters look like flying squirrels – the suits allow you to track forward for a while before you have to open your parachute. With base, I jump "slick", so it's more of a straight drop down.'

'Are you an adrenalin junkie?' I'm trying not to judge him, but the question spills out of me.

'You think I swapped one addiction for another?' He glances at me, his lips tilted up at the corners. He shrugs. 'I guess I did.'

I try to push my concerns aside in order to keep him talking. 'How did you and Logan meet?'

'He was jumping from the Dolomites. I was on the mountain when I saw him and his friends take off. A couple of days later, I saw them again and Logan and I got chatting.'

As we walk, he helps me to piece together some of his back-story that was missing. I knew he ran away from home when he was fifteen and slept rough for a while before falling in with a bad crowd. Now he tells me that one day he had a moment of clarity and walked away. Literally, walked away. He said the only thing he had with him was his passport, which he'd kept safe for years, and the clothes on his back. He kept walking and walking, sometimes hitchhiking – sometimes stealing from people, he's ashamed to say – but always moving forward. Eventually he reached the Dolomites, the stunning mountain range in the Alps. It was the height of summer and he climbed up a mountain and looked down on the most breathtaking view across the valleys, lakes and Alpine meadows. Then, from out of nowhere, a group of base jumpers appeared.

He'd never heard of the sport and he was transfixed, watching them as they got into their gear and strapped on their parachutes. Then, one by one, with only a couple of seconds between them, they launched themselves off the edge of a sheer cliff. One guy did a somersault in the air, another leapt and spun to face the sky, but all of them free-fell for what seemed like forever before they released their colourful chutes and floated to the ground.

Alessandro was sold. When he saw them on the mountain a couple of days later, Logan took the time to talk to him. He knew someone who was selling his parachute and gave Alessandro his number, telling him he'd be happy to put him in touch with another friend about skydiving. Alessandro landed a job at an Alpine restaurant to save up enough money, and then he got in touch with Logan. Logan went with him on his first skydive, and later, his first base jump.

'Where was that?' I ask of the latter.

'Perrine Bridge in Idaho, USA. The bridge spans Snake River in Twin Falls. You can practically take off from your car, it's so accessible.'

'What was it like?'

'The most thrilling thing I had ever done. And also the most terrifying. The bridge is only a hundred and fifty metres high so you fall for only a couple of seconds before parachuting down to the river.'

As he talks, I feel as though I'm seeing the real Alessandro unfold. This is the part of him he's been keeping hidden, but now his expression is open and honest, his forehead free from creases.

'And Giulio, Cristina, Serafina – none of your family know that you've been doing this?' I ask, so as to be clear on that point.

'No. They wouldn't understand,' he replies.

'Why? Is it very dangerous?'

'There's an element of risk involved.' Now he sounds cagey in a way that makes me think the risk is far greater than he's implying.

But I know I must be careful. I don't want to give him a hard time if I'm one of the only people he feels he can talk to.

The streets are getting busy again as we approach the centre of Pompeii. I go to move off the pavement to make way for a group of people coming towards us and Alessandro takes my hand to help me down from the high kerb onto the large flat stones lining the roads.

'What was the Zak—'

'Zakynthos Island?' he asks.

'Yes. What was that jump like?'

'Aah, Navagio is one of the most beautiful beaches in Greece. The water is azure blue, it is surrounded by high, white cliffs and at the bottom on the sand is a shipwreck. You take off from a two-hundred-metre-tall rock and freefall for a couple of seconds before parachuting down to the soft sand.'

He's still holding my hand.

'Where else have you jumped from?' I ask, the contact making me feel nervy. Not that I want him to let me go.

'All over the world. France, Switzerland, Norway, America, Canada, Turkey, China, Brazil, Italy, of course. Somewhere you might have heard of... Angel Falls in Venezuela? It's the tallest waterfall in the world – you can feel the spray on your face as you plunge down the rock face into the rainforest.'

My eyes are out on stalks imagining it.

And he's still holding my hand...

'Yosemite National Park? Table Mountain in Cape Town? The view across the town and ocean is spectacular. Mostly, though, I try to stay off the beaten track.'

'So let me get this straight. You work for six months to earn enough money to go base jumping, wingsuit flying and skydiving for the next six months before returning to *Serafina's*?'

'I do other stuff, too, like mountain climbing, hiking and snowboarding. And I don't skydive so much anymore.'

'Why not?'

'It doesn't give me the same thrill.'

'I don't think I could do any of that extreme sports stuff,' I say. 'But I do like the idea of being able to travel for six months a year.'

He shrugs. 'Nothing is stopping you.'

With the hand that is *still* holding mine, he points up ahead. 'See those stepping stones?'

'Yes.' They're large and rectangular-shaped, going from one side of the road to the other.

'They used to pour the waste down the roads – the sewage, everything. People would cross the roads using the stones, but here, look between them…'

We draw to a stop and see long smooth grooves carved out between the rocks.

'These were made by wagon wheels,' Alessandro tells me. 'The stones are spaced apart so the wheels could still run between them.'

'That's unbelievable!' Evidence of traffic from two thousand years ago! 'How have you remembered all of these facts?'

'I read about Pompeii recently. I do a lot of reading when I'm away.'

We walk on and in the silence that ensues, my brain becomes fixated on our palm-to-palm connection. There's a warmth, an energy, that is traversing up my arm from the place where our skin is pressed together. It's all I can think about, and then, involuntarily and entirely accidentally, I squeeze his hand. This prompts him to glance down and I want to kick myself. He looks up at me, but doesn't let me go.

'Is this okay?' he asks.

I nod, my butterflies in a frenzy. 'Yes.' It's about all I can manage to say without blushing.

'The last person's hand I held was my mother's.'

Now my butterflies freeze. *What*? He's looking at the ground, and I have to revert to doing the same so I don't trip on the cobblestones.

'You've never held a girlfriend's hand?' I ask warily.

'I've never had a girlfriend.'

'Never?' I shoot a look at him.

'You heard Lea,' he replies. 'What woman would stand for what I do?'

'But that's such a lonely way to live.'

He shrugs. 'I'm a loner.'

I frown. 'That's tragic.'

He laughs drily. 'There's a lot about me that's tragic, Angel.' And the look in his eye when he meets mine makes me shiver. His expression momentarily sobers and he averts his gaze.

'Have you ever been in love?' I ask.

'Oh, I was *besotted* with Giovanna. She was the first girl I ever kissed.'

Is he teasing me?

'How old were you?'

'Thirteen.'

Yes, he is.

'It was before she ran off with Giancarlo,' he adds, drawing a smile out of me.

It dawns on me that this happened the year before he lost his mother and sister. There can't have been much room for everyday teenage rites of passage after his life catapulted so swiftly downhill.

'Oh, look, the Lupanar is just here,' he says.

'What's the Lupanar?'

'Wolf den. A prostitute was called a *lupa*. It's the brothel, Angel,' he says when I don't put two and two together. 'My mother wouldn't let me go inside when I was a boy.'

I'm not sure I fancy seeing it now, but how bad can it be?

Bad, is the answer.

There are paintings of naked people having sex with each other!

She's riding him, he's riding her, they're doing it doggy style… I don't know where to look.

'Your cheeks have gone red,' Alessandro says playfully.

The fact that we are still walking around with our hands entwined is not helping.

'I'll wait for you outside,' I mutter eventually, my embarrassment overriding everything else as I extract myself from his grip.

In the bright daylight, I lean against a wall and will my cheeks to cool down.

Alessandro emerges, chuckling.

'Stop it,' I mutter with a smirk.

'When did you last have a boyfriend?' he asks casually as we set off again.

'Three years ago.'

He reaches over and takes my hand and this time the contact sends what feels like a jolt of electricity zipping up my arm. It's different to the shock I gave him when my hair was full of static electricity – this is a far more pleasant sensation.

'He was from Bosnia and Herzegovina,' I tell him, trying to sound unaffected. 'Davud. He came to Coober Pedy to mine opal, but he became homesick. I felt sorry for him so I emailed his mother back home to ask for the recipes for some of his favourite dishes and cooked him a meal one night.'

'You got to him through his stomach,' he states.

'I wasn't trying to get him at all, to be fair,' I reply. 'I was only being friendly, but then he kissed me and that was that.'

'You fell head over heels in love.'

Is he mocking me? I remember him calling me naïve the other night and feel a prickle of annoyance.

'I'm sorry,' he says contritely, noticing the look on my face. He lets go of my hand and drapes his arm around my shoulders instead. 'Please don't stop talking to me,' he says quietly in my ear. My stomach flips. 'Why didn't things work out?'

'Things were always a bit difficult, that's all,' I continue when I feel able. 'I hardly ever left the house because of Nan, and I didn't feel relaxed if we were at home and she was asleep in her room. It didn't make for the most exciting love life, to be honest. He got bored quite quickly.'

'I'm sorry,' he says again, and now it feels like he's taking me seriously.

'It's okay. It's just the way things were.'

Davud returned to Bosnia and Herzegovina in the end, but we've stayed in touch.

'You must have felt very trapped at times.'

I nod. 'I did, but Nan had a lot of friends who would come to visit so I wasn't too lonely.'

We wander aimlessly for a while. There's so much to see that it becomes almost overwhelming – I'll have to visit again so I can fully appreciate it.

'I'm about ready to go and get something to eat,' Alessandro says.

'Me too.'

There are a few people going in and out of a building we're approaching. 'Let's have a quick look in here first.' He takes my hand again and pulls me in after him.

We find ourselves inside an incredibly well preserved Roman bath house. The marble baths are in near-perfect condition and in one room there is a domed ceiling, complete with oculus. It's tiny compared to the Pantheon, but it's exquisite.

Lea and Logan appear from the next room.

'Hey, strangers!' Lea exclaims.

I expect Alessandro to let me go, but he doesn't, not even when Lea glances down at our joined hands with surprise.

'We were about to call it a day,' Logan says.

'Same here,' Alessandro replies.

As Lea and Logan caught public transport in, Alessandro offers to give them a lift to their hotel. But first Logan wants a tour of the van.

'Hashtag van life,' Lea says with a good-natured roll of her eyes. 'When I met Logan, he had one of these. It was a later model, but not much has changed.'

'It was very cool,' Alessandro comments.

Logan nods nostalgically. 'I loved that thing.'

'Come on, I'm starving,' Lea hurries them along. 'Where shall we go? There's an Italian restaurant next to our hotel?'

'I'd kill for a burger,' Alessandro replies with a grin.

I love that he's steering them away from going anywhere that would likely be a pale imitation of *Serafina's*.

'Always up for a burger,' Logan states, and Lea and I nod in agreement.

When we're seated at a round table in the middle of the restaurant, drinks in hand, I turn to Lea.

'How did you two meet?'

'Oh no.' She shakes her head. 'You first. I'm curious.'

I wrinkle my nose at Alessandro. Where to start?

'Okay...' I give it a go. 'My mum came over here from

Australia about twenty-eight years ago and worked with Alessandro's stepdad.'

I'm already starting to feel uncomfortable – I hate admitting that my mum had an affair with a married man.

'Giulio,' Alessandro tells Logan and, from the way Logan nods, I'm figuring he already knows part of Alessandro's past, if not all of it. 'Giulio married my mother when I was seven,' he explains to Lea. 'But it was a marriage of convenience. They weren't in love when Angel's mother came along.'

I'm grateful to him for making that clear, but I'm still squirming. 'My mum returned to Australia, not knowing she was already pregnant.'

Lea gasps.

Wait till she hears the next part…

They're both suitably gobsmacked when we've finished recounting the story. We're half a bottle of wine down already.

Logan lifts up the bottle, offering it to Alessandro.

'Not for me,' Alessandro says. 'I'm driving Angel home.'

'Why don't you guys crash in your van?' Logan asks in a way that makes it seem weird that we're not doing that.

Alessandro shakes his head before I can even consider the idea. 'I don't want to give Giulio anything else to worry about. He's already suspicious about my intentions towards her.' He casts me a sidelong look.

I can feel Lea's eyes on us, trying to work us out.

You're not the only one who's wondering what's going on here.

'Come on then, tell us about you two,' I prompt, changing the subject.

'Lea was working for the air ambulance,' Logan says. 'You remember Dave?' he asks Alessandro.

Alessandro nods. 'Yeah, how is he?'

'I'll get to that.' He smiles sardonically. 'So Dave and I were jumping off Half Dome—'

'*Stupid*,' Lea interrupts.

'Yeah, okay, babe,' Logan says, still grinning as he squeezes her shoulder. 'Anyway, Dave's chute got into a bit of a tangle—'

'Was he okay?' Alessandro interrupts to ask.

'Just about,' Lea replies darkly.

'Lea was part of the rescue op,' Logan continues. 'She gave me hell, didn't you, babe?'

'God only knows how I fell for you,' she mutters.

'What's Half Dome?' I ask, yoyoing between concern and amusement.

'A granite peak at the eastern end of Yosemite Valley in the Yosemite National Park,' Lea explains. 'One side is sheer faced and the other three sides are smooth and round, making it look like a dome cut in half. I'll show you a photo of it.' She gets out her phone.

'I remember it well,' Alessandro murmurs, peering over my shoulder.

Logan sighs in awed agreement.

'Don't you go getting all sentimental on me,' Lea cautions her husband.

'Was Dave hurt?' I ask.

'He was pretty badly broken up,' Logan replies, his tone growing serious. 'But he's walking again now.'

Whoa.

'Where are you doing your next jump?' Logan asks Alessandro.

'I'm heading to Norway this year.'

'Kjerag? Trollveggen?'

Alessandro nods and, once more, Logan seems wistful.

'Don't even think about it,' Lea snaps him out of it, pointing a threatening digit in his face.

Logan shrugs at Alessandro, nonplussed.

I turn to Alessandro. 'What's Kjerag and… What did you say?' It sounded like something out of *The Lord of the Rings*.

'Trollveggen. Kjerag is famous for an unusual boulder stuck between two rock walls.'

Lea looks it up on her phone to show me.

'I've got a postcard of it!' I exclaim. Astrid of the hip operation had her son Erik send it to me. 'I'd love to go to Norway.'

Alessandro smiles at me. 'Angel's never been anywhere,' he says softly.

'Have you heard of Pulpit Rock?' I ask him, remembering the other postcard Astrid and Magnus sent me.

'Preikestolen?' Alessandro asks. 'Of course. I've camped up there. It's beautiful.'

'You can *camp* up there?'

'Not right out on the plateau – you're not allowed to do that – but very close by. Norway has a right to roam policy, even in National Parks.'

'Oh wow, I so want to go!'

'Why don't you go with Alessandro?' Lea chips in.

Alessandro looks regretful. 'Angel knows that I'm too much of a loner to keep company.'

Ouch.

He turns to Logan. 'Are you still in contact with Clive?'

Now any residual humour that Logan was carrying dries up completely.

'No.' He shakes his head. 'We lost him, man.'

Lost? What does he mean lost?

'Where?' Alessandro asks gravely.

'Lauterbrunnen,' Logan replies.

He died?

'And this is why I've said *no more*,' Lea interjects pointedly.

'Yeah, enough's enough,' Logan concedes with a sigh. 'We want to start a family soon and I don't want to run the risk of leaving a kid without a parent so it was time to give it up.'

The more I hear, the more my emotions stop yoyoing. I no longer feel any amusement, only a straight, heavy drop of concern.

'I gotta tell ya,' Logan says to Alessandro, 'when I didn't hear from you for a few years, I thought you were a goner.'

'If I'd come to America, I would've looked you up,' Alessandro replies.

'Ever thought about cutting your losses and calling it a day?' Lea asks.

Alessandro shakes his head. 'No.'

'What if you had children?'

I've got to hand it to her for her direct questions.

'I'll never have children,' Alessandro bats back.

Lea's eyebrows shoot up, as do mine.

'No kids, no wife, no girlfriend,' he states obstinately.

'You'd choose jumping over love?' Lea asks, her eyes darting towards me.

'I don't plan on falling in love, either,' Alessandro replies wryly.

The waitress appears, belatedly, with our burgers.

We've been waiting forever and I've been hungry, but strangely, not so much anymore. I struggle to concentrate on the conversation as it moves on to Logan and Lea's recent travels.

By the time we're paying the bill, I've managed to pull myself together.

'It was great to meet you,' Lea says warmly, giving me a hug. 'Let's definitely hang out in Rome.'

'I'd love that,' I reply, glancing at Alessandro.

'Absolutely,' he says, shaking Logan's hand and slapping his back fondly.

'Weekend after next?' Logan asks.

'Sounds good,' Alessandro replies. 'Call me when you get there.'

Up ahead, the sun hangs low over the centre of the road, a brilliant, burning orange disc.

'Thank you for taking me today,' I say, looking across at Alessandro.

'It was my pleasure,' he replies with a warm smile, reaching over and squeezing my knee. I cover his hand with mine and my heartstrings twang plaintively.

I am so confused.

'Thank you for listening today,' he says. 'And for not judging. I like being able to talk to you,' he continues, turning his hand over and lacing his fingers with mine. 'I like being close to you. I like that we've had some time alone today with no one from home around.'

My butterflies have been replaced by grasshoppers. They're

bouncing around the walls of my stomach, making me feel nervy and edgy.

'Giulio wouldn't understand this.' He nods at our entwined hands. 'But I promise that you're safe with me, Angel. We'll never be more than friends.'

My heart stutters.

He glances across at me and I see it in his eyes: honest, open and sincere. Every touch today has been completely platonic.

'*He'll never lay a hand on you*,' Cristina told me. '*Alessandro loves Giulio. He'd never disrespect him by sleeping with his daughter.*'

And how did I reply?

'*I would never have slept with him in any case. I'm no Teresa.*'

I hate that I'm now doubting the truth of that statement.

Chapter 29

That night, I fall into bed feeling too confused and unsettled to sleep. I finally drift off, but a nightmare about Nan has me jolting awake in a cold sweat. I dreamt that I had forgotten her – not posthumously, but in the last stages of her life. I had forgotten to give her water, forgotten to change her incontinence pad, forgotten to turn her over. She had been lying in her bed all night and day, with no one to care for her.

My heart is racing and my cold chills are replaced by a hot flush.

It's okay, I try to reassure myself. *I didn't hurt her. I did everything I could to help her.*

I open the drawer of my bedside table and rummage around for my opal, rubbing my thumb across the surface in an attempt to comfort myself. But I can't shake the feeling of guilt and despair.

It's not even three o'clock in the morning, but I realise

there's no way I'm going to sleep, so I hunt out my laptop and bring it into bed with me.

Base jumping. I type it into Google.

One of the first things that comes up is, 'What percentage of base jumpers die?'

The hairs on the back of my neck stand up.

The more I research base jumping and wingsuit flying, the more terrified I become. I spend hours in a perpetual state of nervous anxiety, clicking on links, watching videos and reading articles.

I'll see names… Like Valery Rozov from Russia, who set a new world record for the highest base jump in 2013 when he launched himself from Changtse, the northern peak of the Mount Everest massif.

And then those same names appear again in headlines:

2017: Valery Rozov has died in a base-jumping accident in Nepal.

This happens over and over again.

Mark Sutton, the man who played James Bond in the 2012 London Olympics Opening Ceremony…

…killed after crashing into a ridge near Martigny at the Swiss-French border: 2013.

Celebrated climber and National Geographic's 2009 Adventurer of the Year Dean Potter…

…died alongside jumping partner Graham Hunt in Yosemite National Park: 2015.

World-renowned Canadian wingsuit flyer Graham Dickinson…

…died while attempting to fly through Heaven's Gate, Tianmen Mountain, in China: 2017.

His friend and fellow filmmaker, Dario Zanon, had died a year earlier.

Ludovic Woerth and Dan Vicary, two of the world's most experienced wingsuit flyers…

…crashed into the ground and killed on impact in the Lütschental valley in Switzerland: 2014.

Fellow flyer, Brian Drake, succumbed to fatal injuries four days later.

In Lauterbrunnen in Switzerland, which I recognise as the place that Alessandro and Logan lost their friend, a farmer despairs of the number of the deaths that have happened on his land, and a local schoolteacher talks about being with the children when a shrill scream prompted them to look at the cliffs in time to see a base jumper slamming into them.

Even the father of modern-day base jumping, a filmmaker called Carl Boenish, who coined the term BASE along with his wife Jean and friends, Phil Smith and Phil Mayfield, died the day after he and his wife set a Guinness World Record for the highest jump from Troll Wall in Norway in 1984.

Base jumpers and wingsuiters have lost their lives at all of the locations the men mentioned at dinner, including Kjerag, the place where Alessandro is intending to jump later this year. That location, at least, is legal, but Table Mountain, Yosemite National Park and God only knows how many other cliffs he's launched himself from are not.

What makes me feel so out of control here is that I don't know how to stop him. He wouldn't agree to quit anyway – I remember his face when Lea asked if he'd thought about calling it a day. It goes against every single one of my natural instincts, but I can't share my concerns with him because he'll stop confiding in me.

I'm still feeling sick with worry when I go into work. Giulio, Maria and Antonio are in the kitchen.

'What you bring for me today?' Giulio asks enthusiastically, his arms outstretched in anticipation.

I shake my head. 'I didn't bake this morning, sorry.'

I didn't have the heart for it.

He looks terribly disappointed, but I think he's putting some of that on.

'Where's Alessandro?'

'He's upstairs, doing his washing. His clothes,' he elaborates at my look of confusion. 'They're dirty, they need a clean.'

'Oh, I see.'

Serafina's was closed yesterday so I set about getting it ready for the day's customers, putting chairs that were upended for cleaning purposes back in place around tables. Cristina is off for the next few days visiting her family in the south, but she'll return on Saturday afternoon, which is also the day of her thirtieth birthday. She's planning to go out with friends that night and has invited me along.

Stefano waltzes in shortly before opening time and goes straight to the stockroom to put on some music.

The door swings open and a tiny blonde, wearing a summery assortment of colours – yellow T-shirt, bright blue shorts, pink shoes – appears, looking hesitant. Giulio spies her and comes over to greet her. I hear her say 'Alessandro' and after Giulio has chatted to her for a bit, he disappears out the back. She doesn't look over at me as she waits.

Soon afterwards, Alessandro appears.

I'm not sure that I'll be able to look at him again without feeling an element of fear, not now that I know what I know.

'*Buongiorno*,' he calls to the girl as he approaches her.

He doesn't glance my way.

'Ah, new waitress,' Stefano mutters as he materialises from the stockroom. 'How long will this one last?'

I'm on edge as I lay the tables, watching out of the corner of my eye as Alessandro chats to her. He's smiling more than he usually does when he's at work, I notice. Eventually he calls down to us in the main body of the restaurant.

'Stefano, Angel!'

We look up at him.

'This is Julia, she starts today.'

'*Ciao*,' Stefano replies, while I forget and greet her in English.

'Angel is from Australia so we try to speak English,' Alessandro tells Julia, adding for our benefit, 'Julia is from Poland, but she's lived in Italy for most of her life.'

She's petite, with delicate features and perfectly arched eyebrows. Her golden-blond locks are tied up into a high, sleek ponytail that swings from side to side as she walks. She's younger than me, I think, probably in her early twenties.

Alessandro gets on with showing her how everything works while Stefano and I finish setting up.

'Why are you so quiet today?' Stefano asks, when his attempt to get me to dance with him fails.

'I didn't sleep very well,' I reply.

'I will make you a coffee,' he decides.

A couple of minutes later, he Latin dances across the

room to the sexy sound of a woman singing about 'Havana' coming from the loudspeakers, and he does all this while trying not to spill a drop. It's impossible to keep a straight face. He presents me with my coffee, but before I can take it, he whips it away and puts it on a nearby table. Then he grabs my hand, spins me around in a circle and starts to do the mamba – a dance I can sort of manage from my teenage years of watching *Dirty Dancing* on repeat, but it's a very, *very* messy version.

Alessandro comes out of the kitchen and stops short at the sight of us, Stefano singing to me while I try to control my laughter.

Julia, who has followed Alessandro out of the kitchen, giggles.

'Stefano!' Alessandro barks.

Stefano lets me go with a roll of his eyes. Alessandro says something crossly to him in Italian, but 'Angel' is the only word I understand. When Alessandro is finished, Stefano turns to me and gets down on one knee.

'Angel, I apologise,' he says, placing his hand over his heart. 'I am very embarrassed about my behaviour on Friday night. It was unacceptable and I will never fall asleep on your bed again.'

Alessandro says something else to him.

'And I will never again be sick in your bathroom. Next time I will use Cristina's.'

I laugh and look at Alessandro. He gives me a small smile, but our eye contact lasts only a second before he gets down to the business of showing Julia how to use the coffee machine.

*

It's a strange day. Alessandro is no different to the Alessandro of last week, but he's so different to the man from Friday night and Monday that I consider checking upstairs to see if he has a twin brother hidden away.

Gone is the hand holding and intimate conversation – apart from the entertaining way in which he chastised Stefano, he's completely professional.

Professional *and* detached.

'Is Stefano your boyfriend?' Julia asks me during a quiet spell between lunch and dinner.

'No, no. We're friends,' I reply.

'He's cute.'

'He is,' I agree, waiting to see if she'll say the same about Alessandro.

She doesn't.

The first time she calls me Angel, I jolt. But Stefano called me Angel when he apologised so I'm not sure whether or not to correct her.

Later, Giulio addresses me as Angie and she overhears.

'Is it Angel or Angie?'

'It's Angie,' I reply. 'Alessandro nicknamed me Angel for some reason.'

'It's cool. It suits you.' She sounds sincere, but then what would I know? I thought I was a good judge of character until I met Alessandro. I can't work him out at all.

One thing that doesn't stack up is how reserved he is about base jumping. Most of those guys on the YouTube videos that I watched are larger than life extroverts keen to show the world what they can do. That's not Alessandro. At least, I don't think it is. The sport jars with his personality.

Is he a different person in the six months that he's not here? Maybe he feels suffocated being around Giulio, as if the past is a noose around his neck. Maybe, away from Rome, he's more like the man he was yesterday: warm and loving. But that doesn't fit with what he's said either.

He's not open to love, so why would he give it? He claimed that he's a loner. Does he really just travel aimlessly, climbing mountains and jumping from cliff edges?

How can anyone live like that?

I wonder if I can ask Logan, when he and Lea come to Rome next weekend, about what Alessandro was like when they knew each other years ago. Surely the Alessandro from yesterday can't be too different to the Alessandro that Logan jumped with – the two men were so at ease with each other.

At about eight thirty on Friday night, a young couple walk into the restaurant, and, hearing their Australian accents, Alessandro calls me over. I take them to their table and strike up a light-hearted conversation about where they're from. Not unpredictably, they want to know where I hail from in return and, as I tell them, I'm struck with an agonising homesickness.

I've been struggling with melancholy all week – Alessandro's distant behaviour has been really getting to me.

I long to be at home, surrounded by familiarity.

Not my room at Cristina's.

Home.

There's a stinging at the back of my eyes as I brightly take their drinks order and go to give it to Alessandro, but I'm so close to tears that I have to duck into the stockroom to compose myself.

Alessandro follows me.

'Angel?' he asks uncertainly.

'I'm fine,' I reply, but it's obviously a lie.

'What's wrong?' His voice is low and deep, not quite sure of itself.

'I'm tired. I haven't slept well this week.' I can't turn around to look at him – I'm too close to tears.

'Do you want to go home?'

You have no idea how much.

'Julia and Nino can handle your tables.' Nino is our new waiter. He started today.

'No, I'll finish my shift.' It doesn't feel fair on the others when they're still finding their feet.

'I'll give you a lift later—'

'No,' I reply sharply. 'I'd rather walk.'

The silence hangs heavy between us.

'I'll be out in a minute,' I add.

The room falls quiet so I get a tissue from my bag and dab my eyes. I assume he's gone, but a glance over my shoulder reveals otherwise. He's leaning against the wall, staring at the floor. I steel myself to turn around.

'I'd better get back,' I say, trying to sound brighter.

He nods, avoiding my eyes as he reaches down to take my hand.

He doesn't hold it properly – he cradles it from beneath – and then he very slowly runs his thumb across the length of my palm.

Goosebumps erupt over my entire body.

A moment later, he meets my eyes.

I have absolutely no idea what he's thinking.

'Okay,' he says, squeezing my hand once before walking out of the room.

'I see you tomorrow?' Giulio asks as I'm gathering my things at the end of the night.

I shake my head. 'Weekend off.'

'Aah, I see. You gonna do some baking?' he asks hopefully.

I smile at him. 'Yes, actually. I'm baking a cake for Cristina's birthday, but I could also make something to take to Tivoli on Monday?'

'*Fantastico*!' he exclaims. 'I will pick you up at nine o'clock pronto.'

He doesn't ask me what else I'm getting up to this weekend, nor does he ask if I'd like to do something with him.

I'm okay with that.

Alessandro is nowhere to be seen so Giulio unlocks the front door to let me out. My heart is heavy despite the cheery farewells from him and Nino. Julia has already left, gone off to meet her boyfriend, blessedly. That, at least, is something.

I'm about to cross the road when I hear the sound of footsteps pounding the pavement.

'Angel!' Alessandro calls, catching me up. He's wearing his leather jacket, which I'm assuming he's just retrieved from his van.

'What are you doing?' I ask.

'Walking you home,' he replies with a frown as if it were obvious.

'I told you I wanted to be alone.'

'No, you told me you wanted to walk.'

He has a point. We set off across the pedestrian crossing in silence.

'Why do you want to be alone?' he asks when we reach the other side of the road. He seems genuinely perplexed.

I shrug. 'I don't know. I felt like a bit of breathing space.'

'I won't talk if you don't want me to.'

I can't help but smile. 'I don't mind if you'd like to talk to me.'

But he doesn't. Not for the next five minutes. At first the silence feels awkward, but after a while I begin to relax.

We pass the bistro on our left and I look across the road to the short cut before glancing at Alessandro.

'That way?' he asks, meeting my eyes.

'Is that okay?'

He looks hesitant, but he nods.

We cross over the road and head down a street lined with apartment blocks.

'Which one did you live in?' I ask tentatively.

He doesn't ask how I know. Maybe he thinks Giulio told me.

His tone is subdued when he replies. 'The third building on the left.'

It's identical to the ones on either side of it and not at all dissimilar to the block I'm living in with Cristina – six storeys, cube-shaped, with balconies out the front.

'Which floor?' I ask as he comes to a stop in front of his former residence and looks up.

'Fifth. The one on the right.' His tone is leaden.

The confusion of the last few days dissipates – I unthinkingly reach for his hand.

'I was in my bedroom when Carlotta...' His Adam's apple bobs up and down. He's still gazing up at his apartment. 'I came out and… she wasn't there.' When he looks at me, his eyes are full of horror. 'I saw the open door and called out to her. She wasn't on the balcony so I searched the house.'

'Where were Giulio and your mother?'

'Giulio was at work; my mother was asleep.'

'Carlotta wasn't your responsibility,' I say softly but adamantly.

'I should have been looking after her.'

'It was not your fault.'

He averts his gaze.

'Alessandro,' I state firmly. 'It was not your fault.'

'She seemed happy in front of the television,' he tells me in a choked voice. 'I had only gone to my room for a few minutes. When I came out, she was gone.'

It actually hurts to look at him, to see those emotions; the memory dredged up before my eyes.

'My mother woke up when she heard me shouting her name. She went straight to the balcony. And started screaming.'

I need to make it stop…

Grabbing his arm, I turn him to face me and slip my hands beneath his leather jacket so I can give him a hug. A moment passes before he returns the gesture. His breathing is ragged. I hold him tighter and he tightens his grip on me too, burying his face against my neck.

I can smell leather and the orangey scent of his shower gel, mingled with his warm skin.

My arms are around his slim waist, gripping his muscled back. His hips are pressed against mine, our stomachs flat against each other, my chest flush to his – it wouldn't be possible to get any closer fully dressed.

I don't know how long we stand like that, but it's a while before his breathing settles into a regular pattern.

'Are you okay?' I whisper and feel him nod against me.

He lets out a heavy rush of breath as he releases me.

The cold air hits my body and I shiver, craving his warmth as we continue our walk to Cristina's apartment. My head is racing through everything he's told me.

'When does Cristina get home?' he asks as we arrive at the apartment block.

'Tomorrow. Do you want to come in for a bit?'

'Sure.'

Inside, I kick off my shoes and he takes off his jacket, then I set about switching on lights and lowering blinds while he grabs himself a beer from the fridge and makes me a cup of tea. When I spy him about to fish my teabag out, I call to ask him to leave it in a bit longer.

'You take your tea the British way,' he says.

'It's also the Australian way,' I reply with a smile. 'You've never been to Australia, have you?' I think I recall him saying that it was the one place he hadn't visited.

He shakes his head. 'I'd like to go sometime, see where you grew up. Do you have any photos?'

'Yes. Do you want to have a look?'

'I'd love to.'

I'm not sure this is going to do my homesickness any good, but I retrieve my photo album anyway. Alessandro brings my tea over to the sofa, sitting close but far enough away from me that we're not touching.

'I like that you have a photo album,' he says.

'What else would I have?' I'm baffled.

'A phone.'

I laugh. 'I'm a bit behind when it comes to mobiles. I never needed one in Coober Pedy as I never went anywhere. Even my new phone is as basic as they come. I'll use my proper digital camera if I want to take pictures.'

I begin to flick through the photos of friends to try to find some of the town and my dugout, but he stops me. 'Tell me about these people.'

I revert to the beginning. It's only a single-photo-per-page album, each photo secured inside a plastic pocket. I wanted it to be as lightweight as possible for my travels.

'That's Bonnie and Mick. They're my next-door neighbours. This is their dugout.'

'The walls are carved straight out of the rock,' Alessandro muses, studying the rough surfaces.

'Yes. Most people paint them to prevent the dust from falling.'

Not that it works. One thing that I've noticed since I've been here is how clean everything is in comparison to home. I keep running my fingers across shelves like my nan used to do, and I'm still surprised at how free of dust they are when they come away.

I turn the page to reveal a couple in their early sixties. 'That's Vera and Laszlo.'

He takes the photo album from me with a smile, bringing the picture closer so he can study it.

'You're playing a board game?'

'Yes, in my kitchen. Scrabble was our thing.'

'Scrabble?'

I explain the gist of the game.

'The Italian version is called Scarabeo,' he says. 'It's a little different. Sorry, go on.'

'Laszlo would only be allowed to do English words, while Vera and I could only do Hungarian.' I smile, thinking of the trouble we had trying to remember new vocabulary. Laszlo wasn't the greatest at spelling anyway so we always had to check everything against the Hungarian dictionary that I'd had the bookshop order in for us.

'We should play this to practise your Italian,' Alessandro says.

'No way, you'd win.'

'Are you competitive, Angel?'

'I am when it comes to Scrabble, yes,' I reply with a laugh. 'And probably also Scarabeo.'

'Who are they?' he asks of the next picture.

'That's Magnus and Astrid on the hill behind my dugout.'

'Krumkake,' he says, remembering the Norwegian waffle cookies that I brought in last week.

'That's right.' I'm impressed.

'What are these things?' he asks of the pipes protruding out of the sandy earth behind Magnus and Astrid.

'Air vents,' I reply. 'It's how you can tell if a hill is a home or just a hill. They circulate the air in the dugout.'

'Fascinating.'

He turns the page. Jimmy's one eye stares back at him, so dark brown that it almost looks black in this picture. His other is hidden behind a dusty eye patch, and his grey beard is long and unruly, contrasting with his coffee-brown skin.

'That's Jimmy,' I say.

'Your grandfather's mining partner and Patricia Cornwell fan.' He remembers the postcard.

'Some of the girls at school used to say he was my dad.'

He gives me a funny look.

Jimmy is an Antakirinja Matu-Yankunytjatjara man.

The land Coober Pedy sits on belongs to his people. The town name itself comes from the Aboriginal word: *kupa-piti*, meaning white man's hole or burrow. The miners used to sleep down the shafts to escape the desert heat, and of course, they – we – still do.

'I know, it doesn't really stack up. My skin is even lighter than yours.' I pull up the sleeve of my cardigan and press my arm against his. We both stare at our connected skin and then I pull my sleeve down again. 'But Jimmy's hair *is* kinda similar to mine. Nan cut my hair off when I was at primary school. She said it was too hard to drag a comb through, but it didn't stop the teasing. If anything, it made it worse because I ended up looking like a scrawny boy.'

'These girls sound horrible,' Alessandro comments darkly.

I shrug. 'They're not really. They were only kids. We're friends now.'

He glances at me with surprise. 'You're friends with them?'

'With some. Others left town.' I take the album from him and flick through until I come to a picture of Trudy and Rita on their wedding day. 'This is Trudy and Rita with Jan and Jakub, the Polish brothers that I told you about.'

'These are the two couples you brought together?'

'That's right.'

'You have a big heart, Angel.'

'Not really. I just don't bear grudges.'

As soon as the words are out of my mouth, I think of Nan. 'Not usually, anyway,' I mutter.

His brow knits together. 'Who do you bear a grudge against?'

'I'm finding it hard to forgive my grandparents for hiding the truth about Giulio,' I admit.

'Ah, I see,' he replies gravely.

'How do you cope, knowing nothing about your biological father?'

I've been wondering this, wondering what nationality his father is, wondering where he got his green eyes from…

'I've come to terms with it,' he replies. 'My mother was not proud of the fact that she had had many lovers. In Italy, children take their father's family name even if their parents are not married, and when women marry, they keep their own surnames. My mother was embarrassed that I had to take her family name, Mancini, but she did not regret the consequences of falling pregnant with me. She regretted only not being able to tell me who my father was. As there was nothing she could do to change that, I had no choice but to let it go. In some ways this made it easier to accept the way things were.'

I pick up my tea and take a sip, deep in thought. I will never know what my grandparents were thinking when they withheld the truth about my father. Will I also learn to let it go?

'Have you considered how different your life might have been if your grandparents had told you the truth?' Alessandro asks, as though sensing the direction my thoughts are taking. 'Giulio would still have been married,' he points out. 'If your grandparents had contacted him after you were born, when your mother had passed away, I'm not sure he would have reacted very well.'

'My grandparents would have never let me go to live on the other side of the world, in any case,' I say.

'So they still would have raised you.'

'I wonder what would have happened if my mother hadn't died.'

'Maybe Giulio would have asked her to come back to Italy,' he speculates. 'But if he had, Carlotta would never have been born.'

I turn to look at him. Only now do I realise that my half-sister and I could not have existed together in the same orbit. I thought my grandparents had robbed me of any chance I might've had to know her.

'I am glad your mother didn't return to Italy,' Alessandro says solemnly.

He's thankful for his sister's existence, even though he had to suffer the excruciating pain of losing her.

'I know it hurts that your grandparents didn't tell you about Giulio, even when you were older, but what could you have done?' he asks me. 'You would have left them behind? No. Your heart would have been torn in two.'

'I couldn't have left Nan once she'd been diagnosed,' I agree. 'And if Bonnie had told me what she knew, it would have crushed me to learn that my father was out there somewhere and there was no way I could leave to go and find him. I wouldn't have had any idea where to start; I needed the letter to tell me where he was.'

'So maybe this all happened in the best way for you.'

Everything he's saying is making sense.

'Do you have photos of your grandparents?' he asks.

I nod and take the album, going straight to the end where there's a shot of the three of us sitting under the shade of the palm trees at the front of our dugout.

Alessandro studies it. 'When was this taken?'

'On my sixteenth birthday,' I reply.

We're all beaming at Vicky, Jimmy's wife. She fell ill soon after taking this picture.

'I like your grandad's beard,' he says with a smile.

'Me too.'

It was long and wiry, a mottled patchwork of grey, white and tan-brown. As a child, I used to try to straighten out his whiskers and my hands would come away coated in mine dust. I can picture my grandfather now, his blue-brown eyes merry with laughter as I clean my palms on his shirt. We both knew full well that Nan would've scolded me for getting my own clothes dirty, but she'd long given up on her husband.

I still feel a pang whenever I think about my grandfather. Maybe it's because of the way that we lost him – he was taken from us so suddenly and in such a brutal manner that I'm not sure it will ever stop hurting. I don't feel guilty about his death because there's no relief tied to it. And I'm not as upset with him as I've been at Nan, maybe because he never gave me a hard time about longing to go travelling in the first place. Nan made me feel wretched for wanting to leave her, so when she fell ill, I suppose it almost felt as if she was trapping me on purpose.

There are so many emotions battling it out inside me – I think it's going to be a long time before I can come to terms with them all.

'Are you tired?' Alessandro asks.

'No. Are you?'

'No. Do you want to watch a movie, the one they filmed in Coober Pedy?'

I assume he's talking about *Pitch Black*. 'I don't have it with me,' I reply regretfully.

'Technology, Angel,' Alessandro says. 'I can download the film.'

My eyes light up. *Of course!*

I change into my PJs and drag my duvet out from my bedroom while Alessandro whacks some popcorn in the microwave. He smiles when he sees me all snuggled up on the sofa.

I used to love going to the movies. *Saturday night at the drive-in…* Warm desert nights, parking up beneath a sky full of stars, the smell of popcorn filling the car and the tinny sound of the film coming through the stereo. Grandad used to take me as a child and in later years I'd take Nan – until she started refusing to get in the car and it all became too hard.

I still remember seeing *Up* with Pieter, shortly before he left Coober Pedy. I loved it, but, boy, did it make me cry. Grandad had passed away not long before and my travel plans had been put on hold, so it had a double whammy of grief packed into one and a half hours. *A sad old man with wanderlust being carried away by balloons…* How I wished I had a big bunch of balloons that could take me away like that.

I wanted it even more in the ensuing years, but I was rooted to Coober Pedy.

It's ironic that I'm missing it so much now.

At some point during the film, I must have drifted off

because I wake to Alessandro laying me down on my bed. He disappears out of the room without a word and returns with my duvet.

'Stay,' I whisper. It's too late to walk back to *Serafina's* where his van is parked. Remembering that he doesn't have his sleeping bag, I pat the space beside me. 'I don't mind.'

He hesitates but then walks around to the other side of the bed. I tug on the duvet before he can think about lying on top of it – it's much colder than it was a week ago.

'I hope you're not this trusting with anyone but me,' he mutters, prompting me to smile and edge closer.

He takes the hint and opens his arm, gathering me into his warm, solid embrace.

My heart does a happy dance as I rest my cheek against his chest while my head stamps its foot and gives me an earful.

We fall asleep like that.

Chapter 30

When I wake up, Alessandro is gone.

No, I'm wrong. I can hear him out in the kitchen. By the time I've used the bathroom, he's made me a milky coffee.

'*Buongiorno*,' he says, handing it to me.

'*Grazie*.'

'Did you sleep well?' he asks.

'Really well,' I admit with surprise. 'I usually wake up to the sound of a pin dropping. How on earth did you manage to carry me to my room? I'm not exactly light.'

'Your wings helped me,' he replies with a cheeky grin that reminds me of the boy from the picture of his mother's wedding day.

I throw my head back and laugh. 'You're really happy with that one, aren't you?' I tease.

'It was one of my greatest ever sentences.'

'I'm still not sure about this name you've given me,' I say wryly, enjoying his playfulness this morning. 'I don't think it suits me.'

He frowns, but doesn't say anything.

'Did you watch the rest of the film?' I ask.

He nods. 'It was entertaining.'

Coober Pedy stars early on when a spaceship crashes on a desert planet. After dark, the aliens come out. I must've closed my eyes in terror at one point and not opened them again.

I pick up my recipe book.

'Lamingtons,' Alessandro reads over my shoulder.

'My nan's recipe,' I tell him, recalling how hard it was to get her to recount it. I could have looked it up online, but I wanted it in her words. 'I'm going to make some for Cristina's birthday.'

He reaches around me and flips to the front cover of the recipe book. 'This is the one you put together?'

'Yes.'

'The Coober Pedy Bake Club' is printed in large lettering over nine pastel-coloured squares, each one containing a small painting of a different cake or biscuit. There are more on the back.

'Who painted these?' Alessandro asks.

'A few of us.'

He glances at me. 'Us? You're an artist too?'

'I did the Monte Carlo biscuits and the Jammy Hearts.' I point them out.

The painting was really an attempt to keep poor Astrid entertained in the lead-up to her hip operation. Even Nan enjoyed her stint with the watercolours. She had no idea who any of us were, but she still managed to paint a fairy cake.

'I'll let you get on,' he says.

'You have to rush off?' I'm disappointed as he walks into the hall and grabs his jacket from a hook.

'I've got to get to work.'

'You work so much.'

I'm pretty sure he works every day of the week except Mondays.

'I need the money.'

'For your adventures?' I ask with a sad smile that he doesn't notice.

'Exactly.' His attention has been caught by a postcard that arrived yesterday. 'Aada?' he asks me, unsure if he's reading her handwriting properly.

'And Onni,' I tell him. 'One day I'll make their Finnish Meringue cookies.'

'What's this about their residency?'

'I helped them apply.' They're thanking me; thrilled because it has come through.

He stares at me steadily for a long moment.

'They struggled to read the forms,' I explain. Why is he regarding me like that? 'What?' I ask awkwardly.

'And you don't think your name suits you,' he says with a significant look, before going out of the door and closing it behind him.

Chapter 31

I spend the day making Cristina's birthday card and cake and thinking about Alessandro.

It's hard to keep the joy from my heart, even though my head occasionally trots along to remind me that we'll never be more than friends.

Maybe one day I'll be okay with that. I just need to give my pheromones a chance to settle down, poor sex-starved girl that I am.

With Cristina's love of snowboarding in mind, I come up with the idea of making her a mountain cake out of Lamingtons: ten-centimetre-long rectangular chunks of vanilla sponge, covered in chocolate icing and dipped in desiccated coconut. I make about thirty of these cakes, stacking them into the shape of a mountain peak and piling an insane amount of desiccated coconut on the top to make it look like snow.

I draw two very small snowboarding Cristinas onto

paper – one a front view, the other a rear – and cut them out, sticking them together with a toothpick sandwiched between them. I pop the tiny piece of art into one of the Lamingtons to make it look like she's snowboarding downhill.

Drawing another of these tiny Cristinas, I fix it to the white origami mountain that I've made and stick the whole thing onto a folded piece of sky-blue card.

I adore making cards for people. I'd even occasionally make them for friends to give to family members on special occasions.

Last but not least, I pen a birthday message inside:

Dear Cristina,

HAPPY 30TH BIRTHDAY!

I hope this year is your best yet! You deserve all the love, laughter and snowboarding that life can bring you. Can't wait to celebrate with you later.

Lots of love, Angie xxx

When Cristina walks in at five thirty, the apartment is tidy, the cake and card are on the table surrounded by balloons and streamers, and I'm ready for a night out in skinny jeans, a black lace top and the highest heels I'm capable of wearing, which are not very high at all. I've washed my hair and have dried it with a diffuser, styling it with the green headscarf Valentina gave me. I've also prepared some snacks and there's a bottle of prosecco chilling in the fridge.

'Happy birthday!' I cry when the door swings open.

Cristina emerges, red-eyed.

'What's wrong?' I ask her, my face falling.

She shakes her head, seemingly incapable of speech.

'Is everyone at home okay?' I ask.

She nods, miserably. 'It's Rebecca,' she mumbles. 'She just called to cancel. She's having dinner with her boyfriend,' she adds bitterly.

'Oh, Cristina,' I murmur, going to give her a hug.

She's stiff beneath my grasp and withdraws awkwardly.

'What do you want to do?' I ask.

She shakes her head. 'I don't really feel like celebrating.' Her bottom lip wobbles dangerously and I step forward to give her another hug. This time she accepts the comfort.

'You don't have to make a decision yet. If we end up in front of the telly with a bottle of prosecco and an obscene amount of birthday cake, that's not a bad back-up plan.'

She smiles weakly and glances across at the dining room table. 'You got me balloons?' she asks with surprise.

She bursts into tears when she sees the cake and the card. But then she starts to laugh.

'*Cazzo*,' she curses tearfully, nodding at the two champagne glasses on the table. 'Let's get drunk.'

'Put on some happy music,' I urge as I grab the bottle of prosecco from the fridge and pour two glasses. A few minutes later, we're sitting outside in the warm sunshine, a platter of nibbles on the table next to the Lamington mountain cake – Cristina insisted on bringing it outside so she could look at it.

'This is the best cake anyone has ever made me,' she states.

'You haven't tried it, yet.'

'Doesn't matter what it tastes like. It's the fact that you did it.' She looks at me. 'Thank you.'

'You're welcome.' I chink her glass.

'You look nice,' she says.

I glance down at my outfit. 'Thought I'd make an effort for your birthday.'

'Perhaps we should go out then.'

'You can do whatever you feel like and I'll go along with it, but I do think we should celebrate this milestone. Happy birthday!' I repeat, chinking her glass again.

'Thank you.' Her smile is genuine.

'You want to talk about it?'

'There's not much to say. Rebecca's decided that she wants a nice, easy, *straight* life. Her boyfriend will never make her happy,' she states adamantly.

'Do you think Rebecca could have ever made *you* happy?' I ask.

She thinks for a moment. 'Probably not.'

I wait a little longer.

'No. She's not a very nice person, is she?'

'I barely know her,' I reply carefully. 'But she hasn't treated you at all well so far.'

'I'm done with her,' she states.

I chink her glass again and finally she grins at me. It's followed by a heavy sigh.

'She's just so goddamn beautiful. I know, I know, beauty isn't everything, but God… those eyes!'

'All eyes are beautiful if you take the time to look at them,' I point out. 'Lindsey's eyes, for example.'

'Lindsey?' Cristina is clearly perplexed as to why I've brought her snowboarding buddy into our conversation.

'You don't think her feelings run deeper than friendship?'

'No. Why? Do you think that they do?'

'There was something about the way she was watching you and Rebecca last Friday night that made me think she was jealous.'

I really hope I'm not overstepping the mark, here. I inwardly apologise to Lindsey if that is the case.

'She doesn't like Rebecca much, but that doesn't mean she likes me.'

'On the contrary, I think she likes you very much.'

'As a friend.'

I shrug. I've said enough. If it's meant to be, it's meant to be. Time to butt out. 'How was your trip home?'

'So so,' she says. 'More of the usual. "*When are you going to find a nice man and settle down?*"' she mimics an old person with a squeaky voice, then she cups her hands around her mouth to form a loudspeaker and shouts, '"*I'm gay, Nonna, so that would be never!*"'

I'm assuming she does this because her grandmother has bad hearing, rather than Cristina simply shouting at the ignorant old dear.

'That was what bothered Rebecca above everything else,' she says. 'The idea of telling her family. She's the golden girl. She wants an easy life. An ordinary, normal, *boring* life,' she adds sourly.

'There's something to be said for ordinary,' I interject casually. 'If you find the right person, I mean. Fireworks are exciting to begin with, but they get a bit tired after a while and then all you're left with are charred remains. There's something to be said for a slow burn that keeps you warm as the years go by.'

I think of Bonnie and Mick, and Jimmy and Vicky and Nan and Grandad before they were parted.

'Rebecca is definitely fireworks,' Cristina says darkly. 'And sometimes she's a bloody hand grenade. BOOM!'

She mimes her heart being exploded into pieces.

'That doesn't sound like much fun to me.'

She shakes her head. 'It's not.'

'So do you think it would be better to let her go?'

'I don't have a choice. She's chosen her boyfriend.'

'She's done that before, though, right? If she comes crawling, what will you do?'

'I will try to resist,' she states, chinking my glass. 'Can I try this cake?'

'Of course,' I reply. 'It's yours.'

She wants to know what my week was like so I fill her in, telling her about Julia and Nino, the new servers.

'A couple of Aussies came in yesterday, which made me feel a bit homesick,' I admit.

She's so canny, it won't be long before she realises that I'm struggling. I'd rather she think it something to do with home than confusion about Alessandro.

'I'm sorry.' She's sympathetic. 'That's made up my mind, then.'

'Made up your mind, how?'

'We're *definitely* going out. Pour yourself another glass and turn up the music while I get ready!'

We catch a taxi into the centre and, as I'm already tipsy from prosecco, I don't fear for my life as much as I normally would, even though we're taking corners at crazy speeds and narrowly missing other cars driven by proper, serious mental-heads.

Stefano did the lunchtime shift at *Serafina's* so he comes

to meet us at the bar, along with Lindsey and a few others. Cristina says she didn't bother asking Alessandro because he'll be working and he 'doesn't do clubs'.

We go on from the bar to another bar and then to a club, hitting the dance floor with reckless abandon. I dance like nobody is watching, even though that is not the case, as Stefano keeps telling me.

'I will protect you, Angel,' he declares, swearing at a guy who gyrates against me before proceeding to do practically the same himself.

I edge closer to Cristina and Lindsey – no one is bothering them, probably because Cristina thumps anyone who so much as bumps into her.

We end up back at ours in the early hours of the morning. Cristina drags Lindsey and Stefano into the kitchen and points at the Lamington cake.

'Angel made me a mountain cake,' she tells them, her eyes welling up with tears. They all fall over themselves to gush about it. Lindsey can't get over the tiny Cristina.

'This is so beautiful, Angie! It looks like her!'

'She's very talented,' Cristina says, putting her arm around my waist to give me a squeeze. 'No one has ever made me a cake like this. And did you see the card!' She rushes to the table to get it.

'Oh wow, I would *love* someone to make me a personalised card,' Lindsey says.

'When's your birthday?' I ask.

She tells me and I make a mental note in my not-entirely alcohol-riddled brain. I switched to water about four hours ago, managing to draw on the inner strength I used to need when I actually had responsibilities towards someone other than myself.

I experience a bit of an alcohol low the next day, though, and Cristina is suffering from a pretty hefty hangover. We sit on the sofa and watch old movies together and in the afternoon have another heart to heart.

'What did you want to be when you grew up?' Cristina asks me at one point.

I shrug. 'I didn't know. I was pretty good at school. I assumed I'd go and work for someone one day. And travel. That was all I really wanted to do. What about you?'

'I didn't think I'd be a waitress,' she says drily.

'What are you passionate about?' I ask.

'Snowboarding.'

'And you're good at it?'

She shrugs. 'Yeah. I guess.'

'Could you teach it?'

'It's not a year-round job. Anyway, I'm not sure I'd be a very nice teacher.'

'I bet you'd be fine if you were doing something you enjoyed. If you love the slopes so much, why do you live in a city?'

'I don't really know. I moved here because I wanted out of my small town, but I keep finding myself thinking about the mountains.'

'Why wouldn't you get a job there, then? You could work in a bar or a restaurant at night and snowboard during the day.'

'I'm a bit old. That's the sort of thing people do when they're in their late teens and early twenties: head to the mountains for a season in the snow.'

'That can't be true of everyone. And anyway, I'm not talking about a season. I mean actually going to *live* in the mountains, somewhere that inspires you, living the life you love.'

'I don't know if I'd love it if I lived there full time.'

'So do what Alessandro does. Waitress for six months of the year in Rome and spend the other six months working somewhere snowy.'

'I doubt Giulio would let me do that.'

'Of course he would. You've been with him for so long you're practically family. You're loyal and deserve loyalty in return. You should talk to him about it. See if you can take some time off next year.'

'Maybe,' she says hesitantly, but I can see that she's thinking about it.

Chapter 32

A text from Alessandro arrives on Monday morning at nine o'clock, making my pulse race a little bit faster. Friday night and Saturday morning have taken on a dreamlike quality, and yesterday my joy from the previous day was replaced with a feeling of foreboding. Today I'm somehow removed from it all. It helps to be going another day without seeing him, but I'm on edge as I read his message: *Don't let Giulio drive you home if he drinks today. Call me. I'll pick you up.*

Warmth pushes away yesterday's doubts. I reply with a thank you and he instantly responds with: *And bring your photo album.*

Maybe he thinks Serafina will want to see it, but it's a nice suggestion. I slip it into my handbag.

I'm nervous waiting for Giulio to arrive. He's fifteen minutes late, which doesn't help, but he's his usual exuberant self when he does appear.

'Aah, you bake!' he exclaims when I open the door, my tin of Monte Carlo biscuits in hand.

'Yesterday,' I reply with a nod, opening up the lid so he can see the domed biscuits sandwiched together with jam and buttercream.

'Very good! Mama will love these.'

He leads me outside to a compact greeny-grey car. The badge tells me it's a Fiat Panda 4x4. I haven't been driven by Giulio before.

'This is cute.' I hope that's an okay thing to say.

'Yes. Alessandro say if his van had a baby, this is what it would look like.'

This makes me laugh. I can see what he means – they're the same colour and both sort of boxy and utilitarian in appearance.

'How is Alessandro this morning?' I ask casually when we're buckled up.

Giulio flashes me a black look. 'Being a pain, as usual.'

Have they had an argument about Giulio's excessive drinking? I ask him to elaborate but he brushes me off.

It's weird, I'm never normally stuck for words, but I do find my father hard to talk to. Maybe it's because he rarely asks questions in return. It's not a conversation, it's hardly even an interview, because he's happy to talk without interruption. Thankfully he does this predominantly in English so I can understand him, but occasionally he'll slip into Italian, which is confusing, to say the least.

As we drive east out of Rome's suburbs, he begins to tell me a long and convoluted story about one of his friends who has a very impressive house on the Amalfi coast. He wants to sell up and buy something on the island of Capri, maybe even open his own restaurant.

It's hard to keep up, but I try, my mind wandering only a little as I ponder how to get him to have a two-way conversation about something that might be relevant or interesting to both of us.

It occurs to me that he might be nervous too. He comes across as so confident and outgoing, but maybe part of it is an act to cover up his insecurities.

Once we're on the main road to Tivoli, I take a deep breath and bite the bullet. I think I'm going to have to take control.

If I can get a word in edgeways.

'Lots of rain today.' Way to go, Angie. Talk about the weather. 'We didn't get a whole lot of it in the desert.' How insightful for your father. I press on because at least he's fallen quiet. 'We used to get the most incredible thunderstorms, though,' I tell him. 'The view would stretch for miles and the whole sky would light up with these big lightning bolts cracking down from above – it was almost biblical. Sometimes I'd go and sit in my grandad's car so I could watch the rain pour down. It was one of the only times I wished we didn't live underground in a home without windows.'

'I can't imagine living in a home without windows,' Giulio says. 'I like the light too much.'

'I found it a bit hard to get used to the light here at first,' I tell him. 'Underground it's so dark and quiet, but here it's so bright and noisy. Very different.' I pause, but he doesn't fill the silence. 'We'd get dust storms as well,' I tell him.

'Yes?'

'They were spectacular. The sky could be blue, but the horizon would be red as this huge cloud rolled into town.'

'Oh wow.'

'When it hit, everything would fall dark. It was like the lights being switched off. Kind of exciting, but the clean-up used to push my nan to her limits. The dust would get everywhere as it was, but after a dust storm everything was thick with it. She hated the wind and dust. I don't know how she could stand living in Coober Pedy.'

Nan would only sit out under the palm trees on still days, and even in the later stages of her illness I'd catch her running her fingertips along the dusty leaves and frowning with annoyance. The bench I would clean, but individual palm tree leaves would have challenged the limits of my sanity. It was enough of an effort to water the palms – at least we had plenty of waste water from doing the motel's laundry.

'She must've liked the desert,' Giulio says.

'She loved it, really. She loved the people, the community. She had so many friends. They're a great bunch. I miss them too.'

'Your mother told me about the dust,' he says.

'She did?'

'Yes, the dust and the wind. She said she didn't like them together, but she decided when she was here that she loved the wind. I remember one very breezy day that she stood on the roof of Basilica Papale di San Pietro in Vaticano, facing the wind, and howled.'

'Howled?'

'Yes, like a wolf.' He's smiling. 'She was crazy.'

I turn towards him, wanting to hear more. 'Basilica… Is that St Peter's Basilica?'

'*Si*, yes.'

'Did you go there with her?'

'Yes. Her first time on the roof. We go to watch the sunset.'

'I would like to do that.'

He glances at me. 'Maybe we go too, eh?'

'That would be nice,' I reply, although I can't help picturing Alessandro taking me and holding my hand.

'Did you love my mother?' I ask.

Giulio nods. '*Si*. I fell for her very quickly. First, we were colleagues, then we were friends, but right from the start she make me laugh. She was so young and happy, always joking, very different to how Marta was. I feared I had made a mistake in getting married because I didn't know how to help my wife. I was terrified that we would never find our way out of the dark. But when I came to work, there was only light. I could not help falling in love with Angie because she made me smile. And I wanted to keep *her* smiling, so I decided to show her everything I adored about Roma. That was how we became friends.'

'And the first time you kissed?'

'The night we made you.'

Gosh.

'I thought about following her when she left,' he adds quietly.

He would have abandoned Marta and Alessandro?

'Why *did* she leave?' I ask.

'Because I *told* her that I loved her. Because the situation between us was out of control. We were together only once, and afterwards, I confessed how I felt about her. I thought she already knew. I thought that it was obvious. I knew that she cared for me too. We had become close, but nothing else had happened until that night at *Serafina's* when we kissed and could not stop.' He sighs. 'Your mother felt very guilty afterwards, as did I. Marta rarely came to *Serafina's* so Angie did not know her well, but Alessandro joined me at work often and Angie cared for him. She did not want to see him hurt by our affair.' He swallows. 'So she left,' he finishes huskily. 'Four days after our one night together. She did not even say goodbye.'

'Did you know where she went?' I ask softly.

'She was supposed to be going straight to Barcelona. I knew she wanted to visit Gaudí's Sagrada Família.'

I recall the towering alien-looking spires from the front of one of my postcards.

'I thought I could sit outside the church on the steps every day until she appeared,' Giulio continues. 'But I couldn't leave. I could not walk away from Alessandro and Marta.'

'What was Alessandro like as a boy?'

He smiles. '*Very* cheeky! Marta, her tablets make her sleepy, so Alessandro come to *Serafina's* and play tricks! One day he hid my wedding ring in pizza dough. It come flying out as I toss it and hit my papà on the head!'

'No!' I gasp.

'*Si!* My papà was very angry. But then he thought it funny, so Alessandro get off lightly.'

'Was Alessandro happy when you married his mother?'

'*Si*.' He nods solemnly. 'I was already Zio Giulio to him – Uncle Giulio,' he translates, although I'd worked that out. 'We had fun together. Alessandro was the main reason I agree to marry his mother.'

I'm taken aback. 'Really?'

'*Si*. Alessandro need a papà. He was so sad when Giorgio died.' Giorgio was Alessandro's real uncle, Marta's brother, the one who had a brain tumour. He was also Giulio's best friend.

'For a while, we were happy,' Giulio says and his tone has grown despondent.

Does he mean before he met my mother or after she left? I don't need to ask because he tells me.

'Marta getting pregnant was the best thing to happen to us. And the worst,' he adds. 'We had grown to love each other as husband and wife. Marta's medication was working. She was happy or, at least, she was stable. But the doctor said that she must stop taking tablets or they harm the baby. That year was very hard. She was very low. After Carlotta was born, she didn't want to take tablets again. She say they make her too tired and she was tired enough already. But Carlotta bring her joy. She bring us all joy.'

He falls silent. I wait until he's ready to continue.

'If Marta had not fallen pregnant, she would have continued with her medication and everything would be okay. But then we wouldn't have had Carlotta. I rather have one day with *mio angelo* than no days at all.'

His angel?

'That was what I called her,' he says. 'My angel.' He glances across at me. 'It is what Alessandro calls you. Angel.'

'He doesn't see me as a replacement for her, does he?' I ask apprehensively.

'No, no, no,' he replies. 'But maybe he think you are here to save us all.'

I detect humour in his tone. I hope so, in any case.

'Does it bother you that he calls me Angel?'

I'll ask him to stop, if it does.

'No, not at all. It's different. I had *mio angelo*, you are our Angel. Our angel from the other side of the world.'

I'm able to relax again.

Before I know it, we're driving up the dirt road that leads to the Marchesi family residence. There's a break in the rain, but when I wind down my window, the air is heady with the scent of it. I take a deep breath. I've always loved the smell of rain on the desert – the way the earth would squash flat with each raindrop collecting dust on its way to the ground. Here the scent is earthier, mustier, but just as intoxicating.

Big grey clouds hang over the sky that was blue the last time I was here, and the colours of the land are muted, the grass hills several shades darker. When I catch a glimpse of the river running adjacent to the track at the bottom of the hill, the water looks grey and white as it tumbles over the rocks.

Eliana and Enzo have gone to Venice to spend a few days with their eldest daughter Melissa, but Serafina, Jacopo and Valentina are here, although Serafina stays under the porch because the heavens open again as we pull up. Her grandchildren run forward with umbrellas, sheltering us as we splash through the puddles.

We burst into the house laughing, and within seconds Serafina has me in her arms and is chattering away, half in Italian and half in English, about how happy she is to see me again.

She greets her son as warmly, while I in turn say proper

hellos to Jacopo and Valentina. Valentina is thrilled to see that I'm wearing the blue headscarf she gave me.

The house smells of burning wood and when we go into the living room the fire is lit in the hearth. It reminds me of camping with Grandad out in the bush when I was younger. We would bake damper – soda bread – in the coals of our campfire, just as Australia's early settlers once had: the swagmen, drovers and stockmen who'd had only very basic rations. Grandad would add sultanas to the recipe that was otherwise simply flour, salt and water, and I remember how delicious the bread tasted smeared with butter. The next day, though, the leftovers were as hard as a rock. We'd play catch with them.

Grandad also used to bake. Pies were his speciality, mostly savoury ones, but Nan preferred sweet treats. Every day, when I was at school, I'd find something freshly baked in my lunchbox.

The memories make my heart ache.

Serafina settles me on the sofa closest to the fire and, in grandmotherly fashion, drapes a blanket over my knees before going off to prepare hot drinks. She shuns Valentina's offer of help, but doesn't protest when her son follows.

'What is Alessandro doing today?' Jacopo asks me.

'I'm not sure,' I reply.

I think he's disappointed that Alessandro didn't come.

'What have you two been up to?' I ask.

'The usual. Milking goats, feeding pigs,' Jacopo replies with a shrug.

'Is it very hard to milk a goat?' I ask.

'You want to try?' Valentina asks with glee.

'Sure,' I reply.

'I've already milked them today, so we'll have to wait until later.'

'Maybe when the rain lets off,' I suggest.

'Oh!' Jacopo remembers something and jumps up. He returns with his phone. 'I have to take some photos of you. Everyone has been asking.'

I assume he's talking about the family members I haven't met yet.

'Come and sit next to me,' I say to Valentina, patting the space beside me.

She presses her cheek against mine and beams at the lens. I laughingly do the same.

'And now one with you,' she says to her brother, who takes her place.

Afterwards Valentina makes Serafina and Giulio sit down on either side of me and Serafina makes no attempt to get up again. Giulio, who I think was about to, seems to also have second thoughts.

'I brought some photos with me,' I say, remembering Alessandro's suggestion. 'Would you like to see them?'

Serafina would, very much. Valentina and Jacopo come and stand behind the sofa so they have a better view.

'These are my friends,' I say self-consciously, flicking past them quickly to the centre of the album where the photos become more general, featuring snaps of the town, the landscape and the dugouts.

'It looks like the moon!' Jacopo exclaims.

'People say that,' I reply with a smile.

'Is this your dog?' Valentina asks.

'I was only small when he died, but yes. His name was

Dingo. He's not a dingo, but he kind of looks like one, don't you think?' I glance over my shoulder at her. 'Do you know what a dingo is?'

Valentina shakes her head, flummoxed.

'I'll show you some pictures later,' I promise.

'I recognise this dog,' Giulio says suddenly. 'Dingo. Your mother's dog?'

'Yes,' I reply with surprise. I always thought of Dingo as my grandparents' dog. I was only four when he died so I don't remember him that well, only that he used to perform tricks for my grandad.

'Your mother carried a photo of him in her purse. She missed him very much,' he reveals.

Serafina turns to me. 'Do you have a photograph of your mother?'

'Yes.' I'm uneasy as I hunt it out and I imagine Giulio is too. I doubt he ever brought Mum to Tivoli to be introduced. 'Here she is.'

It's a photo of Mum with my nan in Adelaide. She's sitting on the beach, smiling, her dark hair flowing behind her in the summer breeze.

'I remember now,' Serafina says, while Giulio falls quiet, leaning closer to study the picture.

'Did you meet her?' I ask with surprise.

'She worked for us,' she replies with equal surprise that I didn't know this.

But of course she did! Serafina and Andrea were still running the restaurant when my parents met.

'She was a good girl,' she says. 'Very friendly and nice to the customers. So sad that she died.'

'*Si*,' Giulio murmurs. He's still scrutinising the photograph. 'You have others?' he asks me.

I nod and we slowly work our way through the last third of the album, which also features photographs of me as a child and my grandparents.

Afterwards, I snap a few photos of my own. The Bake Club crowd have been on at me to post some pictures of my family online. I'll remind Bonnie to show them to Jimmy when they're next together. He doesn't have Facebook. He doesn't even have email, or a computer, for that matter. '*I can't be doing with all that*!' But he obviously enjoys penning postcards. I've had five from him so far and his last told me that Bonnie is well and truly addicted to the Patricia Cornwell series. I'm glad she's still keeping him company.

It's a lovely day. Valentina and I spend an hour or so on the piano together – I teach her a duet for us to play together, which delights our grandmother no end. We also have a quiet heart to heart about how she can't wait to go to university in September, but how she's worried about leaving behind her responsibilities. She doesn't think anyone cares for Fiocco and Nocciolina as much as she does. To her, the goats are beloved pets. To everyone else, they're not much more than a source of ingredients.

In the afternoon, as we're preparing to leave, Eliana and Enzo arrive home. Enzo tries to get us to stay a while longer, saying he'll open a bottle of wine from the family vineyard, but Giulio declines.

'Alessandro will be waiting with an alcohol test when I get home.' He humphs, casting his eyes heavenwards.

Once again, it's just the two of us in the car. When I say something about Serafina, Giulio interrupts me.

'She would like you to call her Nonna,' he says. 'And, I don't know, maybe you could call me Papà?' He sounds hesitant. 'But whatever you like,' he adds hastily, filling the awkward silence that has descended upon the car.

'I can call you Papà, if you like.' I'm touched almost to the point of being speechless.

'*Si*, I would like,' he replies.

Chapter 33

On Tuesday morning, it's bucketing down.

'That's going to make walking to work fun,' I say wryly, staring out the French doors at the puddles rapidly forming on the terrace.

'I have a spare helmet,' Cristina says easily, prompting me to shoot her a look of alarm over my shoulder.

'I'll go slow,' she adds.

'No, it's okay.'

'Come on, Angel, live a little.'

'You promise to go very, very slowly?'

'I promise! Jeez.'

'Fine. Let's do this.'

We arrive at work laughing and wet through from our hips downwards. Cristina doesn't care – she's wearing shorts today, typically – but my jeans are soaked.

'Angel!' Giulio exclaims when he sees us.

'*Buongiorno... Papà*.' I say this mischievously, still laughing about the bedraggled state we're in.

His face lights up at the moniker and, to my surprise, he opens his arms to me and comes over to give me a hug and two kisses.

Alessandro walks out of the stockroom while this is happening and comes to an abrupt halt.

'*Ciao*!' I call cheerfully.

'*Ciao*,' he replies in a more reserved manner, heading behind the bar.

Oh great. He's gone back to being detached. I try not to be put off.

'Good weekend?' I ask, propping myself up at the bar.

He nods. 'You?'

'Yeah. We went out for Cristina's birthday on Saturday night.'

'How was that?'

'Lots of fun. And yesterday's trip to Tivoli was nice. You were missed.'

He says nothing.

'I was thinking about taking a few days off the week after next and going to visit the rest of the family in Venice. Would that be okay?'

'Of course. Let me know when you've decided which days.'

I pause. 'You wouldn't like to come too?'

He meets my eyes with surprise, then looks down again, shaking his head. 'I have to work, but Loreta and Boris are very good hosts and your cousin Melissa will enjoy showing you around.'

I try to mask my disappointment.

'What did you get up to yesterday?' I probe.

'I had a quiet day,' he replies and doesn't seem to want to elaborate so I get on with setting the tables.

On Friday afternoon, I go to place a drinks order when Alessandro stops me. The restaurant isn't busy – Stefano and I have the only two tables.

'What are you doing tomorrow night?' he asks.

'Nothing, why?'

'Logan has texted. He and Lea would like to have dinner.'

'Sounds good.'

'What's this?' Stefano interrupts.

'Nothing, just meeting up with a couple of Alessandro's friends tomorrow night.'

Stefano looks at Alessandro with mock surprise. 'You have friends?'

Alessandro stares at him and Stefano shrugs. 'What? I've never seen any.' Stefano slaps my arm as Alessandro gets on with the drinks order. 'I thought we were going clubbing again tomorrow night?'

'When did we decide that?' I ask.

'Last week. You said you would come dancing with me every Saturday night from here until eternity.'

'I did?'

'Yes,' Stefano states adamantly.

'I'd had quite a lot to drink,' I reply apologetically.

'Fine. We can go tonight instead.'

'We'll see,' I say to get him off my back, picking up the drinks tray.

There's no such thing as 'We'll see' when it comes to Stefano. In the end I give in to his badgering and agree to go into town with him – Cristina is also swayed. She's still suffering with post-Rebecca blues so we manage to convince her that she needs another night out with her friends.

She's not the only one. All week I've struggled with Alessandro's detachment, but I know I can't let it get me down, not when I'm finally free to live my life. I'm simply going to have to make some solid friendships so I don't feel dependent on him.

'See you later, Papà!' I call with a cheeky grin.

Again, Giulio looks absolutely delighted as he comes out of the kitchen to give me a hug.

It doesn't come naturally, calling him Papà, but it does entertain me, seeing that look on his face. Such a small thing to do to bring someone joy. How could I not? Ultimately, it seems to be bringing us closer.

Warmth spreads through my body as Giulio squeezes me.

'I pick you up Monday morning, nine o'clock,' he states, looking into my eyes.

'I'll see you then.'

Giulio and I are going to Tivoli again – I'm hoping this will become our 'thing', something we do together regularly.

I turn to Alessandro. 'You sure you won't come for a drink?'

He shakes his head. 'I'll see you tomorrow evening.'

'Shall I meet you somewhere?'

'No, I'll pick you up. Seven o'clock?'

'You'll leave work early?' I ask, pleased.

'On this occasion. Have a good night,' he says, nodding towards the door as Stefano calls out to let us know that the taxi is here.

'Thanks, you too.'

I do have a good night, despite the underlying edginess that comes whenever I think about Alessandro. I feel young and free, and I can't believe it when we arrive home and I see that it's four o'clock in the morning!

For the first time in what feels like forever, I'm acting my age.

Cristina and I sleep in late the next morning and nurse our hangovers in front of the TV for much of the day. I was intending to go into town to do some sightseeing – the weeks will soon turn into months and before I know it, I'll be going home again – but I don't have the energy.

At least Venice is all lined up. I'm going a week on Tuesday for three nights. My aunt Loreta and her husband Boris run a small hotel and they've blocked out one of the rooms for me. It'll be great to meet some more members of the family.

I'm not sure what I expected, but Alessandro is as remote when he comes to collect me on Saturday night as he was at work.

It would probably be stranger if he'd instantly switched to being tactile again, but I'm still a bit thrown by his two cool cheek kisses. Our skin barely connects, and a friendly hug seems like it would be out of the question.

'Are you not drinking tonight?' I ask when we go outside to his van.

He shakes his head. 'I'll sleep in this when you catch a taxi.'

'Oh, okay.'

He puts his music on at a high volume so we don't really

talk on the drive into town. I'm unsettled, wondering whether I've done something to upset him. Eventually I come out with it, turning down the music as I ask, 'Have I done something wrong?'

He looks startled. 'No. Why?'

'You've been aloof all week.'

He shakes his head. 'We're at work. Giulio, too many other people around, but everything is okay. Tonight my head is elsewhere.'

'Where?'

A few seconds pass. 'I'm thinking about what will happen when I go.'

'When you go?'

'Frida and I.'

'Oh. What are you worried about?'

'Nothing,' he replies. 'Everything is fine.'

I don't believe him, but that's all he'll say.

We're meeting Logan and Lea at a bar and they're already there when we arrive. Logan calls out in not quite as loud a voice as he did in Pompeii, thankfully, but still loud enough to get a few looks: 'Allez-Allez-Allez!'

I laugh and glance at Alessandro. 'Where did he come up with that?'

'It's what the spectators shout at the cyclists in the *Tour de France*,' Alessandro explains.

'Go, go, go!' Logan chips in, before shaking Alessandro's hand. 'It's also become a Liverpool football chant since then.' He leans forward to give me a peck on my cheek.

I'm not quite as at ease as I was when I last met Logan and Lea, knowing what I now know about base jumping, but the conversation between us flows, and gradually I begin to relax.

After one drink, we head to a steak restaurant with a dark and sumptuous interior. We're led to a booth table with black-velvet-covered bench seats. Lea slides into one side whilst I take up position opposite her, the men following in after us.

We spend the first part of the evening hearing about Logan and Lea's travels. Alessandro has been everywhere they mention, but I hang on to every word, especially when they talk about Venice and the things they got up to there.

During the break between the starters and the main course, Logan slides his arm around Lea and pulls her close. A few moments later, Alessandro rests his hand on my knee.

I give him a sidelong glance and reach for my wine glass, but leave his hand where it is.

By the time we're eating a shared dessert, we're even closer. Anyone looking at our table would think we are two loved-up couples.

Of course, there's absolutely no kissing, but Alessandro is being very affectionate. Right now, his left arm is around me and he's holding his fork with his right.

I don't know why this is happening again after a week of distance. It's almost as though he's following Logan and Lea's lead. Maybe if I hadn't been drinking, I'd be more on guard. But right now, I'm trying not to overthink it because I'm enjoying it too much.

Far too much.

We pay up and move on to a bar, lucking out when a couple of big comfy armchairs by the window become available.

Alessandro and Logan go to get some drinks while Lea

and I look around for extra chairs. We can't see any so we sit down and she leans towards me.

'Are you and Alessandro a "thing" now?' she asks.

I shake my head. 'Friends.'

'You're very close.'

'Sometimes,' I say with a nod. 'He's not always like that.'

'Logan says he's never seen Alessandro with a woman before.'

'Really?'

'Never.'

I'm not sure what to say.

'It's nice,' she adds with a smile. 'He seems happy.'

I glance over at the bar, but Logan and Alessandro haven't been served yet.

'Has Logan told you what Alessandro was like when they used to know each other?' I ask.

She nods, growing serious. 'A little.'

'What did he say?'

'I'm not sure how much to tell you. I mean, he seems in a pretty good place right now.'

There's something about her tone and the look in her eyes that make me feel nervous.

'I worry about him,' I confide. 'If I can better understand him, I might be able to help.'

She pauses, and then sighs. 'There were a few times when Logan said he acted irresponsibly. Not all the time,' she's quick to clarify, 'but occasionally.'

'In what way?'

'He jumped in dangerous conditions when nobody else was jumping. Logan says it was a miracle that he survived. If the conditions aren't right, it can be suicide. Logan tried to talk Alessandro away from the edge more than once, but he was like, "Three, two, one, see ya!"'

Oh, God...

'Logan was furious. The other jumpers too. Most have had a brush with death or know someone who's had a serious or fatal injury – nobody wants to see their friend come to a sticky end. And when one person acts recklessly, it puts the whole base-jumping community at risk. If people die or get seriously injured, then jumps are liable to become illegal. Lots of thrill-seekers then want to do those forbidden jumps. It's bad for the sport. So after the last time this happened, Logan got Alessandro to join him on a jump in Greece and tried to have a heart to heart with him. Alessandro didn't like it. Logan didn't hear from him again until we ran into you the other day.' Lea gives me a sympathetic look, knowing this is hard for me to hear. 'Logan was so happy to see Alessandro. He's thought about him a lot, wondering what had happened to him. He was disappointed to hear that he's still jumping.'

'What would make him stop?'

'It's not something anyone can force. He has to be willing on his own terms.' She gives me a sad smile. 'You really care about him, don't you?'

I nod, watching Alessandro at the bar. He glances our way. Our eyes lock and his easy expression fades. Logan says something to him to take his attention away.

I excuse myself to go to the bathroom, needing a moment to compose myself before I face Alessandro.

Base jumping is already a death-defying sport. If

Alessandro acts recklessly, how long will it be before death refuses to be defied?

When I return to our table, he's sitting in my seat and Lea is perched on Logan's knee.

Alessandro edges himself as far back in the armchair as he can, patting the space between his legs. I sit down and he wraps his arms around me from behind, resting his chin on my shoulder as he reaches for his drink.

I pick up mine – a cocktail of some sort – and he chinks my glass.

'What's wrong?' he asks in my ear.

'Let's talk later,' I murmur, and feel him tense up behind me.

Lea friends me on Facebook before the night is out so I'm glad I have a way of contacting her if I need to. She and Logan are flying to California tomorrow, and have urged us to get in touch if we're ever in the area.

Alessandro gets his phone out and makes a quick call as we walk. Far away, at the end of the road, the Monument of Vittorio Emanuele II glows with a golden light.

'What did Lea tell you?' he asks as soon as he's finished.

I wasn't expecting to be having this conversation so soon.

'She said that one of the last times Logan saw you jump, you were reckless.'

He doesn't deny it.

'Nobody else was jumping,' I add.

'I wasn't hurt,' he replies. I wouldn't go as far as to say he's angry, but he's certainly not happy.

'She said the conditions were dangerous.'

'I wasn't hurt,' he repeats. 'They can't have been that dangerous.'

'Why didn't anyone else jump, then?'

'You'd have to ask them that.'

'You think they were being too cautious?' I want him to say yes, but he doesn't.

'I don't judge anyone else for their actions, so I would prefer others not to judge me. I make my own decisions. I am no one else's responsibility.' He turns to look at me. 'Do not make me your responsibility, Angel.' He says it like a warning.

'You're not my responsibility, but you've become my friend.' I grab his hand. 'And I don't want to lose you.'

He extracts his hand. 'Everybody loses everyone in the end.'

'What the hell does that mean?' I raise my voice.

'It means we will all die one day. I have accepted death as a part of life. When it's my time, I will go.'

'But you're staring death in the face whenever you jump off a cliff edge!' I protest. 'You don't *have* to do that!'

'You're wrong. Jumping is the only thing that makes me feel alive.'

I regard him with dismay. 'It's the only thing?' What about us? What about friendship?

'Nothing else makes me feel free,' he mutters.

I frown. 'Free from *what*?'

He looks frustrated. 'I'll never stop, so don't ask me to.'

'I'm not asking you to,' I say, even though it's the one thing I want to do right now.

He nods up ahead. 'I think this is your taxi.'

That was the call he made?

He speaks through the open window to the driver and passes him a few notes from his wallet.

'I have money,' I protest, as he opens the back door for me. I climb in and he shuts the door, then turns around and walks in the opposite direction without another word.

I stare out of the rear window as the driver pulls away from the kerb, shocked at the sudden end to our evening. As we're taking the corner, Alessandro stops and spins around.

I know that the tormented look on his face will deprive me of sleep tonight.

Chapter 34

Coober Pedy is a small town and everybody talks.

Not me.

If someone trusted me enough to tell me something, I never broke that trust. Not once in all my twenty-seven years.

So I feel terribly guilty about betraying Alessandro's confidence now.

'He holds your hand?' Louise asks.

At least she's on the other side of the world and it's unlikely they'll ever meet.

'Yes.'

'That's not normal.'

'It doesn't feel strange,' I reply. How can I make her understand what my relationship with Alessandro is like when we're away from *Serafina's*?

'But it's not normal. It's like you're two primary school kids playing at relationships. It's weird.'

I'm starting to wish I'd called Bonnie instead.

'And he's never had a girlfriend?' Louise continues. 'Sorry, Angie, but that's properly freaky. Thirty-five and he's never had a girlfriend? Does he look like the Elephant Man or something?'

'No!' I exclaim. 'He's attractive!'

'What's wrong with him then?'

'His mother and sister died within two days of each other.' I told her this earlier, but she obviously needs reminding. 'He ran away from home. It's not like he doesn't have sex; it's just that his encounters don't develop into anything meaningful.'

'Have you had sex with him?'

'Don't you think that would have been one of the first things I'd have mentioned?'

'Fair point.'

'He's slept with some of the waitresses from *Serafina's*. At least two that I know about.'

'That's a bit dodgy.'

'They've quit now.'

'I have to say, I'm not loving what you're telling me so far.'

I sigh heavily. Louise is far too straight-talking for my liking. 'I'm exhausted,' I say, wrapping up this conversation. It's two o'clock in the morning.

'Why don't you think he wants to get close to anyone?' she asks, reeling me back in.

'I guess he doesn't want anyone to try to stop him from doing what he loves.'

He said as much in Pompeii.

'Why is he allowing himself to get close to you then?' she muses.

'I feel like he shut the door on that tonight. He'll never take it further than friendship, anyway.'

'Holding hands is not friendship, Ange,' she says pointedly. 'If it's really never going to go further, maybe you should put an end to that sort of thing.'

'Why?'

'Can your heart take it?' she asks with surprise. 'Mine couldn't. I don't know how to help you here, I've never heard of anything quite like this.'

'I've got to go,' I say again.

'But he obviously likes you,' she chips in. 'Maybe you should ask him outright how he feels. But, hang on, even if he's up for taking things to the next level, I'm not sure that you should. He sounds like a bit of a dud. Sorry, Angie, but maybe this one is best avoided.'

I'm more confused and stressed than ever by the time we finally hang up.

I *can't* avoid Alessandro. It's simply not going to happen. But I don't want to go into work on Tuesday and have tension between us.

On impulse, I text him.

Are you awake?

He replies within a minute. *Something wrong?*

I dial his number.

The phone rings and then stops, but it doesn't go to voicemail.

I ring again and this time he answers.

'Whasswrong?' He sounds drunk, much, much more drunk than he was when I left him.

'I'm fine. Are you okay?'

'You-got-home-okay?' Every word sounds like it's an effort to enunciate.

'Yes, I'm fine,' I repeat. 'Are you okay?'

'Sshh,' I hear him tell someone in the background, and my blood freezes in my veins at the sound of a girl replying in low, sexy Italian. He says something in Italian in return and there's a giggle. There's no other background noise. They're not at a bar, they're somewhere private, maybe a hotel room or even his van.

'Talk-tomorrow,' Alessandro says to me and then the line goes dead.

Chapter 35

Alessandro does not call me the next day. And I do not call him. I can't quite believe that he put me in a taxi and then went back to a bar to pull a girl.

What's more, I feel incredibly stupid for finding that so difficult to believe.

Cristina wants to know what's put me in such a slump, but I can't bring myself to tell her. I can't tell anyone. I sure as hell don't want to ring Louise and fill her in.

But I can't help but think that Louise is right. I'm out of my depth here. Alessandro is far too complicated for me. I had no intention of getting myself into a relationship, anyway, and certainly not a confusing one like this is turning out to be.

I don't know how it happened. How did I become attracted to the one man that I can't – and shouldn't – have? I'm only twenty-seven! I should be out having fun, going on easy dates and maybe sharing a few kisses. Even I could see that I wasn't short of male attention on Friday night at the club – a couple of guys were quite cute – but I shut them down without a second thought.

On Monday, Giulio and I return to Tivoli and spend a glorious early summer's day in the countryside. Valentina didn't milk the goats fully this morning so we finish the job together, and she dissolves into fits of giggles as she tries to teach me how to wrestle milk from the saggy teats.

Nonna – and it doesn't feel as strange calling her that as I thought it would – teaches me how to make ravioli and I'm riveted watching her form perfect pasta parcels of ricotta, spinach, nutmeg and pepper.

In the afternoon, Valentina and I practise our duet on the piano and my eye is caught once again by the photograph of Carlotta. I ask if there are any more photos of her so Jacopo hunts out the family albums.

With my grandmother on one side and my father on the other, we look through the pictures. There were many taken of Carlotta during her short life and I have to keep swallowing down a lump in my throat as I watch her morph from a scrawny newborn baby with a shock of fuzzy black hair to a chubby-cheeked toddler with big brown eyes fringed with long lashes. There are snaps of Giulio and Marta too, and in many Marta is smiling, looking much happier and at peace than she did in her wedding photograph. And, of course, there are pictures of Alessandro, including one of him celebrating his eighth birthday, his expression gleeful and his green eyes shining in the light of the candles on top of his birthday cake. I'm stunned when Giulio points out my mother in the background, looking happy and pretty with her long dark hair fashioned into a braid. She seems so young and she was. She was only twenty when she returned home, seven years younger than I am now.

Tearing my eyes away from her, I turn to the next page of the album.

I soon realise why Alessandro seems so unfamiliar and it's not merely because he's only a boy. It's because he's wearing colour. There's one photo of him holding Carlotta in his lap that I'm especially drawn to. It was taken soon after her first birthday, Giulio thinks, which means Alessandro was thirteen. His tanned limbs are long and gangly, his dark features overly angular and his teeth slightly too big for his mouth. He's wearing a light-blue T-shirt and is grinning as Carlotta, in a yellow dress, reaches out towards the lens with a look of excitement on her face. I think I'm able to work out what it is that has her attention because the next photograph shows her staring with wonder and delight at a familiar pink bunny clutched in her hands. Alessandro is gazing down at them both with a smile.

Hearing him with another woman was the reality check that I needed, I remind myself as my chest contracts.

If he's distant again with me tomorrow, that can only be a good thing.

When it's time to leave, I ask my father if we can go home via the graveyard to put some flowers on Carlotta's grave.

Standing before her angel statue with him at my side feels in a strange way cathartic. I might not have known my small half-sister, but she *was* my blood, we shared a father and my heart pines for her.

Giulio puts his arm around my shoulders as we turn away and we walk a few steps like that.

'Remind me when you are going home,' he says.

'Beginning of September.'

'Why you have to go then? Why can't you stay?'

'For Christmas?'

'Forever.'

I glance at him and my insides feel funny. 'I do love it here,' I say thoughtfully. 'But I miss my friends. And I need to decide what I'm going to do with my grandparents' home. I'll come back, though, of course I will.'

'We must arrange Italian citizenship for you,' he says. 'I don't want you to have any visa problems.'

'I'm not sure how we'd go about that. You're not on my birth certificate.'

'Then we will get a paternity test. I will speak to my friend who is a lawyer.'

I'm dreading the return to work on Tuesday, dreading seeing Alessandro again. I hate that I feel betrayed when he owes me nothing in the way of loyalty and other women.

But he's reverted to being his usual work self and I'm glad. I'm feeling cool towards him in turn when we exchange our usual good mornings.

In the afternoon, we run out of prawns so I offer to go down to *Bruno's* to collect some the restaurateur is willing to spare.

Bruno himself isn't there, but his son, Carlo, comes out of the kitchen to say hi. He's about my age, tall and slender with a narrow face, long straight nose and dark floppy hair. His eyes are kind – brown and a little droopy at the corners, but in a nice way. He reminds me of a puppy dog.

'Giuseppe is boxing them up,' he tells me. 'An espresso while you wait?'

'Sure.'

He stays and chats to me for a while and notices when I grimace.

'You don't like espresso?' he asks with a small laugh. 'You should have told me, I could have made you something else.'

'I'm trying to get used to the taste. I want to live like a proper Italian, at least in this way, before I return to Australia.'

'There's a great coffee shop not far from here. *Lucia's*. Have you been?'

I shake my head.

'They do excellent coffee cake and cappuccino. Maybe we could go sometime?'

He seems nice and friendly. Why would I say no?

I don't.

We exchange phone numbers as Giuseppe comes out of the kitchen with the prawns. I walk back to work with a spring in my step, feeling positive about taking some control of my life.

I felt out of control enough when it came to Nan. I can't – I won't – let that happen again, not if I can avoid it.

Carlo doesn't play games. He texts me that afternoon and asks if I'm free in the morning.

I grab Cristina on her way to the kitchen. 'Are you familiar with Carlo, Bruno's son?' I ask her quietly.

'A little. What do you want to know?'

'Is he okay? I mean, is he nice? He's not a serial killer or anything, is he?'

She laughs. 'From what I've heard, he's decent. Why? You like him?'

'He's asked me for a coffee.'

'Go!' she urges.

I nod and text him to make arrangements.

The next day, we meet at the coffee shop Carlo mentioned and have a perfectly pleasant morning. He's friendly and likeable, and easy to talk to. The only awkwardness comes towards the end of our time together when he blushes while asking if I have a boyfriend in Australia.

'No, I'm single,' I reply. 'You?'

'My girlfriend and I broke up a few weeks ago.'

'Oh, I'm sorry.'

'It's okay. I'm okay. She's okay,' he adds with an easy shrug of his shoulders.

'What happened?'

'We were going—' He moves his hands away from each other. I nod with understanding and he cocks his head to one side. 'Can I take you out for dinner tomorrow night?'

I wasn't expecting this question so soon, but I find myself agreeing. 'I'll have to check they don't need me at work.'

Giulio and Alessandro are at the bar when I walk in. My father greets me in his usual exuberant manner.

'Do you need me tomorrow night?' I ask Alessandro.

'Why? You got a hot date?' Giulio teases.

I laugh, but don't confirm or deny it.

Alessandro checks the rota. 'No, that's fine.'

'I am happy you are here with me,' Giulio says, 'but I am

pleased you are taking some time off. You should be exploring. Sightseeing.'

'I know,' I reply. 'The weeks are slipping away.'

It's early July now and I've been here a month already. The next two will fly by if I'm not careful. A big part of my reason for coming to Italy was to get to know my father and experience life in Rome and I'm glad that I'm doing that, but I do want to see a bit of the country and possibly even stray further afield.

'You want me to fill some of your shifts?' Alessandro asks.

'Um... Do you need me Friday daytime?' It would be nice to go into Rome without the weekend crowds. 'I can still work Friday night.'

He nods. 'No problem. And when you return from Venice, let's go through the rota.'

'Thank you.' I get on with my work.

Carlo and I agree that I'll meet him at *Bruno's* when my shift ends, but as I'm finishing up, he walks through the door of *Serafina's*. Alessandro greets him with a handshake and Giulio comes out of the kitchen to say a friendly hello.

'Everything okay? You run out of something?' my father asks as I take off my apron. 'What do you need?'

'Just your daughter,' Carlo replies with a smile in my direction.

'I'll get my bag,' I tell him, aware of Alessandro and Giulio's surprise as I hurry into the stockroom.

I feel nervous for some reason and I don't think it's because of my date with Carlo. I stash my apron in the dirty washing basket, grab my bag and return to the bar area.

'See you tomorrow,' I say with forced cheer, kissing my father goodbye and steadily avoiding eye contact with Alessandro.

'See you tomorrow,' Giulio replies.

I don't think he disapproves of my date choice, even if it has come out of the blue.

Carlo takes me to the bistro I went to with Alessandro and my father on my first night in Rome. It's more intimate than I would have liked – I was hoping we'd go into the centre for something a bit livelier – but it's still lovely and we find plenty to discuss. There's no deep or meaningful heavy talk, and although I'm not up for ending our evening with a kiss as I sense he might like, I do fall asleep that night with a lightness of heart.

The next day I venture into town on the urban railway, still finding the whole experience daunting. But when I come out at Flaminio and walk across Piazza del Popolo with blue skies overhead, I'm filled with an incredible sense of achievement. I did it. All on my own.

Today the only person I need to worry about is myself, and even though the thought of Alessandro takes the shine off my mood, I'm determined to push those negative feelings aside. I can go anywhere I want, and I do – I venture all the way to the Colosseum and pay to go inside, wandering around the huge arched enclosure and soaking up the history of the place with a happy heart. From there, I head to the Forum, and afterwards I stroll in the direction of the bustling centre, purposefully wandering off the beaten track to explore. At one point I happen across a quiet square dotted with trees and edged by sand- and stone-coloured buildings. On the far side is a restaurant spilling out onto the pavement, its silver chairs and tables glinting in the afternoon sun. I'm starving, so I pluck up the courage to walk over and take a seat at a vacant table. When a plate of crunchy *calamari fritti* appears beside my chilled, fizzing glass of prosecco, a bubble of joy swells inside me. I can't believe how far I've come.

I feel like calling Jimmy and telling him what I'm up to, but it's the middle of the night in Australia so instead I get out one of the postcards that I bought at the Colosseum and pen a message to him.

Dear Jimmy, I've just been to the Colosseum! It's mind-blowing to think that 2,000 years ago, Roman emperors used to sit there & watch Russell Crowe fight lions... Ha ha – we must watch Gladiator when I get home! Now I'm eating lunch outside in the sun – and, shock, horror, it's not too hot! Loving it here, but I do miss you. Love, Angie xxx

I'm still in good spirits when I go into work that night, but I'm slightly dreading being on my feet after a day of walking.

After a week of mutual coolness, I'm able to greet Alessandro with relative warmth. Stefano, Cristina and I are on tonight and it's the first time the three of us have worked together since Julia and Nino joined.

My Italian is coming along – not very fast and certainly not brilliantly – but I'm up for taking a couple of non-English-speaking tables. Giulio exits the kitchen occasionally to announce to my customers that I'm his daughter, so they give me an easy time and are especially good-natured when he pours them free shots of Limoncello.

Cristina appears slightly put out at this favouritism, but I shrug at her, palms-up, and remind her that we're sharing the tips.

This makes her smile.

Despite my sore feet, it's a good service, but by the end of the night, I am ready for a breather.

Perching on a stool at the bar, I turn and face Stefano, who's doing, bizarrely, a tap-dancing jig in front of me in an attempt to convince me to go clubbing.

'I must've walked thirty thousand steps today,' I tell him with a groan that is only slightly exaggerated. 'How are you feeling?' I ask Cristina.

Rebecca rang her earlier. She cancelled the call.

She nods. 'Okay.'

'She needs to go dancing too! Lindsey is coming,' Stefano says slyly.

'I'm not interested in Lindsey,' Cristina replies.

'I think she's nice,' I say.

'She *is* nice,' Cristina agrees. 'That's why we're *friends*.'

'Friends can have benefits,' Stefano jokes.

Alessandro gently taps me on my shoulder. I turn to see that he's trying to pass me a glass of red wine. He looks straight into my eyes – the first proper eye contact we've had in days – and our fingers brush as I take the glass, making me feel jittery.

'You coming, Alessandro?' Stefano asks, as he does every Friday night. I think he'd keel over with a heart attack if Alessandro one day accepted. He doesn't even wait for an answer, slapping me on my arm. 'Maybe we invite Carlo, eh?'

I shrug. 'Could do.'

'Yay! We're going clubbing!' Stefano cries as though it's the first time in months he's managed to make this happen.

I put down my glass of wine on the bar top and slip off my stool, my feet stinging all the way to the stockroom. I'm crazy for allowing myself to be roped into this after a day of walking, but you only live once, right?

Carlo replies to Stefano's text as we're getting stuck into our pizza. He's keen.

'That's four in a taxi,' Stefano realises. '*Perfetto.* I'll book one now.'

Something makes me look over at Alessandro. He's wiping down the bar top and hasn't joined us at our table. I ignore my better judgement and get up to go and speak to him.

'You can't be persuaded to come with us?'

He shakes his head, still polishing the bar top. 'I'm working tomorrow.'

My eyes drop to his neck where his gold cross pendant has broken free from his black T-shirt. When I look at his face, his expression is hollow, vacant.

No, *lost.*

My hand acts of its own accord, slipping into his.

It's like turning a light on, using a dimmer switch. His hand slowly comes to life in mine and his eyes burn with intensity as we stare at each other.

For that brief moment, before Carlo raps on the door, my heart sings.

Chapter 36

Have you bought a train ticket to Venice? Alessandro asks me by text on Sunday morning.

No, I text back.

Don't.

Why?

He doesn't reply.

I'm still in bed, but I drag myself through to the kitchen to make a cup of tea, only to remember that we ran out of milk yesterday. The shops aren't open yet so I knock back a black espresso before throwing myself in the shower.

Alessandro still hasn't replied when I'm dressed and ready. I'm trying not to fixate on my phone, but that's easier said than done.

Grabbing shopping bags from the stash by the door, I call out to Cristina to let her know what I'm up to and set off out the door.

It's a clear, bright morning. The birds are singing in the

trees and the sun is shining overhead. It rained yesterday and as I walk through the small triangle of green space, the ground beneath my feet squelches with every step.

I soon find myself passing Alessandro's old home. I haven't come this way all week because Cristina has given me a lift on her scooter. She still takes it slowly, and by the end of each journey, I've relaxed a bit. But those first few seconds when she sets off are like a shot of adrenalin.

I could never be an adrenalin junkie. The high does not outweigh the terror.

It's not until I'm standing outside the closed supermarket that I remember Sunday opening hours. I don't mind killing a bit of time because it's such a beautiful day so I decide to go for a walk.

A few minutes later, I find myself strolling past a big, official-looking building that stands out amongst its neighbours. It's fronted with white columns and has white stone steps leading down to the tree-lined pavement. A stream of people begins to pour from its doors and only then do I realise it's a church. Sunday Mass has finished, from the looks of it.

As I'm about to move on, something catches my eye, making me do a double-take. A man dressed all in black is coming down the steps. I watch as Alessandro disappears beneath the trees and walks in the opposite direction from me. He's too far away for me to call out to him and I'm not sure I would anyway.

He goes to church?

What was it that he said in St Peter's Square? *He has a tumultuous relationship with God.*

I don't know why I think it, but I wonder if his necklace belonged to his mother.

A moment later, I finally receive a response to my text: *I can give you a lift. I need to take some time off.*

Seeking instant clarification, I dial Alessandro's number. 'You're coming to Venice?' I ask slightly breathlessly when he answers.

'No, but I will take you there and bring you home via Florence and Siena. I thought you might like to see them.'

'Where are you going?' I'm confused.

'Dolomites.'

I tense. 'Base jumping?'

'Possibly. I need a break from the city.'

'Are you okay?' I ask.

'Fine,' he replies simply. 'Where are you?' I think he's registered the sound of traffic in the background.

'I'm on my way to the supermarket. You?'

'Running an errand.'

That might not be a lie, but it sounds like he's being selective with the truth.

He doesn't ask me about Friday night and I'm not sure how to feel about that. I should be relieved – I don't really want to have to go into detail about how Carlo tried to kiss me at the club or how I turned away before he could make contact. It was mortifying enough at the time.

I thought I was open to some light romance and I like Carlo. He's warm and friendly, an open book.

Yet I can't see us being anything more than friends.

I'm aware of the irony. Alessandro wants to be no more than friends with me, so why am I drawn to him?

I hope I'm not just drawn to the darkness within him. I hope I'm not seeing another problem that I want to solve.

This thought is still spinning round my head that night when I'm getting ready for bed.

Despite already betraying Alessandro's confidence by talking to Louise, I call Bonnie. I need to hear a calm voice of reason.

'Be careful, Angie,' she says when I've brought her up to date. 'He sounds like he could be a very troubled individual. I know what you're like. Your instinct is to help people, but you can't help everyone, love. I hate the thought of you getting mixed up in something on the other side of the world when you're all alone.'

'I'm not alone,' I tell her. 'I've made friends here.'

Not that I can talk to any of them about Alessandro.

'I wish you'd called me earlier, before you'd turned Carlo down. He seems like a nice, uncomplicated boy.'

'There's no such thing as a nice, uncomplicated boy,' I say wryly.

'No, maybe not,' Bonnie agrees. 'But it did sound like you were on the right track, having fun with friends and dating. Why don't you continue to do that for a while, see where it takes you?'

'Maybe,' I reply unenthusiastically.

'You've always said you didn't want to get tied down again, not until you've had a chance to live a little. Try to live a little now, Angie. This all sounds very heavy. And remember, you can come home anytime you want to. Your flight can be changed. We're all still here and we miss you.'

The thought of returning to the desert leaves me feeling surprisingly cold.

Chapter 37

Alessandro and I set off to Venice early on Tuesday morning. It's a five-and-a-half-hour drive and he claims it'll be a boring one. Normally he would avoid motorway routes in his van, preferring to explore on his way to somewhere. But in this case, I think he wants to get me there as quickly as possible so he can continue on to the mountains.

'Tivoli was good yesterday,' I tell him. He hasn't asked.

'I'm glad,' he replies. Not exactly a conversation continuer, but I press on regardless.

'I milked the goats again.'

He grins and shoots me a look. 'You milked the goats?'

'Yes. I did it last week as well.'

'Now *that* I would have liked to see.'

'You should've come.'

He shakes his head. 'You don't need me anymore.'

That's a strange thing to say, but then I recall how I asked him to come with me the first time, how unsure I was of meeting my family.

'It's not only about me, your family like seeing you too. Jacopo especially.'

He says nothing so neither do I. *Maybe if I wait patiently, as I normally do…*

'Shall we put on some music?' he asks, passing me his phone.

Oh.

'Sure,' I mutter, taking it from him and trying to work out what to do.

'It's there,' he says gently, reaching over to point at the music icon. 'You really have been living in a cave for years, haven't you?' he teases, and despite the fact that he's making fun of my incompetence when it comes to hi-tech smartphones, I'm glad to see the return of his light-hearted side.

'Press shuffle,' he says.

'Where's that?'

'There.'

I plug in his phone and music fills the van.

We talk on and off, but mostly stay silent, listening to the music. There's not much to see from the motorway, but I'm still in awe of how green everything is, how pretty the umbrella-shaped stone pines are that pepper the landscape and how tall the cypress trees soar into the forget-me-not-blue sky. I know there's beauty in the desert – the vastness of a sky awash with the colours of a sunset or inky black and sparkling with stars – but here there's so much life, so much succulent greenery. And *birds*! Swooping and soaring in big black flocks above the trees. We cross over brown rivers and blue lakes and off in the distance I can sometimes see villages nestled into the hazy hills, with ornate churches, striking bell towers and houses painted in shades of peach and cream.

As we approach Venice via a busy dual carriageway, the view outside my window becomes quite industrial. I catch a glimpse of the water to my right and see the docks with a variety of different-sized boats, and then we're on a long, straight bridge, running parallel to train and tram tracks, and speeding towards the island of Venice.

The water glistens under the sunny sky and then we come off the bridge, pass by a sea of parked scooters and turn right.

Alessandro stops at a checkpoint and speaks to the woman on duty. She raises the barrier and lets us pass.

'You can't normally drive down here,' he tells me. 'But Melissa has arranged a parking space at the university so I can drop you off near the hotel. It's close by.'

We pull up right by the waterfront and I'm staggered at the size of the cruise liners in the nearby docks.

Cristina let me borrow a big backpack so I didn't have to lug a suitcase around – Alessandro takes it from me after locking his van.

'I'll see you into the hotel,' he says, as if reminding me that he doesn't plan to stay long.

We walk around the back of some converted red-brick warehouse buildings that belong to the university, then take a footbridge over a canal filled with water not dissimilar in colour to Alessandro's eyes. I grin at him, excitement detonating my insides as it finally dawns on me that I'm here in Venice, one of the places I've dreamed about visiting for so long.

I don't think he can help but return my smile.

Loreta and Boris's hotel is in Santa Croce, west of the historic centre. The outskirts are ideal for travellers on a smaller budget, and compared to the flashier central hotels, it's not expensive – only around fifty euros a night.

However, my aunt has insisted that I stay for free. Melissa – Loreta's niece and the twins' older sister – also boards with them. It warms my heart to know how much this family looks out for one another.

The hotel is a white-painted building with green shutters. It's on a corner plot, and one side runs along a canal where several boats are moored. There's not a car in sight; here it's fully pedestrianised.

We enter a dark reception area. No one is behind the desk. To our right is a compact dining room filled with round tables and antique wooden chairs.

'Breakfast room,' Alessandro tells me, pressing a bell on the desk.

The floor beneath our feet is shiny speckled yellow marble.

It smells of cleaning product, but nothing masks the scent of pongy seawater coursing through the canal outside.

A door opens off the reception area and a plump middle-aged man with thinning jet-black hair appears. He recognises Alessandro instantly and throws his hands in the air with delight.

'You are early!' he cries.

'We made good time,' Alessandro replies as the man, who I'm assuming is Boris, clasps his upper arms and shakes him. It's not quite a hug, but it's done with affection. He turns to me.

'Hi, I'm Angie.'

'Aah, Angie!' he exclaims, giving me two kisses. 'Welcome to Venezia! I am Boris. How was your journey?'

After a bit of small talk, he checks his watch. 'Melissa is at classes for another two hours and Loreta is out until four. I can show you to your room and then perhaps you would like to go for a walk into the centre? It takes about twenty minutes. It rains tomorrow so you must make the most of today's sunshine!'

'I definitely will,' I reply enthusiastically. 'Do you have a map?'

'*Si*.' He points at a large pad of maps sitting on the desk. 'This is where we are. You take this path here to Piazza San Marco.' He draws a line on it in blue biro, then tears off the sheet and hands it to me.

'Thank you.'

'I show you to your room,' he states, setting off up the staircase.

I'm on the second floor. My room has oak beams on the ceiling and cream-coloured walls. A dark-red floral bedcover and matching curtains hang at the windows, and the bedhead and wall mirror are ornate and gilded.

'This is great,' I say with a smile as Boris hands over the keys.

'We see you here later. Make the most of the sunshine!' he urges again.

We walk out onto the wide pavement. Alessandro comes to a stop and looks at me, his hands in his pockets.

'Are you going to be able to find your way with that?' he asks, nodding at the map.

I peer down at it. It looks very complicated. The roads are winding and narrow in places and there are canals and footbridges to contend with.

'I'll be okay,' I reply uncertainly.

Alessandro jerks his head in the direction of town. 'I'll come with you for a bit.'

Butterflies fill my stomach as we walk side by side. Alessandro still has his hands in his pockets, but he pulls his right hand out and his phone with it. After a moment, I realise he's using it to navigate.

'Is that easy to follow?'

'Yes, but I'm used to it. We're heading here,' he says, showing me.

I compare his map to my paper one. Hmm. Maybe I *should* have chosen a better mobile phone.

We wander alongside emerald-green canals and beside wooden-shuttered houses in shades of ochre, salmon and cream. We come across another university building – modern and white with a green copper roof – and behind it is a leafy square, edged with pavement cafés.

A painted-faced mime artist in a black suit and bowler hat performs outside a flower stall bursting with colour, and the air is filled with the heavenly scent of caramelised sugar from a nearby crêperie.

I breathe in deeply, my chest expanding with more than mere air. I'm beside myself that I'm here in Venice at last. It's every bit as captivating and unreal as I dreamt it would be. When you see the city in movies, it looks like a film set. But it's not. It's real. All of it. I feel as though I'm walking around inside my own personal fairy tale.

As we draw closer to the historic centre, the crowd thickens. Some of the buildings look quite rundown, but occasionally I'll catch a glimpse through a window of a huge chandelier or an enormous oil painting in a gilded frame and I'll remember again that outward appearances can be deceptive.

Eventually we come to a wooden, stepped bridge that is dense with pedestrian traffic. To our right at the end of a long stretch of sparkling water is a big domed church. Boats carrying passengers and produce for hotels and restaurants pass beneath us and the sight of a couple of gondolas makes me want to squeal with excitement. I am definitely going on one of those while I'm here.

Leaving the river behind, we enter a series of narrow passageways and smaller roads. Shops line the streets: Chanel and Dior and other designer outlets. There are jewellers and purveyors of Venetian glass and shop upon shop selling touristy gimmicks.

I stare down at my map and realise that I'm completely and utterly lost.

Alessandro shows me where we are on his phone. 'This is where the hotel is. We came over this bridge.'

A flurry of fear takes the edge off my joy as I see the long and complicated-looking route. I have no idea how to find my way back. I'm really going to need some map reading lessons if I'm to go anywhere else on my own.

With a sigh, Alessandro presses his phone into my hands and takes my paper map from me, folding it up. 'You can borrow it while you're here,' he says.

I shake my head. 'You don't have to do that. I'll be okay.'

'I'd feel better about leaving you,' he insists. 'Remind me to get my charger from my van before I go.'

I wouldn't normally agree to borrow such an expensive device, but I'm touched that he cares enough to lend it to me.

I also have an odd desire to hang on to something that belongs to him.

He peers over my shoulder and points at the phone screen, nodding up ahead. 'We need to go this way.'

We walk under a dark, colonnaded archway and quickly become separated in the hordes of people. Suddenly my hand is in his and my heart is racing as he pulls me through the crowd into an enormous square.

On the other side of the square is one of the most ornately decorated buildings I have ever seen. It's light in colour and its roof is graced with multiple domes, its front glistening with golden frescoes.

'Basilica San Marco,' Alessandro tells me, and I can feel him watching me as I stare, slightly breathlessly, at the spectacular view all around.

To the right is a red-brick bell tower stretching high into the sky. The colonnade goes around three sides of the square and on our left hundreds of arched windows shine bright white in the afternoon sun.

We set off across the square and I notice that the colonnade to our right is being cleaned and is partly obscured by scaffolding. The rest of the stone is grey and murky.

'This whole square is often under water,' Alessandro tells me.

It seems unbelievable.

But I'm too distracted by the fact that we're still holding hands to fully appreciate my surroundings.

Inside my head, Louise is looking very unimpressed.

I know she's right. My butterflies are going haywire. I don't want them to keel over dead.

Forcing myself to let go of Alessandro's hand under the pretext of adjusting my headscarf, I return my attention to his phone.

He slips his own hands into his pockets and my heart feels a little less happy.

All around the outside of the square, pavement cafés are bustling and delicious-smelling aromas waft through the air, mingling with the scent of the ocean.

'Ooh, check out their lovely white suits.' I nudge Alessandro's arm gleefully as I point out the waiters' uniforms.

'It makes me feel stressed even looking at them,' he replies moodily, but his lips lift in a smile as he glances at me out of the corner of his eye.

'I saw some photos of you yesterday in Tivoli,' I tell him casually.

'Did you?'

I nod. 'You were wearing so much colour, I barely recognised you.'

'Did you see photos of Carlotta as well?' he asks.

'Yes.' My gaze drops to the ground as I add, 'She was adorable.'

When we head behind the bell tower, Doge's Palace – or Palazzo Ducale – comes into view. It joins my list of one of the most ornate buildings I've ever seen, with its myriad of arches and sculpted colonnade. We walk alongside it, sidestepping the other tourists.

The sea is on our right, vast and blue. It's a very different sight to the beaches in Adelaide where my grandparents sometimes took me on holiday. Instead of long stretches of sand, here the water butts right up against this enchanting city.

We come to a bridge and Alessandro points out another perfectly arched bridge further along the canal. It's made of white decorative stone and is entirely enclosed, connecting Doge's Palace with the building on the other side of the canal.

'Bridge of Sighs,' Alessandro tells me. 'That's the New Prison over there.' He points to the building on the right. 'The bridge connects to the interrogation rooms in Palazzo Ducale. Convicts would be allowed one last view of Venice before their imprisonment.'

'No wonder they call it the Bridge of Sighs,' I say. 'I'd sigh too if I thought that might be the last time I saw this beautiful city.'

'Lord Byron gave it the name,' he tells me with a smile. 'That's why it sounds poetic.'

In Venice, even a bridge is capable of being one of the most picturesque things I've ever seen.

When I tear my gaze away to face Alessandro, I'm met with a look of regret.

'I should get going,' he says.

His imminent departure takes the edge off my happiness as we return to the hotel.

Melissa and her boyfriend Otello are waiting for us. Melissa looks like her mother, Eliana, only a younger, cooler version with designer horn-rimmed glasses and thick dark hair pulled up into a messy bun. She jumps to her feet as soon as we walk through the door, enthusiastically greeting us both with hugs and kisses. I gather it's been a while since she and Alessandro saw each other.

Otello is more reserved: a tall thin young man with heavy eyebrows and a pointy chin. He seems nice, albeit shy.

'You won't wait to see Loreta?' Melissa asks Alessandro with dismay when he tries to make a move. 'She hasn't seen you for a year, Alessandro!'

'I really can't stay longer,' he replies. 'But I'll stop for a coffee on Friday.'

'I'll come to your van with you to grab your charger,' I say, asking him to wait for me.

When he realises that I went upstairs to get my own charger so he can take my phone in return, he tells me he can manage without.

'What if you need to call for help when you're on the mountain?' It's a disturbing thought.

'Fine,' he concedes as we set off across the bridge. 'I won't read your text messages.'

'There won't be anything of interest there, I assure you.' After a beat, I add: 'I won't read yours either.'

'There won't be anything of interest there, I assure you,' he repeats my words to me.

'No messages from girls asking why you're not returning their calls?' I mock, finding it harder to force humour into my tone.

'I don't give out my number so that is highly unlikely.'

'You don't give girlfriends your number?'

He gives me a meaningful look.

That's right, he doesn't *do* girlfriends. I think of the woman from a couple of weeks ago and feel ill.

We walk in silence for a bit. He's the one to break it.

'When you called that night, after we'd been out with Logan and Lea...'

I glance at him. Where is he going with this?

'Nothing happened,' he tells me. 'I mean... Nothing happened with the woman you heard.'

I immediately avert my gaze, blushing. I wish I could tell him that it doesn't bother me either way, but I can't bring myself to lie.

'And if Carlo calls?' he asks, not offering up any information about why he carried on drinking that night after he'd put me in a taxi. 'Any message you'd like me to give him?'

I don't know if he's bantering or being serious.

'I think it's highly unlikely Carlo will call.'

'And why is that?' he asks.

'We'll never be more than friends.'

A feeling of déjà vu comes over me and I realise that these are the exact words Alessandro said to me.

'Oh,' he replies, and we both fall silent again.

The walk to his van from the hotel, at least, is fairly straightforward. I think I'll be able to manage the return trip without directions. Alessandro slides open the side door and climbs in to open one of his cupboards.

'How long will it take you to get to the mountains?' I ask.

'About two and a half hours.'

That's not too bad. I don't like depriving him of his music.

He steps out of the van.

'Charger.' He hands me a corded plug. 'And power bank.' He places a small but weighty black device in my hands. 'You'll chew through the battery using the navigation, so charge this up and take it with you in your bag. I know it's a bit heavy, but I don't want to lose you.'

He says it casually, and he's said it to me once before, after I found out about Carlotta, but this time his words turn themselves around inside my head.

I *don't want to lose* him.

When he lifts his eyes to meet mine, I think he's startled by what he sees there.

What if he hurts himself? *I really don't want him to do this.*

'Please don't jump,' I blurt.

His expression becomes very serious. He shakes his head. 'Do not ask that of me, Angel.'

My heart twists and I look away, slipping my bag off my shoulder and onto the ground. Crouching down, I securely stow his charger and get out my own phone and charger, slowly straightening up and handing it over.

'Have a good time,' I mumble.

'I'll see you on Friday,' he replies.

'Thanks again for driving me,' I say without looking at him. 'And for the loan of your phone.'

I feel his eyes on me as I turn away.

Chapter 38

Despite my feelings of confusion over everything Alessandro, I have a great time in Venice. Loreta, my aunt, is as lovely as the rest of the family, and Melissa and I get along like a house on fire.

She and Otello have the attic room, which is small with pine ceilings and Velux windows, as I see when she drags me upstairs to ask my opinion on what she should wear for a night out. As if I'd know!

Otello's shyness evaporates after his first beer and he turns out to be really funny. He and Melissa take it upon themselves to show me the best Venice has to offer. They don't mind doing touristy things – we take a ride on a gondola, which makes me feel like a child in my excitement, and we even have a Bellini in Harry's Bar, the famous 1930s establishment that was once frequented by writers, artists and celebrities such as Ernest Hemingway, Charlie Chaplin and Alfred Hitchcock. The fresh peach puree and prosecco cocktail quickly becomes my new favourite tipple, which is unfortunate, because it's the most expensive drink I've ever ordered at about twenty euros a pop. We only have one.

I am totally taken in by Venice and its ethereal beauty, even though at times I feel like I'm walking around an elaborate theme park. It's quite shabby in places with crumbling walls, flaking paint and lots of graffiti, but I still think it's magical and I definitely want to return.

When Friday comes, I'm in a better place about Alessandro. He texted me yesterday to let me know that he was on track for today, but it's still a relief to see him.

He stays for a coffee with his step-aunt, as promised, but he's stiff and standoffish, so much so that I'm squirming with embarrassment by the time we leave. The last few days have been relaxed and light-hearted, but Alessandro's behaviour dampens the atmosphere. What has this family ever done to him? I don't understand.

Even when we're alone in his van, you could cut the tension in the air with a knife. I thought he'd be relieved to get out of there, but he's being off with me too.

'Why are you like that with them?' I ask, unable to keep it inside any longer.

'Like what?'

'You were so...' I try to think of the right word. 'Cold,' is the one I opt for.

Rude would be more accurate, if I'm being honest.

He doesn't reply. I wait in silence while he stares out the front window with a dark look on his face.

'I don't know them that well,' he says, chewing the corner of his thumbnail.

'Neither do I!'

'I'm not like you,' he mutters, returning his hand to the steering wheel so heavily that it makes a thudding sound.

No one's arguing with that statement.

Minutes pass by. I don't know what to say. Eventually he lets out a long, heavy sigh.

'I'm sorry if I embarrassed you,' he mutters. 'It's been a strange couple of days.'

I turn to look at him. 'In what way?'

He shakes his head, his lips pulled down at the corners. 'I can't explain.'

'Please try.'

'Maybe later.'

'Shall I put some music on?' I suggest after a moment.

He nods and passes me the phone I returned to him earlier.

'Francesca has asked if we'd like to have lunch with her in Bologna,' I mention. Loreta suggested it because it's on the way to Florence. 'I'm not sure you're in the mood—'

'That's fine,' he interrupts me. 'We'll be there at midday – ask her where she wants to meet.'

I'm not sure about this, but he seems to be trying to improve his mood, so I call ahead to make the arrangements.

Both Francesca and her husband Pepe manage to escape from work to join us for lunch. Pepe is a lecturer at the University of Bologna, which is the oldest in the world in continuous operation – it was founded in 1088! – and Francesca is a dentist. She's the eldest of my four cousins at thirty-five and Pepe is ten years her senior.

We go to a small, unimposing Italian restaurant on the

outskirts of the city that Francesca mischievously claims gives *Serafina's* a run for its money. She tells me that I simply *must* have the *tagliatelle al ragu* and I have no reason to disagree.

Although spaghetti bolognese was invented in Bologna, here they simply call it ragu. It's made with at least two different types of meat – usually pork and beef – as well as pancetta and a concoction of carrots, celery and tomato. It's never served with spaghetti, since spaghetti is from the south, but always with fresh handmade egg pasta such as tagliatelle or fettucine.

It's lovely, but I'm not sure it tastes all that different to the one Giulio makes.

Over lunch, I ask Francesca about her pregnancy and she admits that she's relieved to be past the morning sickness stage. Her due date is 18 December, so the baby should arrive before Christmas.

Alessandro chats mostly with Pepe about his work at the university, but I'm just thankful he's warmed up since Venice.

I'd love to explore the medieval centre, but we're also trying to squeeze Florence and Siena into our return journey so we simply don't have time. As we say goodbye under a lavishly porticoed walkway, Francesca urges me to promise that I'll come back one day so she can show me around properly.

When we arrive in Florence, another two hours have passed. Alessandro's mood has continued to improve, but mine has taken a downturn.

It's three thirty in the afternoon. It didn't really occur to me how much we would be rushing today.

Alessandro checks his watch. 'We're going to have to be quick.'

He won't tell me why, but thanks to his deadline we literally have to run through the streets of one of Italy's most beautiful cities. There's no time to stop and take anything in. The streets become narrower and busier and then we turn a corner and *BAM*, right there in front of us is an astonishingly striking building. It's enormous – I have no idea how we didn't catch sight of it earlier – but now it's all I can see. The outer walls are decorated with a stunning grey and white pattern. At one end is a soaring bell tower and at the other, an enormous octagonal-shaped red-brick dome.

'The third largest church in the world behind St Peter's in Rome and St Paul's Cathedral in London,' Alessandro tells me. 'Dedicated to Santa Maria del Fiore, the Virgin of the Flower.'

No one has ever sent me a postcard of *this*.

'I'd love to see inside.'

He checks his watch again. 'It closes at four thirty. Let's go.'

The front of the building is even more striking. It's faced with marble panels in shades of pistachio and apricot, bordered by white.

Once we're through the front doors, we have time to wander and take everything in. The underside of the dome is painted with a representation of the Last Judgement and I stand and stare up at the glorious artwork for a while before realising that Alessandro is no longer with me.

I find him over by a beautiful tree-shaped candelabra. Dozens of tealights flicker prettily at the end of its 'branches', and as I approach, I see him drop some coins into a money-box and pick up two unlit candles. He places them in empty branch spaces and lights them with a match.

It's only then that he notices me, holding eye contact for the briefest of moments. He doesn't seem to mind that I'm there so I continue forward until I've reached his side.

We stand and stare at the flickering candles.

'I was out for a wander last Sunday and saw you coming out of a church,' I admit.

He stiffens and glances at me. 'Why didn't you say anything?'

'You were walking away too quickly for me to call out.'

My gaze drops to the gold chain glinting against his skin. I reach up and gently extract the tiny cross pendant from beneath his black shirt.

'Did this belong to your mother?'

He nods, his expression conflicted. He turns slowly and pulls me into his arms.

At first I can't breathe, but then I melt into his embrace, feeling sick with a miserable sort of happiness as he holds me close.

'I've missed touching you,' he whispers. 'I know we shouldn't.'

I tense up, wondering why he would say that now when he didn't seem to think there was anything wrong with it before.

'Logan thought there was more to us,' he explains. 'He was worried I was sending mixed signals.'

I don't say anything, but I'm frozen.

'I just want so badly to be close to you,' he adds.

I tighten my grip on him because I want that too.

Even though it hurts.

The cathedral is closing so we have to break apart, but he takes my hand as we walk to the exit.

'The dome is open until seven p.m.,' he tells me. 'Shall we walk to the top and look at the view?'

'That sounds perfect.'

Several hundred steps later, I'm feeling less enthusiastic. Alessandro smiles at me as, once again, I have to come to a stop to catch my breath. He's not panting, not even slightly!

'It's all right for you, you climb mountains,' I mutter.

'We're almost there,' he replies encouragingly.

We come out onto the roof and stand amid the white marble pillars that hold up the decorative spire. The cathedral looms over everything else, with the exception of the nearby bell tower belonging to Palazzo Vecchio, and all around us is a city sprawling with red rooftops.

All of a sudden, I feel dizzy. Stumbling backwards, I seek out a pillar to clutch on to.

'You okay?' Alessandro asks with concern, his hand darting out to steady me.

'I've never been anywhere this high before,' I tell him, a cold flush washing over me.

'Are you afraid of heights, Angel?' he asks with mild amusement.

'I don't know. Am I?'

'I think you might be.'

He comes to stand at my side, leaning against the pillar and taking my hand again.

'This dome was designed by a competition winner, Filippo Brunelleschi, in 1418,' he tells me. 'It's still the largest brick dome ever constructed, capable of withstanding lightning and earthquakes and also, clearly, the passage of time,' he adds.

'Are you trying to distract me with your facts?' I ask.

'Is it working?'

'Not really.'

'You want to go down?'

I nod. 'Please.'

My dizziness passes as soon as we reach the staircase. But as we start to descend, I feel like a failure. What a missed opportunity.

We'll never do Florence justice in the time that we have and it's hardly worth visiting Siena at all. I'm sure it'll be lovely in the dark, but I'd like to see it in the daytime.

Maybe I should stay the night in Florence and catch the train to Rome via Siena tomorrow.

'Do you want to stay the night here?' Alessandro asks as we come out into the daylight.

I spin round. 'Could we?'

He smiles at the look on my face as he gets out his phone. 'I'll call Giulio. He shouldn't mind covering me for another day.'

I'm so happy and relieved. I was dreading the thought of trying to work out Florence's train system.

'All fine,' he says when he's ended the call. 'Shall we check out hotel options?'

'Will you stay in one too?' I ask curiously.

He shakes his head. 'I'll sleep in Frida.'

'Can't I—' I stop short.

'You want to sleep in Frida too?' he asks with pleasant surprise. 'You can crash in with me if you want to. The bench seat folds down.'

'Okay.' I grin at him.

With that decision made, we don't have to rush. Alessandro

wants to show me the view from a lookout point at sunset, so we make our way to the van at a leisurely pace, stopping at a cosy Enoteca for a bite to eat.

Back in Frida, we drive a short distance before crossing over the river and winding up a hill. The landscape around us becomes very lush, and then Alessandro pulls off the road into an open-air car park.

'Piazzale Michelangelo,' he says, finding a place to stop. He climbs between the two front seats and opens his tiny fridge, pulling out a bottle of prosecco.

'I thought we might make it for sunset drinks somewhere,' he tells me, grabbing a couple of tin mugs.

Sitting on a wall, we gaze down on one of the most stunning city skylines in the world. Even from this distance, the cathedral looks huge, dwarfing everything around it.

The sun reflects off the river, shining through the bridges' arches as it sets. To the right, behind the cathedral, the hills are hazy, graduating in darkness and colour from inky mauve to bluey-grey.

The cathedral walls glow orange and its dome and all of the red-tiled rooftops flame a brilliant red. I can barely breathe, it's so beautiful.

I realise that Alessandro is watching me.

'You're missing the sunset,' I murmur.

'The look on your face is better than the view.'

I purse my lips at him, but I realise he's not joking.

'I wish I could see the world through your eyes,' he says wistfully.

'I wish you could show me the world,' I reply, and I mean it.

Pain lances his features.

'What's wrong?'

He recovers, but doesn't answer me. Instead he asks, 'Do you like it here?'

I nod. 'This is the country I've dreamed of visiting more than any other and it's everything I wanted it to be.'

'And things are going well with Giulio?'

'Really well,' I reply. 'I'm feeling comfortable with him now and I know we'll only grow closer with time.'

'I noticed how relaxed he is around you. I think he was nervous at first.'

'So was I.'

'I'm glad you're getting to know each other, and also Serafina—'

'Nonna,' I correct him.

'Yes,' he says with a smile. 'The whole family is happy that you're here.'

'Why are *you* so sad?' I ask with concern.

He pauses before answering. 'I have to leave soon.'

'Leave? Where are you going?'

'Roaming. My six months at *Serafina's* are almost up.'

'What do you mean?'

'I set off on my travels in a couple of weeks.'

'But I thought you worked at *Serafina's* all summer?' I can hear the panic in my voice.

He shakes his head. 'I've been there for five and a half months already.'

How did I not know this? He suggested when we first spoke that I spend the summer in Rome and I guess I assumed he would be around, but I realise now that not once has anyone specified the time of year Alessandro comes to Rome.

If he's planning to leave at the end of July, that means I'll be in Rome for over a month without him.

It frightens me how much the thought of this upsets me.

'I wanted to get you settled with Giulio and the rest of the family before I left, so I am glad you are happy.'

'I'm not happy now,' I tell him, my insides churning. 'I don't want you to go.'

'I'm not ready to say goodbye to you either, but I must.'

'Why? What's the rush?'

'I can't explain.'

'Please, Alessandro!'

'I can't. I don't fully understand why things are the way they are, but it's something I'm unable to control.'

I stare at him with anguish, but he's looking straight ahead, his face etched with concentration.

'The city is lighting up,' he prompts me after a moment.

I tear my eyes away from him to look at the view. The lights along the river are coming on, twinkling yellow in the darkening night, and the cathedral is up-lit by a golden glow.

'Let's go and set up for the night,' he says at last.

While I'm brushing my teeth, he puts down the bench seat into the bed position and lays out his sleeping bag and pillow.

'I only have one, so I'll use this,' he says of the orange quilted blanket that usually sits on top of the bench.

'Will you be warm enough?'

'I'll be fine.'

'Stay here with me for a bit,' I say. 'Shall we have another glass of prosecco?'

'Sure.' He barely drank a drop earlier. 'I should have left the bench in the upright position.'

'This is cosier.'

I crawl down to the end of the bed and wriggle into his sleeping bag. Resting my back against the rear window, I pat the space beside me. He joins me, knocking his mug against mine.

After a long drive earlier where we barely spoke, he now wants to know what I got up to in Venice. We talk for a while and sip our drinks. His sleeping bag is cosy and warm and I feel closer to him, knowing that he sleeps in it every night. At some point he draws the blanket over his legs.

'So tomorrow,' he says eventually, 'we will walk into Florence over Ponte Vecchio. It's an unusual medieval covered bridge that still has shops along it, like they did in the old days.'

'Sounds great.'

'Then we'll go to Piazza della Signoria. You would like to see the statue of David by Michelangelo?' he asks.

'Absolutely.'

'There's a replica outside Palazzo Vecchio, the town hall. The original was moved to the Gallerie dell'Accademia, but we could go to see it if you want. Also, the fountain of Neptune, and we should definitely visit Uffizi, the art museum. Am I boring you?' He's diverted when he notices me yawning.

'No! Sorry, it all sounds idyllic. I like listening to the way that you speak. Your voice is so slow and melodic. It's lovely.'

I put my empty mug on the countertop and wriggle down into a sleeping position. I can't be bothered to brush my teeth again.

'I should let you get some sleep,' he says.

'Stay.' I place my hand on his chest.

He doesn't lie down, and after a moment, he reaches beneath my hair and unfastens my headscarf, freeing my curls. He gently strokes his hand over my hair, rhythmically, again and again.

The warmth in my heart spreads outwards into every inch of my body.

I feel it and I know.

I'm falling in love with him.

Chapter 39

'*Sono terrorizzato.*'

I jolt awake at the sound of Alessandro speaking. Lifting my head, I stare at him in the darkness. I'd fallen asleep, nestled into his side, but he's still sitting up, leaning against the rear window. His eyes glint at me in the darkness as he runs his hand over my hair.

'Sorry, I didn't mean to wake you.'

'It's okay, I'm a light sleeper.'

He continues to stroke my hair soothingly, trying to lull me into dreamland again.

'Why did you say you were petrified?' I ask, not ready to be lulled.

His hand pauses. 'You understood that?'

I nod. Only because of its similarity to the word *terror*. I noticed the likeness while trying to memorise a list of vocabulary.

He sighs quietly, but doesn't answer.

I wriggle into a sitting position so we can talk on the same level.

'Why are you scared?'

He stares at me in the dark. 'This scares me,' he whispers, indicating the two of us.

Suddenly I feel insanely jittery.

'Don't be scared,' I say in a wavering voice, as if it were that simple. 'It's okay.'

His eyes drift to my lips and he shakes his head, looking away. 'It's not okay.'

'It *is* okay,' I argue, taking his hand and prompting him to look at me again.

'I don't want to hurt you.'

'Why will you hurt me?'

'I want to be close to you, but this has to stop. It can't go any further.'

'I don't understand.' I'm sure he's thinking about kissing me and I want him to, *desperately*. 'We're adults. We're capable of making our own decisions. If something is meant to be, we can't end it just because of some silly promise to Giulio.'

'It's not my promise to Giulio that I'm worried about.'

'Have you made a promise to someone else?'

He averts his gaze.

'Who? Yourself?'

He doesn't answer.

'I care about you,' I say. 'A *lot*.'

'That's what I'm afraid of.'

'You're worried that I'll try to stop you from doing something you're passionate about? Well, I won't. Not if it means that much to you. I'll hate it whenever you throw yourself off a cliff, but I'll learn to cope.'

'I jumped yesterday,' he divulges and fear zips through my

body. He sounds agonised when he continues. 'Usually it's the only thing that makes me feel free. That moment when I jump, that pure and utter clarity of mind… I'm focused, first on falling and then on surviving. But yesterday…' He shakes his head. 'Yesterday I wasn't focused on the jump. I was focused on you.'

Warmth replaces some of my fear, but then I realise he's not confessing to something he's happy about.

'I thought of you as I fell. I lost focus, lost the ability to count, pulled my chute too late.'

Now the horror is overwhelming.

'I made it down safely, but it shocked me.'

'Maybe that's a sign that you should stop jumping,' I say in as calm a manner as I'm capable of.

He shakes his head manically. 'I can't. I'll never stop.'

His fervour seems almost pathological. I know he won't be able to explain if I ask him to, so I don't even suggest he try.

'I'm sorry for waking you,' he says abruptly. 'Come on, we should get some sleep.'

He shifts down in an attempt to show me that he means it.

Hesitantly I follow his lead, but I can't take my eyes off him.

He's lying on his back, staring at the ceiling. My insides are breaking apart. I don't know how to help him.

I reach over and brush my hand across his jaw before placing it on his chest. He breathes in sharply and covers my hand with his.

He's still staring at the ceiling when I finally allow my eyes to close.

Chapter 40

It doesn't surprise me when Alessandro reverts to diffidence on our return to Rome. But I'm not standing for it. Not now. Not after that conversation in Florence.

'Oi,' I call to him when he walks past the stockroom. I'm inside, getting a fresh apron.

He halts and turns around, standing at the door. 'What's up?'

'Come here.'

He hesitantly walks inside, glancing over his shoulder.

My father is in the kitchen with Antonio and Maria, and Cristina is setting tables. We're the only other ones here.

'What is it?' he asks, his expression unsmiling.

He looks especially gorgeous today, a shadow of stubble gracing his jaw.

I walk over to him and slip my arms around his waist. 'I need a hug.'

'Not here.' His green eyes flash as he takes my wrists and

unloops my arms from around his waist. His gaze drops to my lips before he quickly looks away. I feel skittish as I change the subject.

'Where did you see my parents together?' I ask. It's something I've been wondering.

He frowns. 'When do you mean?'

'That night, when you were a boy. Where did you see them?'

'Here, in the stockroom,' he replies, nodding at the far wall.

A shiver goes down my spine and I turn and look around. *Is this where I was conceived?*

'How come you're not angrier about their affair?' It's another question I've been meaning to ask.

He seems to consider this. 'I guess I understood why Giulio longed to be with someone else, because I did too. I always preferred coming to *Serafina's* to staying at home with my mother. He must have felt very guilty, because *I* felt guilty.'

I take a step towards him.

'Jacopo is coming in today,' he says abruptly. Before I can feel too pleased he adds, 'He and Valentina turn eighteen next week so Jacopo's going to run the bar while I'm away.'

My mouth falls open as he walks out of the stockroom.

It's like watching water tumbling over rocks. The river is determinedly surging onward and you're powerless to stop it.

I thought I had two weeks to soften Alessandro up and make him think twice about leaving, but with every day that passes, the task seems to grow more impossible.

He's putting things in order, getting his ducks in a row. He even takes the time to help me plan a trip to Capri and the Amalfi coast for the week after next, showing me which trains and ferries to catch and talking me through everything on a map.

At least he's attending Valentina and Jacopo's birthday celebrations on Sunday – Giulio is closing the restaurant for the day. They're having a party at home with all their friends and family – Loreta, Boris, Melissa and Otello are coming from Venice, and Francesca and Pepe from Bologna.

Giulio is heading to Tivoli a day early to help prepare the food and Alessandro will drive Cristina, Stefano and me on Sunday. Cristina and Stefano are staying the night with friends who live nearby, and Giulio and I will sleep in the house. I'm bunking in with Valentina. Alessandro, of course, will stay in Frida.

He comes to collect us early on Sunday afternoon. I invite him in because Cristina isn't quite ready.

'More postcards,' he murmurs, picking up a small stack from the dresser.

Quite a few came for me while I was away: Cathy telling me about her daughter's reaction to the personalised wedding card I'd left for her to give; Rita and Jan sharing the wonderful news that she's pregnant after trying for a baby for so long; Pasha, my Russian miner friend, informing me that he'd received an A for the Open University dissertation I was helping him write before I left; Jimmy divulging that he'd shared the wine I gave him with Bonnie, Mick, Vera and Laszlo on his late wife Vicky's birthday – they raised a glass to me.

'Do you miss them?' Alessandro asks.

I nod. 'Especially Jimmy and Bonnie. I worry about Jimmy

at home on his own, and Bonnie. Even though she has Mick, she used to spend much of her time at Nan's with me. Mick still mines every day and Bonnie is retired so she was often seeking company.' I'm glad she and Jimmy have been seeing a lot of each other since I've been away. 'As for my other friends,' I continue, 'Facebook keeps me in touch with most of them, so they don't feel that far away.'

'They message you on Facebook, yet they still send you postcards.'

I shrug and give him a small smile. 'It's my thing.'

'How are you feeling about going home in September?'

My lips turn down. 'Conflicted. I'm looking forward to seeing everyone and there are things I need to sort out, but I do want to come back to Italy soon.' The paternity test returned positive for Giulio so we're on the right track – I'm so delighted. The thought that I might end up with an Italian visa so I can come and go as I like gives me such a thrill, but I'm trying not to get my hopes up until I know for sure it will happen. 'I'd love to spend Christmas in Tivoli,' I say longingly.

His eyes dart to mine and the pain on his face takes my breath away. Before I can ask him what's wrong, Cristina comes out of her room. 'Ready!'

Alessandro puts down the postcards and opens the front door.

The Marchesis have gone all out on this one. Colourful pompoms, paper chains and stars hang from the trees and the large trestle table outside is laden with a delicious assortment of antipasti and bottles of booze on ice. Live music fills the air courtesy of Jacopo and Valentina's school friends, and several dozen people are mingling, chatting, eating and drinking on the top terrace by the house.

Even Carlo and Bruno are here – I've already gone over to say hi, and apart from a slightly awkward moment of Carlo blushing after our double-kiss greeting, we chatted amiably.

Now the afternoon has spilled into evening and the festoon lights hanging from the trees have been turned on. People have started to dance, with Stefano, predictably, leading the charge. He's in a good mood because he got a call-back for the soap opera he auditioned for. I have my fingers crossed for him.

Cristina finds me when I'm on the terrace talking to Melissa. My cousin goes off in search of Otello.

'Hey,' I say to Cristina, scanning the crowd for Alessandro. I find him over by the band, with Jacopo.

'I kissed Lindsey last night,' she blurts.

Now she has my full attention. 'Did you?'

She nods, blushing.

'How was it?'

She shrugs, but her eyes are sparkling. 'It was sort of great.'

'That's a good start!' I say with a laugh.

'I don't know how it happened. One minute we were dancing, the next we were dancing closer and then we were kissing. I don't even know who made the first move, but there you are.'

'Have you been in touch with her today?'

'She texted me earlier.'

'What did she say?'

'She wanted to know if I was free for lunch, but I had this going on.'

'You're free tomorrow though, right?'

'Do you think I should text her?'

'Of *course* you should!'

She grins and gets out her mobile phone.

Alessandro is still standing with Jacopo, but they're not talking.

Stefano comes over to help himself to another beer from the ice bucket and drapes a slightly sweaty arm around my shoulders.

'You love him, don't you?' he asks, following the line of my sight.

'Stefano!' Cristina erupts, overhearing.

I tense and give Stefano a look of alarm.

'It's obvious,' he says with a shrug, taking a swig of his beer.

I glance at Cristina and she also nods and shrugs. 'Very.'

My shoulders slump. Cristina's phone rings and she takes the call, walking away from us a few paces. I have a feeling it's Lindsey.

'It's hopeless, in any case,' I say to Stefano, returning my gaze to Alessandro.

'Well, yeah, we all know that,' he replies flippantly.

Despite myself, I flash him a smile, albeit a weary one.

'How could he have been attracted to Teresa?' I mutter. 'Apart from the obvious…'

'Teresa charmed him like she did all of the customers,' Stefano says facetiously. 'And Susanna is spoiled – she desired Alessandro and she wasn't going to stop until she got him.'

I sigh. 'It doesn't matter anyway. Like Cristina said, he'll never lay a hand on me.'

'Why not?' Stefano asks.

'He wouldn't disrespect Giulio by taking it further.'

'Pfft.' He's dismissive. 'Alessandro will do whatever Alessandro wants to do. Not that I think you *should* pursue him. He's a bit of a strange one, if you ask me. Why don't you find yourself a nice boy like Carlo? Or me?' he suggests cheekily.

'Yeah, yeah.' I pat his chest good-naturedly.

'Fine. If you don't want Carlo, maybe I'll attempt to sway him from the straight and narrow.'

'I knew it!' I exclaim, leaping out of his grasp and pointing at him.

'I like men *and* women, Angel. Don't put a label on me.'

I shake my head at him, amused.

'Enough of this serious talk,' he snaps. 'Let's go dance.' He grabs my hand and pulls me towards the band.

Alessandro is no longer there, but I see him on and off throughout the night. I still get this sense that he's on the outside looking in.

It's how I felt when I first came to Italy, but I don't understand his self-imposed distance. I know he's not cold and standoffish at heart, so why does he project that aura to everyone?

I've been trying to give him some space today, trying to prove to myself – and him – that I can be happy independently, but sometimes I catch his eye, and his expression is a baffling mixture of emotions. He seems content, but also somehow desperately sad, and there's another sentiment there that I can't quite put my finger on.

The next time our eyes meet, I don't look away. And

neither does he. I jolt as he starts towards me, coming to a stop a metre away.

'Walk with me a moment?' he asks, his gaze still locked with mine.

I nod, feeling nervy.

We leave the glow of the party lights behind and set off down the hill, the short grass beneath our feet growing longer and wilder as we near the river.

'I used to love playing in this river,' he confides. 'I'd make boats out of paper and put them in up there.' He points to his left. 'Then I'd try to race them down here.' He nods at his grandparents' house. The whitewashed walls are gleaming under the moonlight. 'I rarely won.'

'Does anyone live here now?' I ask as we come to a stop.

He shakes his head.

I figured as much. There's something about it that feels dark and empty.

'Carlotta also loved the river,' he says. 'I lived in fear of her falling in. You had to watch her like a hawk. She was as quick as lightning when she wanted to do something.' He sighs. 'She would have turned twenty-three tomorrow.'

My chest twinges with sympathy. 'I'm sorry, I feel like I should have known that. Her birthday is so close to Valentina and Jacopo's.'

He nods sadly.

'I'm glad you came to their party,' I say.

'I didn't want to miss it.'

'Alessandro, why are you still so distant with your family?' I ask. 'And please don't tell me that they're not your family, because they don't see it that way. They love you. It's as clear as day. Don't you think it's time you *let* them love you? Don't you think it's time to forgive yourself?'

He stiffens and stares at me, his expression tight and wary.

'Your grandparents forgave you for disappearing,' I continue gently as he turns his attention to the river. 'And it was right of them to do that. No one should have had to go through what you went through. You were only a young boy. You can't be blamed for running away and everything that happened afterwards. Any behaviour would have been understandable considering that level of trauma. And Giulio, Serafina, Eliana, Loreta, they all forgive you too, I'm sure, not that I believe there was ever anything to forgive. I really think it's time you forgave yourself,' I repeat.

He exhales heavily and turns to face me. The festoon lights up at the house glint in his eyes as he gives me a sad smile.

'You've got your halo on again,' he murmurs, reaching up to touch my hair. It must be backlit by the lights. 'You have the purest heart of anyone I've ever known, Angel,' he adds, brushing my cheek with his thumb. 'Please just let me hold you.'

My heart quickens as he draws me into his arms. I tighten my grip on him, but we're still not close enough. I don't know how much more separation my body can take.

Off in the distance, the band is playing a slow song. The hard muscles on his back ripple beneath my fingers as we turn a half circle. I lift my face away from his neck and find myself staring directly at his mouth. His lips have parted and in the closeness of our contact, I can feel his chest expanding against mine in short, sharp inhalations.

But he never runs out of breath.

My eyes dart upwards and my own breath hitches. There's heat in his expression.

'Alessandro?'

He lifts his hands to cup my face and we stare at each other in the darkness.

'*Che Dio mi perdoni*,' he whispers, tormented.

Then he brings his hot, dry mouth down to mine.

My heart had stopped, but now it jolts violently to life, and the bolt of electricity zipping through my veins is so powerful that I feel as though I've been branded.

At first, our kiss is slow and tentative, our tongues exploring each other's mouths, but then something happens – some sort of chemical reaction that kicks in and makes everything speed up.

My hands fist in his T-shirt, our hips pressed hard against each other. I gasp as his body moves against mine, walking me backwards until my back hits the wall of his mother's childhood home. He lifts up my legs and hooks them around his waist, kissing me fiercely. My whole body is overwrought with desire and need, and I know it's the same for him – I can *feel* it. I want him to take me right here and now, and that shows how insane he's making me because the party is happening a hundred metres up the hill.

With a low agonised moan that seems to come from deep in his gut, he rips himself away from me. That's what it feels like – a physical wrench.

'Wait.' I reach out to snag his wrist.

He's panting heavily and shaking his head as he detaches me.

'Tell me what's wrong?' I demand to know.

'Everything's wrong,' he tells me unsteadily. 'I shouldn't have done that.'

'Nothing's wrong,' I state firmly. 'This is right.'

'No.' He shakes his head. 'No. *You are not meant for me!*'

What does that *mean?*

But I don't get a chance to ask because he turns and stalks away, leaving me staring with despair after him, my back still pressed against the cold, crumbling walls of his late grandparents' home.

For the rest of the night, I look for him, but he's nowhere to be seen. In the early hours of the morning, I leave the house in search of his van, only to find that Frida is no longer there.

Chapter 41

Giulio gives me a lift home the next day after a mammoth clean-up operation. I'd never normally shirk hard work, but I'm itching to get going. I can't shake my concerns about Alessandro. He's not answering my calls. All I want is to get to *Serafina's* so I can see his face and reassure him that everything is going to be okay.

When we do finally roll into the car park later that afternoon, his van is not there.

'He'll come back, don't worry,' Giulio tells me, unconcernedly.

The next morning I go into work early and, once again, my blood runs cold at the sight of the empty car park.

I pop my head around the door of the kitchen.

'Where's Alessandro?'

'He's probably at confession,' Giulio replies dismissively.

'Did he come home last night?'

'I don't know. I went to bed early with a headache.'

He did drink a lot at the party.

'What do you mean confession?' I backtrack, registering what he said.

'Confession. Church. He goes every week.'

'What's he confessing to?' I ask aloud, aware as I say it that it's a stupid question.

'I don't know,' Giulio replies with a chuckle. 'It's between him and the priest and the man upstairs.' He points at the ceiling.

'I didn't know he was so religious,' I murmur, wondering how many other secrets the man might be capable of keeping.

Giulio shrugs. 'He never used to be. He once told me that he found God at the top of a mountain. He said he stood way up high in the sky and looked at a church in the valley and decided to go down and confess. I think he's been going ever since.'

I recall the night of the party, when Alessandro uttered something about God – *Dio* – before he kissed me. What was it he said? It sounded like pardon. I remember: '*perdoni*'. I look it up. It means 'forgive'.

And then the rest of his sentence comes back to me: *'Che Dio mi perdoni.'*

'May God forgive me.'

But why?

Another day passes and there's still no sign of Alessandro.

'I'm worried about him,' I tell Giulio.

We're standing on the roof of St Peter's Basilica in Vatican City after climbing goodness only knows how many hundreds of steps to get up here. I was worried about the strain on Giulio's heart, but he managed it with less huffing and puffing than I did.

He's been wanting to bring me here ever since telling me that he once came with my mother. Unfortunately, I'm now too miserable to enjoy it.

'*Si*.' My father sighs, sounding glum. 'I think he might be gone. He's done this before, setting off on his travels without telling anyone. He has a date in his mind that we all work towards and then he ups and leaves. I don't think he likes saying goodbye. That's Alessandro. He can be very selfish sometimes.'

'No.' I shake my head, gazing out past the big white stone statues of Jesus, St John the Baptist and the eleven other Apostles that line the front elevation of the roof. Down below is the vast expanse of St Peter's Square and beyond is the city's skyline and a multitude of church domes glinting under the piercingly bright morning sunlight. We came early to avoid the crowds.

'Alessandro is not selfish,' I protest. 'I don't believe that. There must be another reason he disappears like this.'

'The boy is a mystery,' Giulio declares. 'You will never understand him so it's best not to try. He comes and he goes and he comes and he goes. And he will come again and go again. You'll get used to it.'

I try not to show that I'm fighting back tears.

'He needs to get away,' he adds. 'He's not a city boy at heart.'

Such a simple explanation, but I feel like there's more to it.

*

I don't know how I get through the week. I even drop Lea a line on Facebook to ask if she or Logan have heard from Alessandro, but they haven't. Alessandro is not returning my texts or calls and his phone keeps ringing out and going through to voicemail. I can't believe that he left without saying goodbye, and I can't imagine heading home to Australia without seeing him before I go. I'm due to set off to the Amalfi coast and Capri next week, but my heart isn't in it.

Bonnie calls me that weekend when I'm lying on my bed, turning my opal around and around in my fingers.

'I was just thinking of you!' I exclaim. I've been wanting to phone her, needing to offload to someone about Alessandro, but I knew she'd steer me away from him and that was not something I wanted to hear. I find it a lot easier to give advice than take it, I'm discovering.

'Oh, Angie.' Her voice is choked with emotion.

'What is it?'

'He told me not to tell you, but I can't keep any more secrets from you. Jimmy's not well, darling.'

'What's wrong?'

'It's cancer, Angie. Pancreatic, the same as Vicky. He doesn't have long.'

Oh no... Please, no...

'He didn't want me to say, didn't want it to ruin your holiday, but perhaps you should call him.'

'I will. Right away,' I reply, swallowing down the lump in my throat.

Jimmy sounds tired when he answers. It's only eight p.m. in Coober Pedy.

'Jimmy? It's me, Angie.'

'She didn't bloody tell you, did she?' he gripes. 'I knew she wouldn't be able to keep it to herself!'

'I'm so sorry,' I mumble, tears filling my eyes. 'I'm going to change my flight and come home early.'

'That's the last thing I want you to do!' He is practically shouting. 'The only thing that's making me smile right now is the thought of you running around Italy, enjoying yourself. If you come home early, it'll do me more harm than good, I promise you that.'

'Oh, Jimmy,' I murmur.

'Don't, sweetheart,' he mutters. 'I'm okay. I'm ready. It's time to go and see my Vicky.'

I stifle a sob.

'You know, when your grandad died, Angie, you were the only person who didn't think it should've been me.'

'That's not true!' I gasp. '*No one* thought that!'

'Oh, they all did, darling,' he replies casually. 'And I understood. I had no family to support, I'd lost my Vicky the year before, I didn't have a whole lot to live for, to be honest. But you didn't see it that way.'

'Of course I didn't!'

'You're such a special person, Angie. You were only seventeen years old, but you came to see me in the hospital, do you remember?'

I nod, but realise he can't see me so I mumble a yes through my tears.

'You were so sad about your grandad, but you sat there with me after my op and held my hand and you cried when I told you it should've been me. You actually cried and told me not ever to say that again.'

'I want to come home.'

'Don't you dare!' he yells. 'I don't want to see you, do you hear me? Hearing your voice is enough.'

'It was you, wasn't it? You gave me that opal. The hundred-carat one.' I still have it in my hand and my fist squeezes around it, but it brings no comfort.

'Yeah,' he says quietly after a long pause. 'That one had your name written all over it.'

My heart hurts so much. I long to reach through the phone line and give him a big hug, but I can't.

'I still have it, you know,' I tell him.

'Why the bloody hell haven't you sold it?'

'I like it too much. It reminds me of home, and also of Grandad in a funny way.'

'Well, it did come from our mine. Your grandad used his cut to buy a car and take you on holiday. I always thought my share would find its way into your hands, one day. I only hope it comes in useful.'

'Jimmy?' I ask in a husky voice when I'm ready to speak.

'Yes, love?'

'Try to hang on until September, okay? That's when I'll be home and I want to give you a hug.'

'Deal,' he replies.

I decide to postpone my trip to Capri. I'm still worried about Alessandro, and now there's this news about Jimmy to contend with.

I drop Lea another line on Facebook to ask if Logan can put the word out amongst his old base-jumping buddies to see if anyone has heard of or seen Alessandro.

Logan himself calls me the next morning.

'Lea tells me you're worried about Allez.'

'Have you heard from him?' I ask hopefully.

'No, not a thing. He's probably on his way to Norway. That's where he said he was headed. It's a long drive.'

'Do you know exactly where he planned to go?'

'Kjerag and Trollveggen, I think. There's a base-jumping place at Lysebotn, near Kjerag, so you might be able to call and leave a message for him.'

'That's a great idea! Thank you!'

'No problem.'

'Logan,' I ask hesitantly. 'Can you tell me about how you guys met?' I still feel like there's something I'm missing. 'Alessandro said you met in the Dolomites. He was on a mountain when you and your friends turned up. He saw you again a couple of days later and you ended up having a chat.'

'Yeah, that's pretty much it.'

Logan falls silent, but when I press him, he sighs and comes clean.

'To be honest, I thought he was suicidal,' he admits. 'He was standing right on the edge of the cliff. We thought he was one of us, until we realised he wasn't wearing a chute. My heart stopped. Then he saw us and stepped away from the edge.'

'What did you do?' My heart is in my throat.

'We went ahead and jumped, like the selfish pricks that we were back then. We'd climbed all that way for the pay-off and wanted the adrenalin rush, like, *yesterday*. But later I couldn't stop thinking about that guy on the mountain. I even checked the news to see if there had been any suicides. A couple of days later, I saw him again.'

'That was when you stopped and spoke to him?'

'Yeah. I wanted to make up for my previous mistake. He seemed interested in base jumping so I told him about a mate of mine…'

The rest of the story is as Alessandro told it.

Days later, I'm at work when Giulio blows his top at Jacopo. A customer has sent back coffees because they're not hot enough.

'Are you okay?' I ask my cousin because he looks shaky.

'Yeah.' He nods. 'He's always touchy at this time of year.'

'What is it about this time of year?' I ask with a frown.

'Tomorrow is the anniversary of Carlotta's death.'

It's as though someone has switched on a lightbulb over my head. I go straight outside and ring Logan, willing him to pick up. It's nine o'clock in the morning in LA.

'Hello?'

'Logan!'

'Who's this?'

'It's Angie. Angel!'

'Oh, hey. Is everything okay?'

'I'm not sure. Logan, can you tell me something? Do you remember where you were when you last saw Alessandro jump recklessly?'

'Er, yeah, it was Chamonix in the French Alps.'

'Do you remember what time of year it was?'

'Summer.'

'Middle of August?'

'Could've been.'

'What about when you first saw him up on the mountain in the Dolomites?'

'It was also summer.'

'Can you be more specific? Can you remember any other occasions when he was behaving irresponsibly?'

'I could look them up,' he says. 'Most of my jumps are in my diary.'

'Great!' I exclaim.

'You think there's something about the dates?'

'I'm almost certain of it.'

'Let me check and I'll come back to you.'

He does, only ten minutes later, and he sounds confused when he asks, 'What the hell happened to him on the fourteenth and sixteenth of August?'

Chapter 42

Astrid and Magnus, my Bake Club friends from Coober Pedy, have a son, Erik, who lives in Stavanger, not far from Kjerag, which is the location where Logan believes Alessandro will be doing his first jump tomorrow. When I tell Astrid that it's where I'm headed, Erik gets in touch via Facebook to say that I can use his apartment. He and his family are away for the whole of August, but his neighbour has a key and will let me in.

'It's the least I can do after everything you've done for my parents,' he writes. 'Especially with my mother and her hip operation. My parents are very fond of you.'

I'm touched.

I can't get an evening flight so I book the first available the next morning, hoping I won't be too late.

My father drives me to the airport and, for once, he's quiet. I haven't shared my concerns about Alessandro's planned jumps – I promised that I wouldn't – but he must know I'm worried. He seemed shaken when I told him that I planned to fly to Norway to try to catch up with Alessandro.

'I have been blind,' he says, glancing across at me when he pulls up outside Departures. 'Venice... Florence...'

I shake my head. He thinks we stayed away as lovers. 'It wasn't like that at all. But I do care about him, Papà. A lot.'

'I can see that, but I didn't know how much.'

'I love him,' I say gently, and he flinches. 'It's not something you need to concern yourself with.'

'How can I not concern myself with this?' he erupts. 'Alessandro will do to you what he has done to all of the other girls in the past. He can't keep his—'

He launches into Italian at that point, too angry to continue in English.

'Calm down,' I say, after letting him rant for a while. 'This is not good for your blood pressure.'

He makes a noise of disgust.

'You make sure you're taking those tablets while I'm away.'

He grunts again and I sigh.

'Alessandro is different with me.'

He doesn't think much to this comment, either.

'I've seen a side of him that I don't think he shares lightly,' I continue.

Giulio is still muttering under his breath in Italian and I'm not even attempting to understand. I'd rather not know.

'He is still very deeply affected by his mother and sister's deaths, more than you realise. That's why he goes away like this, not because he's *selfish*.'

He falls silent.

I reach across and press his hand. 'Papà, it will be okay.

Whatever happens, I promise this will not affect our relationship.' I mean his and mine. I lean across and peck him on the cheek. 'I'll see you soon.'

I'm flying back to Australia out of Rome in three weeks.

I know he's not happy about it, but he'll survive.

If it's one thing that can be said about Giulio, he's a survivor.

It's a bright sunny morning when the plane touches down in Stavanger, but my stomach has tied itself in knots. I've worked out that there are ferries all the way down the Lysefjord to the tiny village of Lysebotn where the base jumpers set off from, but it takes two and a half hours and I'm terrified I'm not going to make it there in time. If I can't stop Alessandro from doing this jump, I at least want to try to catch up with him before he leaves for his next, but I might be too late even for that.

There's no way I can go to Erik's apartment first so I'm hot and sweaty when I arrive at the docks, carrying Cristina's borrowed backpack over my shoulder. Boarding the ferry, I go upstairs and stand by the railing, too nervous to sit down. I barely register the Scandinavian architecture: the pitched roofs and gleaming weatherboarded houses that rise up the hill away from the docks.

We leave the city behind and head past rocky islands topped with conifers. Soon we're in the Lysefjord, a long 42-kilometre stretch of water that will come to an abrupt end at Lysebotn.

The granite cliffs on either side of the boat slice straight through the water like knives. At one point, I hear other passengers mention Pulpit Rock and follow the lines of their pointed fingers to a high cliff up on our left that looks like a small stone cube placed on top of the mountain.

Some of the cliff faces are so sheer that nothing is capable of growing on them, but other jagged plateaus are alive with greenery and there are even a few goats living on one steep slope.

It all feels otherworldly, but I'm too stressed to enjoy it.

What if Alessandro is not in Lysebotn? What if he's changed his mind about where he's jumping? I've tried calling the base-jumping place a couple of times, but no one has answered the phone. It's probably best that he doesn't know I'm coming, in any case.

As the boat draws closer to Lysebotn, I go to stand at the front, a nervous, shaking wreck. My heart leaps.

Frida is parked by the shore.

I don't know what drove Alessandro to begin jumping from cliffs on the anniversaries of his sister and mother's deaths, but it's clearly a ritual he goes through every year, regardless of the weather conditions. If it's safe, he jumps. If it's dangerous, he jumps. That was the behaviour that Logan witnessed – a compulsive need to jump, even at the risk of his own life.

It's crazy. Frighteningly crazy. I have no experience with mental illness and the thought of trying to make Alessandro see sense scares the hell out of me. All I know is that I've got to try.

Logan suspected that Alessandro was suicidal when he first saw him on that mountaintop. Maybe he was, and maybe he *still* is. There was something about the way he was with me at the party that felt final.

'I just want to hold you…'

He could have added 'one last time.'

And there was the way I caught him watching me over the course of the evening. So many conflicting emotions crossed his face that I couldn't make sense of them all. I believe I saw joy and sorrow, but most worryingly, I believe I saw acceptance.

I think he considered it his duty to settle me in Rome. He was pleased to hear from me when I first called from Australia, happy to bring me to Italy to be close to Giulio. He's done everything he possibly could to make me feel at ease in an alien environment. From his late-night tour of Rome to the way he reluctantly went with me to visit my family for the first time, to how he came over and watched a film with me when I was feeling homesick. He's taken on the role of protector, settler, comforter.

Yet everyone else sees him as selfish.

Is he selfish? Did he do all of this for his own ends? In what way? How is my existence, my happiness to be in Rome, settled with my father, helping *him*?

And then it comes to me and the fear is so debilitating and dizzying that I have to grip on to the railings to stop myself from passing out.

I don't think Alessandro ever saw me as a replacement for Carlotta.

I think he saw me as a replacement for himself.

Chapter 43

My heart is pounding as I run over to the van and try the side door. It's locked. I peer through the window, not caring if I'm about to give Alessandro a heart attack. I have to know he's okay.

But Frida is dark and empty. I look around and see the base-jumping place, but that door is also locked.

Hurrying around the side of the building, I jolt to a stop at the sight of a lone guy sitting at a bench table, reading a book.

'Hi!'

He looks up.

'Excuse me, I'm looking for a base jumper. Alessandro? Do you know him?'

He shrugs. 'I think so, but the group has already left. They should be coming down in about an hour and a half.'

I'm too late!

'What are the conditions like?' I ask in a panic. 'Are they okay?'

He gives me a funny look. 'They're fine. Great. They wouldn't be jumping if they weren't.'

Relief sweeps through me. If everyone else is jumping, at least I know Alessandro isn't being reckless.

'Where do they come down from?' I ask.

He points at the fjord. 'A little way along there. You can come with me for the boat ride, if you like?'

'Can I?'

'Yeah, you need to buy a ticket from the shop. I'll be leaving in about an hour.'

'The shop is closed.'

'That's fine, pay for it later.'

I have a feeling he wants to return to his book.

There's a small café over by the water so I go and buy myself a cup of tea to kill time, but my hands are shaking so much that it's hard to drink it.

Alessandro is an experienced jumper, I try to reassure myself. *If the weather is good, he'll be okay.*

But until I know *for sure* that he's landed safely, I'm going to continue to feel sick to my stomach.

I'm too fidgety to stay seated so I get up and go for a walk across a stretch of grass that's dotted with purple and pink bell-shaped wildflowers. Someone has built a sculpture out of white pebbles by the shore – I go to have a closer look. A noisy waterfall cascades down the cliff face on my left, and straight ahead is a view of the Lysefjord. The cliffs make a V-shape on either side of the glassy water, sloping diagonally outwards instead of the vertical sheer drops of the cliffs on the way here. Their image is reflected up at them like a mirror.

There can't be many places on this earth that are more idyllic.

Not wanting to miss the boat, I go and wait by the dock.

After a while, the guy I saw earlier comes over.

'Okay?' I ask.

'Yep.' He climbs down the ladder and gets into a small boat, then holds it steady for me to follow.

'Lifejackets are under the bench.'

That's about the most he says to me for the rest of the journey, but I'm okay with that. I'm not capable of small talk.

Very soon, the cliffs become vertical again, and then up ahead I see a windsock fixed to a rock, and a small red and white painted hut. The cliffs on the left fall away to a landslide of rocks which run into a steeply sloping grass patch strewn with boulders. This small piece of land is surrounded on three sides by water and behind it is a sheer cliff face. Once the base jumpers have landed down here, there would be no way to reach Lysebotn other than by boat.

My guide cuts the engine and we drift to a small platform adjoining a huge boulder. From there, a wooden walkway leads directly to the grassy slope.

'You can wait here and watch them come down,' he says. 'I've got to change to the dinghy in case anyone lands in the water.'

I climb out and watch as he motors over to a red inflatable dinghy attached to a buoy, and then I turn my attention to the cliffs above.

I don't know where I'm supposed to look. The top doesn't seem that far away, but I have a feeling the distance is deceptive. I sit on the boulder and, when my neck begins to feel sore from gazing upwards, I decide to lie down, using my backpack as a pillow. The wind is cold and I shiver, listening to the whirling, circling birds crying out, high in the sky. As the minutes tick by, my unease grows. How will Alessandro react when he finds me down here?

He left Italy because he wanted to be alone. I'm gate-crashing a deeply personal experience for him and he might well be upset or even angry at me. But I have to let him know that he's *not* alone, however much he thinks he wants to be.

I'm sure he never meant to develop real feelings for me, but somewhere along the way that happened. I *know* it happened. I think he might have even fallen in love with me, but he isn't capable of admitting it.

He isn't capable of accepting my love, either. He doesn't feel deserving of it – giving or receiving.

And I can't work out why that should be.

Is he still punishing himself for the years that he went away? Does he hate himself that much for abandoning his grandparents and Giulio in their grief?

Or is there, yet again, more to it than that?

'They're getting ready to come down!' the boat captain shouts over at me.

'Where?' I shout back, sitting up with a wave of intense nervous anticipation.

He points to the part of the cliff I need to watch. I get to my feet hurriedly and squint up at it, and suddenly, I see movement. The height *is* deceptive – the figures are so tiny, they're smaller than ants; no more than pinpricks. I can make out three people, no, four. But there could be others out of sight.

It's another few minutes before the first jumper takes off. I see him or her on the cliff edge and then they're no longer there. My eyes scan the cliff face and *there*! A small fleck against the grey granite rock. They're falling at a diagonal trajectory. I try to keep watching, my heart in my throat, and then I catch sight of another person following swiftly behind. All at once, there's a flash of colour and their parachutes burst open into red and blue canopies, tiny still against the grey of the cliffs. Their whoops of delight carry like bird calls across the wind as the parachutes glide through the air, twisting and turning, left and right, as they float towards the ground. It looks like they're going to touch down on the bigger boulders, which seems precarious – surely that's a good way to break bones – but they manage to land safely on the grass, one after the other.

Almost instantly I know that neither of them is Alessandro. I can barely make out their faces from this distance, but I can tell they're a couple of mates by the way they're excitedly calling across to each other as they pack away their parachutes.

I return my attention to the clifftop as another two jumpers launch themselves, one after the other. Are they wearing wingsuits?

I crane my neck as two figures fly right over my head, high, high in the sky. They look like flying squirrels. And then their brightly coloured parachutes open and they glide down to the sound of whoops and clapping from the guys on the ground.

When they land, I realise one of the jumpers is a woman. Still, no Alessandro.

Two more come down, one of whom lands in the water, something I gather he's not happy about from the tirade of swear words I'm hearing. My man in the boat zooms over to help pull him out at around the same time the first two jumpers – a couple of bearded, scruffy-looking lads – arrive at the boulder I'm sitting on.

One of them laughs at his comrade in the water and lifts his hand to high-five me. He thinks I'm a spectator, here to watch like a tourist.

I comply, not wanting to be rude, but I feel like I'm going to throw up. *Where is Alessandro? Have I got this wrong? Has he jumped from somewhere else?*

'Is there anyone else still up there?' I ask the high fiver.

He looks around to see who's come down. 'Yeah, Allez. He likes to jump last,' he adds, slightly mockingly.

We both squint up at the clifftop, and then I see him, a lone figure, standing on the edge.

And then he's no longer there.

He doesn't fly outwards away from the cliff, nor does he come down diagonally.

With air choked out of my lungs, I watch him fall almost straight down.

I don't know how many seconds he falls for: ten, fifteen… They're the longest seconds of my life.

Please, please, please, I beg, my heart in my throat, and then his chute bursts open, devoid of bright colours. I'm standing and watching, not taking my eyes off him for a millisecond as he glides to the ground to the sound of a few cheers and handclaps from the others. He lands right on the grass only thirty or forty metres away, and it's beautiful, graceful, his parachute billowing out behind him, black against the green grass and blue sky.

In that moment, right before he sees me, I know that he's happy and at peace. *Free.*

A wave of love and relief chases away the darkness as I start towards him.

Chapter 44

Alessandro's eyes lock with mine and he freezes.

His parachute is still attached to his backpack, still billowing in the wind, and his arms hang at his sides, his hair lifting from his neck in the breeze. He hasn't shaved since I last saw him, but despite the extra bulk his beard adds, he looks as if he's lost weight.

He's dressed as usual in black – a long-sleeved T-shirt and black pants – but his clothes seem ordinary, not special gear like the padded tracksuits or wingsuits belonging to the other jumpers.

He watches me approach across the rock-strewn grass, his expression fathomless. I'm not seeing anger, nor am I seeing joy. Is it fear? And maybe wariness?

I come to a stop a few feet away, something about his stance warning me to keep my distance.

'That was for Carlotta?' I ask.

His head barely moves as he nods, never once taking his eyes from mine.

One of the guys on the boulder calls out, jolting him to attention.

'I've got to pack away my chute,' he mutters, unclicking his backpack and swinging it around to the ground. I stand and watch, not wanting to distract him as he meticulously folds up his parachute.

The sound of a motor has me looking over my shoulder. Our captain has swapped the dinghy for the bigger boat and the other jumpers are getting ready to board.

Alessandro doesn't say a word to me as we walk across the grass to the boat, but a couple of the others try to make conversation with him, one of them fist-bumping him. I'm not sure they notice or care that Alessandro's response is half-hearted; they're all too caught up in the adrenalin rush.

Alessandro sits opposite me at the bow of the boat, and for most of the return journey he watches me with that same impenetrable expression.

When we dock, he waits for me to climb up the ladder first, but while the others tail off to go around the side of the base-jumping building, Alessandro walks towards Frida.

'Are you coming?' he asks, seeing me hesitate.

'I need to pay for the boat ride.' I jerk my head towards the boat.

'Ah.' He opens Frida, swings his parachute inside, and closes the door behind him.

A couple of the base jumpers are inside the shop. I hear someone say 'troll' and wonder if they're talking about the place where Carl Boenish, the father of modern base jumping, lost his life.

'We're going to grab some lunch,' Alessandro tells the boat captain.

'See you back here this afternoon?' he replies.

Alessandro nods.

'What's happening this afternoon?' I ask as we make our way towards Frida.

'Last jump of the day.'

I'm taken aback. 'You're going up there again?'

He nods. 'Probably.'

Probably isn't definitely.

'Where are you staying?' he asks.

'Stavanger.'

'Hotel?'

'Apartment. It belongs to the son of some friends in Coober Pedy. He's gone away for the summer so said I could use it. I didn't have time to check it out before I came here.'

He doesn't say anything, merely opens up the passenger door to his van and waits until I'm seated before closing it after me and putting my bag in through the side door.

I still have no idea what he's thinking. I can't get a handle on his emotional state of mind at all.

We drive out of the village in total silence, but he doesn't turn right to go up the mountain road. Instead he drives straight on, past a couple of small houses, and parks near a green meadow.

'What are we doing?'

'Picnic,' he replies, slipping between the two front seats and grabbing a few bits and pieces to put in his rucksack.

We walk across a meadow dotted with sheep and flanked by mountains. There's a river tumbling noisily over big grey boulders beside us, and ahead is a wooded walkway, sun streaming down between the trees. We come to a footbridge and cross over, the white foam crashing and splicing between slick, dark rocks beneath. It's so green and lush on the other side of the river that I can barely believe my eyes. Moss as thick as shaggy sheep wool clings to the branches and tree trunks, and the rocks that occasionally cross our track are slippery with river spray. It's like paradise.

We come to a grassy clearing surrounded by enormous boulders. To my surprise, there's a picnic table right here in the middle of nowhere.

Alessandro unpacks his rucksack, getting out a loaf of crusty bread, a chunk of cheese and a couple of cans of soft drink. Using a Swiss Army knife, he hacks off slices of cheese and makes two sandwiches.

'Thank you.' When is one of us going to say something about what I'm doing here?

I don't know where to start.

Finally he meets my eyes.

We stare at each other for a long, drawn-out moment. He still has that same strange, serious look on his face, but I feel less wary of him now.

I begin to speak quietly.

'You jump, every year, on the anniversaries of their deaths.'

There's a pause, then he nods.

'No matter what the conditions. If it's raining, windy, life-threatening, you jump anyway.'

'I'm not suicidal,' he says.

I wait for him to go on.

'I'll never kill myself intentionally.'

'When you were on that mountain in the Dolomites...?'

He nods. 'I thought about it. I was so tired, I wanted to

end it all. I'd had enough. I'd walked so far and then climbed so high and I was ready to keep going.'

In a corner of my mind I'm wondering how we can be talking so calmly, so rationally, considering the circumstances.

'I looked down on this beautiful onion-domed church glinting in the valley, and I had this most overwhelming urge to be there, walking inside. Then Logan and his friends showed up.'

'You were standing right on the edge?'

'I've never been afraid of heights.'

'But you stepped away when they turned up.'

He nods. 'I watched them. I saw them *fly*.' He sounds reverential. 'They took off, right from the edge of the cliff. It was incredible. I don't know how I found the strength but I walked down the mountain, went inside the church and stayed there all night. It was dark and cold but I felt at peace for the first time in years. The priest found me the next morning and got me something to eat and drink, and then he began talking about life in the mountains and I just listened. Eventually I began to talk too.'

'What did you tell him?'

'Everything. I told him I'd thought about stepping off that cliff edge, and he told me that suicide was a sin. He wanted me to entrust my life to God's hands. He said God would take me when it was my time to go and not before. The next day, when I climbed up on the anniversary of my mother's death, I was only intending to look at the view and think about her. And then Logan showed up. That first year, all I could think about was doing what I saw him and his friends do. It was what kept me going. I got it into my head that

I'd jump on Carlotta's next anniversary. I was determined to make that jump. I didn't have enough skydives under my belt, but Logan agreed to take me base jumping if I could get myself to America – that was where he was headed that year. I worked day and night, trying to save enough money, sleeping in a tiny box room owned by the restaurant manager. I lived that way for years, cash in hand, hand to mouth – cleaning, waiting, odd jobs – ducking between Canada and America and trying to avoid the authorities. I saved enough money to travel further afield, only returning to Europe when I heard my grandparents were ill.'

'But this morbid desire to jump on the anniversaries of Carlotta and your mother's deaths... Why? You want to put yourself in their shoes, feel what they felt as they fell?'

He looks at me. 'Yes. That's exactly it.'

My heart squeezes. How could he hurt himself like that? Does he think he's somehow honouring them?

'With wingsuiting, it's like flying. It's pure joy, the best adrenalin rush you could imagine. When I jump "slick", without a wingsuit, the terror is so intense. When you step off the edge, it's... It's *horrific*. Every single hair on your body is standing up because it knows no man should be doing what you're doing. Your head wants what your body really *doesn't* want. Then you pull your chute and find out that it's functional, the lines aren't tangled and you aren't going to get smashed against the rocks. When you're away from the cliff face and you're floating down safely... That's the moment. That's when I feel free. Until the next jump, at least.'

'But why are you punishing yourself like this?'

He looks down, breaking eye contact.

'You're still in mourning for them, aren't you?' I say gently. 'That's the real reason you wear black, not because it's "easy".'

He shrugs and nods, cracking open his can of soft drink. 'Can we eat now? I'm starving.'

I realise I am too. I've been feeling so sick and nervous that my hunger pangs have been sidetracked.

'How did you get here?' he asks as we're walking back to his van.

'Ferry this morning.'

'Is there another one leaving this afternoon?'

'No, so I'm stranded unless you give me a lift to Stavanger. Can you be tempted? Hot shower? Proper bed to sleep in? A shave?'

He rubs his hand over his beard. 'You don't like it?' he asks, glancing across at me and, my goodness, I detect humour!

'Maybe we could visit Pulpit Rock, Preikestolen, whatever it's called?' I ask hopefully.

'Maybe,' he murmurs. 'I was supposed to do another jump here, but I might skip it.'

My relief is immense.

Once we reach the village, he parks in front of the base-jumping shop. 'I might be a while sorting everything out. You need to use the bathroom? It's over there.' He points to a block to the left of the café a couple of hundred metres away.

'Sure, thanks. You want a coffee or anything for the drive?'

'No, I'll be okay.'

I glance over my shoulder at him as I walk away. He's

standing by Frida, watching me go. Some of my anxiety returns at the look on his face. We're not out of the woods yet.

I hear it, when I'm locked in a cubicle, going about my business: the unmistakable sound of Frida roaring by.

Alessandro is gone by the time I make it outside.

Chapter 45

I can't believe it. In a panic, I run all the way back to the shop, jolting with shock at the sight of my backpack on the countertop.

Mr Boat Captain picks up a few notes from the counter and holds them out to me. 'Motel's up there. Room's all sorted.'

'What?'

'Motel's up there.' He jabs his thumb in the opposite direction to the fjord. 'Room's sorted.'

'I heard what you said. I don't understand.'

'Allez left this for you.' He waves the notes at me. 'Said he owed you for the motel and ferry.'

'He's gone?'

'Yeah, he ducked out of the last jump, said he had to get going. He didn't tell you?'

'Where's he gone?'

He shrugs. 'Beats me.'

I'm shrouded by the most horrible feeling of darkness imaginable.

Outside the window, the other jumpers are gathering by a minibus. I see the guy who mentioned the word 'troll' earlier. And then something clicks inside my mind.

I quickly turn to the boat captain. 'Is Trollveggen the same as Troll Wall?'

'Yeah.'

I grab my backpack from the counter and run outside.

'Wait!' I call. 'Are any of you planning to go to Trollveggen? Troll Wall?'

A couple of them look at each other a little shiftily and I remember something else: it's illegal to jump from there.

'Will you take me there now?' I ask desperately. 'Instead of doing this last jump? Can we leave right away?'

They glance at each other again and it's clear that they think I'm out of my mind.

'I'll pay you!' I cry, brandishing the notes Alessandro left for me.

'Sorry,' one of them replies, shaking his head.

I drop my backpack to the ground and hurry to locate my purse, but I don't have enough to compensate them for missing out on a jump from Kjerag.

'How much money would it take?' I ask.

One of them, the guy who high-fived me earlier, shrugs. 'Maybe six, seven hundred euros?'

I frantically rummage around until I find it. 'I could give you this as collateral.' I offer up my opal, my heart tearing at the thought of losing something that would have forevermore reminded me of Jimmy. 'It's worth nine thousand Australian dollars. You can hang on to it until we find a cashpoint machine, but we have to go *now*.'

'Nine thousand?' the high-fiver asks.

I wince as his fingers collect my prize.

'It's a hundred-carat opal,' I tell him.

He glances at his friend again and then at the minibus that was about to take them up the mountain for the next jump.

'Please,' I beg. 'But we have to go now. Right now. I'm worried about Alessandro.'

They nod at each other, decision made.

Jimmy's words from our last conversation come back to me: '*I only hope it comes in useful*.'

If his opal helps me to save Alessandro, it will be priceless.

It's a thirteen-hour drive to Trollveggen without any breaks, but my companions, Friedrich and Paul from Germany, will only go at a pace that suits them.

Paul drove his bright blue Mercedes Vito campervan to Norway from Germany and goodness only knows how long that took him. I must have got used to Italian driving speeds because I'm itchy with frustration as he takes hairpin bends at snail speed up the mountain. We curve between smooth rounded granite rocks that gleam under the sunshine, glittering lake pools that reflect the clouds in the sky and past hundreds of manmade stone-pile sculptures like the one I saw earlier down by the shore. A river crashes white as a waterfall, parallel to the road, and sheep run along beside it, wearing bells that we hear long after we pass. We drive through small villages with strange names that have crosses through the 'O's and circles over the 'A's, and we see waterfall after waterfall cascading down charcoal-grey cliff faces. Some of the houses even have grass growing on their roofs. It could not be more different to the landscape of the desert, and under other circumstances, I would be overcome with wonder. But right now I feel too sick with dread.

The day after tomorrow, I believe Alessandro plans to launch himself from one of the most dangerous base-jumping locations in the world: the highest vertical rock face in Europe.

I want to scream when Paul and Friedrich call it a night. 'We gotta sleep, Angie,' Paul says, unpacking his tent for himself so that I can crash in the roof space. 'It's risky driving around here in the dark, anyway.'

All I can do is hope that somewhere out here Alessandro is sleeping too.

The next day, Friedrich and Paul chat away to each other in German, laughing and joking, while I sit in the back feeling anxious.

I know this is merely another adventure to them; they wanted to go to Troll Wall anyway. They insist on stopping for regular breaks, telling me to chill out whenever I get too antsy. The only thing that reassures me is that I know Alessandro won't jump until tomorrow, 16 August, so we should be able to catch up with him.

I have no idea what I'm going to do when I get there, how I'll go about stopping him. I'm hoping I'll think of something in the next few hours.

During one of our breaks, I ask the guys if they can show me where jumpers might take off from.

They get out a map and talk me through the hiking route to one of the most-used exit points.

'Is it a difficult hike?'

They shrug. 'Depends on how fit you are.'

When we're on the road again, I borrow one of their phones and look it up.

Expert hike, sure-footedness, sturdy shoes and alpine experience required...

I look down at my Converse and feel faint as I read on.

The Troll Wall is part of the mountain massif Trolltindene (Troll Peaks) and is the tallest vertical rockface in Europe, around 1,100 metres from its base to the summit of the highest point. The rock is gneiss, formed into a broken rock wall of huge corners, concave roofs and crack systems topped with a series of spires and pinnacles on the summit rim. The rock is generally loose, and rock fall is the norm on this north-facing big wall.

Carl Boenish, the 'father' of modern base jumping, was killed jumping from the Troll Peaks in 1984, shortly after setting the world record for the highest base jump in history. Base jumping from the area has been illegal since 1986.

I really, *really* hope I can stop Alessandro at the bottom. I have to.

That night, Friedrich and Paul tell me something that chills me to the bone. They think it's good news, that we no longer have to rush.

'There's a storm coming in. No one's going to be jumping from Trollveggen until it passes. He'll be waiting at the bottom with a nice cup of tea.'

'Please put your foot down,' I beg in response.

I'd seen photographs, but nothing prepares me for the sight of Trollveggen in person. Maybe if the sun were shining it would be different, but on the dark and gloomy anniversary morning of Marta's death, the mountain looks sinister and foreboding, a giant black wall thrusting into the sky and topped with sharp, jagged peaks.

'There!' I yell, pointing ahead at Frida, parked up on the side of the road.

Please let him be inside, please let him be inside, please let him be inside...

I leap from Paul and Friedrich's van before it's fully come to a stop and run to Frida.

It's empty. He's already set off.

Tears sting my eyes as I look around wildly. The rain hasn't started yet, but the sky is dark and cloudy and the cold wind is scouring my face. How can I do this on my own?

'Will you take me up the mountain to the take-off point?' I plead with Paul and Friedrich.

'Nobody will be jumping,' they respond, shaking their heads.

'Alessandro will!'

'But that's suicidal,' Paul replies with a frown.

'I wouldn't even hike halfway up in this weather,' Friedrich adds.

'Come on, let's go and find somewhere to have breakfast. I think there's a café around here,' Paul suggests.

'Will you please show me where the hike starts from?'

'Sure,' he replies with a shrug, indicating for me to get in the van.

Friedrich is perturbed when I tell them that I'm going to walk a little way up to see if I can see him. 'Have you got a jacket?'

I nod, hastily slipping it on. 'I'll manage,' I add when I see him scrutinising my shoes.

'Okay, we'll put the kettle on and wait a while.'

'Thank you,' I breathe, surreptitiously throwing my backpack over the bench seat and slipping out of the van.

They're too caught up in what they're saying to each other to notice that I've taken one of their parachutes.

Chapter 46

I don't know if Paul and Friedrich *will* wait. If they drive off, Jimmy's opal will be lost to me forever, but I can't think about that now. This is about survival – mine and Alessandro's. Like it or not, my heart has chained itself to him, and if he's going down, I'm going down with him.

I took the map with me, but the route is marked and there's a rocky mountain track to follow. It's a three-and-a-half-hour hike to get over to the exit point and I have no idea when Alessandro set off. I just have to believe that I'll reach him before it's too late.

I trudge through alpine meadows, pass mountain pools with grey shingle shores and I even see my first snow, but I don't stop to touch it. Occasionally I'll glimpse the view across the valley and the higher I go, the smaller I feel, but I'm too concerned about Alessandro to register my fear of heights.

The exercise is keeping me warm, but what would happen if I stopped? Would I freeze up here? I push the thought aside and press on against the bitterly cold wind, praying that the rain holds. There isn't a single other person up here – no one else is crazy enough.

Inside my head, I recite recipes to keep me going…

Mix together one cup each of plain flour, oats, desiccated coconut and brown sugar.

Melt half a cup of butter with two tablespoons of golden syrup.

Mix one teaspoon of bicarbonate soda with two tablespoons of boiling water and add to the butter mixture.

Pour the liquids into the dry ingredients and mix well.

It's the recipe for Anzac biscuits, one of Nan's favourites.

What would she and Grandad say if they could see me now? They loved me as if I were their own daughter – it would break their hearts to see me putting my life at risk.

I come to a steep section of rock and my heart almost jumps out of my chest. It looks so precarious, so impassable.

I'm going to kill myself doing this.

I'm too scared even to cry. My feet slip and slide as I try to cross the rocky terrain, slicing my fingers open on sharp rocks.

When I should be focusing on each and every treacherous step, my memories drag me away to another time, another place…

I'm opening my lunchbox at school and the heavenly aroma of biscuits wafts out, making everyone around me sit up and take notice. I share like always and everyone tells me how lucky I am to have a nan who bakes for me every day.

I understand why you did it, Nan, I say to her now. *You loved me, just as you loved my mother, and you were terrified that you'd lose me too.*

I forgive you for not telling me the truth.

A wave of peace washes over me, and then I see Grandad, his beard white with mine dust, and I tell him also that I forgive him.

He takes me into his arms and gives me a hug and I hold him, one last time, before returning my attention to the perilous path ahead.

The mountain peaks are all around now, jagged dark triangles piercing the clouds.

And then I see him, a black shape against the stormy sky.

Hope blasts away the cold grip of fear, but the feeling is fleeting: he's standing near the edge and I know he's committed to jumping.

'Wait!' I scream, but the sound is snatched away by the wind. I lose my footing and stumble to my knees. Gripping hold of the slippery rock with ice-cold fingers, I push myself back up.

I've come so far: from the driest, flattest of lands to the soaring peaks of windswept mountains. I'd go to the ends of the earth for him – and beyond.

I still don't know if I stand a hope in hell of changing this tortured man's mind, but I had to try, whatever the cost, whatever the consequences.

God knows how I'll make it down from here alone.

Drawing as much air into my lungs as I can, I open my mouth and give it everything I've got…

'*SANDRO*!'

His name rips through the elements.

He glances over his shoulder and I know I will take that look on his face with me to the grave. It's haunted, hollow, bleak. In his head, he's already jumped, already committed his life to God's wretched hands. And he *will* die. The wind is so strong that I'm struggling to stay upright.

Then his expression transforms and he's disbelieving.

'Angel?'

'Don't jump!' I beg.

He takes a few steps towards me and halts abruptly, a mask coming over his features.

'You don't keep your distance from your family because you don't love them,' I cry. 'It's because you don't want *them* to love *you*. You're trying to protect them because you don't expect to live. Every anniversary, every year, you think this might be the jump that kills you. You *know* that will be the case now. But it hasn't mattered how much you've pushed them away: Serafina, Jacopo, everyone… they all love you anyway. They'd be distraught if anything happened to you, and it would kill Giulio.'

Alessandro turns his face away.

'Is that why you go to confession?' I ask. 'Because you know you're hurting the people who love you? You don't need to confess to a priest; you need to speak to a counsellor! Look at me!'

He does so, reluctantly, but his eyes are cold and dead.

I press on, urgently: 'If I have to see your broken, bloody body, the way I had to see my grandfather's body, the way you had to see Carlotta's and your mother's… I will never forget it. It will live with me for the rest of my life. It will *destroy* me.' He flinches and closes his eyes. 'I know you're not a selfish person, so please *don't do this*. Please *stop*. I'm not asking you to stop doing what you love – that has to be your decision – but please stop doing these anniversary jumps, stop putting your life at risk so recklessly.'

I don't know if I'm getting through to him or if everything he's hearing is simply white noise. When he opens his eyes, my gut lurches. He looks as though he's in some sort of trance.

'I made a promise,' he says in a low flat monotone. 'Every year I would honour them by jumping. If I survived, it would be God's will. I would be free to live without guilt, at least for another year.'

What was it he said to me once? *I don't do it to die... I do it to survive.*

'That's insane!' I cry, a cold knot of fear crushing my insides. 'You're talking like you've made a pact with the Devil!'

'Not with the Devil, with God,' he replies, his voice growing in strength.

'So when you jump, you're challenging God? Is that who you've made your promise to?'

'Yes. I'm giving God a chance to take my life. If He wants me to live, then I'll live.'

He sounds fanatical, zealot-like. I feel as though he's lost his grip on reality. How can I make him see sense?

'But so far you've been lucky! Maybe you're a survivor. Maybe you're good at it! But we all fail at what we're good at sometimes! This isn't right. You don't deserve to die! Why would you even think that? Everyone could throw themselves off a cliff and tell God to take them if it's their time. Why are you so different to the rest of us? What makes you so special? Should *I* throw myself off a cliff? *Would that make you see sense*?' I thump my chest and he pulls his eyes away from my face and looks at what I'm wearing.

When I thought, *If he's going down, I'm going down with him*, I meant it metaphorically. There is no way I would ever have used the parachute I've strapped on, but I did think I might be able to trick him into believing that I was capable of jumping.

My plan worked because, right before my eyes, his spell shatters.

'ARE YOU FUCKING CRAZY?!' he bellows, and the next thing I know he's shoving me backwards and knocking me to the ground as he unclicks the parachute from my body.

'*Stop*!' I shout as he goes to launch it over the cliff edge. 'I stole it!'

He glances at me, his expression ripped and stricken and tormented and, also, *really quite confused*.

'I stole it from Paul and Friedrich,' I tell him, my hands in the air.

He stares at me with disbelief, and then he lets out an empty laugh. 'I've reduced you to a thief too?'

'I would do anything to save you. Anything,' I repeat fervently. 'Please, Alessandro,' I implore, shivering uncontrollably and hoping against hope that he doesn't slip back into his trance. 'I won't make it down from here alone.'

He blinks at me. And then the remnants of his mask slip away as his eyes rove over my body.

'You're freezing.' Fear clouds his features as he drops to his knees and places his hands on my arms, making me jolt at the contact. 'I've got to get you back to Frida.'

'You're coming with me?' I ask, daring to hope.

He nods, a little dazedly. 'Yes. I'm coming with you.'

I burst into tears.

Chapter 47

I don't know how we make it down safely. The rain comes, drenching us, and I slip multiple times, sometimes too fast for Alessandro to catch me.

We don't speak, we're too focused on every step. By the time we make it to Frida, we're both soaked to the bone.

'Get your clothes off,' Alessandro commands as he cranks up the heat in the van.

He glances over to see me struggling. My fingers are so cold and numb, they're useless. There's a sense of urgency as he comes to my aid, helping me out of my coat and my shoes. I'm shivering violently and he's muttering about hypothermia as he hurriedly strips off my T-shirt and peels off my wet jeans, then quickly shifts the bench seat into a bed position.

'Get into my sleeping bag!' he orders, and I shakily do as I'm told, watching as he strips off his own wet gear and grabs a towel.

He's down to his underwear too, now, and he's scared, I can see it on his face as he wraps the towel around my wet hair and climbs into the sleeping bag with me, zipping us into the snug space together and dragging the quilted blanket over for an extra layer. And then I'm in his arms and he's engulfing me, rubbing my back and my arms, holding me tight against his chest and trying to bring me warmth.

I don't know how long this goes on for – the storm outside is raging, rain is pounding down on the roof and the wind is blowing so hard that the van occasionally rocks with the force of it. The air around us heats up and, within our cocoon, so, eventually, do we.

When I finally stop shivering, Alessandro is rocking me gently, cradling me against his chest as though I'm something precious. I lift my head and stare at him.

His eyes are wide and full of terror. He's still rocking me, still not letting me go, still absolutely petrified.

'You scared me,' he whispers.

'You scared me too,' I whisper in return.

And then his face crumples.

'*Alessandro*...' His name sounds like a prayer on my lips. Slipping my arms out of the sleeping bag, I pull his face against my chest and wrap my legs around his waist, somehow managing to bring him even closer than he was before.

His body begins to shake as I hold him, and it's the most gut-wrenching thing, listening to him sobbing his heart out.

He clutches hold of me desperately and I'm shushing him and rubbing his back, tears streaming down my face as I brush away his. There's no end to them. He's wrecked, completely and utterly wrecked. But he's safe. He's alive. He's here.

Finally his cries soften to ragged breathing. I slide down into the sleeping bag and we lie side by side, gazing at each other.

His expression is heartbroken and my heart is breaking in turn. How can I help him?

'I love you,' I whisper, my eyes welling up and my vision turning blurry.

He thumbs my tears away and stares at me, his eyes burning with intensity in the low light.

'I love you too,' he replies, and my battered heart leaps out of my chest for a moment and slams back into place.

Cupping my face with his hands, he very slowly brings our mouths together.

Kissing him makes my head spin in the most delirious fashion. I'm dizzy with love, dizzy with need, dizzy with desire as our lips slide against each other, our tongues entwining and our bodies coming ever closer. The kiss becomes deeper, more loving, increasingly passionate and desperate. In the confined space that we have, we somehow manage to shed the last of our clothing and then Alessandro is pressing against me and I'm pulling him closer and we're both gasping into each other's mouths at the intensity of the skin-to-skin connection. At some point during the next couple of minutes, he comes to his senses and hastily retrieves a condom, but the ensuing reconnection feels no less intense, and those final moments when we find our release are so breathtakingly beautiful that I feel emotional all over again.

When we've both recovered, I lift my head to stare at him and see that his eyes are shining.

We gently kiss each other's lips, our arms and legs still entangled, our hips locked together. I don't want him to let me go.

I rest my head in the crook of his neck, feeling better than I have in a long time.

His voice cuts through the noise of the storm.

'It was my fault that they died.'

I lift my head to warily meet his eyes.

'It was my fault that they died,' he repeats.

His expression is hollow again, lost. He's back in the past.

'I used to sit out on the balcony,' he tells me in a low, wretched voice. 'Right out on the ledge with my legs dangling off. I wasn't afraid of heights. I felt comfortable, I liked it there. Sometimes I would stand up on the ledge and I felt invincible. I was never scared.'

I brush away his tears with my thumbs, cradling his face with my hands as we lie on our sides, staring at each other. When he's ready, he continues.

'The first time my mother saw me, she screamed and screamed.' He shudders. 'That didn't stop me. In some ways, I think it made me worse. I wanted her attention. She was so fixated on Carlotta. But then she made it *about* Carlotta. "If she sees you, she will copy you. Her blood will be on your hands, Sandro!"'

Oh holy, holy hell…

'But she was right. Carlotta did see me. More than once. I told myself it didn't matter. I always shut the balcony door behind me. But one day I was careless and I left it open. She climbed up onto that ledge because of me. She fell because of me. My mother was right. Her blood is on my hands.'

His tears have become uncontrollable, so I take him in my arms and hold him while he shakes with whole-body-racking sobs.

My mind is racing.

It was an accident… That's what Giulio said. He was trying to reassure Alessandro that it was an accident. But Alessandro doesn't believe that. He never has. He's always thought he was to blame for what happened. And he's right: Carlotta would most likely never have climbed out onto that ledge if she hadn't seen her beloved brother do it first, and his mother would never have jumped in grief if she hadn't lost her little girl two days earlier.

It's no wonder he finds it so hard to forgive himself.

But *anyone* could forget to close a door – I know that from my experience with Nan. Some mistakes have tragic consequences, but that makes him desperately, *desperately* unlucky, not wholly culpable or unworthy of absolution.

'I thought it was a sign, you turning up when you did,' he tells me in a choked voice. 'I thought you were a gift from God, here to release me from my obligations to my stepfather. I thought that was the reason God was keeping me alive, because He couldn't take me from Giulio. And I believed it would be such a relief to go at last, knowing he would have you. I thought you were here for him, not me. That's why I felt so guilty about loving you. I thought it was my time, time to do my penance, but then you… you… you…' He stares into my eyes and his expression is so earnest, so full of love. 'You're like no one I've ever known. So open and honest and true and pure and good and loving and forgiving and so beautiful, inside and out. I thought maybe you really were an angel.'

'I'm not an angel,' I whisper. 'I'm just a girl who loves you. And this girl would really love you to give her a chance – to give *life* with her a chance – and to love her back.'

His lips lift into a small smile.

'I do love you back.'

Chapter 48

We don't head to Stavanger straight away. Alessandro wants to drive me further north, but first we return the stolen parachute.

Paul and Friedrich didn't even realise I'd taken it in the first place – we find them at a café having breakfast, seemingly without a care in the world.

When Alessandro explains that my opal has personal value, Paul hands it over easily.

'We wouldn't have kept it,' he says amiably, accepting the four hundred euros Alessandro offers instead. 'We could see how much it meant to her.'

'Thank you.' I'm so grateful to have Jimmy's opal in my possession again. 'If you give me your bank details, I'll transfer the rest of the money to your account.'

'Don't worry about it,' Friedrich brushes me off. 'We only missed out on one jump from Kjerag. And we wanted to come here anyway.'

They're eagerly anticipating today's jump. The storm passed quickly and the weather is fine.

'Thank you,' I say again, and they stand up to give me a hug. 'Be careful.'

I desperately hope not to read about them on the news later.

We take it slowly on the drive up through Norway, making the most of the country's relaxed rules about roadside camping. I lose count of the number of times we make love, but it's perfect: life-affirming and bonding. I can't think of anywhere I'd rather be than lying in Alessandro's arms, looking out of the darkened windows of the van at the views across glistening fjords and gleaming mountaintops.

This is the Land of the Midnight Sun and as the sun dips and rises again, sunsets and sunrises blur into one, the sky flashing red, pink and orange, as brilliant as the colours of Jimmy's opal.

But when the Northern Lights light up the sky, it's like watching the blues and greens of the opal coming to life.

Alessandro had hoped we would see the aurora borealis, even though it's rare in late August, and it's an experience I'll treasure forever.

I've been keeping my opal close during our long days of driving and Jimmy is often on my mind. Sometimes grainy flecks of sandstone come free as I work my thumb across the rough surfaces, revealing the depths of colour beneath. Alessandro looks worried when he sees me doing this, knowing that I'm fretting about Jimmy and how he might be faring.

Finally, we head back to Stavanger. Erik's apartment is

simple and stylish with views across red-tiled rooftops to the water. A cruise ship is gliding past when we arrive and the sun is beginning to cast a golden glow across the sky.

Alessandro smiles at me. 'I'm going to very belatedly take you up on your offer of a shower and a shave.'

'Then I will get us a drink,' I reply, thinking that the balcony looks like an ideal spot for aperitivo.

I change my mind, however, when I catch a glimpse of his gloriously naked body in the bathroom mirror. Drinks can wait. I hope the shower is big enough for two.

We spend a few days in Stavanger, walking into town past brightly coloured weatherboarded coffee shops, bars and restaurants, and exploring the old part near the docks, with its white cottages, cobbled streets, boutiques and galleries.

We do a lot of talking and we don't kid ourselves: we're aware the path ahead might be difficult. Alessandro knows he's got some seriously deep-seated issues to sort out, but by not doing his last jump, he feels as though he's broken a spell, that insane need to challenge God on those two morbid days every year. He's agreed to seek therapy to help himself learn to live with what happened.

On a bright, sunny morning, we decide to hike to the top of Preikestolen, but only after we've been shopping to buy me a proper pair of hiking boots.

We catch the ferry across to the other side of the Lysefjord and make the short drive to the car park for Preikestolen. It takes about two hours to get to the plateau from here.

We walk uphill on dirt tracks through forests, traipse across rocky stone paths and amble along blissfully level wooden platforms over squelchy mountainous bogs. But soon it becomes all about the steps: chunky, rocky steps carrying us ever upwards.

The sun beats down on our heads, making it hard work, but at least it's not as slippery as it would be if it were wet. Alessandro waits patiently whenever I need to stop to catch my breath, never once even so much as smiling with amusement at my woeful levels of fitness. It's as if he can't shake the memory of me climbing Trollveggen on my own. He keeps taking my hand and I keep letting him go because I'm hot and sweaty enough as it is.

Eventually our path levels out to larger slabs of rock and we're rewarded with some far-reaching views. There are dozens of people up here, behind us and up ahead.

'I thought you didn't like crowds,' I tease, panting. There's still a bit of a way to go before we reach the plateau.

'I don't. I'm doing this for you.'

The path narrows to only a few metres across. I stop short and look at Alessandro.

'Come on, it's only around the corner,' he encourages.

'I can't walk on this path.'

'It's three metres wide, you're not going to fall.'

'It's too narrow.'

'Angel, you're so close,' he chides. 'You're not giving up now.'

He takes my left hand and directs me to put my right on the rock wall to centre myself, holding on every step of the way.

I'm scared, even as we catch sight of the famous platform up ahead, but soon the path widens out again and Alessandro guides me to a rock wall that's a more comfortable ten metres or so away from the cliff edge. He lifts me up and plonks me on a ledge and I scoot backwards until I'm pressed right up against the wall, as far away from the cliff as I can possibly get. He chuckles, then stands in front of me and kisses me, centring me much more than holding on to any stupid rock ever could.

'Okay?' he asks after a moment.

I nod, slightly breathlessly.

He grins and unclicks his rucksack, placing it on the ledge beside me before climbing up to sit on my other side. I distract myself getting out the picnic things we brought with us.

'How do you feel?' he asks when we're well into our lunch.

I'm growing accustomed to the height now and can finally appreciate the view. We can see right down the Lysefjord, all the way to Lysebotn. The distant mountains fade away in a purple-grey heat haze and the water in the fjord below is as sparkling and as blue as the sky.

'Like I'm on top of the world,' I tell him with a smile.

Over on the square-shaped platform there's a queue – *a queue*! – of people going, one by one, to stand beside the 600-metre sheer drop to pose for photographs.

'Would you do that without a parachute?' I ask with a side-long glance at Alessandro.

He nods. 'I'm really not afraid of heights.'

My mood deflates without warning. I might have claimed that I could learn to cope with him going base jumping, but that was before I fell so deeply in love with him that the thought of him getting hurt makes me feel as though I'm being impaled by a hundred knives.

Alessandro turns to look at me.

'Angel,' he prompts when I continue to stare at the queue

of people, even though I can feel his eyes on me. 'Hey,' he whispers, reaching out and gently taking my chin between his forefinger and thumb. He turns me to face him. His expression is concerned. 'I'm going to quit base jumping,' he tells me in a quiet voice. 'I'm done with it. I *have* quit.'

My heart leaps, but then I remember he's said things before that he didn't mean, including telling me he'd drive me to Stavanger only to abandon me instead.

'I swear to you,' he says seriously. 'I'll never jump again.'

I find my voice. 'How can you say that? It's what you're most passionate about. I can't make you give up what you love.'

'*You* are what I'm most passionate about,' he tells me fervently. '*You* are what I most love. I don't want to do anything to hurt you. I've hurt you enough and I will not do it again.'

His green eyes are glittering with emotion.

I give him a small smile. 'You can't promise that you won't hurt me. It's impossible to promise such a thing.'

'I can promise you that I will try. I want to protect you, not cause you pain.'

'I don't want to cause you pain either, yet I know it will hurt you to never go base jumping or wingsuiting again.'

He sighs and gazes down the Lysefjord before turning back to me. 'I can't honestly say that I won't miss the adrenalin rush,' he tells me. 'But *you* are the greatest adrenalin rush of my life. You mean more to me than anything else.' He brushes my cheek as I blink away tears. 'I've been thinking a lot about what Logan said. His reasons for quitting. He and Lea want to start a family and Logan doesn't want to risk leaving his son or daughter without their dad.'

I nod. I remember that conversation well.

'He's not the first base jumper I've heard say that,' Alessandro continues. 'Base jumping and wingsuiting are selfish sports, purely driven by what that one person – the jumper – wants. For most, it's all about the thrill. For me, on those two significant days a year, it was about something else. But I'm *not* going to do anniversary jumps again. I *can* promise you that,' he says. 'And as for thrill-seeking, I don't need it. I don't want to be selfish. I have so much to live for and I want to be here. For you. For Giulio. For my family. I want a future with you. I hope that one day *we* will get married and have children.'

At this, my heart soars higher than the Lysefjord, but he's not finished.

'The only reason I claimed I'd never quit base jumping is because I expected to do it until it killed me.'

I flinch. It's agonising to hear him say this out loud, even though he's not telling me anything I didn't already know.

He leans forward and presses a tender kiss on my forehead before going on.

'I don't want to die. I want to *live*. Not only for you, but for *me*. When I think about my anniversary jumps now, it's like watching a version of myself through fogged glass. I can't actually believe I did that. It seems so surreal. It's like I was drugged or in some sort of trance. I wasn't myself. I really don't feel like I'm that person now. I feel like *this* is me.' He touches his hand to his heart. '*This* is the person I want to be, the person I'm *meant* to be, the person I believe I *would* have been if Carlotta and my mother hadn't died. I feel like you've helped to bring the real me to the surface and I don't want to let that person slip under again.

I know I'm finally free of whatever crazy curse I thought plagued me.'

'Alessandro,' I murmur, reaching forward and touching my fingers to his lips.

He slips his hand behind my neck and tangles his fingers in my hair, still staring at me steadily.

'I love you. Utterly. Deeply. Profoundly.' His lips curve upwards as he slowly stresses each word. 'Boundlessly. Ceaselessly. Infinitely.' He's properly grinning now and I'm sure he's going to run out of words. 'Acutely. Desperately. Unequivocally.'

I start to laugh. 'Will you stop showing off with your excellent vocabulary and kiss me?'

'I can do that.' With the hand that is still holding the nape of my neck, he draws me closer. Our lips meet and I feel familiar sparks heating up the blood in my veins and making me feel heady. With some effort, I withdraw.

'You're bringing on my dizziness,' I tell him breathlessly. 'I don't want to feel giddy up here.'

'It's all right, I've got you,' he murmurs, giving me one last lingering kiss.

I press my face against his warm neck, breathing him in.

'Will you come travelling with me?' he asks in my ear.

I lift my head, my eyes lighting up. 'Really?'

'Yes. In Frida. Do you think you could handle it for an even longer stretch?'

'Living in such a small space? Oh, sorry, I forgot,' I say with a grin, adopting his voice, 'You don't live *inside* the van, you live *out there*...'

He laughs and takes my hand as I dramatically wave it before me.

'I would love you to show me the world,' I say to him, growing serious. 'But I do think we need to focus on getting you better first.'

'I've never felt better than I do right now,' he tells me earnestly, and I believe him, I honestly do.

'Where would you want to take me?' I ask with a smile, indulging him for a moment.

'Cappadocia in Turkey.'

I raise my eyebrows. 'That's random.'

He shakes his head. 'It's not. Cappadocia is one of the best places in the world for hot air ballooning. You fly over the Göreme National Park and look down on the most incredible landscape of fairy chimneys and colourful volcanic valleys. The people there even live in caves carved out of the rocks like in Coober Pedy. I've seen pictures, but I've never been. It's magical. I know you'd love it.'

'And how exactly do you think someone who is scared of heights will cope in a hot air balloon?' I ask wryly.

'We have almost twelve months to work on that,' he replies. 'I thought we could go there next year on the fourteenth of August.'

My heart melts. He wants to mark the next anniversary of Carlotta's death *with me*? How can I not kiss him for that?

A phone is ringing somewhere nearby.

'That's yours, Angel,' he says, smiling against my lips.

'Oh!'

He reaches past me to grab his rucksack, holding it while I retrieve the device.

'Hello?'

'Angie, love, it's Bonnie.'

'Bonnie! You would not believe where I am right now!'

'I'm afraid I have some bad news, darling.'

My heart stops.

'Jimmy's gone, sweetie. He passed away in the early hours of this morning.'

Chapter 49

Alessandro comes home with me to Australia. We manage to change my flight, staying one night in Adelaide with Louise to break up the journey before hiring a car and driving the nine hours up to Coober Pedy.

My friend told me very matter-of-factly that she was reserving judgement about my 'new man', knowing what she knew about him, but she'd come round by the time we said our tearful goodbyes – tearful because she knew how much Jimmy meant to me.

Jimmy's funeral is the day after tomorrow so it was a rush getting out of Stavanger – an unhappy end to what had been a life-affirming stay.

But despite the tragic circumstances that have brought me back to Australia a week early, I'm glad to be able to show Alessandro where I grew up.

'It really is like Tattooine,' he says with astonishment when we drive into Coober Pedy.

We pull up in front of the wire fence that was a necessary evil for keeping Nan safe from wandering off and falling down a mineshaft.

To my surprise and delight, the garden is still thriving.

Alessandro looks around curiously as we walk up to the front door. I knock loudly.

A minute or so passes before Aada answers.

'Angie!' she exclaims. 'It's so good to see you again! I'm so sorry about Jimmy.'

Aada and Onni have been living in my dugout since I left. Things have been a bit tight for them and they were being threatened with eviction, so it made sense for them to move in while I was away. Hopefully Onni's luck will look up soon. That's the thing with mining: it's completely unpredictable. He could find a million dollars' worth of opals tomorrow.

'This is Alessandro.' I introduce them, the sound of a screen door stealing my attention away. I look over to see Bonnie coming outside.

'Angie!' she cries.

I run to give her a hug.

The funeral dredges up a lot of memories of my grandfather's service – his and Jimmy's old mining buddies all attend – but it helps having Alessandro there to hold my hand.

He seems so solid mentally, as though my grief is giving him strength to help carry *me* through.

The wake is being held at the pub and Alessandro stands and stares with wonder at the dozens of postcards, mostly of Italy, stuck to the wall.

'You sent all these?' he asks me.

I nod. My friends must've put them up here for everyone to see.

Bonnie wanders over and slips her arm around my waist. 'This is my favourite.' She points at the beautiful big fountain set within an Italian Renaissance garden.

'Villa D'Este,' I say. 'Alessandro grew up nearby.' I glance at her. 'I keep meaning to tell you this: remember how the kids at school used to think Jimmy was my dad because we had the same frizzy hair?'

She nods. 'Your nan cut it all off so they'd stop harassing you.'

'Was *that* why she did it?' I ask. *Bloody hell. And instead I ended up getting teased because I looked like a boy!*

She smiles. 'You were determined to grow it again anyway. You *liked* Jimmy's hair.'

'I did,' I agree with a sad smile.

'Why do you bring it up?' she asks, reminding me that I had a point to make.

'When I went to Tivoli for the first time to meet Alessandro's family,' I squeeze his hand as I say this, 'Serafina, my grandmother, was amazed. I have the same frizzy, curly hair as my cousin Valentina! She herself had the same hairstyle when she was younger. I'd always wondered where I got it from. Of course, their hair is dark and mine is light. I still have no idea which of my ancestors was blond.'

Bonnie looks at me with surprise. 'But, darling,' she says, 'didn't you know that you take after your nan?'

'Pardon?'

'Your nan had exactly the same shade of hair as you. She was blond as well.'

I stare at her. I've only ever seen black-and-white photos of Nan from when she was younger.

'You take after *both* of your grandmothers,' Alessandro states.

This day is already emotional enough, but that's just about the end of me.

We stay in Coober Pedy for a couple of weeks because there's so much to sort out and so many people to catch up with. I think Alessandro enjoys meeting my friends – he's a different guy to the person he was in Rome. His aloofness has been replaced by a warm kindness and a light-hearted sense of humour. My friends are fans.

Jimmy has left everything to me on one condition: that his dugout goes up for sale without delay. I think he was worried that I'd let his place out for free, as I've done with Nan's. He wants me to use the money to go travelling and also to buy myself somewhere to live someday, if I'd like to.

He had a substantial opal stash, including some very precious black opals that he mined in Andamooka many years ago. I don't know why he never used his money to go anywhere. Maybe his heart has just always belonged here on Antakirinja Matu-Yankunytjatjara land.

Aada and Onni will continue to live in my grandparents' dugout until Onni gets his big win and can afford to buy it from me. I'm leaving the furniture for them, but I'm taking some of my personal possessions – my photo albums, a few books that I can't part with, the rest of my postcards and Nan's jewellery, including her and Grandad's wedding rings. I'm also arranging for my piano to be shipped to Italy. It's not particularly valuable and I could easily buy a new one, but it belonged to Grandad and I'd like to have something to remember him by.

My final farewell is not meant to be a final farewell, but it feels like it. It may be years before I return. Maybe my friends will see me in Italy or somewhere else first. We certainly have enough people to drop in on when we're driving through Europe: all those travellers who went home again, and of course the families of the other settlers who are still tied to Coober Pedy.

'Will you be okay?' I ask Bonnie as we say goodbye.

'I'll be fine, love. Mick is making noises about retiring, believe it or not. Maybe we'll finally get around to booking that round-the-world cruise.'

'Just make sure you hop off in Italy.'

'Oh, we will,' she promises. 'Now, what about you two? Have you decided where you're off to first?'

'The Great Barrier Reef,' I reply, smiling at Alessandro.

Australia is one of the few places he hasn't explored and it seems only right that I should see some of my own country before heading to Europe for who knows how long. It's exactly what Mum did all those years ago.

We've brought Giulio up to date over the phone, and Frida is safe in storage in Norway where we left her, so there's no need to rush back.

We have only one deadline to work towards and I'm determined to make it...

Chapter 50

We roll into Tivoli on a wet and windy Christmas Eve, almost four months after Jimmy's funeral. We're really cutting it close – we had some trouble driving through the Alps with the recent snowstorms so we didn't tell anyone we were coming because we weren't sure we'd make it.

I don't know if he heard Frida – it's hard not to – but Giulio is outside when we pull up. His mouth drops open and he shouts out, although I have no idea what he says.

Before I get out of the van, I place the pink bunny that once belonged to my small half-sister on the dashboard. I like to imagine her sitting there and watching the world go by. It came as no surprise to discover that her name is Frida.

The whole household is outside when Alessandro reaches my side of the van. He gives me a slightly pensive smile as I take his hand.

'It's time to let them love you,' I whisper.

He nods, his eyes shining.

Serafina gets to us first.

'You brought him home for Christmas!' our grandmother cries at me as she grabs Alessandro with one hand and me with the other. When she finally lets us go, tears are streaming down her cheeks.

I turn to Giulio. 'Hello, Papà,' I say with a cheeky grin.

'*Mio angelo*,' he utters, grabbing Alessandro and me simultaneously, and then we're pulled away and separated from each other as we say hello to everyone else. The whole family is here, including Francesca and Pepe with their newborn baby boy. We are completely and utterly surrounded – by family, by friends, and most of all, by love.

Epilogue

We live in Alessandro's grandparents' house by the river in Tivoli. It had been sitting empty for years, steadily falling into disrepair because Alessandro couldn't bear to sell it, nor stay in it. I wasn't aware that his grandparents had left it to him, but that's Alessandro. I'm sure he will continue to surprise me.

Just as he says I continue to surprise him.

Together we decided to do up the house and it has been a labour of love for both of us. We've worked hard since Christmas, but now we can finally enjoy the fruits of our labours and we adore living in the countryside, even if it does mean a commute to *Serafina's* for Alessandro on the days that he's working.

As for me, I've taken up residence in Nonna's country kitchen, helping her to make pasta and pickles and all the things *Serafina's* is famous for. I also milk Valentina's beloved goats when she's at university and feed Jacopo's poor doomed pigs now that he's moved to the city. He's currently renting Cristina's apartment and looking after it while she's in Chamonix with Lindsey. She decided to take a year out to see if she wants to make a life for herself in the mountains and so far she's loving it – it's heart-warming to see.

Stefano is himself, still working at *Serafina's* and still going to auditions. He was cast in a men's haircare advert recently and it makes me smile whenever it comes on the telly, seeing his glistening, shiny locks. He didn't get the part in the soap opera, but I have no doubt he'll make it one day.

As for Papà, despite his initial reservations, he's now absolutely delighted that Alessandro and I are a couple. He encourages us to take regular breaks from work to go travelling, but he's glad when we stay in touch and send him the occasional postcard. Alessandro has reassured him that he'll never again disappear for months on end with no word.

Therapy has helped Alessandro to see that his poor teenage self deserves forgiveness, but it will probably be a long time before he feels truly at peace, if ever.

He didn't want to burden Giulio or Serafina with the whole truth, dark and twisted as it is, but he has explained that he's been carrying a debilitating guilt over the deaths of his mother and sister and has on occasion felt the need to punish himself for it.

Giulio and Serafina were heartbroken to hear this and have showered him with love ever since.

Life is good, but sometimes Alessandro and I just want to get away from our crazy, noisy, and sometimes annoyingly interfering family, and that's when Frida comes in handy.

We'll hop into her and drive and drive and drive, not always knowing where we want to go, but always happy to be on the lookout for our next adventure.

My Italian citizenship has been granted – what a celebration we had when that came through! – and it has made travelling through Europe incredibly easy. So far, we've been to France to see Cristina in the snow, southern Spain for some winter sunshine and, of course, all over Italy. We'd also like to visit Logan and Lea in California one day – they were thrilled to hear that we're finally more than friends.

But right now we're in Turkey, gliding over the Göreme National Park in a hot air balloon. It is the anniversary of Carlotta's death today and Alessandro wanted to do something significant. This year, *together*, we are flying instead of falling.

Down below is the most magical, fantastical landscape of rock formations that I have ever seen.

I couldn't do this with anyone else, but Alessandro centres me, just as I seem to centre him.

He's holding me tightly from behind, his hands clasped around my waist. He whispers something in Italian and I wonder if it's a prayer.

I carefully turn around to face him, brushing the tears from his beautiful eyes. 'What did you say?'

'*Riposa bene sorellina. Anche te Mamma*,' he whispers. 'It means: rest well, little sister. And you, Mamma.'

'Rest in peace,' I whisper in turn, and I'm not only thinking of Carlotta and Marta now, but Nan and Grandad too.

He cups my face and kisses me. My head spins, but I don't want him to stop.

I'm not sure I'll ever be at ease climbing mountains or soaring into the skies, and Alessandro will probably never be at his happiest when he's on low, level ground, but he loves me and I love him and the world is our oyster.

We can go anywhere now. Anywhere at all.

We plan to go there together.

Acknowledgements

Firstly, my lovely readers, thank you for coming on this journey with me – I hope you enjoyed Angie and Alessandro's story! If, like me, you find it hard to let them go, sign up to #TheHiddenPaige at paigetoon.com, as I plan to write a short story for them at some point to see what they're up to…

Thank you to everyone at Simon & Schuster for the stellar work that they do, but especially my amazing editor, Suzanne Baboneau, Rebecca Farrell, Jess Barratt, Sara Jade Virtue, Dominic Brendon, Hayley McMullan, Richard Vlietstra, Joe Roche, Justine Gold, Rachel Stewardson, Danielle Wilson, Maddie Allan and, last but definitely not least, Pip Watkins for her stunning cover design.

Thanks also to my copy-editor, Anne O'Brien, and Dawn Burnett for everything she's done for me over the years – I'll never forget her dressing as an air stewardess for the *Lucy in the Sky* launch party!

Thank you to everyone at Penguin Random House ANZ,

but especially the awesome Ali Watts, Emily Cook and Rosie Pearce. Also, Louisa Maggio for the beautiful ANZ cover design.

Immense gratitude also to Kimberley Atkins who very kindly read an early draft of this book and gave me such helpful feedback. Ditto some other lovely friends, Jane Hampton, Katherine Reid and Katherine Stalham. I owe you all alcohol!

Thank you to my best author buddies who are a great support in more ways than one, especially Lucy Branch, Ali Harris, Dani Atkins, Lindsey Kelk and Giovanna Fletcher.

Grazie mille to my old pal Giulia Cassini for her boundless help with all things Italian – it's been a long time since she helped me with swear words for *Chasing Daisy* and it warms my heart to know that she's still here for me now.

A big cheers to Nick Troisi from Umoona Opal Mine & Museum in Coober Pedy who answered my many random questions and helped bring Angie's surroundings to life. I'd just like to say that Nick didn't share any stories (nor did I ask him to) about real people in Coober Pedy – similarities have occurred with my books and real life in the past, so if that happens to be the case here, it is one hundred per cent coincidental!

Thank you very much to Wendy Dunn from Alzheimer's Society (alzheimers.org.uk) for all of her help with my Alzheimer's research – it is enormously appreciated – and also Eric Magut, a base jumper from Germany who kindly answered my questions when I accosted him in Lysebotn, Norway, whilst on a research trip.

Thanks to my parents, Jen and Vern Schuppan, and my

arents-in-law, Helga and Ian Toon, who all helped me pull
ıis cat out of the bag in one way or another.

Finally, thank you to my gorgeous family: my children,
ıdy and Idha, and my husband, Greg, who probably helped
ıe with this book more than everyone else all put together.
'd be lost without you. Quite literally.